Praise for Jillian Hart and her novels

"Hart's tender love story has strong characters who stay true to themselves and what they believe is the right thing to do."
—*RT Book Reviews* on *Gingham Bride*

"This is a beautiful love story between two people from different stations in life, or so it appears. The characters are balanced and well thought out and the storyline flows nicely."
—*RT Book Reviews* on *Patchwork Bride*

"A sweet, romantic novel, with memorable characters who will do what they must to survive during a bad economy."
—*RT Book Reviews* on *Snowflake Bride*

Praise for Lyn Cote and her novels

"Cote is an amazingly talented author who writes from the heart, and that shines through in this book."
—*RT Book Reviews* on *Her Patchwork Family*

"*Her Healing Ways* is a wonderful love story between two people with different outlooks on life, who together bring out the best in each other. Cote knows what will keep readers interested in the story and uses this knowledge throughout her story. Don't miss this wonderful book."
—*RT Book Reviews* on *Her Healing Ways*

"*Suddenly a Frontier* [...] everything: mystery, dr[...] The two young girls are [...] as they are totally cha[...]
—*RT Book Reviews* o[...]

Jillian Hart grew up on her family's homestead, where she helped raise cattle, rode horses and scribbled stories in her spare time. After earning her English degree from Whitman College, she worked in travel and advertising before selling her first novel. When Jillian isn't working on her next story, she can be found puttering in her rose garden, curled up with a good book or spending quiet evenings at home with her family.

A *USA TODAY* bestselling author of over forty novels, **Lyn Cote** lives in the north woods of Wisconsin with her husband in a lakeside cottage. She knits, loves cats (and dogs), likes to cook (and eat), never misses *Wheel of Fortune* and enjoys hearing from her readers. Email her at l.cote@juno.com. And drop by her website, www.lyncote.com, to learn more about her books that feature "Strong Women, Brave Stories."

Gingham Bride

Jillian Hart

&

Her Patchwork Family

Lyn Cote

♦HARLEQUIN® LOVE INSPIRED® HISTORICAL

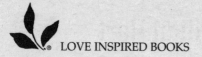

LOVE INSPIRED BOOKS

Recycling programs for this product may not exist in your area.

ISBN-13: 978-1-335-00541-0

Gingham Bride and Her Patchwork Family

Copyright © 2018 by Harlequin Books S.A.

The publisher acknowledges the copyright holders of the individual works as follows:

Gingham Bride
Copyright © 2009 by Jill Strickler

Her Patchwork Family
Copyright © 2009 by Lyn Cote

www.Harlequin.com

Printed in U.S.A.

CONTENTS

GINGHAM BRIDE

Jillian Hart

I trust in the mercy of God for ever and ever.
—*Psalms* 52:8

Chapter One

Angel County, Montana Territory,
December 1883

"Ma, when is Da coming back from town?" Fiona O'Rourke threw open the kitchen door, shivering beneath the lean-to's roof. *Please,* she prayed, *let him be gone a long time.*

A pot clanged as if in answer. "Soon. And just why are you askin'?"

"Uh, I was just wondering, Ma." *Soon.* That was not the answer she had been hoping for. Her stomach tightened with nerves as she set down the milk pail and backed out the door. She wanted to hear that Da had gone to his favorite saloon in town for the afternoon, which would give her plenty of time to fix the problem before her father returned.

"You are still in your barn boots?" Ma turned from the stove in a swirl of faded calico. "Tell me why you are not ready to help with the kitchen work? What is taking you so long outside today?"

The word *lazy* was not there, but the intonation of it was strong in her mother's fading brogue. Fiona winced, although she was used to it. Life was not pleasant in the O'Rourke household. Love was absent. She did not know if happiness and love actually existed in the world. But she did know that if her father discovered the horse was missing, she would pay dearly for it. She had school to think of—five full months before she would graduate. If she was punished, then she might not be able to go to school for a few days. The thought of not seeing her friends, the friends who understood her, hurt fiercely and more than any punishment could.

"I will work harder, Ma. I'll be back soon." She scrambled through the shelter of the lean-to. Wood splinters and bark shavings crackled beneath her boots.

"It will not be soon enough, girl! I've already started the meal, can't you see? You are worthless. I don't know if any man will have the likes of you, and your da and I will be stuck supporting you forever." A pot lid slammed down with a ringing iron clang. Unforgiving and strict, Ma turned from the stove, weary in her worn-thin dress and apron. She raised the spatula, clutching it in one hand. "When your da comes home, he will expect the barn work to be done or else."

It was the "or else" that put fear into her and she dashed full speed past the strap hanging on a nail on the lean-to wall and into the icy blast of the north wind. Outside, tiny, airy snowflakes danced like music. She did not take the time to watch their beauty or breathe in their wintry, pure scent as she plunged down the steps into the deep snow. She hitched her skirts to her knees and kept going. The cold air burned her throat and lungs as she climbed over the broken board of the fence and into the fallow fields. Snow draped like a pristine silk blanket over the rise and fall of the prairie, and she scanned the still, unbroken whiteness for a big bay horse.

Nothing. How far could he have gone? He had not been loose for long, yet he was not within sight. Where could he be? He might have headed in any direction. Thinking of that strap on the wall, Fiona whirled, searching in the snow for telltale tracks. The *toot, too-oot* of the Northern Pacific echoed behind her, a lone, plaintive noise in the vast prairie stillness, as if to remind her of her plans. One day she would be a passenger on those polished cars. One day, when she had saved enough and was finished with school, she would calmly buy a ticket, climb aboard and ride away, leaving this great unhappy life behind.

In the meantime, she had a horse to find, and quick. But how? It was a big job for one girl. She lifted her skirts, heading for the highest crest in the sloping field. If only her brother were still alive, he would know exactly what to do. He would have put his arm around her shoulder, calming her with kind, reassuring words. Johnny would have told her to finish her chores, that he would take care of everything, no need to worry. He would be the one spotting the hoofprints and following them. He would know how to capture a runaway. She lumbered through the deepening drifts, watching as the snow began to fall harder, filling the gelding's tracks.

How could she do this alone? She missed her brother. Grief wrapped around her as cold as the north winds and blurred the endless white sweep of the prairie. She ached in too many ways to count. It would be easier to give in to it, to let her knees crumple and drop down into the snow, let the helplessness wash over her. Snow battered her cheeks, stinging with needle sharpness. If she wanted the future she had planned, the promise of a life on her own and alone, so no one could own her or hurt her, then she must find the gelding. She must bring him in and finish the barn work. Those were her only choices.

What would her friends say? She plunged deeply into the snow, following the set of telltale tracks snaking through the deeply drifted snow. She sank past her knees, hefting her skirts, ignoring the biting cold. She imagined sitting in Lila's cozy parlor above the mercantile her parents owned with the fire crackling and steeping tea scenting the room, surrounded by those who were more family to her than her own parents.

"Fee, you ought to stay with one of us instead of leaving town," Kate might say in that stubborn, gentle way of hers. "I'm sure my folks would put you up if I told them what your home life is like."

"Or you would stay with us," Lila would offer with a look of mischief. "My stepmother would be more than happy to take you in and manage your life."

"Or with me," Earlee would say. "My family doesn't have much, but I know we could make room for you."

Fiona's throat ached with love for her friends, and she knew she could not share this with them. Some things were too painful and besides, her parents would come for her if she stayed anywhere in Angel County. The new sheriff was one of Pa's card-playing buddies. She feared for her friends. There was no telling what Pa might do if he were angry enough. It would be best to find the horse.

A plaintive neigh carried toward her on the cutting wind. Flannigan was easy to spot, standing defiantly on a rise of the prairie, a rusty splash of color in the white and gray world. Thank heavens! She faced the brutal wind. If she could get to him fast enough, she could lead him back to his stall and no one would be the wiser. The strap would remain on the lean-to wall untouched and unused. Relief slid through her and her feet felt light as she hurried on. The deep snow clutched at her boots as if with greedy hands, slowing her progress.

On the rise ahead, the gelding watched her brashly. Now all she had to do was to hold out her hand and speak gently to him, and surely he would come to her as he did in the corral. To her surprise, the gelding tossed his head, sending another ringing neigh echoing across the landscape. He turned and ran, disappearing into the folds of land and the veil of snowfall.

No! She watched him vanish. Her hopes went with him. What if he kept running? What if she could never catch him? What if she had to return home and face Da's wrath? She plunged after him. She reached the crest where he'd stood and searched the prairie for him. Her eyes smarted from staring into the endless white. Panic clawed at the back of her neck, threatening to overtake her.

Get the horse, her instincts told her. Run after him as far as it takes. Just get him back before Da comes home. She closed out the picture of the dark lean-to and her father's harsh words as he yelled at her, listing everything she had done wrong. Desperation had her lunging down the steep rise, sobbing in great lungfuls of wintry air, searching frantically for any movement of color in the vast white.

There he was, flying through an empty field, black mane and tail rippling, racing the wind. What would it be like to run as far and as fast as you could go, to be nothing but part of the wind, the snow and sky?

"Flannigan!" she cried out, praying that her voice carried to him. But it was not her voice that caused the giant workhorse to spin and turn toward town. A distant neigh echoed across the rolling fields and like a death toll it reverberated in her soul. Would he keep running? How would she ever catch him?

"Flannigan!"

The horse hesitated, his tail up and his black mane fluttering in the wind. Proud and free, the gelding tossed his head as if troubled, torn between galloping over to her and his own freedom.

She knew just how he felt, exactly how attractive the notion of fleeing could be. Please don't do it, she begged with all her might, but it made no difference. The gelding rocked back on his hooves and pivoted, running like a racehorse on the last stretch. She took off after him, wishing she could do the same, her skirts fluttering in the winter wind.

Ian McPherson sat up straighter on the hard wooden edge of the homemade sled's seat, trying to get a better look at the young woman in the fields. Flecks of white stung his eyes and cheeks and the storm closed in, turning serious, as if to hide her from his sight. He caught flashes of red skirt ruffles beneath the modest dove-gray coat and a mane of thick black curls flying behind her. "Who is that running through the snow?"

"If I tell you the truth, you will have a mind to get back on that train." O'Rourke was a somber man and his hard face turned grim. "We couldn't beat common sense into that girl. Don't think we didn't try."

Ian gulped, knowing his shock had to show on his face. He could find no civil response as he turned his attention back to the young lady who hiked her skirts up to her knees, showing a flash of flannel long johns before the storm and the rolling prairie stole her from view. "She's got some speed. Can't say I have seen a woman run that fast before."

"Likely her neglect is the reason the gelding got out. That girl hasn't got a lick of sense, but she *is* a good worker. My wife and I made sure of it. That's what a man needs in a helpmate. She will be useful. No need to worry about that."

"Oh, I won't." Useful. Not what he wanted in a wife. He didn't want a wife. He had more than enough responsibility resting on his shoulders.

Aye, coming here was not the wisest decision he had ever made. But what other choice did he have? Creditors had taken his grandparents' house and land, and he still felt sick in his gut at being unable to stop it. Gaining a wife when he was near to penniless was not a good solution, even if his nana thought so. A better solution would be to find his own wife sometime in the future, even though, being a shy man, courting did not come easily to him.

"Don't make up your mind on her just yet." O'Rourke hit the gelding's flank fairly hard with his hand whip. The animal leaped forward, lathering with fear. "You come sit down to eat with us and look her over real good."

Look her over? The father spoke as if they were headed to a horse sale. Ian strained to catch another glimpse of her, but saw only gray prairie and white snow. What would the girl look like up close and face-to-face? Probably homely and pocked, considering her parents were desperate to marry her off.

"Remember, you gave us your word." O'Rourke spit tobacco juice into the snow on his side of the sled. "I don't cotton to men who go back on their word."

"I only said I would come meet the girl. I made no promises." Although he did have hopes of his own. He couldn't explain why his eyes hungrily searched for her. Maybe it was because of the pretty picture she made, like a piece from a poem, an untamed horse and the curly haired innocent chasing him. It was his imagination at work again, for he was happier in his thoughts than anywhere. Hers was an image he would pen down later tonight when he was alone with his notebook.

"Your grandfather promised." O'Rourke was like a dog with a bone. He wouldn't relent. "I knew this would happen first time you caught sight of her. Fiona is no beauty, that's for sure, but I'm strapped. Times are hard for me and my wife. We can't keep feedin' and clothin' her and we don't want to. It's high time she was married and your family and me, we had this arranged before you both was born."

He had heard it all before. Nearly the same words his grandmother had told him over and over with hope sparkling in her eyes. After all that she had lost, how could he outright disappoint her? Life was complicated and love more so.

Would the girl understand? Was she already packing her hope chest? She swept into sight, farther away, hardly more than a flash of red, a bit of gray and those bouncing black curls. From behind, she made a lovely pose, willowy and petite, with her flare of skirt and elegant outstretched hand, slowly approaching the lone horse. The animal looked lathered, his skin flicking with nervous energy as if ready to bolt again.

"Fool girl," O'Rourke growled, halting the horse near a paint-peeling, lopsided barn. "She ought to know she'll never catch the beast that way."

Her back was still to him, distant enough that she was more impression than substance, more whimsy than real with the falling snow cloaking her. If he had the time, he could capture the emotion in watercolors with muted tones and blurred lines to show her skirt and outstretched hand.

Ian vaguely realized the older man was digging in the back for something, and the rattle of a chain tore him from his thoughts and into the bitter-cold moment. He did not want to know what O'Rourke was up to; he'd seen enough of the man to expect the worst. He hopped into the deep snow, ignoring the hitch of pain in his left leg, and reached for his cane. "I shall take care of it. I have a way with horses."

"So do I." O'Rourke shook out a length of something that flickered like a snake's tongue—aye, a whip. "This won't take long with the two of us."

"No need to get yourself cold and tired out." Under no circumstances was he going to be involved in that brand of horse handling. Best to placate the man, and then figure out what he was going to do. What his grandparents hadn't told him about their best friend's son could fill a barrel. The ten-minute drive from town in the man's company was nine minutes more than he felt fit to handle. He gestured toward the ramshackle shanty up the rise a ways. "You go on up to the house where the fire is warm. Let me manage this for you."

"Well, young fellow, that sounds mighty good." O'Rourke seemed pleased and held out the whip. "I suspect you might need this."

Ian looked with distaste at the sinuous black length. "I see a rope looped over the fencepost. That will be enough."

"Suit yourself. It will be here if you need it." O'Rourke sounded amused as he tossed down the whip and sank boot-deep into the snow. He gestured toward the harnessed gelding, standing head down, as if his spirit had been broken long ago. "I'll leave this one for you to stable."

It wasn't a question, and Ian didn't like the sound of mean beneath the man's conversational tone. Still, he'd been brought up to respect his elders, so he held his

tongue. O'Rourke and how he lived his life were not his
concern. Seeing his grandmother through her final days
and figuring out a way to make a living for both of them
was his purpose.

He ought not to be giving in to his fanciful side, but
with every step he took he noted the gray daylight falling at an angle, shadows hugging the lee side of rises and
fence posts, but not over the girl. As he loosened the harness and lifted the horse collar from the gelding's back,
he felt a strange longing, for what he did not know. Perhaps it was the haunting beauty of this place of sweeping prairies and loneliness. Maybe it was simply from
traveling so long and far from everything he knew. There
was another possibility, and one he didn't much want to
think on. He led the horse to the corral gate, unlooped the
coiled rope from the post, used the rails to struggle onto
the horse's back and swiped snow from his eyelashes.

Where had she gone? He breathed in the prairie's
stillness, coiling the long driving reins and knotting
them. He leaned to open the gate and directed the horse
through. No animal stirred, a sign the storm setting in
was bound to get worse. Only the wind's flat-noted wail
chased across the rolling and falling white prairie. Different from his Kentucky home, and while he missed the
trees and verdant fields, this sparse place held beauty, too.

"C'mon, boy." He drew the gate closed behind them.
The crest where he'd last spotted the girl and horse was
empty. He pressed the gelding into a quick walk. Falling
flakes tapped with greater force and veiled the sky and
the horizon, closing in on him until he could no longer
see anything but gray shadows and white snow. He wel-
comed the beat of the wild wind and needle-sharp flakes.
The farmer in him delighted in the expansive fields and
the sight of a cow herd foraging in the far distance. Aye,

he missed his family's homestead. He missed the life he had been born to.

When he reached the hill's crest, hoofprints and shoe prints merged and circled, clearly trailing northward. A blizzard was coming, that was his guess, for the wind became cruel and the snowflakes furious. At least he had tracks to follow. He did not want to think what he would find when he was face-to-face with the woman. He could only pray she did not want this union any more than he did. And why would she? he mused as he tucked his cane in one hand. The girl would likely want nothing to do with him, a washed-up horseman more comfortable chatting with his animals than a woman.

Perhaps it was Providence that brought the snow down like a shield, protecting him from sight as he nosed the horse into the teeth of the storm. Maybe the Almighty knew how hard it was going to be for him to face the girl, and sent the wind to swirl around him like a defense. He could do this; he drew in a long breath of wintry air and steeled his spine. Talking to a woman might not be his strong suit, but he had done more terrifying things. Right now none came to mind, but that was only because his brains muddled whenever a female was nearby. Which meant that somewhere in the thick curtain of white, Miss Fiona O'Rourke, his betrothed, had to be very close.

He heard her before he saw her. At least he *thought* that was her. The quiet soprano was sheer beauty, muted by the storm and unconsciously true, as if the singer were unaware of her gifted voice. Sure rounded notes seemed to float amid the tumbling snowflakes, the melody hardly more than a faint rise and fall until the horse drew him closer and he recognized the tune.

"O come all ye faithful," she sang. "Joyful and triumphant."

He wondered how anything so warm and sweet could be borne on the bitterest winds he'd ever felt. They sliced through his layers of wool and flannel like the sharpest blade, and yet her sweet timbre lulled him warmly, opening his heart when the cruel cold should have closed it up tight.

"O come ye, oh come ye…" The snowfall parted enough to hint at the shadow of a young woman, dark curls flecked with white, holding out her hand toward the darker silhouette of the giant draft horse. "To Bethlehem. Come and behold him…"

The horse he rode plunged toward her as if captivated. Ian understood. He, too, felt drawn to her like the snowflakes to the ground. They were helpless to take another course from sky to earth just as he could not help drawing the horse to a stop to watch. Being near to her should have made his palms sweat and cloying tightness take over his chest, but he hardly noticed his suffocating shyness. She moved like poetry with her hand out to slowly catch hold of the trembling horse.

"Born the king of angels. O come let us adore him." Her slender, mittened hand was close to touching the fraying rope halter. "O come—"

"Let us adore him." The words slipped out in his deeper baritone, surprising him.

She started, the horse shied. The bay threw his head out of her reach and with a protesting neigh, took off and merged with the snowy horizon.

"Look what you have done." Gone was the music as she swirled to face him. He expected a tongue-lashing or at the very least a bit of a scolding for frightening the runaway. But as she marched toward him through the downfall, his chin dropped and his mind emptied. Snow-frosted raven curls framed a perfect heart-shaped face.

The woman had a look of sheer perfection with sculpted high cheekbones, a dainty nose and the softest mouth he'd ever seen. If she were to smile, he reckoned she could stop the snow from falling.

He took in her riotous black curls and the red gingham dress ruffle peeking from beneath her somber gray coat. Shock filled him. "*You* are Fiona O'Rourke?"

"Yes, and just who is the baboon who has chased off my da's horse and will likely cost me my supper?" She lifted her chin, setting it so that it did not look delicate at all but stubborn and porcelain steel. She looked angry, aye, but there was something compelling about Miss O'Rourke and it wasn't her unexpected beauty. Never in his life had he seen such immense sadness.

Chapter Two

Who was this strange man towering over her and what was he doing in her family's fields? Fiona swiped her eyes, trying to see the intruder more clearly. The storm enfolded him, blurring the impressive width of his powerful shoulders and casting his face in silhouette. The high, wide brim of his hat added mystery; he was surely no one she had seen on the country roads or anywhere in town. He did not seem to have a single notion of what he had just done, scaring off Flannigan again, when she'd almost had his halter in a firm grip.

"What possessed you to trespass into our fields?" She was working up a good bit of mad. Time had to be running out. She had not been watching the road well, but Da's sled might come down the road at any moment. She had no time to waste. "Why are you here?"

"I heard your singing."

"What? And you felt you had to join in the caroling?" Men. She had little use for them. Aside from her brother, she did not know a single one without some selfish plan. "Go sing somewhere else. I have a horse to catch."

"Then hop up." He held out his hand, wide palmed,

the leather of his expensive driving gloves worn and thin in spots.

"Hop up? You mean ride with you?" Was the man delusional? She took a step back. Angel County was a safe, family place, but trouble wandered through every now and then on the back of a horse. The ruffian in front of her certainly looked like trouble with his quality hat, polished boots and wash-worn denims. And his horse, there was something familiar about the big bay who was reaching out toward her coat pockets as if seeking a treat.

"Riley?" Her chin dropped in shock, and she knew her mouth had to be hanging open unattractively. She could hear her parents' voices in her head. *Close your mouth, Fiona. With your sorry looks you don't want to make anything worse, for then we'll never be rid of ya.*

She snapped her jaw shut, her teeth clacking. "What are you doing on our horse?"

"I know your father" was all he said.

"My da was driving Riley. Does that mean he is back home so soon?"

"Aye." His brogue was a trace, but it sent shivers down her spine. Something familiar teased at the edges of her mind, but it wasn't stronger than the panic.

"My father is home," she repeated woodenly. "Then he must know the other workhorse has gone missing."

"Afraid so. We had a good view of you racing after the horse from the crest of the road." His hand remained outstretched. "Do you want me to catch him for you, or do you want to come?"

She withered inside. It was too late, then. She would be punished even if she brought the horse back, and if not, then who knew what would happen? This strange man's eyes were kind, shadowed as they were. Yet all she could see was a long punishment stretching out ahead of her. After the strap, she would be sent to her tiny attic room, where she would spend her time when she was not doing her share of the work. And that was *if* she brought the horse back.

If she lost Flannigan, she could not let herself imagine what her parents would do. This man had no stake in finding the horse. She did not understand why he was helping her, but her hand shot out. The storm was worsening. There wasn't a lot of time. "Take me with you."

"All right, then." He clasped her with surprising strength and swept her into the air. Her skirts billowed, the heel of her high barn boot lightly brushed Riley's flank and she landed breathlessly behind the man, her hand still in his.

"Who are you?" The storm fell like twilight, draining the gray daylight from the sky and deepening the shadows beneath the brim of his hat. She couldn't make out more than the strong cut of a square jaw, rough with a day's dark growth.

"There will be time enough for that later. Hold on tight." He drew her hand to his waist. He could have been carved marble beneath his fine wool coat. With a "get up!" Riley shot out into an abrupt trot, the bouncing gait knocking her back on the horse's rump. She slid in teeth-rattling jolts, each bump knocking her farther backward. Her skirt, indecorously around her knees, slid with her.

A leather-gloved hand reached around to grip her elbow and hold her steady. "Never ridden astride before?"

"Not without a saddle." The words flew out before she could stop them. If her parents knew she had ever ridden in such an unladylike fashion, they would tan her hide for sure. But the stranger, whoever he was, did not seem shocked by her behavior.

"Just hold on tight to me and grip the horse's sides with your knees."

Did she ask for his advice? No. Her face blushed. She might not have been bashful riding this way with her brother watching, but this man was a different matter. She fell silent, bouncing along, staring hard at the stranger's wide back. Riley's gait smoothed as he reached out into a slow canter, and she raised her face into the wind, letting the icy snow bathe her overheated skin.

Lord, please don't make me regret this. Yes, she was second-guessing her impulsive decision to ride with this man, this stranger. Maybe he was the new neighbor down the way. The Wilsons' farm had sold last month. Or maybe this was the new deputy come to town. Either way, she needed to find the horse.

"Hold up." The stranger had a resonant voice, pleasantly masculine. He leaned to the side, studying the ground. The accumulation rapidly erased Flannigan's hoofprints. "I think he's turned northwest. There's a chance we won't lose him yet."

"We can't lose him." Terror struck her harder than any blizzard.

"I'll do my best, miss. Are you sure you don't want me to turn around and take you back to your warm house?"

"You don't understand. I can't go back unless I have the horse." She shivered and not from the cold. No one understood—no one but her best friends, that was—how severe her life was. She had learned a long time ago to do her best with the hand God had dealt her. She would be eighteen and on her own soon enough. Then she would never have to be dominated by anyone. She would never have to be hurt again. "Please. We have to keep going."

"You sound desperate. That horse sure must mean something to you." Gruffly spoken, those words, although it was hard to tell with the wind's howl filling her ears. He pressed Riley back to a canter. The storm beat at them from the side now, brutally tearing through layers of clothes. Her hands hurt from the cold.

Night was falling; the shadows grew darker as the stranger stopped the horse to study the ground again and backtracked at a slow walk. With every step Riley took, her heart thudded painfully against her ribs. *Please, don't let me lose Flannigan,* she begged—prayer was too gentle of a request. She should have been more vigilant. She should have realized something was amiss when the horse hung back in the corral instead of racing to the barn for his supper. Had she been quicker, this never would have happened. And she wouldn't be fearing the beating to come.

You could just keep on going. The thought came as if whispered in the wind. They were headed away from town and toward the eastern road that would take her straight to Newberry, the neighboring railroad town. She could send word to her friend Lila, who could gather the girls and find a way to unearth her money sock from the loose floorboard in the haymow.

"There he is." The stranger wheeled Riley around with a confident efficiency she had never seen before. The huge animal followed his light commands willingly, this gelding who had lost his will to care long ago.

It was impossible to see around the broad line of the man's back. When he unlooped the rope and slip knotted it while he directed Riley with his knees, hope burrowed into her and took root. Maybe catching Flannigan would be quick and painless, if the stranger was as good with a lasso as he was with the horse.

"Hold on. He's bolting."

That was her only warning before he shouted "Ha!"

and pressed Riley into a plunging gallop. Snow battered her from all directions, slapping her face. The horse's movements beneath her weren't smooth. He was fighting through the uneven snow and she jounced around, gripping the stranger's coat tightly.

"Can you stay on?" He shouted to be heard over the cadence of the horse and the roaring blizzard.

She wanted to but her knees were slipping, her skirt had blown up to expose her red flannel petticoats and long johns and she was about to slide off the downside slope of Riley's rump. "No," she called out as she slid farther. A few seconds more and there would be nothing beneath her but cold air and pounding hooves.

"I'll be back for you." To her surprise, the stranger twisted around, caught hold of her wrist and swept her safely to the side, away from the dangerous hooves. She landed in the snow on her feet, sinking in a drift past her knees. Horse and rider flew by like a dream, moving as one dark silhouette in the coming night.

Cold eked through her layers and cleaved into her flesh, but she hardly noticed. She stood transfixed by the perfect symmetry between man and horse. With manly grace he slung the lasso, circling it twice overhead before sending it slicing through the white veil. Without realizing it, she was loping through the impossible drifts after them, drawn to follow as if by an invisible rope. Perhaps it was the man's skill that astonished her as the noose pulled tight around defiant Flannigan's neck. She could not help admiring the strength it took to hold the runaway, or the dance of command and respect as the horse and rider closed the distance. A gloved hand reached out, palm up to the captive gelding. The stranger's low mumble seemed to warm the bitter air. Her brother could not have done better.

"Our runaway seems tame enough." He emerged out of the shadows, towering over her, leading Flannigan by a short lead. He dismounted, sliding effortlessly to the ground. "He got a good run in, so he ought to be in a more agreeable mood for the journey back. Let me give you a foot up."

He was taller than she realized; then again, perhaps it was because her view of him had changed. He was bigger somehow, greater for the kindness he had shown to Flannigan, catching him without a harsh word or a lash from a whip, as Da would have done. She shook her head, skirting him. "I'll ride Flannigan in. He ought to be tired enough after his run. He's not a bad horse."

"No, I can see that. Just wanted to escape his bonds for a time."

Yes. That was how she felt, too. Flannigan nickered low in his throat, a warm surrender or a greeting, she didn't know which. She irrationally hated that he had been caught. It was not safe for him to run away, for there were too many dangers that ranged from gopher holes to barbed wire to wolves, but she knew what it felt like to be trapped. When she gazed to the north where the spill and swell of land should be, she saw only the impenetrable white wall of the storm. Although the prairie had disappeared, she longed to take off and go as fast and as far as she could until she was a part of the wind and the sky.

"Then up you go." The stranger didn't argue, merely knelt at her feet and cupped his hands together. "I'm sure a beauty such as you can tame the beast."

Did she imagine a twinkle in his eyes? It was too dark to know for sure. She was airborne and climbing onto Flannigan's back before she had time to consider it. By then the stranger had limped away into the downfall, a hazed silhouette and nothing more.

You could take Flannigan and go. It was her sense of self-preservation whispering at her to flee. It felt foolish to give in to the notion of running away, right now at least; it felt even more foolish to lead the horse home. Da had fallen into an especially dark mood these last few months since he had lost much of the harvest. Thinking of the small, dark sitting room where Da would be waiting drained the strength from her limbs. She dug her fingers into Flannigan's coarse mane, letting the blizzard rage at her.

"I'll lead you." His voice came out of the thickening darkness. There was no light now, no shades of grayness or shadows to demark him. "So there will be no more running away."

Her pulse lurched to a stop. He couldn't know, she told herself. He might be able to lasso a horse, but he could not read minds. That was impossible. Still, her skin prickled as Flannigan stepped forward, presumably drawn by the rope. His gait rolled through her, and she felt boneless with hopelessness. The wind seemed to call to her as it whipped past, speeding away to places unknown and far from here, far from her father's strap.

This was December. She had to stick it out until May. Only six months more. Then she would have graduated, the first person in her family to do so. That meant something to her, an accomplishment that her parents would never understand, but her closest friends did. An education was something no one could take from her. It was something she could earn, although she did not have fine things the way Lila's family did, or attend an East Coast finishing school as Meredith was doing. An education was something she could take with her when she left; her love of books and learning would serve her well wherever she went and whatever job she found.

It will be worth staying, she insisted, swiping snow from her eyes. Although her heart and her spirit ached for her freedom and the dream of a better, gentler life, she stayed on Flannigan's broad back. His lumbering gait felt sad and defeated, and she bowed her head, fighting her own sorrow.

"I know how you feel, big guy." Going home to a place that wasn't really a home. She patted one mostly numb hand against his neck and leaned close until his mane tickled her cheek. "I almost have enough money saved up. When I leave, I can keep some of it behind for payment and take you. How would you like to ride in a boxcar? Let's just think of what it will be like to ride the rails west."

Flannigan nickered low in his throat, a comforting sound, as if he understood far more than an animal should. She stretched out and wrapped her arms around his neck as far as they could reach and held on. Come what may, at least Flannigan would not be punished. She would see to that. She would take full responsibility for his escape.

And what about the stranger? She couldn't see any sign of him except for the tug of the rope leading Flannigan inexorably forward. There was no hint of the stranger's form in the gloom until they passed through the corral gate and she caught the faintest outline of him ambling through the snow to secure the latch. Flannigan blew out a breath, perhaps a protest at being home again. She drew her leg over the horse's withers and straightened her skirt.

"I'll help you." His baritone surprised her and he caught her just as she started to slide. Against her will, she noticed the strength in his arms as she was eased to the ground. She sank deep and unevenly into a drift. His helpfulness didn't stop. "Can you find your way to the house, or should I take you there?"

"I have to see to the horses."

"No, that's what I plan to do. Let me get them sheltered in the barn and then I'll be seeing you safely in." Stubbornness rang like a note in his rumbling voice.

She had a stubborn streak, too. "I'm hardly used to taking orders from a stranger. These are not your horses, and what are you doing on this land?"

"Your da invited me."

"A drinking buddy, no doubt. It must be poker night already." She shook her head, plowing through the uncertain drifts and trailing her mittens along Flannigan's neck until she felt the icy rope. She curled her fingers around it, holding on tight. "I don't allow intoxicated strangers to handle my horses."

"Intoxicated?" He chuckled at that. "Missy, I'm parched. I won't deny, though, I could use a drink when I'm through."

Was that a hint of humor she heard in his lilting brogue? Was he teasing her? He had a gentle hand when it came to horses, but he could be the worst sort of man; any friend of her father's would be. Birds of a feather. She saw nothing funny about men like her da. She pushed past him, knocking against the iron plane of his chest with her shoulder.

"Go up to the house, then, and you can wet your whistle, as my da would say." Why was she so disappointed? It wasn't as if she cared anything about this man. She didn't even know his name. It just went to show that men could not be trusted, even if they were prone to good deeds.

"That's it? I help you bring in your horse and now you are banishing me from your barn?"

"Yes." Why was he sounding so amused? A decent

man ought to have some semblance of shame. "Likely as not, my da already has the whiskey poured and waiting for you."

"Then he'll be a mite disappointed." The stranger grasped the rope she held, taking charge of Flannigan. "Come along. The barn is not far, if I remember, although I cannot see a foot in front of me."

"Just follow the fence line." She was tugged along when she ought to stand her ground. There was something intriguing about this stranger. It was not like one of Da's fellows to choose barn work over cheap whiskey.

"This is better." She heard his words as if from a great distance, but that was the distortion of the wind and the effort as he heaved open the barn door. She realized she was the only one gripping Flannigan's rope and held him tightly, leading him into the dark shelter of the main aisle.

"Where is the lantern?" His boots padded behind her, leading Riley into the barn.

"I was just getting to that." Really. As if she expected them all to stand around in the dark. She wrestled off her mittens, ice tinkling to the hard-packed dirt at her feet, and felt with numb fingertips for the match tin.

"Need any help?"

"No." Her hands were not cooperating. She balled them up and blew on them, but her warm breath was not enough to create any thaw. She must be colder than she thought. Boots padded in her direction, sure and steady in spite of the inky blackness. Although she could not see him, she could sense him. The scent of soap and clean male skin and melting snow. The rustle of denim and wool. His masculine presence radiating through the bitter air.

The shock of his touch jolted through her. She stumbled backward, but he held her hands, warming them with his. The act was so unexpected and intimate, shock muted her. Her mouth opened, but not a single sound emerged. He was as if a part of the darkness but his touch was warm as life and somehow not threatening—when it should be.

We're alone, she realized, her pulse quickening. Alone in the dark, in the storm and with a strange man. She felt every inch of the yawning emptiness around her, but not fear. Her hands began to warm, tucked safely within his. She wanted to pull away and put proper distance between them, but her feet forgot how to move. She forgot how to breathe.

"There. You are more than a wee bit chilly. You need better mittens." He broke the hold first, his voice smooth and friendly, as if unaffected by their closeness. "Now that my eyes are used to the dark, I can almost see what I'm doing."

Her hearing registered the scrape of the metal match tin against the wooden shelf on the post, the strike of the match and Flannigan's heavy step as he nosed in behind her. Light flared to life, a sudden shock in the blackness, and the caress of it illuminated a rock-solid jawline and distinctive planes of a man's chiseled, rugged face.

A young man's face. Five o'clock shadow hugged his jaw and a faint smile softened the hard line of his sculpted mouth. He had to be twenty at the oldest. As he touched the flame to the lantern wick, the light brightened and highlighted the dependable line of his shoulders and the power of his muscled arms. A man used to hard work. Not one of Da's friends, then, or at least not one she had seen before.

"How do you know my father?" Her voice scraped along the inside of her throat, sounding as raw as it felt.

"I don't." He shrugged his magnificent shoulders

simply, an honest gesture. He shook out the match and stowed it carefully in the bottom drawer of the lantern's base. "I never met him until this day, although I grew up hearing tales about him and my father. And I know who you are, Fiona O'Rourke."

A terrible roaring filled her ears, louder than the blizzard's wail, louder than any sound she had ever known. The force of it trembled through her, and she felt as if a lasso were tightening around her neck. Her dreams cracked apart like breaking ice. "Y-you know me?"

"Aye." Gently came that single word.

"But how? Unless you are—" Her tongue froze, her mind rolled around uselessly because she knew exactly who he was. For she had grown up hearing those same tales of her da and another man, the man whose son now towered before her. "No, it can't be."

"Ian McPherson. Your betrothed." Since the lantern was lit, he seized a cane that she now noticed leaning against the post. He leaned on it, walking with a limp to snare Flannigan's lead rope. "Come, big fellow. I'll get you rubbed down. That's a fine coat of lather you have there."

Ian McPherson. Here? The ground beneath her boots swayed, and she gripped a nearby stall door. For as long as she could remember, Ma and Da would talk of better times when they were young and of their friends the McPhersons. Sometimes they would mention the old promise between older friends that their children would one day marry. But that was merely an expectation, a once-made wish and nothing more. Whatever her parents might think, *she* was certainly not betrothed and certainly not to a stranger.

The barn door crashed open, startling the horses. Flannigan, now cross tied in the aisle, threw his head and tried to bolt, but the lines held him fast. Riley, who was not tied, rocked back onto his hindquarters, wheeled in the breezeway and took off in a blind run.

Da grabbed the reins, yanking down hard enough to stop the gelding in his tracks. The horse's cry of pain sliced through her shock and she raced to Riley's side. Her hands closed around the reins, trying to work them from her father's rough hands.

"I'll take him, Da. He needs to be rubbed down—"

"McPherson will do it." His anger roared above the storm. "No need to see how the gelding got loose. You nearly lost the second one, fool girl. If I hadn't been standing here to stop him, he would have gotten out. Come to the house."

Fiona wasn't surprised when he released his iron hold on the reins to clamp his bruising fists around her upper arms and escort her to the door.

"McPherson, you come on up when you're done. Maeve has a hot supper ready and waiting."

Fiona heard the low resonance of Ian's answer but not his words. The hurling wind beating against her stole them away, and she felt more alone than ever as she was tugged like a captive along the fence line toward the house. Her father muttered angrily at the storm and at her, promising to teach her a lesson. She blocked out images of the punishment she knew was to come, her feet heavy and wooden. As Da jerked her furiously along, the wide, endless prairie, hidden in the storm, seemed to call to her. She stumbled but did not fall.

Chapter Three

The lean-to was black, without a single flicker of light. Da's boots pounded like rapid gunshots across the board floor, the sound drowning out her lighter step. The sharp scent of coal in the far corner greeted her as the door slammed shut behind her with a resounding crack. Even the blizzard was angrier, beating at the closed door with immeasurable fury.

At least she was numb now. She had tucked her feelings deep so that nothing could really hurt her. The inky darkness made it easier. She heard Da's steps silence. The rasp of leather as he yanked the strap from the nail came louder than the raging storm.

"You're darn lucky that McPherson hasn't changed his mind outright and hightailed it back to Kentucky." Low and soft, her father's voice was deceptively calm as he ambled close.

Although she could not see him, she sensed his nearness as easily as she sensed the strap he clutched in both hands. "You didn't tell me he was coming."

"Doesn't matter if you know or you don't. You will marry him."

"But why?" She choked against the panic rising like

bile in her throat. Her instincts shouted at her to step back and run. The door wasn't far. A few quick steps and she would be lost in the storm. Da couldn't catch her, not if she ran with all her might.

But how far would she get? The storm was turning deadly, with the temperature well below zero. Even if she could make it to Earlee's house, her friend lived more than half a mile away. She would freeze if she tried to walk that far.

"It's not your place to ask questions, missy." Da grabbed her roughly by the shoulder and shoved her. "It's your place to do what yer told."

Knocked off balance, Fiona shot her hands out, but she couldn't see the wall. Her knuckles struck wood and she landed hard against the boards. She hardly felt the jolting pain, because it wasn't going to be anything compared to what was coming.

"Let me tell you what, girl." Da worked himself into a higher rage, smacking the strap against his gloved palm. "If McPherson changes his mind and won't have you, you'll be the one to pay. I'll make this look like a Sunday picnic—"

She gritted her teeth and closed her eyes, breathing slowly in and slowly out, ready for the bite of the strap. She heard the rustle of clothing, imagining her father was drawing his arm back for the first powerful blow. This won't be so bad, she told herself, gathering what strength she had. She could endure this as she had many times before. She braced herself for the worst. It was best if she thought of being elsewhere, maybe astride Flannigan galloping toward the horizon. She imagined the strike of snow on her face and freedom filling her up. If only she could ignore the hissing strap as it flew downward toward her.

The lean-to door burst open with a thundering crack, and the strap never touched her back. Footsteps hammered on the board floor and Da cursed. Her eyes had adjusted enough to make out the shadowed line of two up-raised arms, as if locked in battle. But the taller man, the stronger man, took the strap in hand and stepped away.

"It's over, O'Rourke," Ian McPherson's baritone boomed like an avalanche. "You won't beat this girl again. You hear me?"

"This is my house. You have no call giving me orders."

"If you want me to consider marrying the girl, I do." Warm steel, those words, and coldly spoken. He unwound the strap from where it had wrapped around his hand. Had he caught it in midstrike? Was he hurt?

It was hard to think past the relief rolling through her and harder to hear her thoughts over her father's mumbled anger. He was saying something, words she couldn't grasp, while Ian stood his ground, feet braced, stance unyielding. His words echoed in her hollow-feeling skull. *If you want me to consider marrying the girl...*

She squeezed her eyes shut. *Marry.* She wasn't yet eighteen; her birthday was nearly five months away. The last thing she wished to do with her life was to trust a man with it.

"What is going on out here?" Ma's sharp tone broke through whatever the men were discussing. Fiona opened her eyes, blinking against the stinging brightness as lamplight tumbled into the lean-to, glazing the man with blood staining his glove.

"Just setting a few things straight with the boy." Da pounded past her. "Don't stand there gawkin', woman. Get me a drink."

The door closed partway, letting in enough light to see the tension in his jaw. Ian McPherson hung the strap on the nail where it belonged, his shoulders rigid, his back taut. She inched toward the door, torn between being alone with an angry man and feeling responsible for his bleeding hand. He'd caught the strap, taking the blow meant for her.

Warmth crept around her heart, but it couldn't be something like admiration. No, she would not allow any soft or tender feelings toward the man who wanted to bridle her in matrimony. She would be less free than she was now; this she knew from her mother's life. Still, no one aside from Johnny had ever stood up for her. It wasn't as if she could leave Ian McPherson bleeding alone in the dark.

"Is it deep?" She was moving toward him without a conscious decision to do so; she reached out to cradle his hand in her own. Blood seeped liberally from the deep gash in his leather glove. It had been a hard strike, then, if the strap had sliced through the material easily. She swallowed hard, hating to think that he was badly cut.

"I believe I shall live." Although the tension remained in his jaw and tight in his powerful muscles, his voice was soft, almost smiling. "I've been hurt much worse than this."

"If you have, then it wasn't on my behalf." She gingerly peeled off his glove, careful of the wound, which looked much worse once she could clearly see it. Her stomach winced in sympathy. She knew exactly how much that hurt. "Come into the kitchen so I can clean this properly."

"I left the horses standing, and that's not good for them in this cold." He withdrew his hand from hers, although slowly and as if with regret. "I'll bandage it myself when the horses are comfortable."

"This should not wait." Men. Even Johnny had been

the same, oblivious to common sense when it came to cuts and illnesses. "You need stitches, and you cannot do that on your own."

"I might surprise you. I have some skill with a needle."

"Now you are teasing me." She caught the upturned corners of his mouth. He wasn't grinning, but the hint of it drew her and she smiled in spite of her objections to the man. "I'm not going to like you. I think it's only fair that I give you honest warning."

"I appreciate that." He didn't seem offended as he pulled away and punched through the door, holding it open to the pummeling snow. "It's only fair to tell you that I don't dislike you nearly as much as I expected to, Fiona O'Rourke. Now, stay in the house where it's warm. I'll be back soon enough and you can minister to my cut to your heart's content."

The shadows did not seem to cling to her with their sadness as he offered her one lingering look, and reassurance washed over her. She could not explain why she felt safe in a way she never had before; nothing had changed. Not one thing. Da was still drinking in the kitchen, Ma was still worn and irritable with unhappiness and exhaustion as salt pork sizzled in a fry pan, and yet the lamplight seemed brighter as she followed it through the door and into the kitchen where more work awaited her.

He had not bargained on feeling sorry for the girl and bad for her plight. Ian took a drink of hot tea, uncomfortable with the tension surrounding him. Other than the clink of steel forks on the serviceable ironware plates, there was no other sound. Mrs. O'Rourke, a faded woman with sharp angles and a sallow face, kept her head down and shoveled up small bites of baked beans, fried potatoes and salt pork with uninterrupted regularity. Mr. O'Rourke was hardly different, his persistent frown deepening the angles of his sharp features.

These were not happy nor prosperous people. What had happened to the family over the years? What hardships? While it wasn't his business, he was curious. This was not the wealthy family from his grandparents' stories. Not sure what to say, he kept silent and broke apart a sourdough biscuit to butter it. Searing pain cut through his hand. He'd used a strip of cloth as a bandage, but judging by the looks of things the cut was still bleeding. He would worry about it later. His mind was burdened, and he had greater concerns.

A single light flickered in the nearby wall lamp, but it was not strong enough to reach beyond the circle of the small table. He'd caught a glimpse of the kitchen when he'd come in from the barn, but Mrs. O'Rourke had been in the process of carrying the food from the stove to the table in the corner of the spare, board-sided room. A ragged curtain hung over a small window, the ruffle sagging with neglect. The furniture was spare and decades old, battered and hardly more than serviceable. Judging by the outline of the shack he'd seen through the storm, the dwelling was in poor repair and housed three tiny rooms, maybe four.

Nana is never going to believe this, he thought as he set down his cup. What happened to the O'Rourke family's wealth? Times looked as if they had always been hard here. His chest tightened. He had some sympathy for that. Recent hardships had broken his family. But he reckoned in the old days when they had all been sitting around the peat fire dreaming of the future, his grandparents could not have foreseen this. There was no fortune here to save the McPherson family reputation. His grandmother was going to be devastated.

"More beans?" O'Rourke grunted from the head of the table, holding the bowl that had barely one serving remaining.

Ian shook his head and took a bite of the biscuit, his troubles deepening. What of the marriage bargain made long ago, in happier times? How binding was it? It was clear the O'Rourkes wanted their daughter married. But what did Fiona want? Not marriage, by the way she was avoiding any evidence of his existence. She stared at her plate, picking at her food, looking as if in her mind she were a hundred miles away. Her features were stone, her personality veiled.

His fingers itched to sketch her. To capture the way the light tumbled across her, highlighting the dip and fall of her ebony locks and her delicate face. She could have been sculpted from ivory, her skin was so perfect. The set of her pure blue eyes and the slope of her nose and the cut of her chin were sheer beauty. There was something about her that would be harder to capture on the page, something of spirit and heart that was lovelier yet.

"I see you've taken a shine to the girl." O'Rourke sounded smug as he slurped at his coffee, liberally laced with whiskey by the smell of it. "Maeve, fetch us some of that gingerbread you made special. Fiona, get off your backside and clear this table right now. Come with me, McPherson. Feel like a card game?"

"I don't gamble." He pushed away from the table, thankful the meal had finally ended. The floor looked unswept beneath his feet, the boards scarred and scraped.

"Didn't figure you for the type, although that grandmother of yours was a high and mighty woman." O'Rourke didn't seem as if he realized he was being offensive as he unhooked the lamp from the wall sconce and pounded through the shadowed kitchen, carrying the light with him. "Your old man knew how to raise a ruckus. The times we had when we were young."

O'Rourke fell to reminiscing and in the quiet, Ian hesitated at the doorway, glancing over his shoulder at the young woman bent to her task at the table. New light flared in the corner—the mother had lit another lamp—and in the brightness she was once again the lyrical beauty he had seen on the prairie trying to tame the giant horse. He realized there was something within Fiona O'Rourke that could not be beaten or broken. Something that made awareness tug within him, like recognizing like.

"McPherson, are you comin'?" The bite of impatience was hard to miss, echoing along the vacant board walls.

Ian tore his gaze away, trying hard not to notice the shabby sitting room. A stove had gone cold in the corner and the older man didn't move to light a fire, probably to save the expense of coal. He set the lamp on a shelf, bringing things into better focus. Ian noted a pair of rocking chairs by the curtained window with two sewing baskets within reach on the floor. A braided gingham rug tried to add cheer to the dismal room, where two larger wooden chairs and a small, round end table were the only other furniture. He took the available chair, settling uncertainly on the cheerful gingham cushion.

"You've met Fiona, and you like what you see. Don't try to tell me you don't." O'Rourke uncapped his whiskey bottle, his gaze penetrating and sly. "Do we have a deal?"

"A deal?" Hard to say which instinct shouted more loudly at him, the one urging him to run or the one wanting to save her. Unhappiness filled the house like the cold creeping in through the badly sealed board wall. He fidgeted, not sure what to do. His grandmother would want him to say yes, but he had only agreed to come. His interest, if any, was in the land and that was hard to see buried beneath deep snowdrifts. Still, he could imagine it. The rolling fields, green come May, dotted with the small band of brood mares he had managed to hold on to. "Shouldn't we start negotiating before we agree to a deal?"

"No need." A sly grin slunk across his face, layered in mean. "Your grandmother and me, we've already come to terms. Ain't that why you're here?"

Warning flashed through him. "You and my grandmother have been in contact?"

"Why else would you be here?"

Oh, Nana. Betrayal hit him like a mallet dead center in his chest. Had his grandmother gone behind his back? "What agreement did the two of you reach?"

"Six hundred dollars. My wife and I stay in our house for as long as we live. Now, I can see by the look on your face you think that's a steep price. I won't lie to ya. The girl is a burden, but like I said, she's a hard worker. That's worth something. Besides, I saw you looking her over. A man your age needs a wife. I ought to know. That's why I settled down."

Horror filled him; he couldn't say what bothered him more. He launched out of his chair, no longer able to sit still. He thought of his frail grandmother, a woman who had lost everything she once loved. Her words warbled through his mind. *It won't hurt a thing for you to go take a look. The land might be just what we need—what you need—to start over and keep your grandfather's legacy living on.*

Legacy? That word stood out to him now. At the time, the plea on his grandmother's button face had persuaded him to come, that and the doctor's dim prognosis. Nana's heart was failing. So, he'd reasoned, how could he disappoint her in this final request? Not the marriage agreement—he had been clear with her on that—but in taking a look and in agreeing to meet the people once so important to their family.

Now, all he saw were broken dreams—his grandmother's, his grandfather's and his hopes to start again.

"What are you up to, young man?" O'Rourke slammed his bottle onto the unsteady table—not so hard as to spill the liquor—and bounded to his feet. "Your family agreed to this. The girl and six hundred dollars *and not a penny less.*"

"Six hundred for the girl?" Ian raked his good hand through his hair, struggling with what to say. The truth would probably make the man even more irate and if that happened, would he take it out on Fiona? He thought of his return ticket on tomorrow's eastbound train and shivered. His palm burned with pain, a reminder of how hard O'Rourke had meant to thrash his daughter. His stomach soured.

"I feared this would happen. She's no prize, I grant you that. I'm sorry you had to see how she can be. She could have lost that horse, and that ain't the first time she's done something like that. Trouble follows that girl, but she can be taught to pay better attention. I'll see to it."

He felt the back of his neck prickle. He glanced over his shoulder and noticed the shadow just inside the doorway to the kitchen. A glimpse of red gingham ruffle swirled out of view. She had come to listen in, had she? And what did she think of her father trying to sell her off like an unwanted horse?

"It costs to feed her and shelter her. Her ma and I are tired of the expense. Since we lost our Johnny, we don't have anyone to work the fields in the summer or in town for wages in winter."

And that's what a child was to these people? A way to earn money without working for it? "I don't have six hundred dollars, Mr. O'Rourke. My grandmother is ill and she isn't aware of how precarious our finances are. My grandfather made some bad investments. We are nearly penniless as a result."

"You have no money?" Fury rolled through the man, furrowing his leathery face and fisting his hands.

"Not a spare six hundred dollars. I didn't come to renegotiate for the girl." He had hoped he could bargain for the land with the little savings he had left. He had traveled here with a hope that O'Rourke would be willing to sell at a bargain to his friend's son. That a wedding would not have to be part of the deal.

"If you don't have the money, then this is a waste." O'Rourke cackled, the fury draining, but the bitterness growing. "Tell your grandmother the arrangement is off."

"That's for the best." Ian heard the smallest sigh of relief from behind the shadowed doorway. Again he caught sight of a flash of red gingham as she swirled away, perhaps returning to the kitchen work awaiting her. Disappointment settled deep within him. He told himself it was from losing out on land he had hoped to afford, but in truth, he could not be sure.

Chapter Four

Ma turned down the wick to save kerosene, and the small orange flicker turned the kitchen to dancing shadows. Darkness crept in from the corners of the room like the winter's cold. "Don't forget to wipe down, Fiona, after you throw out the dishwater."

"Yes, Ma." She dried her hands on the dish towel and hung it on the wall behind the stove to dry. Tiny tremors rippled through her, as they had been doing for the last half hour or so, ever since she'd heard her da's fateful words. *Tell your grandmother the arrangement is off.*

Thank the heavens. Gratitude and relief pounded through her. A terrible fate avoided, and she was grateful to God for it. As she unhooked her coat from the wall peg by the door, she caught sight of her mother pouring a cup of tea in the diminished light at the stove, her one luxury. She worked with great care to stir in a frugal amount of honey. Fiona winced, turning away from the sight, fighting pity she didn't want to feel. She herself had narrowly missed that kind of fate although her feet remained heavy as she slipped into her coat and hefted the basin of dirty wash water from the table. How could her parents do such a thing? And why? With the way Da was asking for six hundred dollars, she might as well be livestock up for sale.

Angry tears burned behind her eyes as she buttoned her coat, blurring the image of her ma's threadbare calico dress and apron, of her too-lean frame as she took a first soothing sip of tea. Fiona didn't have to look to know exhaustion hollowed her mother's face. That she would spend the rest of the evening sewing quietly with her head down while Da ranted and raved about their troubles.

Tiredly, she trudged through the lean-to and, sure enough, her father's voice followed her.

"You get that look off your face, woman." Da's shout rang too loud and slurry. "You keep that up and you'll be living in the back of a wagon. Is that what you want?"

"I didn't mean anything by it—"

"I don't care what you mean. I thought that boy had money. His family was richer than Midas. What in blazes did they squander it on? We have need of it, and that pipsqueak shows up whining about being broke. Time to get back the money we put into that girl, if you ask me. If McPherson won't take her, there's others who will."

And just who would that be? She stumbled into the brunt of the storm. The blizzard had grown, beating at her as if with enraged fists, her face full of ice so that she couldn't breathe. Her father wasn't making any sense, as usual. But he did sound determined to find a husband for her, someone who could hand over money to them. How could they do this to her? Could they actually force her to marry? No, this was America, not the homeland. It was modern times, not 1700.

But that was no comfort, none at all. The storm seemed to cage her in, blocking out the entire world. As if drowning, she knelt and upended the basin, letting the hot water steam and spill safely away from the pathway. She had underestimated her father's callousness again. Ever since Johnny's death, she had taken over all the chores Johnny used to do. His criticism had become unrelenting, and now he expected her to marry just so he could get some gain from it? She thought of her money sock tucked safely away, the savings she had set aside one coin at a time that no one knew about. Not even Johnny had known.

"Still at work?" The rugged baritone startled her.

She dropped the basin, shocked, as the hammering storm diminished. An unmistakable shadow appeared, standing between her and the fierce gusts, towering above her like righteousness. Ian McPherson.

"I couldn't hear you because of the storm." She straightened on unsteady legs. She felt beaten and battered. Did she have to face this man now, when she felt ready to crack apart? "What are you doing out here? Shouldn't you be in with my father trying to barter him down to a better price?"

"You're angry with me."

"You're smarter than you look, McPherson." Anger was easier. It was the only thing keeping her strong. She swiped annoying amounts of snow from her lashes and squinted. Yes, that was a pack slung over his left shoulder. "Why aren't you inside with a whiskey bottle? Or are you on your way to buy another bride?"

"No, not tonight. Maybe tomorrow when the storm breaks." He knelt and retrieved the basin. Night and shadow shielded him and his voice was layered, too. She could not be sure, but maybe a hint of dimples teased at the corners of his mouth. "Sorry. I see this is no joking matter."

"To you, maybe. I don't know how anyone could think—" She stopped, biting her bottom lip. This had to be a nightmare, a bad dream she would wake from at any moment, wipe the sweat from her brow and thank the heavens above it was just a dream. But it wasn't. The cruel wind gusted, chilling through her layers of wool and flannel, and she shivered, hard. Her teeth chattered. "Just get away from me, McPherson. I'm not fooled by you any longer."

"I am sorry." He lumbered close, gripping his cane tightly as he leaned on it. He remained straight and strong. "I didn't come here to hurt you."

"I'm not hurt." Devastated. Betrayed. Disillusioned. Sure, she was all of those things. She knew her parents were not the best of people, but never had she believed they would bend this low. "I'm perfectly fine."

"You're lying more than a wee bit." His leather gloves brushed her brow. His thumb rasped across her lashes, wiping away the snow because it could not be tears.

She reared away from his touch, pulse thumping as if with fear. It was too dark to see the expression on his granite face. She snatched the basin from him. "Just get going. Go on. Town is that way. Just follow the fences."

"Eager to be rid of me?"

"More than you can guess."

"I cannot blame you for that." His hand fell to her shoulder, his baritone dipping low with regret. "You're freezing out here. Let's get you back in the house."

"No, I can't go there." She thought of the four walls closing in on her and the darkness pounding with the blizzard's wail. Her ma would not look at her, and her da, if she were lucky, might already be deeply drunk with his feet up on a stool. They would be sitting here as they did every evening, as if everything were the same as it always had been.

But it wasn't. She could not stomach the notion of

looking at them, or of knowing how wrong about them she had been. Sure, they were strict and often harsh. But deep down she had never thought they were this cold. She could not step foot in the sitting room, knowing what she was to them.

"You cannot be staying out here, pretty girl." Well-meaning, he shielded her from the brunt of the wind as he steered her toward the fence line. The wooden posts were nearly buried, but offered dark bobbing buoys to follow in the strange, pearled darkness.

He was taking her to the barn. Her knees went weak with relief. She turned her back on the house, gripped her skirts and followed his tall shadow through the drifts. Snow needled her face, crept down her collar and over the tops of her shoes. The prairie was out there, still and waiting, calling like an old friend. Did she listen to it? Should she set aside her hopes to finish school and leave while she could?

"Careful. It's deeper here." Nothing but a shadow ahead of her blocking the worst of the storm, Ian stopped to reach back and take her elbow. Shadow became flesh and bone, and a stranger's compassion softness in the brutal night. His grip was firm, a band of strength holding her as she struggled to lift her boot high enough to step out of the impossible drift. Her boot scraped over the berm of snow and then it was like falling, trying to find where the earth began. She went down and Ian held her safely until her toe hit ice and she found her balance.

"Want to head back?" he asked, releasing her.

The thought of being in the sitting room made her throat burn. She shook her head, letting him lead her through the darkness, and shivered deep inside, where no cold wind could possibly touch her. The image of her mother bending quietly to her task of stirring a drop of honey into her tea became all that she could see.

What if her parents thought they could pressure her to marry? Already they pressured her into doing so much. A good daughter would do more for her parents. A Christian girl would honor her parents with her obedience. Only a selfish girl would think of her own future when her family was running out of money for food and coal. Like they always did, would they talk at her and team up and make her feel as if helping them by marrying was the only right thing to do? She could hear their voices as if part of the brutal wind, chipping away at her like water against rock until she thought they might be right.

But this? Marrying a stranger against her wishes? How could that ever be right? She let the strong grip on her arm keep her upright, forcing her legs to keep moving and her feet to lift and fall into the unbearably cold snow. If her parents had their way, she could imagine her life twenty years from now: worn down by hardship and thankless work and hardened by a harsh marriage to a joyless man. That wasn't the future she wanted. That wasn't the way she wanted to live.

"Fiona?" Ian's rough voice brought her back, straining as he fought the powerful wind to hold open the barn door. He was waiting for her, a kind presence on a heartless night.

"Sorry." She stumbled across the threshold, passing so close to him she could feel the warmth of his breath. Tiny shivers skidded down her spine, from closeness or warning, she didn't know which.

"You have a lot on your mind, lass." The door banged shut, echoing in the dark.

"I wish I didn't." What she wanted was to go back to believing her future was bright. She wanted to turn back time and start over the day, armed with answers she did not now have. She knew her parents were hurting financially, but with every step she took all she could hear was her father's words. *If McPherson won't take her, there's others who will.*

"I know the feeling." His kindness could drive the cold from the air and the hopelessness from the night. Heaven help her, for she could turn toward him in the inky blackness as if she saw him. The thud of his rucksack hitting the ground and the pad of his uneven gait only confirmed it. His hand found her shoulder. "It's a tough night you've been having. Let's get you dry and warm. Come with me."

"I can take care of myself." Her deepest instinct was to push him away, to shrug off his comforting touch and turn away from his offer of help. Except for her friends, whom she trusted, she was wary of help from others, for there was always a price that came with it.

"Aye, I'm sure of it, but tonight you are heart weary. Let me help." The smoky layers of his voice could charm away the winter. His fingers brushed her chin, tugging at the hood ties until they came free. Bits of snow rained off the edge, but before they could hit her in the face, he brushed them away, every one, as if he could see them quite clearly. "You, Miss Fiona, are in worse straits than I have ever seen."

"I know. My father said—" She squeezed her eyes shut, unable to speak aloud the horrible words. "Why are they doing this? Why now?"

"Your teeth are chattering." He eased down her hood and knocked the driven ice from around her collar. "There are blankets in the corner. Come with me."

"Are you still considering marrying me?" She stood her ground.

"Not anymore." The full truth, he couldn't deny it. From the moment he had spotted her in the fields looking like snow-speckled poetry, he had been drawn. He didn't want to admit it, but something had changed. Maybe it wasn't anything more serious than pity for the girl— there was certainly a lot to feel sorry about in her circumstances—but he knew his awareness of her was not that simple. His eyes had adjusted to the darkness and he could see her wide, honest eyes, the cute slope of her nose and the new sadness on her face that tonight's events had drawn. "I came here hoping you would feel the same as I did about our betrothal."

She turned away. Her hair tumbled like a curtain shielding her from his view, but he could sense her smile, small and thoughtful and pure relief. He was able to herd her down the main aisle. The runaway horse stretched his neck over his stall gate and nickered in greeting.

"Hello, handsome." She stopped with a spin of her skirts and a stubborn set to her jaw. Tension tightened the muscles of her shoulder beneath his gloved hand, and he let her go. She breezed away from him, ice crackling in her clothing, a lithe shadow that was like a spring breeze moving through him.

Just ignore it. The feelings are bound to go away. He set his teeth on edge, tucked his cane against the post and lifted the match tin off the ledge. He needed a moment, that was all, and the feelings would pass. At least, he prayed they would pass.

"You are such a good man." Her quiet praise made the horse nicker and the other animals peer around their gates to call out for her attention. A meow rang from the rafters above. Sure enough, a black-faced cat crept into the shadows, eyes shining, to preen for the girl below.

"Mally, where have you been? I haven't seen you all

day." Her greeting made the feline purr and the cow moo plaintively, as if anxious for Fiona's attention, too.

The emotions stirred within him like embers coming to life in a hopeless place. He struck the match and lit the wick, unable to keep his gaze from following her as she reached up to touch the cat's paw. The feline's purr grew rusty as he batted at her playfully.

His fingers itched to capture this image, the Cinderella girl with her patched clothes and her Midas heart. Everything she touched seemed to love her. The cow leaned into her touch with a sigh, and the other gelding—the one he had ridden earlier—leaned so far over his stall that he cut off his air supply and began to choke.

"Riley, you poor guy. I won't forget you." She unwrapped her arms from the gelding's neck and the lantern light found her, highlighting the curve of her face, gleaming on her ebony locks and revealing her gentle nature.

He grabbed his cane and followed his shadow down the aisle. The melody of her voice trailed after him. He was not surprised when the cat bounded along the wooden beam overhead, hopped onto the grain barrel and plopped to the ground. Hurrying for more of Fiona's affection, no doubt.

Ice spiked into his skin and crept in fragments beneath his collar, but he ignored the cold and discomfort. He gathered a patched wool blanket from the end stall, where it sat on top of an equally old quilt, and stepped around the pillow and the small sewing basket tucked in the soft hay. He had spotted this private corner when he had been rubbing down the horses before supper.

"Let's get this around you before you freeze." He shook the folds from the blanket.

"Oh, I can take care of myself." Her chin came up

and her eyes squinted, as if she were trying to judge his motives.

"I don't doubt that, lass, but let me." He swept close to her, near enough to breathe in the softness of her hair. She smelled like roses and dawn and fresh snow. He swallowed hard, ignoring a few more unexamined feelings that gathered within him. Emotions that felt far too tender to trust. He stepped around the cat rubbing against her ankles to drape the blanket around her shoulders. Tender it was, to tuck the wool against her collar so that she would be warmer. "I have an unexplainable need to take care of others."

"A terrible flaw." Amusement crept into the corners of her mouth, adding layers of beauty.

He felt sucker punched. Air caught in his chest, and his hand was already reaching before he realized what he was doing. His fingers brushed the curve of her cheek, soft as a spring blossom. Her black hair felt like fine silk against his knuckles. Shyness welled up, stealing all his words. It was too late to pretend he didn't care and that he could simply walk away without a backward glance come morning.

"How is your hand?" Her fingers caught his wrist, and it was like being held captive by a butterfly. Now he knew how runaway Flannigan had felt, forced to choose between Fiona and his freedom.

"It's been better." His voice caught in his throat, sounding thick and raw. He ought to step away now, put a proper distance between them and keep it that way. Best to remember he had not come here to get sweet on Fiona O'Rourke.

"Are you trying to go back on your promise?" Humor tucked into the corners of her pretty mouth.

Captivated, he could only nod. Then, realizing he had meant to shake his head, gave a half shrug.

"Too bad, McPherson. You will do as I say or pay the consequences." She tugged him across the aisle with the wash basin in one hand and the blanket cloaking her like a royal robe. "You promised I could doctor your cut to my heart's content, and I fully intend to. You need a stitch or two."

"It'll be well enough with a cleaning and a bandage," he croaked in protest. Perhaps she didn't notice the croaking or, worse, the bashfulness heating his face.

"So you're a tough guy. I should have known." She didn't sound as if she approved of tough guys. "Sit down and stay while I fetch the iodine."

A more dashing man would have the right thing to say, meant to charm and make the lass toss him a beautiful smile. A smarter man wouldn't tempt fate and would sit quiet and stoic, determined to do the right thing and not stir up feelings he had no right to. But sadly, he was neither dashing nor smart because he eased stiffly onto the pile of bagged oats stacked against the wall and savored the sight of her. His eyes drank her in, memorizing the slight bounce to her walk, the life that rose up within her here, in the safety of the barn. Gone was the withdrawn and pale girl who'd sat across the table from him. His fingers itched for his pen to try to capture the fairy-tale woman and the adoring cat weaving at her ankles.

What harm can come of this, boy? Nana's voice replayed in his memory. *Time to face your duty. You marry the girl, and you have property. Think of it. Our champion horses would be grazing on McPherson land again. Our name will have the respect it once had.*

But at what cost? He still reeled from his grandmother's betrayal. She was the only family he had left, and he loved her. But if she were here, she would have sold her wedding ring for the money to seal this deal, holding on too tightly to what was past.

"Are you all right?" Fiona waltzed back into the lantern's reach. The light seemed to cling to her, bronzing her as if with grace and illuminating the gentle compassion on her sweet face.

"I've been better."

"Me, too." Every movement she made whispered through the darkness. She knelt before him and set a small box down on the floor, the straw crinkling around her. "Why did you do this? Why did you come?"

"Because my grandmother is dying and I could not say no to her." He fell silent as she gathered his injured hand in her soft, slender ones. Tender emotions tugged within him. "She wants to find what is lost, and I—" He could not finish, the wish and the words too personal.

"I overheard you. You're penniless."

"Aye, and that's not good when you have a sick grandmother needing care." He winced as she untied his bandage and the wound began to bleed fresh. "I regret coming. I've made things worse for you."

"No, you were not the cause." Dark curls tumbled forward like a lustrous curtain, hiding her face. "I will be all right."

"I fear you won't. You cannot look at your parents the same way after tonight."

"True." She searched through the dim interior of the small box at her knee, focusing too hard on the task. She had such small, slender hands. Too tender for what lay ahead of her.

He could sense the hardship she tried to hide because it was too painful to speak of. He knew that feeling well. There was more hardship to come for her and her family, and he didn't like being the one to bear the news. "Before your father told me to get out of his house, he admitted something. The bank is ready to take back the property. At month's end, you all will be homeless."

"So that's why." She shook her head, scattering dark curls and diamond flecks of melting snow. Stark misery shadowed her innocent blue eyes. "Most of the harvest fell in the fields without Johnny to harvest it. Ever since then, we have been scraping by."

"Your father let the harvest rot?"

"He says he is not a working man. He lives as if he still has his family's wealth, although he has not had it since he was probably our age." She uncapped a bottle and wet the edges of a cloth. "Now he needs money to stop an eviction. I see. He ought to know he isn't going to find any takers that way. Who would buy a woman? Especially me."

He bit his lip, holding back his opinion. He was not an experienced man by any means, but Father's lack of decency had given him more than a glimpse of the bad in the world. The land was ideal but mortgaged beyond its value. A man could work himself into the ground trying to keep up with the payments. How did he tell her it wasn't the land that would attract a certain kind of man?

Unaware of the danger, she leaned closer. Her face was flawless ivory and he could not look away. He did not feel the sting of the iodine. There was only her, this beauty with her gleaming midnight curls and soft pink mouth pursed in concentration. Her touch was the gentlest he had ever known, like liquid gold against his skin. When she drew away, he felt hollowed out, as if darkness had fallen from within.

"I don't know how to thank you for your act of mercy."

She cast him a sidelong look through jet-black, lush lashes as she rummaged in the small box once again.

"Just doing the right thing." He remembered how small she had looked in the lean-to, and the horror filling him when he realized she was about to be hit and hit hard.

"And do you often do the right thing, Ian McPherson?" A needle flashed in the lantern light.

"It can wear a man to the bone trying. If only life were more cooperative." He cast her a grin, choosing to keep his stories private. What would she think of him if she knew how he had failed his loved ones? How he had lost his future trying to hold on to the past? He cleared his throat, struggling to let go of things that could not be changed. "I see you were serious about the stitches."

"Is that a note of fear I hear in your voice?"

"Not me. I'm not afraid of a needle and a bit of thread."

"Yes, how could I forget you are a tough one? Grit your teeth, then, for this will do more than sting."

"These will not be my first stitches."

"No, I suppose not." The corners of her mouth drew down as she threaded the needle, and he could easily follow her gaze to where he'd left his cane leaning within easy reach.

Thank the Lord, it was a question she did not ask and so he did not have to answer.

Chapter Five

Homeless by month's end? Fiona's hands trembled as she tied the last knot. The needle flashed in the lamplight as she worked it loose and used her sewing scissors to snip the thread. One last douse of iodine to Ian's wound, and she wrapped it well with clean bandages from the roll she kept on hand in the barn. She could not bear to think of the times her kit had come in handy, for Johnny had been always getting a cut here or a gash there. She could almost hear his voice echoing in the pitch-black corners of the barn, as if whispering beneath the beat of the wind.

No wonder Da wanted her married. It all made sense now. She rose on weak knees, clutching the box. Ian cut quite an impression, even in lantern light. The single flame did little more than chase away a bit of the dark, but it accented his fine profile and the powerful line of his shoulders. What had he given up to come here? A trip from Kentucky was expensive, and if he was all but penniless then this trip had been a risk, too.

"What kind of work have you been doing?" She fit the lid on the box and stood with a rustle of straw.

"Barn work, mostly. Horse work, where I can find it." He glanced briefly at the cane leaning near to him, and the flame chose that moment to flicker and dance, casting him in brief shadow and stealing any hint of emotion that passed across his granite face.

Sympathy welled up within her. That had to be difficult work with a lame leg—or was it simply injured? She stowed the box on the corner shelf, unable to forget how he'd ridden to the rescue. The poetry of him on horseback with the snow falling all around him like grace clung to her, as did the memory of her cheek against his solid back as they rode together through the storm.

"Truth be told, I'm grateful for any work I can get." The shadows seemed to swallow him.

"Me, too." She bit her lip, but it was too late. The words were already out, her secret already spoken.

"Where do you keep the kerosene?" He moved through the darkness, his uneven gait commanding.

It took her a moment to realize the lantern had sputtered out. "Here, on the shelf, but there isn't much left in the can."

"It will be enough." He stood beside her, close enough to touch. "You work for wages in town, too?"

"I shouldn't have said that. I didn't mean to." She shivered, not only from the chill air driving through the unceiled board walls. "Ian, you won't say anything to them."

"To your parents? No, I will not."

"Good. It will be our secret." She glanced upward into the dark rafters and thought of her savings buried there. An uncontrollable urge to go check on it rolled through her, and she fisted her hands. She could not do so now, not with Ian here.

"What sort of work do you do? Wait, let me guess." His voice smiled, making her wish she could see the shape that grin took on his face. His boots padded across the barn. "You sew."

"How did you know?"

"The extra sewing basket in the empty stall." His footsteps silenced and the lantern well squeaked as it was opened. "I noticed it when I was putting up the horses. You come out here after supper and sew when you can."

"Some afternoons and most evenings." She wrapped her arms around her middle like a shield. "I realized that without my brother, I was as good as on my own. If I wanted something better than my life here, I had to work for it."

A match flared to life like a spark of hope. Although darkness surrounded him, the light bathed him in an orange-gold glow as he closed the glass chimney and carefully put out the match. The single flame struggled to live and then grew, brightening like a blessing on the cold winter's night, a blessing that touched her deep inside. Even standing in the shadows, she did not feel alone.

"Now that our agreement is broken, you are free to marry someone else." He came toward her empty-handed, except for his cane on which he leaned heavily. There was no disguising the tight white lines digging into his forehead.

Was he in pain? The new, gentle light within her remained, growing stronger with every step he took. She didn't know what was happening or why she felt as if the vast barn were shrinking and the high rafters coming down to close her in. Everything felt small—she felt small—as Ian opened the stall gate next to her.

Realizing he was waiting for her answer, she cleared her throat. "I don't want to be any man's wife."

"You don't want to marry?"

"No. I've always dreaded the notion. Our betrothal has been hanging over my head since I was a little girl."

"Were you that frightened of me?" His fingers brushed

a stray curl from her face. "I hate to think the thought of me worried you all these years."

"Yes. No." She swallowed; her throat had gone unusually thick. Her thoughts scrambled, too, and she couldn't figure out what she wanted to say. The caress of his thumb against her temple could soothe away a bushel of her fears, and the way he towered over her made her feel safe, as if nothing could hurt her. "I don't want my mother's life."

"Aye, I can understand that." He pushed the strand of hair behind her ear. "What about children? Don't you want a family?"

"I want a real family more than anything." The truth lifted through her, a force she could not stop around Ian McPherson. "When I was a little girl, I would pray every night as hard as I could for God to use His love to heal my family. To make my mother smile and to want to hug me, and to make my father kind. But, as you can see, it did not work. Apparently God's love cannot fix everything that is broken here on earth."

"And that makes you afraid to believe."

"If God's love is not strong enough to heal what's wrong, how could a mere man's be?"

"That's a puzzle I can't answer." He withdrew his hand, but the connection remained. "There is a lot wrong in this earthly life and more challenges than a man feels he can face. But I believe God will make it right in the end. Maybe you will find your family one day, Fiona."

A family? She squeezed her eyes shut, fighting to keep a picture from forming, an image of dreams she once held dear. Loved ones who loved her in return, little children to cherish and raise. Her friends all had hopes for their futures, dreams of a husband and marriage they sewed into their pillowslips and embroidered on their tablecloths to tuck away into their hope chests. But she had no hope chest to fill.

"I don't know if I have enough belief for that. I'll keep faith that you find what you're looking for, Ian McPherson." She did not know what pulled within her like a tether rope tied tight, only that she did not have to think on it. Tomorrow, God willing, the storm would be over and McPherson gone and she would have a new set of problems to face.

She gripped the edge of the door tightly so the wind wouldn't tear it from her grasp. She then slipped out into the bitter night before Ian could move fast enough to help her. Her last sight of him was striding down the aisle with the lantern light at his back. If his kindness had followed her out into the stinging cold, she pretended she didn't feel it.

He had *not* affected her, not in the slightest. Truly. She clung firm to that belief as she battled the leveling winds and sandpaper snow. The blizzard erased all signs of the barn behind her, making it easier to pretend to forget him. She would not let her heart soften toward him. Not even one tiny bit.

But hours later, tucked in her attic room working on her tatting by candlelight to save on the kerosene supply, her mind did return to him and her heart warmed sweetly. Yes, it was a mighty good thing he would be gone tomorrow. She bent over her work, twisting and turning the fine white thread as if to weave dreams into the lace.

Ian stripped the last of the milk from the cow's udder and patted her flank. "There's a girl. All done now."

The mournful creature chewed her cud, narrowing her liquid eyes reproachfully.

"Aye, I'm not Fiona and sorry I am for it." He wagered

the animal was sweet on the woman. Who wouldn't be? He straightened from the three-legged stool, lifted it and the bucket with care and climbed over the low stall rails. The black cat let out a scolding meow the instant Ian's boot touched the ground.

"I have not forgotten you, mister." His leg gave a hitch, sending pain streaking up and down his thigh bone. He set his teeth on edge, concentrating on slinging the stool into place on the wall hook and missing the cat underfoot. "You're acting as if you've not seen food for a week. I know you snacked on my beef jerky last night. I caught you in my rucksack."

The cat denied all knowledge of such an event, crying convincingly with both eyes glued on the milk pail. He crunched through fine airy inches of snow and followed the feline to a bowl on the floor. He bent to fill it and received a rub of the cat's cheek to his chin.

"You're welcome." He left the tomcat lapping milk and wondered how he could get the full bucket through the high winds to the shanty without spilling. Snow drove through the boards and sifted between the cracks in the walls. He'd never seen snow do that before. And the cold. His teeth chattered as he set the pail down to bundle up. How did delicate Fiona do all this barn work in harsh winter conditions, and without help from her father?

Anger gripped him, strong enough that he didn't notice the bitter air when he hauled open the barn door.

"Oh!" A white-flecked figure jumped back. Fiona, mantled in snow and sugar-sweet. "You startled me."

"I seem to be making a habit of it." He ignored the meow of protest from the cat at the sweep of below-zero air into the barn. All he saw was Fiona. Her face had followed him into sleep, haunting his dreams through the night. The hours he had spent in the low lantern light with his notebook and charcoal had not made him grow tired of her dear face. She was only more lovely to him this morning with her cheeks pink and her jewel-blue eyes sparkling.

"Come in." He held the door for her, drawing her into the relative warmth with a hand to her wrist. She felt delicate this morning, as if last night's shock had taken a piece of her.

She brushed past him into the aisle, little more than a slip of a shadow, leaving the scent of snowflakes and roses in her wake. Why such a strong reaction to her? he wondered. Why was being near to her like a bind to his heart? His chest warmed with strange new emotions, and he did his best to ignore them as he let the door blow closed. He was a man with problems, not one in a position to care about a woman or to act on what had troubled him the night through. Best to stick to the plan. He squared his shoulders and faced her. "I was hoping to spare you a trip out into the cold this morning, but I'm too late."

"The milk." She glanced at the two buckets by the door and down the long aisle. She tugged her icy muffler from her face, revealing her perfect rosebud mouth and chiseled chin. "And you've tended the livestock."

"The animals have been fed, watered and their stalls cleaned." He was glad he could do that for her and make her burden lighter, even for this one morning.

"You did my chores." Delight and surprise transformed her. Her flawless blue eyes were compelling as any lyric, her vulnerability captivating as any poem. She waltzed to the nearest stall, her small gloved hands brushing Flannigan's nose. "And done well, too. Oh, Ian, thank you. This is wonderful."

"It's nothing I haven't done every morning at home. Or used to." Sketching her for hours last night had not been enough. He planted his feet, longing to capture the snow glinting like jewels in her midnight-black hair and her shining happiness. "When our stables were full, the morning chores took me from before dawn to noon."

"My grandmother spoke of your family's horses." She swept off her snow-dappled hood. Ice tinkled to the ground at her feet. "I met her when I was a little girl, hardly knee high. She took me on her lap and told me about the thoroughbreds."

"There was never a more lovely sight than a pasture full of them grazing in the sun, their coats glistening like polished ivory, gold, ebony and cherry wood."

"We have never owned animals like that. Just work-horses. My friend Meredith's family has a very fine driving team, some of the nicest in town, and a few of the wealthier families have horses like that. It's like poetry watching them cross the street."

"Aye, and to see my grandfather's horses run, why, that was pure joy." He ignored the bite of emptiness in his chest, longing for what was forever lost. Failure twisted deep within him, and he couldn't speak of it anymore. "So as you can see, tending two horses and a cow was no trouble at all."

"It hurts you to talk of what is past."

"Aye. Just as it is painful for you to talk about what is to come." He wished he were a different man, one who knew the right thing to do. Leaving could not be right, but staying could be no solution. Fiona wasn't his concern, although he'd spent his life hearing of the pretty flower of a girl he was expected to marry. Perhaps that was bond enough. He cleared his throat. "It was hard when we lost the last of our land. We sold off parcels one at a time, but we could not stave off losing all of it. The hardest part was letting go of the good memories that happened in the house where I was raised. Where my ma would bake cookies for me before she passed away and my grandmother would play the piano in the afternoons. When I was working with my grandfather in the corrals, the music would drift over to us on the wind."

"You are a rich man, Ian McPherson, although I do not think you know it. To have had a family who loved you and memories to hold close like that has to be the greatest wealth there is."

"I've never thought of it that way before." Material wealth had always been a great source of pride in his family, and the loss of it was a great humiliation that had taken the fight out of Grandfather and weakened Nana's heart. He had been fighting so hard to restore his family's wealth, he had not taken the time to consider anything more. But seeing what Fiona had here and how loveless her life was, he saw his childhood with a new perspective. His nana's kindness, his safe and secure upbringing in spite of his father's excesses and tempers and a long apprenticeship with his grandfather, who had taught him more than a profession but a way to face life, as well.

What would you do, Grandfather? He asked, knowing there was no way to be heard, that heaven was not that close. But he thought of the man who had taught him the difference between right and wrong and who had understood his failures, in the end. Failures he felt as powerfully as the bite of pain in his bad leg. He had spent a good part of the night drawing her face and trying to capture her spirit on the page, and those hours stuck with him. When he ought to leave, his feet did not move and a farewell remained unspoken, lodged somewhere near to his heart.

"How is your hand after all that work?"

Not a single word rose up to rescue him as she breezed

closer through the gray shadows. With no lantern to light her way, she came like dawn after the night. Sweetly she gathered his hand in hers. Lord help him, because he could not move. As if paralyzed, he stood helpless, captive to her featherlight touch and compassion.

"It doesn't look as if you broke it open." She bent close, scattering dark curls and diamond flecks of melting snow. "Let me change the bandage."

He shook his head, his only protest, and struggled to clear his throat. She affected him, there was no doubt about that, when he didn't want to be. He knew her by memory, those big, wide-set eyes framed by lush black lashes, the slope of her nose speckled with a light scattering of freckles, the curve of her cheek, the shine of her smile and her gentleness that touched him now as she prodded at his wound. A line of concern creased her porcelain brow.

"It will only take a minute and then you can be on your way back home. Come, sit on the grain bags and I'll get started."

The thought of sitting close to her, breathing in her rose-and-snow scent and fighting emotions he didn't want to feel choked him. Panic sped up his uneven pulse. "No need to go to the trouble."

"What makes you think it would be any trouble?"

Aye, there would be trouble if he gave in to the need to stay near her. Trouble in the form he hadn't reckoned on.

A shy man, he said no more, even when she continued to inspect his hand. He stayed the urge to brush the stray untamed curls before they tumbled in her eyes. He fought to wrestle down soft emotions coming to life within him, feelings he did not want to name or examine too closely. "You have taken care of me well enough, Fiona."

"It looks good, so I'll let you have your way, tough

guy." She gently relinquished control of his hand. "I should fetch some breakfast for you before you go. Town is a long walk on an empty stomach."

"Is this what you always do? Take care of everyone else? Do you have no one to care about you at all?"

"There's no other family. No one else left alive but my parents." She shook her head, scattering gossamer curls that fell back in place around her perfect heart-shaped face. What a picture she made with her simple gingham dress peeking out beneath her long gray coat and her silken black locks. "Are you starting to worry about me, Mr. McPherson?"

"We are back to being formal, are we?"

"We *are* strangers."

"And yet I've heard of you all my life, lass. I did not think you would be so beautiful."

"Beautiful? No wonder you've never married. You have terrible eyesight and poor judgment."

"Aye, I have been accused of the latter more times than I'd care to admit." He chuckled, a warm coziness coming to life within him. "You enjoy insulting me?"

"What other course do I have?" Her chin went up. "Da might decide to lower his price and then where would I be? It's best to make sure you can't stand the likes of me."

"Wise thinking." He hefted his rucksack from the shadows and settled the strap on his shoulder. "Times might get harder for you, Fiona. You can come to me if you need help, if you need a friend."

"Perhaps I should offer you the same. You might have need of a friend, too."

"That I do." They were too alike, Ian realized, as he buttoned his coat. With family burdens and financial hardships and no clear way to turn, and he wished there was more he could offer her. He grabbed his hat from a nail in the wall and settled it onto his head. His feet did not want to move, although the rest of him was ready. He had not bargained on caring about the girl. He cleared his throat. "I left something for you on your sewing basket."

"A gift?"

"Aye. It was your grandmother's." He hesitated with his hand on the door. "A promise was made long ago that it would be given to you on our engagement day. I think we can agree that you should have it anyway."

"May God go with you, Ian McPherson."

"And with you." He shouldered open the door and the fierce snow pounded against him, cloaking him with white. "Goodbye, Fiona."

"Take care of that hand." She wrapped her arms around her waist, watching as he braced his cane and ambled into the storm. The thick veil of white stole him from her sight long before the door slammed shut, leaving her in darkness.

That was one burden off her shoulders. Ian McPherson, the man chosen for her long ago, had come and gone and her family duty was over. She ought to feel jubilant, or at the very least relieved. She was neither as she knelt to rub the top of Mally's head and dodge him underfoot. She stopped to pat Flannigan and Riley and the emptiness dogged her, a vague feeling that something would never be the same.

Her sewing basket sat tucked in the darkest shadows of the stall, in the soft hay that Ian had freshly stirred and beside the quilts and blankets he had neatly folded. She couldn't make out the two items sitting on the woven basket lid until she knelt close and Mally knocked the edge of a paper with his cheek. The paper flew into the hay like a giant maple leaf, and something sparkled as it fell, too. A small gold locket gleamed dully, the heart shape intricately etched with rosebuds and petals.

The instant her fingers closed around it, she heard Ian's words. *It was your grandmother's. A promise was made long ago that it would be given to you.* The richness, the meter, the lilting kindness of his words rolled through her, one sweet wave at a time, and reminded her of his caring. Of how he had swept a lock of hair behind her ear, how he had stepped out of the darkness to save her from being punished, how his concern for her was as true as an old friend.

She closed her hand around the delicate piece of jewelry and felt the cold metal warm against her palm. Why did the man affect her so much? Why did she remember the richness of his timbre and the character in his voice? She hardly knew him. She would never see him again. He was nothing to her, not really. He was only a story her parents told, a man she had always dreaded meeting, and yet it was as if he had taken something of her she could not replace, something she would always miss. It made no sense, not at all.

What else had he left her? A note? She slid the locket in her pocket and leaned across Mally, who bumped up into her hand. The paper rattled as she drew it out of the straw. Not a note, she realized, squinting at the dark slash of lines and fragile curves. She turned the page around and her pulse skidded to a full stop. Everything within her stilled and she feared it would never start up again. She stared at the exquisite drawing. Airy delicate snow-flakes swirled across the snowy white paper, crowning a defiant runaway and a girl with her hand reaching toward the horse. She recognized her own full black curls and the gingham ruffle showing beneath her coat.

His initials were in the right-hand corner, etched next

to a snowbound fence post. *Captivated,* he had written below like a title. She closed her eyes, but the image remained as if burned on the back of her lids. *Captivated?* She had almost felt that way with him, when she had held his hand and tended his wound, when he had kept secrets and shadows had darkened his eyes, and when he told her she could turn to him for help. And why did the emptiness he left behind seem so vast?

Mally's meow broke through her thoughts. She opened her eyes to see the cat glaring up at her and yowling again in reprimand.

"Yes, I'm right here and so why am I not petting you?" Fiona ran her fingertips through the cat's long, thick fur. "You are perfectly right. I should never ignore such a good friend."

The feline purred rustily, rubbing her skirts with his cheek. She spent a few moments with Mally before tucking the picture carefully in her sewing basket, and tucking her sewing piecework into her book bag. The locket jingled in her pocket as she went to fetch the milk bucket by the door. It was gone. He must have taken it with him when he left the barn, but she hadn't even noticed. No, she had been far too busy noticing the man.

More proof it was a good thing he was gone. If there was one man who could ruin her plans for the future, it would be Ian McPherson.

Since the work was done, she had no reason to linger in the barn. Her ma needed help with breakfast. She squared her shoulders, drew her muffler around her neck and faced the dying storm.

Chapter Six

"Mornin', Fiona." Lorenzo Davis sauntered down the aisle, his boots ringing on the wooden schoolhouse floor. "You're here bright and early today."

Great. Why was he coming in her direction? If she didn't acknowledge him, would he change direction and decide to go somewhere else? Why didn't he try to charm another girl? She poked her needle through the fabric, the click of the needle point against her thimble holding more of her attention than poor Lorenzo ever would. When the toes of his boots came into sight beside her desk, she could no longer ignore him. "Good morning, Lorenzo."

"What are you working on?"

She peered up at him through her lashes. Surely he wasn't interested in hearing about sewing. She pulled her thread through and considered what to say to him that would be polite but not encouraging, and yet not too friendly to give him any kind of hope. Judging by the clean-combed look of him and that hopeful glint in his polite eyes, he wasn't simply being courteous. She had noticed Lorenzo's interest for a while now.

"A dress," she said simply, and turned her attention back to her next stitch.

"Oh. Uh, you wouldn't be going to join the caroling group at the church, would you?" Nerves hopped in his voice, making it rough and squeaky.

"No, I'm sorry."

"Oh. Okay. Well, you have a nice morning." He took a step back, a wide-shouldered, strapping young man with hurt feelings.

Not what she wanted to do, but she had to be honest. "You, too, Lorenzo."

He nodded once, apparently choosing not to answer, and walked with great dignity back up the aisle. She felt terrible.

"I can't believe you said no." Someone dropped onto the bench seat beside her, occupying the vacant side of the double desk. Lila dropped her calico book bag on the desktop. "Lorenzo is the cutest boy in school."

"Cutest?" She hadn't noticed that, although he was rather good-looking, she had to admit, as she watched him join the popular crowd, headed by their nemesis, Narcissa Bell, near the potbelly stove in the front of the classroom. But his clean-cut good looks could not compare to a certain man's rugged handsomeness and dependable presence, a man she could not get out of her mind. She slipped her needle into the seam to secure it. "Lorenzo is all right."

"He's a complete dream. There isn't one girl in this school who isn't sweet on him, and you turn him down. I heard him. He was going to ask you to join the caroling group with him." Lila, keeping her voice low, opened her bag and pulled out a comb. She began to fluff at her sleek cinnamon-brown hair. "I would have said yes before he could have finished asking me."

"I wish he would have asked you." A terribly tight pressure grew behind her sternum, and it wasn't her cor-

set constricting her breathing. It was Ian. Why did the
emptiness inside remain every time she thought of him?
It was a mystery for sure.

She folded up her sewing. She had checked on the
animals after he'd left her, and they were happy and fed
and well cared for. Their stalls spotless, their water bin
scrubbed and filled with fresh water. Even the barn cat
had been grinning ear to ear while he washed the milk
from his whiskers.

Yes, it was a good thing Ian had gone. She pulled off
her thimble. "I don't want a beau."

"I know, I know." Lila rolled her eyes lovingly as always. She believed that love happened to everyone when
you least expected it, like smallpox attacking when you
were vulnerable. Poor Lila. Then again, everyone knew
her mother and father had been blissfully happy for a
time. She came from an entirely different view of things.
"But I would have said yes. Lorenzo is just too too. What
are you sewing on? Another piece for Miss Sims?"

"Yes. I almost have the collar set. If I can work the
entire lunch hour, I can finish up and get this to her after
school." It would be another dollar for her money sock;
she might need it sooner than she'd once thought. If her
parents were going to lose the farm, then what would
happen to them? Where would they go? And what if they
found a man they wanted her to marry instead?

I'll run, she decided, thumbing her thimble. The silver
gadget winked in the lamplight like an affirmation. It was
the only thing she could do. To run away from her best
friends and this schoolhouse where she had always been
happiest. Snow still fell beyond the windows, reminding
her it was a cold world. Making it on her own too soon
and with too small of a savings would not be easy. But

it would be better than marrying a stranger, than living a life without freedom.

"What? You're going to work through the entire hour again? You've got to eat." Lila's voice drew her back to the classroom. Worry furrowed her oval face. "You're going to ruin your health."

"I've got to get as much work done as I can."

"You work too hard, Fee."

"I don't know what choice I have." Her best choice was still to strike out on her own. So why, then, was she wondering about Ian? With all the snow, would the train arrive on time or not at all? Would he be forced to stay in town awhile longer?

"All right, you have to tell me what's going on." Lila slid her comb into her bag and set it on the floor. "You look like you barely slept a wink last night."

"Sorry. I have a lot on my mind."

"Yes, and why aren't you sharing it?"

How did she tell part of the story without telling all of it? If she spoke of Ian, would it make this strange yawning behind her sternum worse? If she told of why he had left, then would she have to confess what her father was trying to do?

"Just tell me, Fee. Maybe I can help."

"I wish you could." A true friend. Her heart squeezed with thankfulness. Whatever hardships that came into her life, she was grateful to the Lord for softening those blows with caring friends. "Remember Ian McPherson? He came to meet me yesterday."

"What?" Lila's jaw dropped. "You mean that Tennessee guy?"

"He's from Louisville." Mentioning him had been the wrong decision. The emptiness that he had left intensified, like a wound festering. She bowed her head, star-

ing at the folds of delicate green fabric on her lap, but
what she saw was the picture Ian had drawn for her.
Captivated, he'd written. The expert strokes, the skilled
rendering of a girl who was too lovely and lyrical to be
plain old Fiona O'Rourke. But how she wanted it to be.

"So, what happened? Do you really have to marry
him?" A familiar voice spoke out from behind her. Kate
dropped her armload of schoolbooks onto the desk.

"Your parents can't make you, can they?" Scarlet demanded as she took the seat across the aisle.

"No, they can't force me to. Guilt me into it, pressure
me into it, scare me into it, yes. But that's not going to
happen." Fiona slipped the folded fabric into her book
bag with care. "Ian is catching the morning train."

"He's leaving? Without marrying you?"

"Lucky me." Why didn't it feel that way? She didn't
want to get married—that had not changed. But something within her had—the belief that there could never
be a man she could trust even a little bit.

"Whew. Thank God." Lila's hand flew to her throat.
"It might sound romantic in my dime novels, but really
having to marry a stranger is downright frightening."

"I'd be scared," Kate put in. "Well, not scared exactly. More like wary. You would want to know that he
is a good, honorable man who would never hurt you."

Yes, that was what she was afraid of. Fiona tied the
ribbons on her bag, holding her feelings still. Images
tried to fill her mind, images of him, noble and fine, but
she stopped them. "I was surprised that Ian seemed to
be a nice guy."

"That was unexpected." Lila leaned closer. "So, tell
us more. Was he good-looking?"

Fiona's face heated.

"He was!" Kate clasped her hands together. "So, did you like him?"

"Why did he come in the first place if he was just going to leave?" Lila asked.

Fiona held up her hands. "Wait. He's gone, so we don't have to talk about it, do we?"

"Yes," her friends answered together, looking shocked that she didn't want to share information about the man they had been wondering about forever.

"It's over. He is not a horrible obligation hanging over my head like a noose anymore." Now he was simply a feeling of loss she couldn't explain or make sense of. He had carried the milk pail to the lean-to before he left, because she had found it was waiting for her inside, safely out of the storm's reach when she'd returned to the house. Only his footsteps and the faint track of his cane in the snow were proof he had been there. A fair walk on an empty stomach and a cold one without a thicker winter coat than his. Why was her stomach coiling up with worry over him?

"What did I miss?" Earlee wove around and plopped into the seat beside Kate. Bits of driven snow still hung to her blond locks and her face was flushed red from her walk to town. "What's not hanging over your head?"

"Ian McPherson." The name simply popped out and why? Because her stomach had been coiled up with worry over him all the morning through. Had he found a warm place in town? How had his injured leg fared? Was he feeling like this, a confused tangle of sadness and relief?

"The arranged marriage is off," Lila announced.

"And you are free." Kate bounced in her seat.

Free? Her midsection cramped up in knots as she remembered her father's threat. How did she begin to explain that she wasn't free? Not by a long shot.

"Oh, Fee, your parents finally changed their minds!" Earlee clapped her hands with excitement. "That's great news. Yay. You don't have to get married now."

"I feel like celebrating," Kate chimed in. "I'm going to make cookies. No, a cake. I'll bring them tomorrow and we'll have a party at lunch. Just the five of us."

"I'll get some candy from my dad's store," Lila added. "We need to mark this occasion. Fiona is free to find her own beau. Look around, Fee, think of the possibilities."

Her face heated, because she was not looking for a schoolyard crush.

"Class." Miss Lambert strolled to the front of the room and rang her handbell. "School will begin now. Please take your seats."

Saved from having to comment on any of the boys in the room, Fiona gave thanks for the perfectly timed interruption, shrugged apologetically to her friends and slipped her sewing beneath the lid of her desk. Beside her, Lila sighed wistfully as handsome Lorenzo lumbered by and took the back seat two aisles over.

Apparently she was the only girl in school not sighing wistfully. Three other sighs rose around her. When she glanced over her shoulder, Kate, Scarlet and Earlee were all star-struck, their attentions fixed on Lorenzo as he sorted through his stack of schoolbooks.

"I still can't believe you turned him down," Lila whispered. "He could be your beau right now."

"I'm not interested in a—" She started to explain, for probably the nine hundredth time.

"In a beau," Lila answered. "I know."

She had never been one of those girls prone to going sweet on a boy and daydreaming about a future with him.

Innocent crushes were fine, her best friends were certainly prone to them, but Fiona was immune. She prided herself on her strength of will and control over her heart.

So why were her feelings about Ian tangled up like a knot in a length of thread? It made no sense. There was so much she wanted to know about him, questions she should have asked. Now she would never know about his grandmother or what his hopes for his future were. While the classroom quieted, she pulled her spelling book from her piles of texts and laid it on top of her desk. It was eight o'clock, but she hadn't heard a train's whistle yet this morning. Had she missed it, or did that mean Ian was only blocks away, still waiting?

Miss Lambert called the twelfth-grade spelling class to the front of the room, so there would be no more wondering. Fiona tucked her book in the crook of her arm, smiled at Scarlet and followed her down the aisle. She passed the frosty windows. Snow was still falling with fury. *Watch over Ian, Lord,* she prayed. *Please touch him with Your grace and make his road easier.*

She thought of the man who had offered her a place to go should she need it. Gratitude, stubborn and tender, crept into her eyes, blurring her vision. She followed Scarlet across the front of the classroom toward the teacher's desk, and she still thought of him.

"I'll be sure and send the telegraph right away for you, Mr. McPherson." The man behind the depot's counter gave an efficient nod as he gathered the coins and the note. "Word is the train is slow, but she's comin'. Just not sure when. If you wander through town, keep an ear out for the whistle."

"Thanks." Ian tipped his hat, pocketed his change and grabbed his cane. His leg hadn't taken kindly to the bitter-cold mile's walk, and while he had thawed out hours ago the healed break in his thigh bone was still putting up a protest.

He ought to be itchy to start the long journey home, but his feet were dragging as he cut across the train station's small waiting room. A crowd gathered around a red-hot potbellied stove, but he wasn't in the mood to sit with a dozen strangers and make small talk. He shouldered open the door, bowed his head against the drum of snow and headed across the street.

Was it luck or Providence that the storm was slowing? Either way, he didn't know, but as sure as it was a December day, there was the steeple of a church a few blocks away and beyond that the bell tower of the schoolhouse.

Fiona. Warmth, unbidden and unwanted, curled around him. He could picture her bending studiously over her schoolbooks with her dark curls framing her flawless face and a little furrow of concentration right above the bridge of her nose. She had been haunting him all morning. Did he get on that train when it came? If he did, what might happen to Fiona? Should he stay behind? And if he did so, what would it cost him and his grandmother? Nana was his only family, surely his responsibility was to her.

That had to be the correct thing to do, he reasoned, trudging through the ruts of ice and snow in the street. But it didn't feel right. He wiped snow from his face with his free hand, squinting against the twirling snow. The shadowed steps were hard to spot covered in white, and trickier to climb up once he was there. The school bell chimed one long merry toll to announce the noon hour. Children's shouts and squeals of freedom rose above the street noise and the dying note of the bell.

Don't think of her, man, he ordered. But his rebellious

thoughts went straight to her, wondering if she was with friends, talking intently the way girls did over her pail lunch. Hard not to imagine dark ringlets tumbling down to frame her face and her blueberry eyes flashing with laughter. His heart cracked a little as he hiked down the snowy boardwalk. Hard to say exactly why, because she was not his to care about.

It felt as if she was. He paused in front of a boarding-house's window. The day's menu was written on a black-board. Roasted chicken and dumplings looked mighty good, and his stomach rumbled as if it thought so, too. But the sharp note of a train's whistle pierced the falling snow, drawing him away from the window. Looked like God had interceded. It was time to head home.

O'Rourke didn't mind a bit that his poker buddy, the town's sheriff, was paying for his whiskey. His funds were lower than they had been in that long hard stretch before he'd married Maeve. The money from her father's farm, which he'd sold as soon as he'd married her, was long gone, and his plans for McPherson's son to take Johnny's place in the family had come to naught.

"I've got a set amount due the bank or I lose my land." He knocked back the tumbler and waited for the first swallow to burn the back of his throat. "I can't take less than six hundred. Sorry, Dobbs."

"You sure you want to go through with this?" The sheriff, old friend that he was, wasn't the judging type. He tipped back his hat, frowning in thought. "I could get you more, but it'll take a bit. I'll telegraph a few bud-dies of mine."

"I only got till month's end. Eighteen days."

"Well, that changes things."

Just his luck. O'Rourke drained the glass and banged

it onto the scarred wooden bar, thirsty for more. Hard to think in all this noise. One of the dancing girls was tickling the ivories of the warped piano in the corner, and the out-of-tune rendition of "Oh! Susanna" was hard to recognize. Folks in the saloon talked above the music. When a fight broke out at one of the poker tables, he banged his tumbler on the bar to get the barkeep's attention. If Dobbs couldn't help him, then he was going to need much more than another drink.

"I wish you had come to me sooner, Owen." Dobbs rubbed his beard, still mulling things over.

"You can't help me." Should have known. Luck had been against him at every turn. An O'Rourke shouldn't have to be worrying about living out of the back of a wagon in the dark days of winter. Time was the O'Rourke name put fear into folks. When he was a kid in Lochtaw Springs, no one dared look at him crossways. It was a good thing his daddy wasn't alive to see how the family's outlook had changed. "I've got the horses and the girl. That's all I got, unless I want to hire Maeve out to work in someone's kitchen."

"Now, I didn't say I couldn't help you." Dobbs grinned—slyly, O'Rourke didn't miss that—and tossed a few coins on the bar to pay for their drinks. "I know of someone."

"He'll pay for the girl?"

"Sure. As long as you aren't concerned about getting a wedding ring on her finger."

"I want a son-in-law to work the farm for me."

"Sure, I know, but the man I'm thinking of is always looking. He can pay you right away and, as they say, beggars can't be choosers."

That he knew for a fact. His mouth soured thinking of McPherson wasting his time and that old woman making promises her grandson couldn't keep. He hadn't even thought to doubt her claim. The family had always had deep pockets. It wasn't his fault that he'd been fooled, and it wasn't his fault that Johnny had died to leave him in this predicament. He would send another telegram to that old woman in Kentucky, and in the meantime it was time to do what was best for himself. That's all a man could do in this world.

"As long as she can help out around our place, I don't much care about a ring." He thought of Maeve, sallow-faced and a burden to him. One woman to support was all he saw fit for. "Time to make that girl of mine useful."

"He'll want to get a good look at the girl before he decides." Reasonable, that's what Dobbs was. "He'll want to make sure she's innocent, as you claim. Got a problem with that?"

"Nope, not as long as I get my money."

"If he's happy with her, you'll get it." Dobbs reached into his vest pocket for a cigar. "How about I bring him along to our poker game tonight?"

"I'll have Maeve bake up that bean soup you like." He searched through his pockets for the last of his tobacco. Either way, it looked like he wouldn't be having to skimp and save when it came to his little luxuries, not anymore. After tonight, his problems would be at an end for some time to come.

Chapter Seven

While the bell tolled in the tower overhead, signaling the end of the school day, Fiona slipped into her wraps in the crowded foyer. She was all thumbs trying to button up. She had to hurry if she wanted to drop by Miss Sims's dress shop on the way home. She had finished her sewing over lunch, and she wanted to pick up more work for tonight. After what Ian had told her, it would be best to make as much extra money as she could before—

Well, maybe she would function better if she didn't look ahead. She fit the last button through, pulled her scarf around her neck and reached for her hood. She would keep walking her path step by step, trusting that she was going in the right direction. Trusting that she wasn't alone.

"I'm definitely going to caroling practice." Lila shouldered close, ignoring the jostle and tussle of the crowd. "Are you sure you don't want to go?"

Oh, it was simple as pie to read what her friend was thinking. Fiona shook her head. Really. She did not want the opportunity to be any closer to Lorenzo. She tucked her hood in place and tied a quick bow. "I'm too shy to sing in front of people."

"You sing at church."

"Yes, but everyone sings there. Even tone-deaf people." Fiona couldn't help it. She cast a glance down the row of hooks and shelving to where Earlee was gathering up her family's lunch tin.

"Hey, I'm not exactly tone deaf. More like tone–hard of hearing." When Earlee smiled, it was like the sun shining. Everyone around her smiled, too. "You'll be glad to know that the caroling group will not have to suffer through my attempts to sing this year. Ma needs me at home."

Smallpox had been hard on Earlee's family, too. Fiona held the door open as her friends paraded through, reminded that rain fell in everyone's life. She should not dwell overly on her own hardships. The snow struck her face like a punch; the storm was still putting up a fight. She thought of the cold walk home and sighed.

"I won't be there, either." Kate swept down the steps. "It's too long of a drive. We wouldn't get home until well past supper and the evening chores. So you town girls will have to tell us country girls all about singing with Lorenzo tomorrow."

"Shh! There he is." Lila gripped the closest girls to her by the arms. Both Kate and Scarlet winced, turning pink as Lorenzo lumbered past.

"Fiona." The strapping young man gave her a brief nod as he headed in the direction of the church. He was persistent, she had to acknowledge that.

The second he was out of earshot, Lila, Kate and Scarlet squealed. "That's it. He likes you."

"Definitely."

"I would die if I were you. He is so nice."

What was she going to say to that? She wasn't interested in a schoolyard crush. And if she pointed out that

Lorenzo wasn't nearly as handsome as another man she could think of, then she would have to explain all over again about Ian. Surely her friends knew her well enough to guess at what she might—just might and only a very tiny itty bitty bit—be feeling for her former betrothed.

"Hurry up, Kate," Mr. Schmidt called out from the road, where he was tucked in the family's small, home-made sleigh.

"Coming, Pa!" Kate tossed her braids behind her shoulders. "I'll see you all tomorrow. Lila, don't get into trouble at singing practice. Or if you do, you have to tell us all about it. Fiona, you ought to change your mind about Lorenzo. You're free now!"

Free? That word mocked her. She felt as if chains shackled her to the ground while Kate and her father zipped away behind their fast horse. The falling snow still hid any glimpse of the prairie beyond town, silent and waiting like a reminder. If Da found another groom for her to marry, then she had a plan. She clutched her schoolbag tightly. She would do what she had to.

"Fiona?"

Someone touched her arm. She shook her head to scatter her thoughts, realizing they had taken her away. Earlee was at her side, concern on her heart-shaped face. Her friends watched her with similar worry.

Shame flooded her, scorching her face. How could she tell them what had happened? That her father was more concerned with having a roof over his head than his daughter's welfare? Lila might not get along with her stepmom, but she was safe and loved. Earlee might not have much, not with nine children in her family, but her father would give his life to keep her safe. Scarlet's family might be unhappy, too, but they would never dream of harming her. As for Kate, her father drove her five miles

and back every day so his daughter could have an education. Her caring friends would all support her, but if
she told them, then it would bring her sadness into their
circle of friendship.

"Fiona?" Earlee touched her sleeve again. "That man
there, the one with the black horse and the sleigh, I think
he is looking at you."

A man? What man? Panic skittered through her. She
swirled toward the road, her mind turning. Ian had gone
on the noon train—then again, maybe he hadn't. She
had thought of him when she'd heard the train's departing whistle. Had he stayed? Gladness swept through her,
as cheery as a Christmas candle. She longed to see his
grin and the spark of his poetic blue eyes, but the figure in brown leather standing beside a fancy red sleigh
was not Ian.

He hadn't come for her. Logically, at the back of her
mind, she knew there was no reason for him to have. But
her hopes cracked like a heart broken. Foolish, really, to
care so much about someone long gone. It was her decision not to care for any man so much. So it had to be the
relentless snow making her eyes tear and not emotions.
She was quite in control of her feelings. Really.

"Do you know him?" Lila stepped close, as if to protect her from the stranger's assessing stare.

"He's tipping his hat." Scarlet dropped her schoolbooks. "I don't like the way he's looking at you. Does
he know your father?"

"I don't think so." She blinked, trying to bring the man
into focus. He was rather short and lean, his features hidden beneath the brim of a black hat. Her da's words replayed in her mind. *If McPherson won't take her, there's
others who will.*

No, he wouldn't have found someone so soon. Her

bones turned to water. She shook so hard, her lunch pail rattled. No, she reasoned. Certainly not so fast, or someone older than her father. Silver locks peeked out from beneath the man's hat as he tipped it one last time, grinned not entirely nicely at the group of them and climbed back into his sleigh. See how he was leaving? He wasn't approaching her, so she was safe.

Then why was she trembling? Her lunch pail continued to rattle. They all watched the man drive away. Although he never looked back, she couldn't get rid of the strange feeling taking her over, as if her blood had turned to ice.

"Fiona, are you all right?" Lila wrapped an arm around her shoulder.

"You've gone completely white." Earlee did the same.

"He's turned the corner. He's gone." Scarlet tromped back through the hip-high drifts. Only then did Fiona realize her friend had taken off toward the stranger, probably to confront him. That was Scarlet, ever fearless. "I didn't like the way he was looking at you."

"How did you know he was looking at just me?" Her words came out scratchy, like she had a sore throat.

"It was pretty clear." Scarlet was flushed, as if she was ready for a fight. "It was scary."

"Maybe he thought she was someone he knew?" Earlee wondered.

"Maybe." Lila didn't look convinced. "Should we all walk Fiona home?"

"No." She spoke loud enough to drown out their resounding yeses. She had a suspicion she knew what the man had been doing. Her lunch pail was still squeaking and rattling as she knelt to pick up Scarlet's books. "You can't miss singing practice. What about Lorenzo? This might be your big chance to get close to him."

"There will be other chances," Lila answered, stubbornly loyal.

"He's not likely to even notice me," Scarlet confessed.

This was why her throat stayed raw. Her friends were the best part of her life. She looked from Lila and her chin set with determination, to Scarlet dusting snow off her schoolbooks with more ferocity than necessary, to Earlee standing protectively at her side. Surely, this was not the last time she would see them.

"You can't risk it." She shook her head, and snow rained down off her hood. "This might be the turning point. The critical moment when Lorenzo notices one of you and falls deeply in love. So you have to go sing."

"But what about you?" Lila asked.

"I'll be fine knowing my friends are right where they are supposed to be." It was hard forcing her boots to move; the first step away from her friends was the hardest. "Have fun, you two."

"Yeah," Earlee called out. "But not too much fun! Hey, Fee, wait up. You're going too fast."

"Am I?" She was. She'd charged through the snow and onto the broken path by the road like a runaway bull. Her skirt hem and the bottom half of her coat were caked white, and she was huffing as if she'd run miles. Goodness, she was more upset than she'd thought. "Sorry. I've got to stop by the dressmaker's shop. That might take some time, so if you want to head home, I'll understand."

"Ma needs me, but I can spare a few minutes. Besides, poking around the dress shop is fun. There are so many pretty things to look at." Earlee sighed wistfully.

Fine, so she sighed, too. What Earlee hadn't said was that there were so many beautiful things in that shop, things they could never hope to afford. "It is nice dreaming a little, isn't it?"

"Being wealthy isn't what's important in life. It's not what makes you rich. I know that. But it would be something to be able to own one of those dresses."

"It would." It didn't hurt to dream a little, to wonder what if, right? "If you could have any dress, which one would you pick?"

"The white one in the front window display, with the tiny rosebud pattern. What about you?"

"There's a yellow gingham dress hanging on one of the racks. That's the one I would pick." They turned the corner and tapped down the boardwalk. The town passed by in a blur of lamplit windows and merchants out sweeping the snow off their walks. She dodged a boarding-house worker with a broom, preferring to think about the possibilities of her daydream, of being someone else with a different life, whose greatest worry was choosing between the exquisite dresses in Miss Sims's shop instead of where she would go, where she would sleep, if she would be safe when she left on tomorrow's train.

"Do you think your pa is going to try to find you another husband?" Earlee's question came quietly, with great understanding. "Was that why that man was staring at you?"

"I don't know for certain, but I'm afraid so." She gripped her book bag more tightly, but she was too frozen inside to feel anything.

"I think I've seen him somewhere before. Like maybe around town, but I couldn't say for sure. Now, if he were Lorenzo's age and half as cute, I'm sure I would have noticed." She flashed her contagious smile, obviously wanting to lighten the mood.

Fiona couldn't help grinning, but it felt like a fake one and it died quickly. Miss Cora's shop was down the next street. It would be hard to tell the kindly lady that this was the last piece she could sew for her. It was time to tie off the loose threads of her life in this small railroad town.

"Look. I think that's him." Earlee nodded once at the red sleigh and black horse parked just up Main. "He's going into the bank, so he must be from around here. We just haven't noticed him before."

That didn't explain the icy ball of dread sitting in the middle of her stomach. She had a bad feeling, and she walked faster down the next street. She didn't feel safe until the man's horse and sleigh were out of her sight.

A nicker rang out from the back of the stables the moment Ian set foot in the Newberry livery stables.

"She's one fine horse." The owner met him with a pitchfork in hand. "She kept lookin' me over like I wasn't good enough to take care of her. But after I gave her some of my best warmed oats, she at least deigned to let me rub her nose."

"She's a character, all right." He'd missed his girl, his best friend. "I raised her from a foal."

"That right? There are few bonds closer, except for the human kind." The burly man nodded with understanding as he led the way down the main aisle. "Had someone stabling a horse ask if you'd be interested in an offer, but I can see you wouldn't. Don't blame you there."

"No, I want to keep her." Grief cut him deep at all the other horse friends he'd been forced to sell. That made it harder to think of letting another go. The mare caught sight of him, tossing her head and scolding him, as if the last thing she approved of was that he had taken an adventure without her. "Sorry, girl. You'll forgive a poor fellow, won't you?"

Duchess gave him a hard look and blew out a breath through her lips. She lowered her head, allowing him to rub her neck and ears. "Looks like you took good care of her. Thanks, Russell."

"My pleasure. I'll go fetch your saddle," he called over his shoulder.

Alone with his favorite girl, he leaned close, resting his forehead against her warm velvet neck. "You feel up to heading back home?"

Duchess didn't complain, although he thought of the deep drifts, much higher now than when they'd first arrived. She'd struggled with them, which was why he'd stabled her in the first place. He hadn't liked leaving her, but the notion of taking her back out in the hazardous cold and difficult snow gave him pause. Did he leave her here one more night and start fresh come morning? He could always curl up in the stall with her for the night. It was something to consider.

"You would have liked Fiona." He stroked the velvety curve of his mare's nose, just the way she liked it. She sighed deep in her throat, a contented sound. Calm filled him like still water, as it always did when he was around the animals he loved. He missed his horses. He missed his way of life and his calling. *That's* what he ought to be thinking about. That's where his concerns should be. But they weren't. He could not get Fiona O'Rourke out of his mind. She had burrowed beneath his skin and claimed a part of him.

Duchess nickered low and sweet, leaning into his touch as if she were asking to hear more.

"Nana was right about her." If betrayal panged deep within his chest, he paid it no heed. Whatever his grandmother had done, she had done it for him out of love. He could not fault her for that. And if places new and surprising within his heart seemed to open for the first time upon thinking of Fiona's dear face, then he denied that well and good. Aye, a smart man would not acknowledge anything that could not aid his life's plans.

"The farm was not in good shape. The barn poorly maintained, the fence posts sagging in the fields. But the land was something. I like these wide-reaching plains. What do you think, Duchess?"

She tossed her head up and down as if in agreement. He supposed the endless prairie called to her spirit, too, calling her to race the wind. Unbidden, the image of Fiona sprang into his mind, the one that had kept him up much of the night trying and failing to get it down on paper. He had captured the curve of her cheek as her dark curls brushed it, the bold set of her porcelain jaw and the swirl of her skirt when she had first turned in that storm to face him. The first moment he had seen her face was emblazoned in his mind, and he'd been able to replicate her big, honest eyes, perfect sloping nose and rosebud mouth. What he'd not been able to capture was the strength and radiance of her spirit.

Somewhere a bell chimed, muted by snowfall and distance, marking the time. Didn't sound musical like a church bell. A school bell, he figured, announcing the end of the school day. Ten miles down the rails, Fiona would be leaving the warm schoolhouse. Would she be walking with friends? Did she get her sewing done?

His gut twisted tight, a sure sign he was acting against his conscience.

"Sure is a nice saddle you've got." Russell lumbered into sight. "Don't see gear like this in these parts."

"Don't tell me you've got an offer for it, too."

"If you're interested, let me know. No pressure." With a friendly grin, he hefted the saddle onto a nearby sawhorse. "If you're in these parts again, I hope you drop by. I sure would appreciate your business."

"I will." His mind had already decided. He had lost all reason and erased the long list of his obligations back home. Of his grandmother depending on him. What about the debt he was in the middle of settling, the horses needing his care and the weight of his family's fallen dreams? They felt like nothing against the image of one woman he could not forget.

Duchess bumped his shoulder to get his attention.

"It's all right now, girl," he told his mare. "I won't be leaving you again."

In the distance he heard another sound, the approaching blast of the westbound train. The train that would take him back the way he'd come and back to Fiona's door.

What do I do, Lord? He glanced upward, hoping that the Good Father could see him in spite of the storm. There was a choice he had to make—one was sensible, the other borne on emotion alone. Only God would know the consequences of each. Only God could lead him the right way. He bowed his head to pray.

Another dollar. Fiona tied the top of her money sock into a knot. It wasn't a fortune, but the twenty-three dollars in coins would have to be enough. Her stomach knotted tighter as she tucked the thick bundle into the little wooden box her grandmother had gotten her. It was meant to be a jewelry box, but she'd had no jewelry to store in it until now.

She brushed the locket with her forefinger. The memory of her grandmother was dim, but she'd been a smiling, gentle woman who smelled of cinnamon rolls. Maybe it was because she had been baking them that day Fiona's family had come to visit. There had been an argument, and she had never seen the woman or heard from her again.

Let me tell you about the man you will marry one day,
her grandmother had said in her quiet way. Like music
the words came, although she did not sing them. Fiona
remembered being a little girl, snuggling close to her
grandmother's side, wanting to hear more of the story.
Her grandmother had obliged. *Ian is a mere boy, barely a
year older than you, but I hear he already has his grandfather's gift with horses. He's a born horseman. They say
McPherson thoroughbreds are the prettiest sight in all of
Landover County. You will live there one day, my dear,
and gaze upon the green fields where the magnificent
horses race in the sunshine. What do you think of that?*

Remembering the love that had shone in her grandmother's words drove the cold from the air. She realized
she was smiling as she closed the box's fitted lid. She
had forgotten the musical sweetness of the story; over
the years the family's agreement to marry the McPherson heir had lost all wonder. Da spoke of his exploits of
drinking and gambling and pranks done together as boys
until she began to see Ian's father and Ian himself as the
worst nightmare she could dream up.

She'd been wrong. Her smile lingered, remembering
the kind, strong man. It was tempting to want to turn to
him. She *almost* altered her plans to run westward and
go to Landover County instead.

Foolish, though, wouldn't it be? She slid the small box
beneath the loose floorboard and laid the wooden planks
flat to hide her treasures. She knew Ian's offer of help
had been a genuine one, but he had troubles of his own.
He did not need her to add to them.

The barn door flew open, startling her, and cracked
against the wall. The animals cried out in alarm, tram-
pling nervously in their stalls below. Mally flew from
his soft bed in the hay beside her with his claws out and

tail bristling to dive for cover. Likewise, she covered the floorboards with an old burlap sack and a hunk of hay.

"Fiona!" Da's shout didn't sound as angry as it usually did, echoing in the shadowed rafters. "Get down here. We're having guests to supper."

"Guests?" Her knees weakened as she pushed to her feet. What guests? A man like the one today? Fear gripped her. She still had time to grab a few things and meet the four o'clock train. If she hurried and ran most of the way, she could make it.

"My turn to host the poker game." Da came to the base of the ladder, his gaze pinning her in the half-light. There was warning in his eyes and in the hard set of his jaw. That always spelled trouble for her. "I'll expect you to help your ma."

"It's Thursday," she realized. One of Da's regular poker nights. Her knees turned watery with relief.

"Get your lazy self down here. I brought you up to work, and it is work you'll be doing or else. I don't want any nonsense tonight. You hear me, girl?"

"Yes, Da." She cast one last look toward her hidden box. The wind gusted against the north wall of the barn, howling as if in protest. She gripped the top rung of the ladder, wishing she could ignore the clench of nerves deep inside.

It's going to be all right, she told herself, but in truth, she could not be sure.

Chapter Eight

The distant *toot*, *too-oot* of the westbound train called across the prairie, muffled by the lessening snowfall and by the thick, panicked pulse thudding in her ears. Was it four o'clock already? Fiona stopped stock-still in the middle of the yard, forgetting the empty buckets in both hands, forgetting that Ma had a sharp eye on her. She shivered, but not from the cold penetrating her coat. Her parents had kept her busy with one task after another, and every time she slipped away to pack a few necessary clothes, they called her to do some other chore. And now here she was, home and not on the depot's platform with a ticket in hand.

And why was the train on time in this weather, instead of running behind? Oh, why couldn't it have been fifteen minutes late, just today? That was all she needed to get the water from the pump and slip back out of the house.

"Fiona!" Ma's shrill anger rang loud enough for the neighbors, a quarter of a mile away, to hear.

Or at least it seemed that way. Fiona jumped, her heart thudded and the bucket handles slid from her grip.

"What are you doing, standing around like a loon? Get to work." Face ruddy, mouth drawn tight in anger,

Ma stood at the top step, her spatula raised as if ready to strike. "An important visitor is to come, and if he sees you lolling about like an idiot, your father will have your hide. You understand?"

A visitor? What visitor? Surely this could not be another would-be husband for her, and so soon. "I thought it was just Da's poker night."

"And he is coming to play cards, too."

All the daylight drained from the sky. Winter's cold burrowed deep within her. "I won't do it, Ma. I'm not going to marry anyone."

"We are your parents, and you will honor us as the Bible says. You will do what you're told." Ma's face sharpened, and a harsh look twisted her features.

What could she say to that? Anything would be seen as disrespectful, and even God's word was clear. A child must honor her parents, but surely He did not mean for her to obey in this. Snowflakes struck her face like tears. In town, a mile away, the train was at the depot, idling on the tracks. Each moment that passed was one moment closer to the train's departure. If she hurried, left her belongings but grabbed her treasure box, she could run to town before the train left. But if her parents spotted her, then Da would come after her on one of the horses. She could not run fast enough to evade him.

"Fiona!" Ma's voice hit like a slap to her cheek.

She knelt to retrieve the fallen buckets, but she missed one of the metal handles and had to reach for it three times. Out of the corner of her eye, she caught her mother turning with an economical swish of her skirts and disappearing inside the lean-to. Time and defeat had stooped her spine, and misery covered her like a shawl.

If she did not run, would that be her one day? She shivered, despair heavy within her. Snow grabbed at her boots just like dread at her heart. If she married as her parents said it was her duty to do, would life always be this way? Would one day follow another, filled with hard work and a cold man's cruel words? When the color in her hair had faded to gray and her face became roughened with deep lines, would she, too, speak harshly with unhappiness?

She reached the well and fit one bucket's handle into the groove. If she squinted, she could make out the shadowy boxes of the town's buildings. *Run.* The wish rose up as if from her soul, and longing filled her. She wanted to hitch up her skirt and take off through the fields straight to the depot. To her surprise, she was already twisting away from the hand pump, reaching for her skirts when a hard voice stopped her.

"Fiona! Stop fooling around." Da appeared around the corner of the shanty. "Come stable this man's fine animal."

She swirled to a stop, vaguely noticing the bucket had fallen from the pump and hit the snow with a ringing clank. Her gaze went straight to the black horse standing obediently at Da's side and the short, bony man next to it.

The man from the schoolyard. The wind seemed to push at her, urging her to run. But it was too late.

"Come here, child." A wide hat brim shaded the man's face, but he reached toward her, holding out his hand. The glove he wore looked to be of the finest leather. "Come meet my horse. He's a purebred. There isn't one finer in all of Angel County."

"You had best not trust him to me, then." She did not know exactly why she feared the man. Perhaps it was his small smile that didn't look genuine, or the jovial way Da tried to wave her closer.

"Come on, lass. You're sweet on the critters. Come take care of this gentleman's horse so we can get started with our game." Da nodded to her, as if everything was going to be all right. He wasn't even angry with her for the fallen bucket or the fact that she'd been dawdling when it came to fetching water for his supper.

Warning enough that something was wrong. She could not make her feet move.

"Don't make me come get you." The warning came subtly and with a cold promise. "I'll be makin' sure you regret it if I do."

"Yes, Da." She left the buckets where they lay and tried to uproot her shoes from the earth. Her pulse rattled like dried leaves in a wind and she shuffled forward. She felt afraid, although she couldn't say exactly why.

"Nice to meet you, miss." The stranger tipped his hat to her, as a gentleman might. He looked dapper with his tailored clothes and long duster. But there was something in his cold liquid eyes, something she didn't understand.

"Sir." Her curtsy was shaky under her father's watchful eye. The wind swirled against her as if to grab her away, and the departing train's whistle mocked her with what might have been. She gripped the reins her father held out for her and turned on her heels.

It wasn't a terrible thing—surely this would go as before. The man would stay to supper and then speak with her father. She still had time. Relieved, she clucked to the horse and he followed her obligingly. She was panicking for nothing. It wasn't as if the minister was coming. Wedding preparations took time. She swiped the snow from her eyes with her free hand. If this really was a man wanting to marry her, she could take her money to school with her tomorrow morning and walk to the depot. Her parents would think she was at school. And chances were this man wouldn't be interested in a wife less than half his age. What were her folks thinking? It just went to show how desperate they were.

She wrestled the barn door open and ignored the flickering anxiety in her midsection. She had to stay calm. Rational, instead of acting on fears that weren't real. She led the horse into the aisle. Flannigan neighed out a warning, for this was his barn. Riley reached out as far as his stall would allow, straining against the groaning boards. The cow, chewing her cud, seemed unimpressed with the newcomer. By the time Mally let out a meow from the overhead rafter and reached down to try to bat at her, the knot in her stomach had eased.

See? Everything was fine. Likely as not, this evening would turn out much like Ian's visit. The instant Da mentioned that money would be part of the bargain, the old guy would head out the door so fast he would be nothing more than a blur.

The hinges creaked, and the inside of the barn went dark. It took her a moment to realize someone had shut the door. Flannigan trumpeted in protest. The horse she held tugged at his bits. They were no longer alone.

"Hello?" She dropped the reins and felt her way to the first main pole. She groped for the match tin, bumping the lantern. It rocked on its nail with a scraping sound, like fingernails on a blackboard.

"I thought we oughta get better acquainted." A stranger's voice lifted out of the shadows. Footsteps padded toward her on the hard-packed earth. His voice sounded closer. "I hear you're lookin' for a man."

"You heard wrong." She found the edges of the match tin and lifted the lid. "My father is looking for money."

"A pretty penny, too, but then you are a very pretty girl." His shadow hulked out of the blackness, within arm's reach.

Tiny fissures of alarm snaked through her. She struck the match, chasing away the darkness. Sure enough, the black-horse guy was within hand-shaking distance. She touched the flame to the lantern's wick. "You aren't really interested in me, are you? It's the farm. Is that why you're here?"

"I'm a lonely fellow, and lookin' to settle down. I got my own place east of here."

"Lonely?" She blew out the match, wishing she could extinguish her bad feeling as easily. "I would make a terrible wife. You ought to find someone else. Maybe someone your age? Maybe you could attend church. There are plenty of nice older ladies there."

"Now I know why your pa is desperate to get rid of you." A sour expression crossed the man's ruddy features. "You've got a smart mouth. That can be cured."

"I doubt it." She closed the lantern's squeaky door. "Why don't you go play cards. I've got work to do, and I—"

"Did I say you could talk?" His temper flared, as if out of nowhere. "I like what I see, but you have some learnin' yet to do."

"Leave me alone, you—" She didn't see the blow coming, it was so fast. His palm shot out and connected to her cheek. Pain bulleted through her skull, and white stars danced in her head. Her knees no longer held her upright. He'd hit her, she realized, as her head cracked against the wood post, and she hit the ground on her back. She tried to focus on the rafters overhead, but they were blurry. Her ears rang like church bells.

"I don't like sass and I don't take orders." He towered over her, fists clenched, ready to swing again. "Listen here, missy. You will do what I say."

Fear crackled through her nerve endings as she inched

backward. Her father was in the house, and she knew the sheriff was, too; she'd seen him arrive. "I don't understand why you would want to marry me."

"Who said anything about marrying you?" He grabbed for her arm and she rolled away. "My last gal run off, and I have need of someone to cook and clean and keep me warm."

Shock choked her. She gasped for air, but nothing came. Just a garbled sound, a terrified sound. Dimly she wondered what would happen to her. If he intended to take her with him tonight, with her father and the sheriff watching to make sure she obeyed. She would have no chance to say goodbye to her friends. They would go to school tomorrow and know nothing of why she wasn't there. The future she'd wished and saved for, the one with hopes for a happy life working at some pleasant job in a nice town and her own little house one day—all that would vanish.

"Git up!" The stranger grabbed for her again.

She leaped to her feet, evading him. Flannigan neighed angrily. Riley lunged and reared in his stall. They sensed the danger, too. What else did this man intend to do to her? Her fingers closed around the worn smooth wood of the pitchfork handle. She presented it, tines out.

"Go away." She might be able to scare him off, or make him angry enough to run and get her da. That would give her the time she needed. Time to run and hide in the falling darkness.

"How dare you give me orders!" His face twisted with rage and he lunged toward the pitchfork as if to rip it from her hand. But he was jerked off his feet from behind.

"Fiona? It's me." Ian McPherson emerged from the shadows, as strong as a hero, as shadowed as twilight. "It's all right now, I promise you that."

"I'm dreaming you up, aren't I?" She started quaking so hard the pitchfork shook. It was a cruel trick her mind was playing on her.

"The last thing I am is anyone's dream, lass." He looked real enough as he hauled the cursing man to the door by the back of his collar, handily, as if he were carrying a varmint by the scruff of the neck. "Reckon it's a good thing I've come back."

"I'll not argue with that." A good thing? A blessing it was. He had come just when she needed him most. She watched in disbelief as he deposited the man outside in the storm, exchanged heated words with him and strode inside to grab the black horse by the reins. When he slammed the door shut, they were alone.

"It did not take long for you to get into a wee bit of trouble." He ambled toward her, his limp pronounced, as if he'd strained his injury. "I was right. Your father wasted no time finding a man to take my place."

"You were the far superior candidate."

"Your nose is bleeding. Sit down." He took a handkerchief from his pocket and shook out the folds. "Tilt your head back. Pinch the bridge of your nose."

"I don't have time." Her head might be foggy and now that Ian mentioned it, blood was running down her face, but she couldn't stand here. The man—with Da—would be back. "Could you saddle Flannigan for me?"

"Saddle him? What for?" He dabbed gently at her nose, close enough that she could see the day's shadow whiskering his chin and smell the winter wind on his coat.

"I don't think I can do it. My legs are like water." She let him tilt her head back, the metallic taste of blood on her tongue. His callused fingertips pressed against the bridge of her nose and pinched it, a gently soothing touch. Why was he doing this?

"You can't go anywhere while you are bleeding hard. I hope you weren't sweet on that fellow."

"Hardly. I was prepared to introduce him to the sharp end of the pitchfork when you came."

"So I saw. I'll have to remember that the next time I think about making you angry." A dimple teased at the corner of his mouth.

Had he always been so very handsome? His perfect blue eyes had lighter blue speckles in them. How on earth had she not noticed that before? Or how comforting the sheer size of him was, that when he stood between her and the rest of the world, she felt safer than she had ever been. She longed to lay her cheek against his chest and rest, to know that nothing would hurt her as long as the moment lasted. She watched him through her lashes, noticing the squint of concern at his brow and his wince as he wiped the last of the blood from her chin. How noble he looked, burnished by lantern light and framed by darkness.

There was something about him that stirred up emotions she didn't understand. Gentle, hopeful feelings that were surely simple schoolgirl silliness. She saw it all the time, girls going sweet on a boy. Look at her best friends; as much as she loved them, it was so easy for them to fall into an innocent crush. But she was not that girl. She did not believe in love. She could not believe in noble men. So why was she leaning toward him? Why did she wish that he could be what she needed?

I don't need any man, she reminded herself. What she needed was to gather her common sense, toss these foolish thoughts right out of her head and make wise use of the time she had to escape. Da would be coming, and then it would be too late.

Please, God, she prayed, *just a little help.*

"The bleeding is slowing." He pressed a clean, folded handkerchief into Fiona's free hand. "In case it starts up again."

"Thank you." Her fingers squeezed his before she let go. "Something bad would have happened to me. I know it."

"You never figured on being glad to see me." He pushed a lock of hair out of her eyes.

"I'm grateful, Ian."

"Grateful is how I'm feeling, too." He could make out the pain on her delicate features. Far too much sadness for one small woman. She broke him, that's what she did, changing him as surely as stars changed the night. "Where are you going?"

"Away from here. My father will be pounding through that door, and I don't intend to be here when he does." She grabbed hold of a rung and started to climb, her skirts swishing and her face ghostly white in the half-light. "Why did you stay, McPherson?"

"Thought I would stick around and do some sightseeing. This is mighty pretty country."

"Did you miss your train?"

"No. I got as far as Newberry, where I stabled my horse."

"Your horse?" Her voice echoed like a stretch of music in an empty church, drawing him closer.

"I rode horseback all the way from Kentucky." He grabbed a rung and followed her into the rafters.

"It's winter outside."

"Aye, I was well aware of that as I slept night after night on the frozen ground." He climbed over a low beam, and the sight of her kneeling in the hay was a sweet sight. Her hair was atumble, bits of dried grass and seed clung to her clothes. She looked like a lost orphan in need of a home and a hot meal. Wanting nothing more than to be her shelter, he knelt beside her. "What? You think I have money to waste on comfortable hotel rooms?"

"Then how come you arrived on the train?" The question crinkled her forehead, completely adorable.

Hard it was to look at her bruised and swollen face and fear staining her perfect blue eyes. He would do anything to take away her fear. He would give up everything so she could be safe. "I got as far as Newberry, but the drifts were too much for Duchess. She's expecting a foal come spring, so I stabled her in town and bought a ticket here. It was only twenty miles, so the journey did not cost much."

"You rode the train out of consideration to your horse?"

"Aye, it was a dollar I did not want to spend, but she is the best friend I have. What is a fellow to do? You, on the other hand, cannot catch a train until tomorrow."

"I'm not going to take the train." She swept hay from the floorboards in front of her. "Why did you come back?"

"It seems I had no choice." He thanked the Lord for leading him back. What would have happened had he not followed his conscience? His stomach knotted. He couldn't stay the urge to caress the side of her soft cheek with his knuckle. A gentle touch, and he wished it could take away her pain, heal what was bruised and battered.

"Did you leave something behind?" She hauled up a small length of board.

"You might say that." There was nothing to say but the truth. "I could not make myself ride another step east, so I followed my heart back to you."

"Back to me? I don't understand." She pulled out a small box, which she hugged to her. The first hint of moonlight streamed over her as if it, too, wanted to hold her dearly.

"I'm here to help you." It was the deepest truth he had ever known on this earth, a commitment that bound him as surely as God was in the heavens. "I'm going to make sure you are never frightened like that again."

Duchess chose that moment to whicker, a low nervous sound in her throat. Flannigan neighed, and a thud of steeled horseshoe connected with a wood wall. Sounded like trouble was coming. Ian was already rising when the barn door slammed open like a hammer-strike.

"Fiona! What in blazes is going on in here?" O'Rourke's color was high from fury and whiskey, made brighter by the lantern he carried. "McPherson. What are you doing here?"

"I've reconsidered the offer." He pushed the wooden box back into the hiding place. "Fiona is my fiancée from this moment on."

He heard Fiona's gasp of shock, and if he feared she would hate him for it, then he ignored that fear. He wanted to give her time to hide what had to be her money, so he climbed over the beam and down the ladder to discuss the rest of his terms with O'Rourke.

Chapter Nine

Fiona is my fiancée from this moment on. Ian's words rang in her head like a funeral bell with every step she took carrying the water buckets back to the house. Da had ordered her out of the barn and the rise of temper ruddy on his face made her knees knock. She'd fled into the frigid twilight, longing to know what the men were discussing.

How could she feel so much gratitude toward Ian and hate him even more? How could Ian do this to her? She'd trusted him. *I followed my heart back to you,* he'd said. Trying to charm her, no doubt, when he really saw her as a means to get the land he couldn't buy any other way.

Wasn't that a man for you? She felt torn apart, like the aftermath of a twister leaving rubble in its path. The edge of the bucket slammed against her shin with a clang and a snap of pain.

Pay attention, Fiona. She shook her head, trying to scatter her thoughts, but it did no good. Her mind looped straight to Ian, how tenderly he had cared for her and his kindness in the loft. Before he'd announced he intended to marry her against her will. What happened to being friends?

"Hurry up, you lazy girl," Ma bellowed from the doorway. "You have caused enough trouble for one evening. That man, the one who came to meet you, he left angry. You have much to make up for, young lady."

Miserable, she stumbled up the steps, spilling water as she went, hardly able to see where she was going. Her vision was still blurry, and her nose was throbbing. She let the kitchen door slam shut and heaved the buckets onto the small counter.

"You are getting snow everywhere." Ma whirled from the stove. She had to notice the blood and the swollen cheekbone, but she simply pointed her spatula at the mess on the floor. "I have enough to do. You clean that up and then you get to work."

"Yes, Ma." She grabbed the broom and dustpan and knelt to swipe snow chunks into the pan. Her pulse thundered in her ears, drowning out Ian's remembered words. *I've reconsidered the offer.* He had gotten as far as Newberry and what did he do, start thinking about what awaited him in Kentucky? His family lands—gone. His family fortune—spent. What did he care about her future when he was more concerned with his?

"You had best be on your good behavior when your da gets in this house. We are not happy with you, Fiona." Ma turned the ham slices in the fry pan one by one. "We've a house full of your father's friends and Mr. Newton storms into the house saying you've attacked him. We're to lose our home because of you. You're a thoughtless, selfish girl, Fiona, and I can't stand the sight of you."

She leaned the broom in the corner by the door and emptied the snow into the waste bucket. She had done the right thing all her life. She had been quiet when her parents told her to be. She did the work her parents told her to do. She prayed day and night. She studied her Bible, she lived faithfully and she did well in school. And for what?

She washed her hands in the corner basin, breathing in the sharp scent of the plain lye soap. All she could see was her life in this kitchen, working in the half-light of a turned-down wick to save on the cost of kerosene day after endless day. That was her future unless she decided on another course. With twenty-three dollars to her name, how far could she get? She dried her hands on the small towel and hung it neatly on the stand's hook. Ian was the problem. Would he let her go?

"Stop lollygagging." Ma checked on the simmering soup with a slam of a pot lid. "Supper's almost ready."

She grabbed a towel and knelt to rescue the biscuits from the oven. They were golden-topped and fluffy, so she carried the sheet to the table and filled a waiting basket.

As she placed the basket on the table, an uneven gait tapped outside the kitchen door. Ian. Her mind looped to him like a lasso arcing through the air. Seeing him towering over her protectively, hauling the man away, feeling his caring touch to her cheek, hearing the kind rumble of his voice made her feel confused—angry and used and needing his tenderness again. What had he promised her? *I'm going to make sure you are never frightened like that again.* That's what he'd said, probably thinking that by marrying her he would be keeping her safe. That was probably his justification for his broken promises.

The door squeaked open, and there he stood looking like goodness itself. Her hatred peaked. A pressure built inside her throbbing head. If only part of her still didn't care—the stupid, needy part of her that had believed in him. And it hurt worse than any blow.

"Smells good in here, ladies." He stepped into the room as if he belonged there.

"The men are in the front room." Ma glanced at him with what passed for surprise, but after a huff went back to her cooking. That would change once Da told her what Ian had done.

Fiona ignored the silent apology that radiated off him and hefted the ironware from the shelf. The rattle of the stacked dishes betrayed her. She was not calm. She was not unaffected. She wanted to hurl the plates at him; she wanted to turn time back like resetting a clock and stay in that place where she had trusted him, where he was her friend.

Hurt and outrage blazed through her, staining her vision red, making the top of her head feel a strange pressure. She turned her shoulder and passed the plates around the table, holding back two for her and Ma. They would eat in the front room, out of the way of the men. Their loud raucous language and laughter roared through the thin board walls. Da's voice joined then, jovial. Then, why wouldn't he be?

The last plate hit the table with a clink. She kept her gaze down and her back turned. Sure, she could feel the sensation of his gaze traveling over her face, trying to make eye contact, perhaps wanting to exchange a smile or two. Maybe he was even hoping she would forgive him. He had no notion she was breaking inside, losing the little drop of faith she ever could have had in a man.

She yanked open the drawer and counted out forks, knives and spoons. She told herself she didn't care as his step tapped close and he waited for her attention. Turning her back, she didn't acknowledge him. If she felt his hurt feelings like a slap to her cheek, she ignored it. She did not care at all. Absolutely not. Not a little bit.

She sorted through the flatware, aware when his slow step left the room. Shame filled her. She laid a fork and spoon on a plate with a clatter. She was lying and, worse, it was to herself.

Seeing how Fiona despised him made something within him die a little. All through the meal at the kitchen table, with men he neither knew nor liked, he thought of her in the front room, eating quietly with her mother. There had been nothing quiet about the anger flushing her cheeks and flashing in her eyes. He could still hear the echoing clatter and clinks and clanks as she'd set the table, angry sounds he could not dismiss.

"That woman. Gettin' slow." O'Rourke ambled back to the table like a king settling onto his throne. "Don't know why I keep her some days."

"She's a fine cook, Owen." One of the men patted his belly and leaned back in his chair. "Can't say my Martha can make biscuits like that."

Footsteps padded closer and the rustle of skirts grew louder. Fiona was coming. He felt her nearness like a touch to his spirit. He knew the exact moment she entered the room because the sharp edge of her anger hit like a dagger's blade to his back.

She will understand, he argued with himself, but it did not ease the bad feeling in his gut. He'd hurt her with his actions. O'Rourke had burst into the barn before there was a chance to explain, to try to make things right with her. Now, he feared it was too late. The damage had been done.

"Hurry up!" O'Rourke spat to the women, his features turning narrow and mean as he pulled a deck of cards from his pocket. "We don't got time to waste."

Ian's fists curled, but he stayed in his seat. He was too

reactive where Fiona was concerned. Too involved. Too invested. He didn't know how it happened, but it took all his self-discipline to sit still. The need to protect Fiona beat inside him with a blizzard's fury. But judging by the way she kept her back to him as she snatched his plate and bowl from the table, he guessed she didn't want him coming to her aid any time soon. Maybe never.

Looked like he'd made a mess of things, and he was sorry for it. He pushed out of his chair.

"Stay and play, McPherson," O'Rourke commanded.

"I'm not a gambling man." He snagged his coat from the row of wall pegs. He may have been talking to her father, but his gaze stayed fixed on Fiona. Red stained her face, and the muscles in her jaw bunched and jumped. She kept her head down as she worked, taking plate after plate and stacking them into the fold of her arm. Her nose was swollen, her cheek was bruising, her face ashen. Some emotion too elusive to name tangled within him. He shrugged into his coat, wishing he knew how to make things right for her. All he saw was a long string of heartache for them both.

God may have led him here, he realized, but it was not the easiest path. Maybe not even a possible path. He could lose what little he had left of his dreams and his grandmother's hopes for the family.

"We're all gambling men." O'Rourke's tone might have been jovial, but something glittered in his eyes. Something mean and cold. He wasn't happy that the low-life varmint who'd attacked Fiona had decided he didn't want her after all. Too cantankerous, he'd said. That meant O'Rourke had to settle for what Ian was offering or wait for another offer for his sorry piece of land and his innocent daughter.

Bitter fury filled him, and Ian's mouth soured as if he'd tasted something vile. He did not have time to examine it because Fiona stayed on his mind. The stubborn jut of her delicate chin was the only sign of her fury as she swept to the small corner counter and set the plates down next to the wash basin.

"Every day is a wager," O'Rourke was saying. "You never know if you're going to win, draw or fold."

"A man's lot in life is uncertain." Hard not to agree with that. "But if he works hard, trusts God and does the right thing then most times it turns out."

"I've learned it's better to take matters in your own hands. Sit down, McPherson. I'm bein' hospitable."

"I'm not interested in your brand of hospitality." He tipped his hat, settled it on his head and wrapped his hand around the battered wooden latch. Fiona was within reach, hating him. Everything within him yelled to go to her, to lay a comforting arm around her delicate shoulders and whisper in her ear. Let her know it was okay. The misery pinching her battered face destroyed him.

But he feared O'Rourke's wrath. The man was not happy with the bargain struck; well, he wasn't alone in that. Ian didn't like it, either. Enough responsibility weighed on his shoulders, and now he had another. Fiona, carving shards from the bar soap, each falling into the steaming basin with a plop. Tenderness gathered like a storm within. If he comforted her now, her father would see it and guess how much the girl meant to him.

Worse, he feared Fiona would push him away, so he drew open the door. Regret clawed at him. He'd hurt her every bit as much as the man responsible for the dried blood staining her collar. He hated that. He forced his feet to carry him out of the room feeling less than the man he strived to be.

Alone in the lean-to, the cold and dark wrapped around him like a shroud.

* * *

Her parents' voices murmured through the floorboards as she moved in the half dark of her little attic room. Moonlight filtered through the small window enough for her to see. She folded her last pair of woolen long johns into the top of the secondhand satchel her friend Meredith had given her.

However was she going to stand to leave her friends behind and without saying goodbye? She snapped the top closed and wished she could close her feelings as easily. But no luck. Her gaze strayed to the window and across the darkness to the barn, where the faint lick of a candle danced and flickered between the cracks in the plank walls. Ian was still awake. She didn't want to wonder what he was doing. Thinking of him made her miserable in too many ways to count.

She'd been the foolish one to believe in him and to think he didn't look at her and see a good worker or a means to get something for nothing. Fresh fury flowed through her, growing stronger with each wave. So huge she became tall with it, strong with it. She curled her fingers around the smooth wood handles of the satchel so hard her knuckles burned. Anger made the pounding behind her cheekbone worse as she laid her ear to the door. Conversation floated through the ill-fitted boards.

"I don't like it, either, Maeve. But we're better off than we were. We might not have the money, but we more than likely will get to keep the house and get a strong back to work around here. It's the best offer we're gonna get, considering she ran off the one man who would pay more."

"That girl cost us a good opportunity."

"And I won't be forgettin' it."

She wrapped a bubble around her heart to protect it from her parents' words. She eased the satchel to the floor, packed and ready to go. All she needed was to wait for her parents to go to bed and Ian's light to go out. The night silenced, as if waiting, and the enormity of what she was about to do frightened her. This was not her plan, running away when there was no train to whisk her away quickly and without enough money to see her far. Her stinging cheek and throbbing head reminded her of how serious it was to be alone in the world. If Ian had not come along—

She blinked back the hot wetness in her eyes. She was not a girl given to crying or sentimental foolishness. She did not feel anything more than a distant gratitude for the man—really, and if that wasn't the truth, then it would be. She would think of all his faults until this confused need to like him disappeared. She would do everything she could to forget the apology in his eyes back in the kitchen. It wasn't working. Beneath her anger wasn't really hatred at all, but recognition. They were two like souls, one who had lost his dreams and one who intended to find hers.

All she wanted was a safe place to thrive. *It has to be out there somewhere, right, Lord?* The prayer rose up from the truest part of her spirit, from the place within her that no one could break. *Please lead me toward it tonight. Please stay with me so I am not alone.*

The sky outside stretched as if to infinity, the darkly shining prairie vast. Although the storm had stopped, frost hazed the edges of the window panes, a sign of a bitterly cold night ahead. She had dressed warmly in three layers of woolen long johns. Surely that would see her through until morning. She did not know how far she would get, but if she and Flannigan rode until dawn they would be far enough that no one—not even Ian—would come after them.

Time crept slowly until the voices downstairs silenced and the light in the barn faded. This is it, Fiona. She rose, gathering her courage. In the inky darkness, she seized her satchel, eased open the door and crept down the ladder. Her father's muffled snoring from the next room told her the faint creak of the boards had not wakened him. She tiptoed across the icy floor, hearing every loose board. Her rustling skirts and the whisper of her movements echoed in the small, dark kitchen.

Almost there. She took her shoes in hand and her wraps from the wall peg and faced her biggest obstacle: the lean-to door. The latch caught, and she laid her coat over it to muffle the sound. The door creaked open—she moved it slowly, inch by inch, until she could squeeze through—and then eased it closed. The latch clunked like a shot in the night. Her pulse stopped. But when she leaned her ear against the door, her father's steady snoring continued to drone.

Whew. Teeth chattering, she slipped into her coat, cinching the sash tightly, and sat down to yank on her shoes.

Small hope steadied her as she waded through the luminous snow. Moonlight shone like a dark pearl, guiding her way to the still barn. Only one hurdle left—she surely hoped Ian was a sound sleeper. She opened the door with care and hoped the rush of icy wind would not be enough to wake him. She waited a moment until her eyes adjusted to the thick darkness.

Down the aisle, the horses dozed. Their rhythmic, heavy breathing was a dependable cadence that hid the light pad of her shoes against the hard-packed earth. She set her satchel near the bottom rung and gripped the thin wood slat. The wood creaked faintly as it took her weight. A small sound, hardly noticeable. She eased her foot onto the ladder rung and climbed to the next board. One step closer to her freedom.

"Where are you going, lass?" A voice rumbled like thunder out of the night. Ian McPherson, not asleep, not at all.

Chapter Ten

Her hand slipped, she lost her balance and her feet hit the ground. The shock of the hard landing traveled up her bones. It was nothing like the shock at seeing him emerge, hands fisted, brawny shoulders set, a man twice her size and strength. He could easily stop her.

"You wouldn't be heading up into the loft to get your running-away money, would you?" His footsteps marched closer, uneven and with the accompanying tap of his cane. "That wouldn't be a satchel at your feet, would it?"

"I'm not interested in having a conversation with the likes of you." Not only had he traded her future for his, he was going to stop her chance to escape. Would he drag her back to the house and her father?

Probably. But instead of grabbing her, he stopped. The lantern well eked open. He was taking the time to strike a match instead of stopping her. He must think she would be too afraid to run now. Or, more likely, that he had her trapped. Well, she was not so easy to defeat. She seized the handles of the satchel, slid them over one wrist and leaped onto the ladder. Rung by rung she rose into the rafters as the match struck and flared, casting light into the darkness like hope, a hope she would not lose.

She could still get away. She felt the pull of his gaze as she tossed her satchel into the hay and tumbled onto the loft boards. She glanced over her shoulder—a mistake. He was a striking sight, bathed in the flicking orange light. Standing tall in that square-shouldered way of his, he appeared to be all that was good and right. A strange glow within her caught and came to life like a flame to a wick. Her eyes teared and she could not explain it. She did not like this man. In fact, she detested him. Ian McPherson pretended to be something he was not. Lying, when he ought to have told her the truth. Befriending her and telling her she was safe with him, when he ought to have admitted he was using her. He was a man she could never trust again.

She had to do her best not to forget that. She hated the wish rising up within her. Foolish, that's what her feelings were. A schoolgirl's stubborn clinging to a fairy tale, one which could never be true. She wrenched away, stinging in deep places she had never known before— yes, she cared about him and her heart knew it. But her mind was more rational and smarter than her heart. She climbed to her feet, determined.

"What are you going to do, Fiona? Run off into the night? Walk down the road all the way to town by yourself?" The sincere concern layering his rich baritone chased up the ladder after her. "You have no protection. Tonight you saw a bit of what can happen to a young lady alone in this world."

"I doubt Da's friend is waiting outside the barn." She scrambled over the beam, catching her hem in her haste. She winced at the ripping sound and dropped to her knees in the sweet, fragrant hay.

"No, but there are plenty of men of his ilk in the world. Do you want to risk being trapped like that again? Or worse? Anything could happen to you. Lass, you do not know how much worse you could be harmed."

How did he get the perfect ring of caring into his tone? She marveled, pawing away shanks of dried grass. He was attempting to play on her fears, on the truth neither of them could deny. Was it smart to run off on her own in the dark? No, but it was better than the known danger here—the danger of losing her freedom and her dreams. She swept off the burlap and pried it off the floor, working as fast as her fingers could go.

"I'm asking you to stay. I'll keep you safe. I won't let any harm come to you. I vow it, on my honor."

Why did her emotions respond? What was wrong with her? She pried up the boards with a clatter. Why did she want to believe his concern was real? He was simply pretending he cared. That was the real Ian McPherson. Sure, he was sorry he had hurt her, but it hadn't stopped him. Now he was trying to talk her out of leaving for his own sake, not hers.

She hardened her heart and dug out the box. Wasn't it odd that Ian wasn't coming up after her? Why wasn't he trying to stop her? There was no telltale squeak of the ladder, no groan of wood beneath his weight.

"I know what you think of me, Fee, and I'm sorry." His voice came from down below at the ladder's base where he waited for her. "Come down and let me take care of you. Let me tell you what I've planned."

She hesitated, brushed by moonlight, feeling the luminescence against her cheek, and it was like the emotion within her, longing to be cared for. But that was only another one of her foolish notions and she could not give in to it. She hated that her fingers trembled too hard to open the box on first try, and it felt as if a sob lodged in her throat. Why did she feel torn apart? What was he doing to her? The sincerity in his tone, the affection in his words were like an unimaginable treasure that lured her; it was what she wanted most. But he was not a man she could trust.

She wedged open the lid. It was too dark to see. Her pulse fluttered wildly. Was her money gone? She bit her lip, forced her hands to stop shaking and held the box up to a slat of moonlight slanting between the boards.

The sock was still there, the contents of the box untouched, the locket glinting faintly in the starlight. What a relief. She grabbed her stash of money, and there was the picture he had drawn. An illustration of a girl and her horse, but on this night she saw something more. The swirl of the wind-driven snow, the stretch of the unseen prairie, the spirit of freedom that somehow came from lashing lines of ink on a page. Almost as if he understood. As if he knew her spirit's longing.

And if he knew that, surely he would understand. She had to leave. She stuffed her savings into the top of her satchel, the hay crackling beneath her step. "I have an offer to make you, McPherson."

"Do tell." A smile crept into his tone; he thought he had won.

She crept deeper into the mow. He still waited for her to come down the ladder. He must think there was no other way out of the barn. It did not feel right to trick him, but then wasn't that what he had done to her? A few more paces brought her to the loading door. "You stay here with the land, and I'll go where I please. Da will be rid of the expense of me, and you won't be forced to marry to get what you want."

"Is that what you think? That I am using you to get the land?"

"Why else would you accept Da's offer?" She shouldered open the heavy door and prayed no boards would creak.

"Have I said a single word about marriage?"

"Not directly."

"And surely you do not think there will be a wedding tonight or tomorrow?"

"Not if I can help it."

"Then why the rush to leave? You will be safe here, lass. This is your home."

"And you're using *this* for an argument?" The icy air felt welcome against her face. She gripped the rope and gave it a testing tug. "I've been hurt enough here. I shall take my chances in that big, dangerous world you are afraid of."

"Do you know what a boardinghouse costs by the week? What of your meals? What if you have trouble finding work? What will you do then? Your savings isn't enough. It won't see you far." Caring rang like a true bell, perfect in pitch and honesty.

A part of her longed to stay, if only for the promise of caring in his voice. As much as she longed to be truly cared for, she did not trust it. The rope held, so she transferred her weight. The door swung closed, bashing her in the shoulder. She bit her lip, ignored the pain and dug her shoes into the hemp. She had to stop thinking of Ian. She inched downward, gritting her teeth as the door bashed her again. She caught it and waited a beat, easing it closed with what she hoped was the smallest of sounds. How long would it take for him to figure out she was gone?

Probably not long. She tossed her satchel. It landed with a muted thump in the soft remnants of hay left over from the morning's feed. The platinum moonlight focused on her like a beacon so she went fast, sliding some of the way, going hand over hand the rest. No time to waste. She hit the ground, grabbed her satchel and ran. Was Ian still talking at her, waiting for an answer? Still trying to convince her that marriage was the best of her choices?

Her breath rose in white clouds as she skidded to a stop at the first stall door—Flannigan's. All she had to do was to release the latch, and the horse would come running. She'd catch a handful of mane, swing up onto him and they would be off, following the call of the prairie and the lure of the moon. She would be free.

A footstep crunched in the snow behind her—Ian, larger than life and radiating fury. She stared at him, disbelieving. Was that really him and not a figment of her fears?

"Going somewhere, lass?" His anger boomed in the empty corral, resounding against the flawless night.

"How did you—"

"I've done the same a time or two when I was a boy." He wrenched the gate open and pounded into the silvered light. Every strong line of his powerful form and the curves of his muscles were highlighted; he looked like a knight of old, mighty and invincible—a very angry knight. "I'm not as dim-witted as you think."

The stars faded; the moonlight waned. Maybe that was simply her hopes hitting ground. She could run, but how far would she get? A few beats of his step and his hand curled around her nape, holding her captive by her coat collar and ending all possibilities.

"Come back inside." His command was not a harsh one.

"I cannot."

"Planning on staying here in the corral all night, are you?" He did not relent, his grip on her steadfast. "You have to go somewhere or you will freeze. It may as well be with me."

"You could let me go." She turned in his grasp, enough to show the plea in her eyes. Such immense sadness. It was what had struck him hardest about her.

"If I did, do you even know where you would go?"

"Far away as fast as I can."

"That's no sound plan." It pained him to say so.

"I had a good one, but you ruined it." Defiance painted her like the moonlight. "And that means you owe me. Please, Ian, walk away."

A smart man would not care so much. A wise man would lock away his feelings and never let them see light again. He felt sorely alone, although they stood together in the platinum night. "I cannot."

"I could give you half my money. It's not much, but it's something. To just look the other way while I ride Flannigan."

"No." The thought of her alone in this world destroyed him. He reached deep inside for the courage to hurt her more and tugged her toward him. "You must stay with me, lass."

"There has to be something you want, some bargain we can agree to." She dug in her heels. The frost clung to her dark hair and lashes, making her look like some lost winter sprite of ancient lore, a sweet bit of goodness too fragile to be captured for long. "You said we were friends, Ian. If you ever meant that, if you have any honor at all, then close your eyes and when you open them again, I'll be gone. It won't be your fault. You won't know where I am. Please. I can't do what you're asking."

"You're going to have to find a way to, my friend." He

softened his words, wanting to make her defeat easier. He did not like the agony taking her over inch by inch—the slump of her shoulders, the tuck of her chin and the way she drew inward just a little. Aye, but she was killing him as surely as if she held a dagger to his heart.

He watched her gulp, watched fear flicker across her face. She came with him haltingly, her feet seeming heavy. For one moment the rebellion remained etched on her like starlight on the wild, endless prairie; the wind lashed her dark curls as if trying to blow her away from him. She was calculating her chances of escaping him, no doubt, measuring the dark corners of the corral and wondering if she broke his hold could she outrun him?

"If you run, then I would be out the money I promised your father. It's in a lawyer's trust in Newberry." He hefted her along, gently but firmly, and prayed his soft—and secret—feelings did not show. "I had a contract drawn up. Fortunate it was there was an attorney in town with the spare time to help me."

"Yes, lucky you." She choked back a sob, but he felt it roll through her, pure agony as if straight from her soul.

He was sorry for it. "It was Providence watching over you, lass. Your father's back payments and fees will be paid, so that you won't lose your home come month's end."

"I intend to lose my home just the same. You can't keep me here, Ian. You can't watch over me every second."

"That's not my wish." He hauled her through the gate, leaving it open rather than release his hold on her. Not because he feared her escape but because he liked holding her close. Being at her side, knowing he was what stood between her and sorrow, knowing he could give her what she wanted most—he and no other man—made his sadness easier to abide. He loved the girl, aye. It was the first blush of emotion but it was love all the same— a love she would never feel for him.

"I sold my saddle," he confessed as they crossed the yard together. "I pawned my grandfather's pocket watch and gold fob, which he gave me for my sixteenth birthday. Both had been his father's. I had hopes of giving them to my son one day."

"And why are you telling me this? Using guilt to keep me here?"

"I only want you to understand my sacrifice." The path the moon made on the snow felt blessed, extraordinary, as it glittered and gleamed at their feet. Hard to believe there could be any shadows on a night like this, and ones so deeply dark. "I sold my riding coat, the one my grandmother sewed for me before her hands were crippled with arthritis. I found a buyer for Duchess's unborn foal. I did all of that so no man would come along and try to hurt you. Try to break you."

Looking as lost as the shadows, she trembled once, as if she were hesitating, as if she were remembering what had almost happened this night. He saw the strength of it as her chin dropped, and she remained unbowed and unmoving. Not fleeing, after all.

"If I betrayed you, then it was for a good reason." The house loomed above them, silent and still, blocking out a chunk of the star-strewn sky. He nudged her toward the back steps. "You will stay, Fiona. Let's get you back inside."

He ignored the choke of a sob catching in her throat. His grip didn't relent, nor did the unhappiness burrowing like the cold into his chest. Although they walked side by side, a great divide separated them. One he feared could never be crossed.

"I was wrong about you." Her voice was strained, her words tight with defeat. "You are a much more horrible man than I thought."

"You would not be the first to say so." He wished he knew how to shield his heart better, to turn off his feelings so that he did not care, so that nothing could hurt him. Impossible. Fiona O'Rourke had stripped him bare of armor and shields, leaving him defenseless. As he tugged her through the last of the incandescent snow and into the house's shadow, he had to face the truth. Few things in life hurt as much as Fiona's hatred for him.

Why the kitchen? That's what Fiona wanted to know. This small, unhappy room symbolized everything she feared most. Her mother spent most of her life in this room.

Although the cook stove was cold, the scent of the night's supper and the cigar smoke from Da's card game stained the air. In the corner stood the washboard and tubs, the broom, cleaning buckets and dish basin, reminders of all the unhappy hours here doing chores. It was not the work that troubled her, but the lack of choice. That was what happened when a woman married a man who dominated her.

"Sit here." His order could have been gruff. It should have been. Anger or something similar to it tensed the muscles in his jaw and delineated the angles of his cheekbones. His grip on her arm ought to have been bruising— she knew, for Da had hauled her into the house countless times—but it was not. He drew a chair away from the table and eased her into it. "Don't move."

"You're comfortable giving orders. I suppose this is a hint of how you would treat a wife?"

"Aye." Grim, as if fighting smoldering rage, he set her satchel on the small counter and knelt before the stove.

At least he admitted it. He could have lied to her. She straightened her spine and ignored the burn of her vertebrae against the unyielding wood. She hurt everywhere. Her head, her shoulder, her ankle, her soul.

"Here. Put this against your cheek and hold it there." He pressed something cold into her hand. A cloth wrapped around chunks of ice from the water bucket. "I've never seen a woman climb a rope like that."

"Technically I wasn't climbing. I was going down."

"Aye, but it was hand over hand. Same difference." Towering over her, he looked as stalwart as a legend and twice as difficult to defeat. "Did your brother teach you that?"

"Who else?" For the life of her, she could not be nice to him.

"You two were close?" His hand curled around hers to press the ice tenderly against her cheek. Her wide eyes pinched, and he felt the answering emotion within his chest, as if her grief were his own. "I guess that's obvious, too."

"Johnny was the only real family I had. My folks..." She said nothing more. She didn't have to.

"That's not the way parents are supposed to be." It felt as if they were the only two people on earth, for the silent night and his affections were vast. He pushed away from her. "My grandparents had the real thing. Enduring love and respect and devotion to one another that strengthened day by day. An inspiring sight to see, and a soft comfort to grow up in."

"Surely you want to find the same thing one day."

"Lass, I know what you are about to say." The lamp casing creaked as it opened. "You are hoping I will break my agreement with your father and go off to find such a love."

"Why not? You will not be happy with me, and here? There is no happiness in this home."

"Your reasoning will not work with me." The flare of a match caressed his stony features. "I'm not staying to find happiness."

"I don't understand you, McPherson."

"Aye, this I know." He did not turn from the stove. "You told me that if you wanted something better than your life here, you had to work for it. What would that be?"

"And I should tell you?"

"Why not? I'm curious." A cup rattled in a saucer as his gait whispered near. He leaned close, bringing with him the scent of winter snow and hay and the musty wool of the old coat he wore.

Not the same one he'd arrived in. He had been telling the truth. She spotted a small tear in the collar seam and a patch on the elbow. The ironware clinked against the tabletop, and the warm scents of honey and chamomile curled against her nose.

"That will warm you." He brushed a lock of hair from her forehead, his touch as gentle as a blessing, his kindness unmistakable. "You need another bit of ice for that bump."

"I don't need your pity, McPherson."

"It's not my pity you have."

She did not want his kindness, either. She wanted to hate him. She wished she could see him as the enemy he was. Taking her money as handily as he wanted to take her freedom. And yet, as she listened to him breaking more ice in the water bucket, and the glasslike tinkle as he gathered it into a dish towel, strangely tender emotions glowed within her like banked embers. With any luck, her affection for the man would turn to ash and darkness.

"When I was a little girl sent to my room without any supper, I would close my eyes and dream. Not of story-books and romance, like I know my friends did, but of the house I would have when I was grown." She didn't know why, but the truth swept out of her. Ian, as if he saw and heard only her, came toward her with an intense focus that both frightened and calmed her.

"I suppose this was a fancy house?" He grabbed an empty chair by the rung and hauled it over, facing her. "Did your grandmother tell you of McPherson Manor, then?"

"My future home was not a fine place, but simple with four walls and plenty of windows to let in cheerful sun-shine." She took a sip of the steaming brew, savoring the sweet, liquid comfort. It warmed her and she went on. "It was a place with flowers surrounding it, so that when the wind blew, the whole house smelled like lilacs and roses. It was a place where I was and always would be safe. There was no strap hanging from a nail on the wall."

"And you were in this house alone?" He laid the ice against her temple. "So you could not be hurt?"

How did he know? She blinked hard, for the ice stung, but something secret and deep within her smarted more. "I would have to work hard and save my earnings to af-ford my own place."

"You hope to find work sewing?"

"Why not? Miss Sims has promised I can use her for a reference. She is pleased with my work. And before you say it, such work might be hard to find right off. I would be happy to do laundry in a hotel or wash dishes in a busy kitchen. I know I can find a job."

"It is winter, and few are hiring this time of year. Did you consider that?"

"You're still not going to let me go?"

"Not on my life."

"You said you would help me."

"And so I am."

You're imagining tenderness in his words, she told herself, knowing it could not be true. And she did not want it to be. Look at the proof of his character as he opened her satchel, removed her money stash and stuffed it into his coat pocket. Warm when he could be cold; mellow when he could be commanding.

"Is there anything more I can do for you tonight?" he asked, as if he cared about her answer.

What she wanted, he would not give her. Exhaustion crept into her like a heavy fog; the numbness of the evening was wearing off. Her head throbbed. Her cheek pounded. Every muscle she owned felt strained and sore.

"No, there's nothing I want from you."

"Then up you go." He carried her satchel to the base of the ladder. He waited in silence while she gripped the rungs in her cold hands, realizing she still wore her mittens and coat. She didn't want to spend the few moments it would take to remove them in Ian's presence, so she climbed into the cold attic and darkness. The moonlight had vanished: perhaps clouds were moving in.

"I'll see you in the morning, pretty girl." He tossed her satchel into her hands, and something about the man pulled at the deepest places within her. As if it were her soul that longed after him, wishing for what could not be.

As his uneven gait padded softly through the house, she heard a muted grunt of pain. The kitchen door creaked closed, leaving her alone. She wanted to hate him, but she could not.

Chapter Eleven

"Fiona? Yoo-hoo."

"That must be some daydream."

"About Lorenzo, no doubt. She's smiled the whole time I've been talking about him."

Lorenzo? Fiona frowned, pulled herself out of her thoughts. The cold night—last night—frothy with snow and moonlight vanished from her mind, and she was sitting in the warmth of Lila's pretty parlor filled with sunshine, as she did every Friday afternoon. She poked her needle through the seam of the dress she was basting. Ian might have taken her savings, but she intended to keep earning. Her amused friends were staring at her. Scarlet's grin stretched ear to ear, and Lila covered her hand with her mouth to keep from laughing out loud.

"He does cause a girl to dream, doesn't he?" Kate was busy sighing in agreement. "I don't blame Fee a bit."

"Neither do I." Always faithful, Earlee looked up from threading her needle. "Now that her engagement is broken, why shouldn't she start to consider the possibilities?"

Goodness, was *that* what they thought? That she was daydreaming about Lorenzo courting her? Heat stained her cheeks. What did she say? If she denied it, then it would only make them disbelieve her more. And in truth, she *had* been thinking about a man. Ian—to be precise. But she had *not* been smiling. She was nearly sure of it.

"Look, she's blushing. It's cute," Kate cooed, going back to her embroidery work. "Fiona's first crush."

"It had to happen sometime," Lila said as she studied her hem work. "It may as well be Lorenzo. Every girl in school has gone sweet on him at one time or another."

"He *is* a perfect tenor." Scarlet looked enraptured; having missed paying attention to the story of church caroling practice, this was news to Fiona.

"Plus, he is perfect." Lila sighed airily in agreement.

"Lorenzo and Fiona would make a good couple, don't you think?" Trouble twinkled in Earlee's eyes. "I know you don't want to marry, Fee, but that could change, now that you have a choice."

"Uh, there's really something I need to tell you all." Really, she had to stop them before they began planning her and Lorenzo's wedding. Honestly. She rolled her eyes at the thought. "He came back."

"The Kentucky guy?" Lila put down her needle. "He came back for you and you didn't tell us?"

"You didn't say *one* word. All day at school? All day long?" Scarlet chimed in.

"You could have told us, Fee," Kate added gently.

Why, exactly, was her face feeling hotter? She had to be blushing furiously because her nose was as red as a berry. This was why she'd been afraid to say anything. Even her closest friends would misunderstand the situation and see in Ian's return something that could never be. Why did he have to come back? Why did he have to decide their broken-down farm was so important to him? He should have simply kept going east, back to wherever he belonged. That's what he should have done.

And, if he hadn't, then what terrible thing would have happened? She wouldn't have been able to fight off Da's friend for much longer, although she would have tried her hardest. Ian had saved her from unspeakable things. She felt a needle prick through her thimble, and the sharp sting reminded her of where she was. Maybe she ought to pay better attention to her sewing.

"I understand, some things are too personal to say out loud." Earlee knotted her thread with care. "Ian must be a very special man."

Special? Her tongue tied, and she realized she might as well tell the whole truth. How Ian had taken her savings and forced her to stay. How confusing his kindness to her was, how nice his protection. This morning, all the barn work had been done by the time she'd come downstairs. Her parents hadn't scolded her once as she helped with the kitchen chores. She stared down at her work, at the luxurious velveteen fabric Miss Sims had entrusted her with, and realized her stitches were crooked. How had that happened? She hadn't stitched so badly since she was six years old.

"But private or not, we're your friends," Lila pointed out lovingly.

"Your *best* friends," Kate emphasized.

"You're obligated to tell us." Scarlet leaned forward, eager for the real story.

"We care about you, Fee," Earlee sympathized. "I'm sure you will tell us when you're ready."

"I just might never be ready to talk about *him*." She couldn't even say his name. Her vision blurred—with fury or confusion, she didn't know which—as she took her needle and began ripping out her stitches.

"She's blushing harder," Lila reported.

"How romantic." Kate's voice was pure glee. "Look at her, ready to deny it. But it *is* romantic."

"It's like something out of a novel." Scarlet set down her hoop. "Grandparents who were friends make a solemn vow their grandchildren one day will marry. When hero and heroine meet, they take a fancy to one another and live happily ever after."

"You're like a fairy tale, Fee." Kate sighed. "Earlee could pen a story about you."

"It would be a story with a joyful ending," Earlee agreed. "With love triumphant."

"It is an arranged marriage. Trust me, there is nothing romantic about that." The thread snapped. Fiona glared at the frayed edges and realized she'd been using far too much force. It was all Ian's fault, because she had been thinking about him. Now she was talking about him. How had he come to dominate her life so fast and thoroughly?

"Lila?" Mrs. Lawson, Lila's stepmother, rapped her knuckles lightly against the open parlor door. "It's four o'clock. Kate's father and Fiona's beau are outside waiting to take them home."

"My *what?*" She couldn't believe her ears. Mrs. Lawson smiled decorously as if nothing could possibly be wrong.

"Your beau." Scarlet winked. "Who would have thought you would be the first of us to have a young man walk you home?"

"No one is more surprised than me." She tucked her needle into the remnants of the seam and folded her work neatly, but she didn't stand up to shrug into her wraps with the same speed as everyone else. She was in no hurry for the pleasant hour to end. Not only had this been the best time of her whole week, but Ian was outside waiting for her. Already wanting control of her, no doubt.

"Next week is our Christmas party," Lila reminded everyone as they clambered down the staircase. "Can everybody stay longer for supper?"

"I can, but then I live two streets over." Scarlet pushed ahead, leading the way past the back door to the mercantile to the alley entrance instead. "Kate, you have the farthest to come."

"It depends on the weather." Kate paused in the vestibule to pull on her hood. "If there's no blizzard, then yes. I'm sure Pa will let me. What about you, Earlee?"

"I'll just make a meal ahead. I know Beatrice will warm it in the oven and get the food on the table for everyone." Earlee wrapped her muffler around her neck. "Will your pa let you come this time, Fee? You can't miss our last party."

"Da is awfully mad at me." She tugged at her muffler. "I don't know if I will be able to come."

Everyone fell silent. What was there to say? Her friends knew well her father's disposition. Scarlet opened the door and led the way into the brisk air. The magenta blaze of the sinking sun turned the typical small town into a breathless wonderland, like a picture in a children's Christmas book. The snow in the alley gleamed like a rare opal. The violet light dusted the store buildings and the man waiting by a single horse-drawn sled. Sure, there were others in the alley, but all she noticed was the tall, stalwart shadow, radiating integrity so substantial it could be felt and seen in the ethereal light.

"Who is *that?*" Lila breathed.

"Is it *him?*" Scarlet whispered.

Ian. Something strange was happening to her. Her throat had closed up, and it was as if she had forgotten how to breathe. She stammered, unable to say yes or no.

"That's your betrothed?" Kate's jaw dropped.

"He's the one you were supposed to marry? He's the one you were dreading all this time?" Earlee's whisper was a hush of astonishment. "He's utterly well—"

"Handsome. Incredible. Manly," Scarlet finished as if in awe. "No wonder you are letting him court you. That is a man a girl can dream on."

"I didn't think any fellow could be cuter than Lorenzo, but I was wrong," Lila agreed.

"I'm so glad he came back for you." Earlee squeezed Fiona's hand. "How romantic."

"Utterly," Kate agreed.

Lila sighed as if too overcome to speak.

Could anyone have better friends? They were happy for her, thinking the boy she'd dreaded meeting all these years might actually be a once-in-a-lifetime kind of man. From their perspective, she knew that's how Ian looked with those granite-cut shoulders and striking good looks. But he ambled closer, the tap of his cane easy and his reserved smile friendly, and there was no time to tell her friends the truth. That this was no romantic match, and Ian had not returned because of his affections for her. She felt like a miserable fraud.

"Ladies." Ian tipped his wide-brimmed hat, exposing thick dark locks that only enhanced his manliness.

Not that she was noticing such things. Fine, maybe she was, but only as a casual observation. She could not forget what he had done to her.

Her feet stumbled forward and she was aware that her friends were curtsying in greeting, but all she wanted to do was to push him away and out of her sight. He had no right walking into her life like this. He was supposed to be at the farm, perhaps riding the fields, proud of his soon-to-be acquisition.

"Why are you here?" She didn't mean to sound sharp. The words simply came out that way.

"I was in town and about to head home. When I realized the time, I figured I would stop by." He didn't seem perturbed by her tone, not at all. "It would save you the walk."

"I would rather." Oh, she knew what he was up to. Asserting his authority over her, as if she was one of his horses. "Besides, Earlee and I walk part of the way together."

"Then I would be happy to have your friend join us. The wind is kicking up. It's bound to be a mighty cold hike."

"I'm used to walking in the cold. It doesn't bother me. In fact, I prefer it." Her chin hiked up; she couldn't help it. She felt her friends' curious glances and, in Lila's case, a shocked look. More misery filled her up. This man was already making her sound like her mother.

Instead of getting angry, like Da would have done, instead of putting her in her place or shaming her in front of her friends, Ian shook his head. His rich chuckle was like to warm the chill from the twilight air.

"Whatever you want suits me just fine, lass. I thought you would prefer to take a ride behind Duchess. I was going to let you drive her, but maybe another time. If you change your mind, let me know. Nice to meet you, ladies." With a gentlemanly tip of his hat, he turned and strode away, his boots crunching in the icy snow.

"Fiona!" Scarlet whispered, scandalized. "Look at his horse. It's the nicest one I've ever seen."

"Much finer than ours," Lila agreed. "Meredith's family's horses, as amazing as they are, couldn't hold a candle to that one."

"Plus, your Mr. McPherson is quite dashing." Kate gave her a nod. "I would say yes."

"I don't mind walking on my own." Earlee gave her a shove. "Go ahead. You can tell us all about it before church on Sunday."

They all meant well. Fiona studied each dear face, shining with happiness and hopes for her. With McPherson watching, there was no way she could explain. Nor was there time to.

"C'mon, Earlee." She grabbed her friend's hand and tugged her along. "You're not walking home alone in the dark, and Ian's right. It's getting colder by the minute."

"I don't want to intrude." Earlee dragged her feet and looked to everyone else for help.

"Go with her!" Scarlet ordered. "Or she won't say yes to him."

"Have fun, Fee!" Lila called out.

"Your beau will have to bring you early to church!" Kate had reached her father's sled and was beaming. "Don't let him forget."

Oh, he wasn't about to. She could see that as plain as the grin on his face. That dimpled grin, the one that made the setting sun fade in the sky and the earth fall away from beneath her shoes. Proof that the man had entirely the wrong effect on her. She was determined to keep him well away from her heart. She wouldn't stop trying until she had accomplished that goal.

"Wait, Fee." Ian stopped her, sounding far too happy, more proof he was a scoundrel of the worst sort. Taking delight in her discomfort. Using her friends' good intentions to his own advantage. "Let your friend in first, and then you can sit in the middle."

"Next to you?" She would rather have a tooth pulled. But neither did she want poor Earlee to feel uncomfortable being forced to sit next to a stranger. Well, fine. She waited next to him while he helped Earlee onto the board seat.

"Don't even think about it," she warned him, jerking her hand away. She did not need his help getting into the odd-looking sled. "Where did you get this?"

"I made it with scraps I found around back of the barn."

"Yes. That explains it." Only Ian would have the finest horse in the county *and* the worst vehicle. She ignored his chuckle as she scooted onto the seat beside Earlee.

"It's sort of cute," Earlee whispered. "It's fun."

"Yes, I'm in stitches I'm having so much fun."

Why did Ian have to laugh—again? This was not funny. Not from her view, anyway. He settled in beside her, his arm pressing against hers. She was safe and protected, and that was completely the wrong way to feel. No, she had to stop these sorts of troubling emotions. This was horrible, she decided. It was like sitting next to a big pillar of immovable steel. If she tried to scoot farther away from him, then she would risk inching Earlee off the end of the seat.

"Good meeting you, Schmidt." He tipped his hat to Kate and her father as they trotted by.

"Hope to see you Monday." Mr. Schmidt said nothing more and in moments the Schmidt sleigh was out of sight.

What, exactly, had he been discussing with her friend's father? The man was infiltrating her life. How did she stop him? He hauled a folded blanket from beneath the seat and shook it. Rich wool tumbled over her, and somehow it was his caring she felt, warm and strong like a hand curled in hers. She found the hem and stretched out the blanket to full length, making sure Earlee had enough to keep her warm. Ian filled her senses, the pleasant male scent of his skin, the rhythm of his breathing and the rustle of his movements. He was the only color she saw in the twilight world.

She barely remembered to wave goodbye to her friends standing shoulder to shoulder in the alley. The sled jerked forward roughly on the rutted snow. Ian's arm moved against hers as he handled the reins. She didn't want to notice his tensile strength and his kindness when he spoke to his mare. The wind knifed through her with shocking cold and stung her eyes. The street flew by in a blur.

"Why are you seeing Mr. Schmidt on Monday?" Earlee asked as the horse and sled stopped at the busy intersection. "Is it because you plan on taking Fiona to school?"

"I'm hoping to get a job at the mill. Mr. Schmidt said he would put in a good word for me with his boss."

"You're going to find work here, in Angel Falls?" It sounded permanent, as if he was entrenching himself not only in her life but in town. The more he did that, the better the chances were that he would never leave.

"You don't want me lounging around like your father, do you?" Gently, as he did many things, he smiled at her.

"The less you are like Da, the better."

It all made perfect sense. Getting a job showed he was responsible—not that she wanted to see any bit of him in a positive light. She refused to like him, and that was that.

Thank heavens there was a break in the traffic. Ian eased his mare into the bustle. The wind gusted, making it too cold to speak, so they glided down the street, decorated for Christmas, in silence.

"Thanks for the ride." Fiona's friend climbed out of the sled, clutching her bag. "I hope to see you again, Mr.

McPherson. If you're a churchgoing man, you might want
to come with Fiona on Sunday. We have a fun Sunday
School class. There are lots of young people our age—"

"I might like that, thank you." It sounded mighty fine
to him. He noticed he was alone in that opinion. Fiona
retreated to the far edge of the bench seat, and he felt her
horror as simply as if she were still pleasantly against
his arm.

"Earlee!" She choked, turning as white as snow. "How
could you?"

"I just thought he might want to beau you to church—"

"I'm starting to really dislike that word." She looked
as if she were being torn apart, and he knew why. The
wind had carried to him her friends' whisperings, and
he had heard enough to know they assumed a bond had
formed between them.

They were not wrong. On his side, at least. A blind
man could see the pretty lady's disdain for him.

"What word? 'Beau'?" Fiona's friend asked inno-
cently. "Oh, I see what you mean. You're right. 'Beau'
is the wrong word. You're engaged now. How exciting.
I should not tell you this, but I'm going to start a little
present for your hope chest. I know you haven't started
filling one yet, and you need help before your wed—"

"That is really sweet of you." Fiona looked over her
shoulder, and he could read the longing on her face as
she searched the shadowed, endless prairie. The falling
twilight hid the scattering of houses and barns, making it seem lonely and vacant. As if a person could be
lost from her problems there forever. "You are the best
friend, Earlee."

"No, *you* are the best friend." The girl bobbed a curtsy
in his direction. "Nice meeting you, Mr. McPherson. I
hope to see you both on Sunday. Bye, Fee!"

Well aware he was that his intended opened her mouth to argue, but her friend was already trudging up the snowy driveway to a ramshackle shanty, windows glowing like a beacon in the gathering dark. Her brow furrowed as she studied him. The bruise and swelling beneath her eye was like a bayonet to his chest. Tender emotions set his teeth on edge, because he could not brush those unruly curls from her face and caress the bruise away.

"You are staring at me. Why?" She looked ready for a fight, but he was not fooled.

"How is your head feeling?" He gave the reins an easy snap and Duchess stepped out, choosing her own pace in the difficult snow.

"You don't need to pretend you care. Actually, I prefer that you didn't."

How could such a slight lass hold such fierceness? Not cruel and not harsh, but fiery, like a filly who did not want to be bridled. She reminded him of someone, another female he was fond of, although in a very different way.

He guided Duchess around the sharp bend in the road and directly into the raging wind. He couldn't say why he hardly noticed the stinging temperatures. His gaze, his senses, his very essence were glued to her.

"I know you are mad at me." Well he understood, so he did not fault her for it. "I've treated you unfairly, coming back like I did. Bargaining with your father for you."

"For the land," she corrected him. A less attentive man might have missed the deep well of pain beneath the surface of her words. "You don't want me. I'm just the means to land you can't buy any other way."

"And what makes you think that, little filly?"

"Filly? I am not a horse. Have you not noticed?" She

whirled to face him, and although the darkness and shadows cloaked her, it was as if he could see the pain on her face, hidden beneath her anger.

He could not argue with her. He shrugged, unable to deny it because he feared to say the wrong thing. He could not make her hurt worse.

"Hard to believe once I *almost* thought you were a decent man. You are much more horrible than I ever guessed. Then you went and took—" She fell silent.

He heard emotion catch in her voice, hurting with her. "You mean when I took your money?"

She did not answer, but he sensed it. Deep inside it was like a door opening, and he could see her clearly in a way he had never perceived anyone before. The shadows tried to hide her as nightfall descended more deeply over the land and over them, but he didn't need light to see that her anger was meant to push him away.

"I'm not like your father, Fiona."

"Maybe, but you seem a lot like him to me." Her disdain was layered, as if it did not come to her easily.

Her opinion of him weighed heavily. He swallowed the sting in his throat, adjusted the reins into one hand and drew the small packet from his coat pocket. "I'm not completely like the man," he argued.

She didn't answer, but he heard a distinctive harrumph, as if she highly doubted his statement. She had every right to her opinion, but did she have no belief left?

The last of the sunset's blaze disappeared from the underbelly of the clouds, the sky darkened and night fell grim and bleak. The cruel wind moaned, and he could only hope he was doing what God wished. It was hard to tell. He reined Duchess off the main road and onto the narrow drive.

"Here." He held out the small ledger.

"What is it?" She took it, uncomprehending.

"The record of your savings account at the bank. It's in my name, but yours is on there, as well. It is safer than stashing it in the barn. You can keep adding to your going-away fund." He halted them in front of the barn and turned to her with his feelings veiled. "That's what you wanted, right?"

Chapter Twelve

She wished she could see his face to read his emotions. The darkness hid all, making it impossible to see if a lie or the truth shone in his gaze, if he was offering her a dash of hope or taking it away. She clutched the little book tightly. "Is this really mine?"

"Every penny." The winter air vibrated with his honesty.

He hadn't taken her savings. That single thought rolled around in her mind, first with disbelief and then acceptance. The hard shell she'd put around her heart cracked a fraction, leaving vulnerable places unprotected. "But if this is in your name, it is technically yours."

"Aye, by law that would be an argument." The blanket rustled, and his shadow rose as if into the star-strewn sky. "But this way your father cannot touch it, and you can. You can withdraw the full amount any time you wish. This means you can run. I won't stop you, lass."

"You make no sense, McPherson. Last night you dragged me back to the house—"

"Aye, so you would listen to what I'm asking you." His strong, warm hand curled around hers, warm and significant, and held on tight. His fingers twined between hers were companionable, right. As he helped her from the sled, her fear of him began to drain. She landed beside him, defenseless and small. Snow slid over the tops of her shoes, wetting her stockings, but the sudden cold did not steal her breath the way Ian did.

"What are you asking?" she asked.

"To let me help you."

"You want to help me run away from you?"

"Aye, why else do you think I have agreed to stay?" He shouldered open the barn door, waiting for her to enter first. "I intend to help you, Fee. I promise you that."

"And I suppose like any man you think that really means you are helping yourself?"

"I came back for you." As substantial as truth, as intangible as dream, and yet real all the same. "Why else would I have pawned what I had on me, all but my horse, to come back here?"

"It was for the land."

"Which is no prize. It comes with a mortgage a man would have to break his back working to pay off. Surely you must know that."

"Johnny used to talk about it. He said Da was bad with money."

"I am not." He waited, his feet planted, his legs braced, and in the shadows the starlight found him. "I came back to help you find a better life. I do not think I can go on with my own unless I know you are safe and well. Only the good Lord above knows why."

"I almost believe you." Why was he doing this to her? How did he strip her defenses away with a few honest-sounding words?

Only the Lord knew why she was susceptible to him. She wrenched away, having the advantage of knowing the inside of the barn by heart, and moved through the darkness faster than him. The horses whinnied, moving around in their stalls, and the cow lowed in greeting.

"I pity the man who does marry you." Amused now, his brief chuckle rang cozily through the barn. His chest bumped her shoulder blade as he reached around her to take the match tin before she could grab it.

"You mean you pity yourself?" She whirled to face him.

"I do, and the man who wins your heart. For he will fall in love with you so hard and strong he would give up anything for you. And you could crush him with a word and that temper of yours." He struck the match, and the flame worshipped him as he lit the lantern.

Why did he have to be so appealing to her? Why was he tearing her into pieces? When she suspected the worst of him, he proved to be a better man. The small book she clutched felt like a weight on her soul. "I don't understand you. You make no sense."

"I'll not argue with you." He tugged the ledger from her grip. Outlined as he was by the golden, glowing light a more fanciful girl could imagine him the hero of a dime novel, a man who stood for all that was good in the world, who was both unwaveringly tough and endlessly gentle. He folded open the first page of the booklet and tipped it toward the light for her to clearly see.

There was her money, all twenty-three dollars and forty-six cents. Not that she had doubted him. A strange aching emotion built in her throat, something she couldn't swallow past—something she was afraid to look at too closely. Because then she would no longer be able to keep trying to hate him. Now there was no way to keep him safely away from her inexperienced heart.

"Let us make a deal, you and I." His rugged voice vibrated with layers too dangerous to think about.

"I do not make bargains with men of your ilk."

"Perhaps just this one time, for tonight, you can amend that and come to an agreement with me. Better to deal with me than with your da, right?"

"For a man who does not gamble, you know which cards to play."

"As your father says, life is a gamble. I have learned much with the losses I have been dealt." His richly layered words drew both the light and the darkness.

His honesty and sorrow touched her. The earth beneath her shoes tilted—again. She forgot to breathe—again. Every word she knew clumped into an incomprehensible ball in her brain. She hated that he was hurting. What was wrong with her that she wanted to comfort him? She knew sorrow well, and knew, too, that he had lost more than she had ever known. But his betrayal remained, and she could not afford to be kind. "What do you want, McPherson?"

"I want you to stop worrying. You're not alone. Not anymore." Tenderness hid in the layers of voice, a tenderness she must be imagining. "Now that you and I are engaged, at least as far as your father is concerned, he will not be trying to hand you over to the next man who comes along."

"I do not intend to marry you."

"You can go to school, spend time with your friends, sew to your heart's content." He tucked the ledger into her coat pocket. "Hide that. Add to it. When you're ready, I will help you go. Wouldn't it be better if you left with a job waiting and someone looking out for you?"

"I don't need you, McPherson."

"Aye, I see that. But I need you." There he went, tricking her with his tenderness and kindness.

He could not be telling the truth. She backed away

from him. "I sincerely doubt that. What about the land? That's why you came and that's why you are saying these things."

"Wrong." He drew himself upright, steeling his spine and setting his jaw. His tenderness vanished, leaving behind a formidable man, one who looked strong enough to defeat any foe. "Fiona, I didn't come back for the land. That was not the true reason I am here. I will vow it on a stack of Bibles if you want me to. I vow it on my honor."

"You don't want to marry me?"

"Now, I never said that. But marriage between us always has and always will be your choice, pretty girl." He cupped her face with the curve of his hand, tenderness real and tangible, not imagined. The sweetest longing spilled up from her soul. Everything within her wanted to believe him. She squeezed her eyes shut, and the image of the man remained etched in her mind. As did the caring chiseled into his stony features, and his concern reaching out as if to rope her in.

When she opened her eyes, he hadn't moved. In his secondhand coat, rumpled shirt and trousers he did not at all look the horrible man he that she wanted him to be.

A friendly meow filled the silence between them. A furry paw reached down from the rafter above and batted at Ian's hat. His buttery chuckle warmed the cold air, and his amusement beat at her falling defenses.

"Hello to you, too," he crooned to the cat. "Come to see if there's any milk, have you?"

Mally's answering meow left no doubt, and while the feline tossed a glance Fiona's way, it was a mere glance, nothing more.

"You have gone and stolen my cat," she accused. "I don't think I shall ever forgive you, Ian."

"At least you are using my first name, lass. It is an

improvement." He batted playfully at Mally's paw. The cat, apparently thrilled, grabbed hold of his rafter and reached down to wrestle with Ian properly.

"It's not an improvement. Simply resignation." It was easier to let him think she still loathed him than admit the truth. She grabbed a small pail from the nearby shelf. "As you insist on playing, I'll get started on your work."

"I left Duchess standing in the doorway." He chuckled again, dodging the cat's attempts to knock his hat off. "I'll take care of her, don't you worry."

"You are hardly trustworthy." She let the mare scent her hand. Once the beautiful mare nodded in greeting, she dared to run her fingers over the rich velvety nose. Softer than it looked, she marveled. "You are like the finest satin."

Duchess nickered low in her throat with great dignity and dipped her nose in the bucket. Her lustrous red coat seemed to gleam, as if holding light of its own. Breathtaking to be so close to her. She was perfection. Not the kind of horse you leave standing. No, judging by the perturbed look, Duchess was used to immediate attention. She stomped her foot, not at all pleased to find the bucket empty.

"It's hot water I'll be fetching for you. I suppose you are used to your oats warm," she told the mare, fully aware of Ian coming closer. The nerves on her nape tingled in warning at his approach.

"That would be kind of you, lass." His warm breath fanned across the back of her neck. His hand landed next to hers on Duchess's silken nose. "I have left her too long already. She's used to receiving all of my regard."

"Poor Duchess." Fiona sympathized. "It must be hard to endure so much of Ian."

The mare tossed her head up and down as if in perfect agreement.

"I guess that puts me in my place."

His chuckle followed her out into the bitter cold; she couldn't rightly say she was running from it. Just as it was not his warm, cozy company she would be missing. It was *not* the promise of hearing his laughter again that had her hurrying down the path toward the shanty's glowing window.

At least, that's what she told herself.

A strange power had overtaken him, there was no denying it. Ian ran his hands down Duchess's legs, checking knee and fetlock and hoof. No warm spots, no swelling, nothing out of the ordinary. Everything his grandfather had taught him about horse care was ingrained, and as he lowered the mare's hoof onto his knee to check her shoe, the old man could have been with him, standing as he always did with a bit of advice to offer. Fine when Ian was a six-year-old, but how it had annoyed him as a teenage boy.

Warm memories curled around him like his grandfather's loving presence used to. He almost glanced over his shoulder to see if the older gentleman stood there. Impossible, of course, his grandfather had been gone a full year, but perhaps he was looking down from heaven. And if he was, would he be glad of what he saw? Relieved he was falling for the granddaughter of his best childhood friend? Or would he be ashamed of her circumstances?

Duchess blew out a breath through her lips, a sort of horsey huff. How long had he been kneeling here, with her hoof in his hand? Ian blinked. He had no notion how much time had passed.

"Sorry, girl." He eased her hoof to the ground and

straightened. Duchess forgave him with a low, affectionate nicker.

The barn door creaked open, and Fiona waltzed in.
He would have liked to say that his every sense wasn't
attuned to the woman. But no matter how hard he tried,
his ears picked up the light, padding rhythm of her boots
on the ground and the rustle of her skirts.

The animals turned toward her. Flannigan whinnied
in welcome and the cow lowed mournfully. Even Duchess watched with eagerness, and he was able to rise and
brush the straw from his trousers as if he were too busy
to notice the change in the air or in his heart. Fiona murmured low to the animals. Her sweet voice could melt
the frost on the walls.

Aye, it was a strange influence she had over him, but
not an unwelcome one. He laid his hand on his mare's
neck to lead her gently, wordlessly to her stall. Duchess
trusted him, walking confidently beside him, but her
attention, too, remained on the dark-haired dream of a
woman in her green gingham dress as she stooped to pet
the cat eagerly curving about her heels.

*Lord, I am trusting where You lead me, that this will
all be well in the end.* He had to turn to prayer, because
he could not see. It was like standing at a crossroads in
the dark. Trails led off in many directions, and there
was no way to know what lay ahead or which was the
one that would bring him home. There were no dreams
here to be had; he had more money to earn if he were to
buy the deed from O'Rourke, and that would be no easy
path. Fiona despised him, and that would not change. He
did not miss the difference in her, now that she understood his cause. She sparkled, her step was light, happiness warmed her voice as she stopped to rub Flannigan's
nose and explain the hot mash was not for him. The horse

leaned into her touch, closing his eyes. When she skipped away, he leaned after her, yearning for more than he could have.

Aye, he knew how Flannigan felt. The light pad of her step and the scrape of the bucket as it landed on the barrel top—every movement she made glanced through him. He could not say why she was dear to him, only that he was alone in that regard. His feelings would never be returned. Aye, he did not need to be a genius to know this. When he ambled close to her, her brightness dimmed as if she were drawing herself in. Clearly whatever friendship they'd had was damaged. Perhaps beyond repair.

He was sorry for it but not for helping her. Not for what it was costing him. He rested his cane against the side of the grain barrel and watched tension creep into the delicate line of her jaw because of his nearness. She was quick to swirl away and put distance between them.

"Thank you for bringing the water." He prayed no wounded feelings crept into his voice. He pried the lid up and stirred oats into the few inches of water. Fiona had thought to leave a spoon in the bottom of the pail, so he stirred, the scraping filling the silence between them when she did not answer.

Aye, there would be no easy laughter between them again. He was sorry for it, too. More than he ever wanted to admit. He gave the plumping oats a final stir. "I'll finish up the chores if you want to go in where it's warm."

"You have invaded my haven." She scooped up the cat in her arms, cradling him like a baby. "Now I must choose between spending time in the shanty with my parents or out here with you."

"Sounds like a difficult choice, lass." He wagered she might think so. He lifted the pail, crossing the aisle with a limping gait. "I'm sorry if I'm the least of two bad choices."

"You are not the worst choice."

Was that a grin threatening to tug upward at the corners of her mouth? He could not be sure. Maybe it was his hope making him see what wasn't there. He lowered the bucket over the stall gate and held it as Duchess dunked her nose in and lapped at the good food daintily. The other horses pricked their ears and scented the air, straining against their doors, hoping for the same. Flannigan nickered. Riley kicked the wall. The cow mooed sadly.

"Where did you get that coat?" She watched him through narrowed eyes. There was no telling what the lass was thinking, but she made a pretty sight, caressed by the lantern light, her curls tumbling out of her braids and with the cat in her arms.

His fingers itched for his pen and paper. She made a pretty picture, but it was more than drawing her image he yearned for. He wanted to memorize the perfect angle of her cheek, to etch into his soul the sight of her gentle spirit. He was a sorry cause, pining after her so. He focused on the horse in front of him. The mare, done with her oats, licked the bottom of the pail harder and gazed at him with her liquid brown eyes in protest.

"There will be more tomorrow, don't you worry." He rubbed her poll, laughing when she bumped her forehead against his palm, wanting more adoration. He felt Fiona's gaze and the question behind it. "Are you still pitying the horse, lass?"

"Something like it. You two have a deep bond."

"Aye. I helped see Duchess into the world. Her dam was my first horse. I was a boy, hardly school age when my ma and I came to stay with my grandparents. She was my first great responsibility, the gentling and train-ing up of her."

"You did not do too badly."

"Perhaps it was the quality of the horse more than the one who raised her." He could not disguise the pride as he gave his mare one final rub. "She's the best of the best."

"I'll not argue that." She set the cat on the stall rail-ing, and he sauntered away, still purring. Perhaps she watched her feline because it was easier, pretending there was distance between them. "You didn't mention your father. He must have been there, too."

"Pa found being a husband and father difficult. He tried, but he could never settle down." He did not mention the long stretches where they had not known where his father was. How Ma would fret and cry with worry, with no money left to buy bread and staples. How she could cry with heartbreak late in the night when she thought him asleep. He'd been a little guy, but he had been old enough to know his father was a man who loved only himself. "My mother was happier living on the estate, but she died a time later in childbirth."

"I'm sorry. I didn't know you lost your ma." She hesi-tated outside the bright pond of light, as if unsure to stay away or come close.

"It was a long time ago. The Lord made sure I was not alone. My grandparents raised me, and I could not have asked for better."

"What about your grandmother? You must miss her."

"Aye. I sent her a telegram but there has been no news in return. I worry about her." He set the bucket on the floor next to others needing to be washed. "She has been frail enough since Grandfather's passing, but she is happy and well cared for."

"Can she travel?"

"The doctor says only by rail. Which poses a problem, as I do not have that kind of cash, unless I sell the rest of what I have."

"Do you mean Duchess?" She eased into the fall of light, knowing she risked him seeing what she feared was on her face—sympathy, no matter how hard she tried not to care at all. "You don't want to sell her because she was a gift from your grandfather."

"I am surprised you can see that much of me."

"It is not that difficult. You are not such a mystery."

"I suppose not." When his smile played across the contours of his mouth, dimples cut into his cheeks. "She is my prize mare, but there are others. I managed to keep a dozen brood mares from the clutches of the creditors."

"They were what you spoke of, the hopes to rebuild what was lost." She didn't know what drew her toward him, only that he fascinated her. He, with his lost hopes and family; she knew what it was like to be left with broken dreams and no one to comfort you. "Is it true what you told me, about selling your things?"

"I have told you nothing but the truth."

"And you are staying to help me when your grandmother needs you, too?"

"When you put it that way, I sound like a terrible grandson." He swiped at a lock of hair falling rebelliously into his eyes. It would be easy to imagine him a prince in a fairy tale, with his handsome charm and steel integrity.

No, she did not think him such a horrible man. Not anymore. Not at all.

"I didn't have it in me to leave you, Fee. Good friends are with Nana, so she is cared for. But you. You have no one to care for you." He stopped, his face growing stony and impossible to read.

"Those things you sold, that could have been money

to help your grandmother. Yet you spent it for me." She wasn't aware of crossing the aisle; suddenly she was close enough to feel the weight of his regret.

"I do not feel the money was wasted."

"That coat is terrible. It is worn and patched." She cleared her throat but the emotion remained, revealing.

"It was what I could afford." He did not sound sorry.

"When you come in for supper, leave it in the kitchen." Her chin came up; she stepped back, putting distance between them once more. "I will mend that tear when I'm through with the dishes. You cannot leave it like that. The rip will only get worse."

"That's thoughtful of you."

"No, it is not." Emotions deepened her blue irises, ones that looked both soft and ready to fight him. "If you are going to come to church with me on Sunday, then I cannot have you embarrassing me."

"I understand." He saw that she no longer hated him. It was something. A quiet gift in the silence between them on this cold winter's night. She spun on her heel and took the light with her. When she paused in the doorway, she stole the last pieces of his heart.

"Don't think this changes anything between you and me," she warned.

"No worries, lass."

When she left him alone in the barn, it was without hope. Some loves in life were never to be.

Chapter Thirteen

Ian was shivering. Even through the steady snowfall, she could see him trembling on the other side of the sled seat. Ma sat between them, well bundled and staring straight ahead, not overly concerned about the man driving them to church. She wouldn't be. Ma did not like Ian. Whatever agreement he had reached with Da had not made her parents happy.

But she could not forget how thin the fabric when she had mended the tear in his coat or all that he had told her. *I came back to help you find a better life. I do not think I can go back to my own unless I know you are safe and well. Only the good Lord above knows why.*

The Bible cradled in her hands felt reassuring and troubling at once. Snow lashed at her face, burning her exposed cheeks and nose with its needlelike iciness. But she was comfortable enough in her coat, layers of flannel and wool, and with the old blanket draped over her and Ma for extra warmth. At least her teeth were not chattering as Ian's were. What would the book she held have to say about his sacrifice? Or her hard-set determination against him?

The church sped into sight, its spire reaching up into

the hazy snow. Families tumbled out of sleighs or walked along the street toward the church. Little kids, warmly bundled, skipped ahead of their parents, or trailed behind, being gently reprimanded either way. She tried not to notice the patient manner in which Ian directed Flannigan, who was distracted by all the excitement, and the way he guided him to a stop at an available hitching post.

"Ladies." Ian stood to help Ma from the sled. Ma refused his hand with a huff. The way she did it, chin up and a frown darkening her face, was a shocking reminder.

Hadn't she treated him the same way days earlier? Shame filled her. Had she been that coldhearted to him? The man was suffering in the temperatures without complaint. What did it say about him that he offered her his hand, knowing how she felt? Did he expect her to act like her mother again? There was no sign of it on his face as he waited with quiet dignity, palm up.

Surely he deserved better from her. It went against the grain to lay her hand in his, to willingly accept what he offered. It was more than a gentleman's manners, much more, and as his fingers closed around hers, she felt the catch of it deep within her soul, like recognizing like.

I do not want to care for him, she thought, but it did no good. Her shoes sank in the snow and her hand remained tucked in his. Snow sifted around them like grace, like peace everlasting, forcing her to see with the eyes of her heart. How tall and straight he stood, as if no hardship was big enough to break him. His grip on her hand was both binding and reverent, protective but not overbearing as he guided her out of the ice. When he released her, she felt sorely alone although he was a mere foot away, tethering Flannigan's rope.

No, she did not want to care for him, but she did. She cared that he was not dressed well for the frigid morning. She cared that he hid it with a handsome smile. She cared that his limp was more pronounced today. Why had she never asked how he'd been hurt?

He handled the horse with care and competence; Flannigan obediently stood and waited with a swish of his tail. No attempt to fight. No sideways kick. The animal nickered and pressed his nose into the man's touch. Ian double-checked the knot securing Flannigan solidly to the iron ring of the post. "Almost done, boy."

Flannigan nickered, bumping Ian again. Something had changed. The horse no longer tried to bite men. He stood patiently, his defiance gone, swinging his neck to keep an eye on his caretaker as he circled to the back of the sled.

Ian was changing things, changing her. She tucked her Bible into the crook of her arm. While he blanketed Flannigan, working the fastenings and smoothing the wool, she tried not to notice the care he gave the horse, or how handsome he looked with happiness softening the chiseled angles of his face. A born horseman, her grandmother had called him. He surely was that.

"Do you miss your horses back home?"

"Until it hurts. I have cared for them all, most since they were wee foals." He gave Flannigan one final pat and a promise they would return to him soon. He joined her on the side of the road, where sleighs full of families whirred by on the ice. "They are my best friends."

"I can understand that." She brushed a stray lock out of her eyes.

"I thought you might. Nana always worried about me, growing up in the barn the way I did, always with Grandfather and the horses. She feared I would grow up to be an odd young man, and when we met you would refuse to marry me."

"Wise woman, your nana. She was right."

"Hey!" Their laughter mingled together, sweet and a perfect chord. "There's a clearing in the traffic. Careful of the ice."

"I have been crossing icy streets for as long as I can remember. I hardly need help from you." Her words could have been cutting, but they weren't. Emotion hid in the layers, soft and shy.

Maybe it was only his wishful thinking. He ignored the wince of pain in his thigh, leaned on his cane and caught her hand with his. "I'm your fiancé. It's my right to help you across the icy street."

"What else are you thinking you've a right to?"

Oh, he caught that flicker of a grin. She was teasing him, for she had no notion how the torch he carried for her could light up the darkest night. He prayed he could keep those feelings hidden. He suspected the lass would have nothing to do with him—even accepting his help—if she knew. They reached the side of the road, but he kept her hand and did not let go.

"Oh, I was thinking I have the right to control your life. Order you around. Get you to do all the barn work." He could tease, too.

"Funny. You are hysterical, McPherson."

"Sure, but I'm serious. I'm taking charge of your life."

"Go ahead and try." She did not seem alarmed. Perhaps because she trusted he would never leave the barn work to her. No, a mischievous sparkle gleamed within her, a hint at her untamable, beautiful spirit. "I'm not sure, but I think I could take you in a fight."

"You would win hands down, lass." His laughter rang out, and pleased he was that they laughed together. Aye, but the girl was good for his weary soul. "I could not fight you."

"Because you are afraid of losing to a girl?"

"Because I would want you to win." The truth slipped out and hovered in the chilly air between them. He winced, afraid she could hear what he did not want her to know. The churchyard was up ahead, and the crowd that went with it. The cheery rumble of conversations broke the silence that fell between them.

He watched her out of the corner of his eye, wondering if she could guess, if he had been too revealing. He steeled his spine, ready to take the hit if she figured it out and very plainly and fairly rejected him, as he knew she would do.

"Fee!" A familiar voice called out above the hustle and bustle of the busy street. One of her school friends, the one whose family owned the mercantile.

"It's Fiona!" The second girl, the one with the red hair, joined the first one, waving from the snowy churchyard.

"And you brought your beau." The third girl, Mr. Schmidt's daughter, looked so happy she couldn't stand still.

Oh, he saw exactly what they thought. They wanted Fiona happy. As he crunched to a stop on the snowy path, he realized how things looked. Him and Fiona walking side by side and hand in hand, like other serious young men and women headed to church—courting couples. Fiona must have come to the same conclusion. She dropped his hand and stepped away.

"Ladies." He tipped his hat and did his best to smile, so the lass wouldn't guess how her reaction hurt him. "Good morning. If you will excuse me, I'd like to go in search of the minister."

"His name is Reverend Hadly, and you don't have to leave." A crinkle burrowed across the bridge of Fiona's nose, an adorable furrow. "We're going down to the church basement. I was going to introduce you to some other fellows."

"Oh, I think we could all do that, Fiona," one of the girls answered, while another whispered, "Lorenzo," making the first one blush.

Girls. They were a mystery to him. But the only mystery he was interested in was Fiona. An apology shone in her eyes, true and lustrous. She hadn't meant to hurt him, and she was handing him a peace offering to join the rest of her friends.

"I will come find you after a bit." He nodded toward the front steps where a line had formed. Mrs. O'Rourke was standing with another severe-looking lady, he noticed, waiting to speak to a white-collared older man. He tipped his hat, leaving Fiona before he had the chance to say more. He wanted to stay with her, but it hurt too much.

"We have a surprise for you, Fee." The girls grabbed hands. "Where is Earlee?"

"She's not here yet."

"Then we'll show her later. C'mon, Fiona."

"Come where? What surprise could you possibly have?"

He could not say why her voice followed him, or why of all the conversations surrounding him, her quiet alto was the one he heard clearly. The line had grown, and he took his place behind an elderly couple. His gaze strayed to the edge of the yard where Fiona was hopping up and down in excitement as another girl, one he had not seen before, joined the group. Their squeals of happiness and welcome made him smile.

"Henrietta, I see your girls are back from their East Coast school." A voice floated to him from farther ahead in line.

"Yes, they arrived on yesterday's train. With that dangerous storm, I feared they might have troubles with snow on the tracks. There was a terrible crash only last month. Thank the Lord the girls arrived safe. I do not like these modern contraptions, but they are convenient. A coach trip would have taken months."

"It's good your family is all together for Christmas," her friend replied.

Christmas was coming. Aye, living on the joyless O'Rourke farm, he had nearly forgotten. But the memories of the blessed season blew through him like a chinook. As the bell in the steeple rang, he remembered the church back home, which he had attended with his grandparents since he was a boy. He would miss Christmas Eve service there this year, cutting a tree for his grandmother, the carols she would play on her beloved piano and the hymns on Christmas Day. He missed home, the ache soul-deep. He longed for what was—the beautiful horses grazing in the green pastures, the sense of rightness as he worked a colt in the paddock and the history of his family on the land, land now gone. Land his grandfather had loved and his grandmother grieved; land he was still hoping to get back.

He was not the only one clinging to the past. He understood more what his grandmother felt. It was not the McPherson name that she wanted to establish, but the moments of love that time stole day by day, that were only memory now. The caring looks Nana and Grandfather had shared over morning tea, across the blooming fields and beside the fire at the end of the day. As the Bible said, all things had a beginning and an end, all things a season. He felt alone as he stood, a solitary man among groups of family and friends.

Across the way, Fiona was hugging another newcomer, a girl in finely tailored clothes. Must be one of the daughters home from the East Coast school, he reasoned, watching as his betrothed hopped up and down with excitement. He had never seen her this happy. A pretty picture she made with her braids bouncing and the skirt of her blue-checked dress swirling around her ankles. Snow dappled her, sweet as sugar. Gone were the shadows, the sadness and the troubles of her daily life. She was bursting with joy; not only could he see the evidence of it, he could feel it deep within. As if his spirit knew hers. His fingers itched to draw her, to try to capture her elusive spark. But the line moved forward, and the kindly minister was offering his hand.

"I'm so pleased to know you," Reverend Hadly said with great sympathy. "I have worried over and prayed for little Fiona. What a blessing your coming here must be for her."

"I hope so, sir." He shook the minister's hand and when he walked away, he felt something more, something like the notice of God. Nana always said that to find His will, all a person had to do was to look into his heart.

When I do, Lord, I see Fiona.

Her musical voice, wholesome and lovely, stood out from all the others. Aye, she looked her age for a change, laughing and carefree with her friends as girls were wont to do.

Confirmation that the decision he had made was the right one.

Fiona bowed her head for the final prayer, far too aware of the man at her side. The man who seemed to dominate the sanctuary. The man every one of her friends thought was in love with her.

Love? She studied him out of the corner of her eye. With his head down, his rugged face poignant in prayer, he was the perfect image of faithfulness. As if every piece of his soul was focused solely on the minister's prayer for peace and selflessness during this holy season. That's what she ought to be focusing on, too, except her mind could not keep track of what was being said. She concentrated, clearly hearing Reverend Hadly's every word. But did they make any sense? No, of course not. Her brain was like her morning oatmeal, all mush and steam.

"Fiona, stop fidgeting," Ma hissed on her other side.

I'm trying to pay attention, Lord. Even her prayer felt mired down next to the track her mind kept following.

"Look at the way he stared down Lorenzo," Lila had whispered over their Sunday-school table in the basement only an hour before. "Your Ian is serious."

"I'll say. Did you see the way he gazes at her?" Scarlet had to voice her opinion—of course. "He can't take his eyes off her."

"Only to glower at Lorenzo." Kate beamed with happiness, as if that were proof of eternal devotion.

"And the loving way he helped her with her coat and keeps watch over her." Earlee's sigh held with it great romantic hopes.

"He loves her," they all pronounced, practically in unison.

He does not love me, she thought stubbornly. He couldn't possibly. Her friends, as dear as they were, did not know everything. They were slightly unrealistic where romantic love was concerned, bless them. Her stomach twisted up like it did when she was afraid of something. And well it should, because believing something like that would be a big mistake.

Someone touched her elbow and she jumped to stand. Ian.

"Are you all right, lass?" His faint Irish brogue resonated gently.

"Fine." Fine? That was all she could say? She had no trouble speaking her mind usually, except her brain was still oatmeal. She managed to shuffle her feet forward toward the end of the row. It was all her friends' fault for putting these fanciful notions into her head.

She crept forward. The end of the row seemed miles away. Maybe it was because Ian was inches from her back, his six-foot height like a mammoth unwanted mountain behind her. Love, indeed. The man did not love her. Ridiculous idea. That's what came from dreaming about romance all the time—you started seeing it whether it was there or not. Good thing she was not a fanciful sort. It was why she wanted a future she could depend on, relying only on herself.

Finally, she reached the row's end—escape. She slipped into the crowded aisle only to have Ian's hand land on her shoulder, stopping her.

"You aren't going to stay after and help out?" He leaned close, his chin stirring her hair. Goodness, he was near and far too intimate.

"I have to go home," she confessed, but not the reason for it.

Ma, having heard the conversation, whipped around. "Fiona spends far too much time with those girls as it is. Church is serious, not meant for idle play and garishness. Come along, girl."

"Yes, Ma." Why wasn't Ian following her?

"Don't you want to stay?" Puzzled lines dug into his brow as he leaned on his cane. "You can't help decorate the tree if you leave."

She could see why her friends had drawn the wrong conclusions. He was simply a kind man, and it would be easy to see more if you didn't understand. Ian was faithful; he did what was right. That was why he was helping her. He saw it as the correct thing to do. She liked that about him. Against her will, a wisp of admiration ribboned through her, as airy and pure as the daylight hazing the stained-glass window.

Oh, it was something more than admiration, she admitted. She hardly heard Ma's sharp words of reproach, ordering her to hurry up.

"She will stay if she wants to." Ian's tone brooked no argument, but to her, he was gentle. "I will take your mother home and be back to get you."

"But Da will be mad—"

"I will deal with your father, too." Ian looked a great deal older than his nineteen years. He pressed something into her hand. A twenty-five-cent piece. "I heard the group goes up to town for the noon meal before they start decorating."

She stared at the quarter, but it wasn't the gift that touched her. "You will come back?"

"If you want me to."

"I suppose that would be tolerable."

His smile came slow as sunrise. He tipped his hat before he donned it and took a step away. "Have fun, lass."

The church crowd had thinned out; they were alone in the aisle. Ian turned on his heel and strode away, ever so strong and solitary. She did not know why she felt his wounds, the depth and breadth of them. She liked the man. Very much. She couldn't help it.

"I can't believe you get to stay." Scarlet's footsteps echoed in the aisle behind her. "Thanks to your Ian."

"This is going to be so fun, Fee." Lila grabbed her hand.

"And to think, he's coming back." Meredith joined them. "If I were you, I couldn't wait."

"If I were you, I would never let him go," Kate added with a sigh.

Fiona watched Ian as he pushed open the vestibule door. The falling snow tossed him in dark relief, and his silhouette made the real Ian much easier to see. They all thought Ian was a catch, but she knew the truth. There was true goodness in this world—goodness in the heart of the man who ambled out into the winter's cold. The door closed shut behind him and his image stayed with her, at the back of her mind and the core of her soul.

Chapter Fourteen

"Ooh, there *he* is, helping with the Christmas tree." Lila left no doubt as to who "he" was. "Ian is a nice man."

"Nice and good-looking. I approve." Meredith hooked her arm in Fiona's. The group was walking back from a meal at the boardinghouse owned by a church member who had spoiled them all with delicious roast beef sandwiches and chocolate cake. "I hate being away at school. I'm missing the good times and soon they will all be gone. First Fiona, and then one of you is next. By the time I come back in May, every one of you will be married."

"Fiona wouldn't get married so fast, would you, Fee?" Kate locked arms with her on the other side.

"What about finishing school?" Lila asked.

"I *will* be graduating." Thanks to Ian. If she walked on tiptoe she could see a glimpse of him, standing alongside Emmett Sims's teamster's sled, talking with a few other young men. None of them seemed as fine or as handsome as Ian McPherson. "He and I are not discussing weddings. We are strangers. I do not want to marry a stranger."

"Some people you meet right away and know better than someone you have known forever." Kate crinkled her brow thoughtfully. "True love might be like that. At least that's the way it is in all the stories. You find the right one for you, the other half of your soul. It's not about how much time you know someone."

"My parents were like that," Lila confessed, lowering her voice. Up ahead their nemesis, Narcissa Bell, was walking with her friends, within earshot. "They were school sweethearts. Ma said the first time she saw my pa, it was as if she had known him forever. One year later, they were married. They were happy."

"That's not a fairy tale, it's real," Kate said as if proof positive. "I have a feeling the same will happen to you, Fee. The way Ian has changed you—"

"I have *not* changed." Okay, maybe she said that a little too fast and with a telling ring of denial, but she was exactly the same girl she had been before Ian had rode into her life one snowy afternoon.

A note rang in her chest, an emotional pang that felt like the perfect chord played by both heart and soul. It came from simply remembering how he'd galloped after Flannigan with lasso circling, like a myth.

I'm starting to believe, she realized as the road brought her to the churchyard, where he stood talking to other young men near to his age. Every step brought her nearer, making it easy to see the details. The snow building on his hat brim, the dimples bracketing his cheeks, the lean line of his jaw, the laughter softening it.

She forgot that he was only a year older than her. Ian had become the head of his household when his grandfather passed away. He provided for his grandmother. Somehow he had managed his grandfather's debts and survived losing great wealth and valuable land, all with his dignity and spirit intact. He had not walked an easy road, and yet he'd done so without complaint or bitterness and with an injured leg.

Shame filled her because she had never asked him about it. She had wanted to keep distance between them; now, she no longer cared about that. She had been so concerned with what she wanted and couldn't have that she'd failed to see how he had tried to help her. He was having a hard time of it and she could have offered him an ear to listen and a friend to care.

He lit up when he saw her, and something within him was open, like a door letting in the light. He turned from his discussion with the Sims brothers and the reverend's son. Pure blue sparkles twinkled in his irises, like a rare jewel she had never seen before. There was much to admire about this man, more than she had let herself notice. Maybe—just maybe—she had noticed all along. She didn't want tender feelings for him taking root, but her will didn't seem to stop them. Affection for him kept struggling to life.

"I invited your fiancé to join us, Fiona," the reverend's son explained as he hefted the base of a cut fir tree from the teamster sled. "Something tells me you won't mind."

She blushed, feeling the weight of all eyes turning to her. But it was Ian's silent question she noticed, the one that she heard without a single word. She did want him with her. She wanted him to have fun. "I was going to ask him to stay, too."

"Then grab a hand, McPherson." Austin Hadly was joined by the other young men in lifting the tree.

The fresh scent of evergreen sweetened the air, or maybe it was something else that made the afternoon perfect. She was hardly aware of other kids from her class clamoring up the street to help; Ian was all she could see. The ease as he grabbed the tree's trunk midway, his easy conversation with the other men, and the capable way he did everything. His baritone stood out from all the other voices in the yard, deep and rich and far too dear.

"Oh, you really do care about him." Kate squeezed her tightly.

"It's written all over your face." Meredith squeezed, too. "I'm happy for you, Fee."

"We all are," Scarlet added.

"But the real question is who will stand up for you at your wedding?" Lila's question, meant to tease, was a loving one.

"I do not know what I am going to do with the lot of you." Fiona rolled her eyes. "We should be thinking of decorating the tree and raising donations for the orphanage. Not thinking about something that will never happen. You all are putting the cart before the pony."

"Sure, but we keep hoping for you, Fee." Scarlet led the way to the front stairs.

"Hoping and praying," Kate added.

"Just because you have planned one future, doesn't mean something better can't happen." Meredith sounded as if she spoke from personal experience. "God might have other plans for you, Fee. Better ones."

"That's right. Maybe He is planning to give you a good family," Lila added as she followed Scarlet up the steps. "Maybe He wants you to have true love in your life, after all."

But I don't believe in true love. She bit her lip to hold back the words. The last thing she wanted to do was to spoil her friends' good cheer. Besides, they knew how she felt about placing her life in a man's hands. Even if they were Ian's. She slipped through the doorway toward him. He and Lorenzo were holding the tree upright while the reverend's son drove nails through the base and into the stand.

When his gaze met hers, she did not need words to know what he was thinking. She started to chuckle, just a little, and across the sanctuary he joined her. It felt as if their laughter lifted like prayers all the way to heaven.

He could have dreamed up the afternoon, drawing it with the soft slants of light through the windows—not harsh straight lines, but gentle, broken ones. The scene could have been something he had captured on paper, the regal tree and the hopeful young people surrounding it. The dance of lamplight on happy faces. Handmade and donated ornaments, some of fine crystal and porcelain, others of calico and lace, twirled on strings of red satin ribbon amid the dark stands of small white candles.

He moved the chair over a few feet and climbed back onto it. Through the boughs, he caught Lorenzo frowning at him. It took a bit to fight off another surge of jealousy. Those had been plaguing him all afternoon, ever since Fee stepped into church, snow dappled and luminous, more beautiful in her simple gingham dress and coat than he had ever seen her before. He feared he would never tire of seeing her; forever would be a long dark place when she was gone from his life. So he intended to cherish this time he had with her.

Judging by the adoration on the smitten Lorenzo's face, Ian was not alone in that wish.

"You have a good eye, McPherson," Austin Hadly commented from the next chair over. He finished twining a small candle holder to a sturdy bough and gave it a test to make sure it held tight. "Next year you should volunteer for the Christmas committee. We could use

more men. I feel mighty outnumbered with all those matrons in the group."

"I suppose some of them will be by to inspect our
work?"

"Without a doubt." Good-natured, the reverend's son
chuckled, as if he enjoyed his work. "I saw that fine mare
you were driving around town on Friday. I've never seen
an animal like her."

"She is rare, my Duchess." He absently hung a porcelain angel on a branch. He heard Fiona's name murmured
in the chorus of voices. His senses sharpened, aware
when she spoke. In the dull roar of conversations, her
alto was the one he heard above all the others.

"They did turn out very well this year." Fiona held up a
snowflake, a fragile lacy concoction of thin white thread
and air. He had hung ornaments just like the one she held
up, one she had made, he realized. "I am finally getting
the knack of tatting. Thanks to you, Scarlet."

"You are better at it than I ever was. I should have
made snowflakes, too."

"I love your little embroidered manger scenes." Fiona,
bent over her work on the front pew, tied a red ribbon
into an ornament and fussed with the bow, tugging until
it was perfect.

She made a picture with her china-doll face flushed
pink and relaxed. Only the fading bruise of her black eye
remained. He hated that she'd been hurt, but it would be
the last time. He vowed it.

"Uh, Ian?"

He blinked. Austin was waiting, as if for an answer.
Embarrassed to be caught watching the lass, with his
feelings—he feared—revealed.

"The candles are up. Why don't you go fetch the last
of the ornaments from the girls, and then we will all be

done." Austin cleared his throat, probably trying not to laugh.

Sure, he felt like a sap as his feet hit the polished wood floor. The rest of the men gathered around the tree knew it, and he didn't miss the choked-back laughter as he walked away. Just wait, he wanted to tell them. Wait until a pretty lass comes along who turns your priorities upside down. Until there wasn't anything a man wouldn't give to make her life better.

"Are you glad you stayed to help?" Fiona asked, unaware of how vulnerable she made him with that curve of her smile and her sweet spirit.

"Aye. I haven't had this much fun since I was in school." Before Grandfather's illness had taken him out of the classroom for good. Life had been far too serious.

"You have made friends." She looked pleased, as if that was her hope. "I mean, if you are going to be staying here, it might be nice for you to know people. So you aren't so alone."

His throat closed, and he could not speak. Ah, but her caring touched him and made the losses in his life smaller and the hardships easier.

"That is the last of them." One of the girls—the red-haired one—shoved the box into his hand. He suspected Fiona's friends saw right through him to his eternal devotion. To his enduring, lifelong love.

A love that likely would never be returned.

He clutched the box, realizing he still could not speak. He feared Fiona, too, could see far too much. It was for her that he gave a shrug, as if to make up for his silence, and turned away.

"I will take those." Lorenzo took the ornaments, his manner gruff, although Ian sensed he did not mean to be. He knew how it felt not to have affection for Fiona returned. He felt an odd empathy with the young man as they stood side by side, hanging the last of the decorations in the uppermost branches.

The chairs were pulled away and all in the room gathered close to admire the tree. Everything passed in a haze for him: the cacophony of movement and noise, the joyful discussions, the call to join hands in prayer. Fiona slipped into line beside him, her soft hand finding his. That surprised him, as did her tight grip. All through the prayer, he did his best to keep from asking the Lord above for what he wanted most. As the group prayed for compassion and peace and for the welfare of others, he did, too.

He prayed for Fiona. Not that he would win her love, but that she would have her heart's desire. Beyond all that he wished for himself, none of it mattered a bit in comparison with all he wanted for her.

Coziness clung to her and chased away the shocking cold as they sped toward home. The town was a shadow in the falling twilight behind them, and the road ahead ribboned across the gently rolling prairie. Tonight the wind did not whisper to her as she drew the blanket up to her chin. Whatever the world held out there could not be as rosy as what Ian had given her here.

"Do you think you will like staying in Angel Falls?" She felt shy, her voice strangely thin, but she attributed it to the bitter temperatures.

"I like it just fine. This place will be a new start for me, different from all that I knew. Maybe I can find my future here in this land of wide-open prairie and of mountains that hold up the sky."

"Spoken like a man who is thinking of drawing those mountains."

"How did you know?"

"You are less and less a stranger to me."

"I feel as if you never were, lass."

It was pure kindness, plain and simple, a sign of his compassionate nature, that was all. Fiona fisted her hands inside her mittens, determined to be practical and sensible.

"What kind of start did you have in mind?" Snowflakes sifted through the air between them, perhaps hiding what she really wanted to know. "Will you move north if you get a job at the mill?"

"I need wages, lass, but I can ride the five-mile stretch and live here."

Why could she see the colors of his dreams? Green like the fields in May, sapphire-blue like the Montana summer sky and dotted with horses of every color, their velvet coats gleaming in the sun. "You will work to buy horses again. To build another stable."

"Once, we had more than two hundred horses grazing on our land. More than a few of them were champions. Now, the twelve are all I have left."

She felt his loss, not for the former prestige of his family but for the horses he had loved. "You helped to raise and train them, didn't you?"

"The hardest losses are of the heart, it's true." His throat worked, and his jaw turned to iron. "The horses I have left were the ones I could not part with."

"Where are they now?"

"A neighbor is boarding them for me. He's a good friend, and he bought all of my family's land. It is his house where my grandmother is staying."

"Have you heard from her?"

"No, but I expect a letter in the mail any day. This is the first Christmas we will spend apart."

"What was Christmas like for your family?"

"Nana would always serve a roasted duck, candied yams and her mother's baked bean recipe. Buttermilk biscuits light enough to float in midair. Hot chocolate and angel food cake afterward by the fire. That was Christmas dinner."

"You mean there is more?"

"Presents piled under the tree. Christmas Eve service the night before, of course. We would have dinner in town at the hotel after a day of stringing popcorn and making cookies. When I was a little tyke, I would help my mother decorate the Christmas cookies. After she passed, Nana and I carried on the tradition. Nana would spend part of both days playing Christmas carols on her piano. We would gather round with eggnog or tea and sing until we were hoarse."

"You have lived a dream, Ian. Or at least, a dream to some people."

"I'll not argue." The rundown shanty where Fiona's friend lived came into sight, the few windows glowing across the ever darkening landscape. He gave Flannigan more rein, letting the horse run some, as he seemed to want to do.

"One day I pray you have that again." Her hand covered his, and through the layers of wool and leather, he could feel the depth of her wish for him.

The heavens were kind to him and saved him from answering, for the driveway rolled into sight and beyond that the joyless shanty with one window aglow with light.

"We're home." She breathed the words out like a sigh, and it was as if the twilight fell with her happiness.

"I pray that one day home will be a welcome place for you, pretty girl." He reined the horse toward the barn, drawing him gently in from his run. Because he did not want to reveal anything more, he let silence settle between them. Her hand remained on his until the sled came to a stop.

"Next time, Fee, be kinder to the poor young men who have lost their hearts to you." He dragged away from her side, hating to put distance between them.

"What are you talking about?" She scowled, her face scrunching up adorably.

Sad that he was falling ever harder for her. Love was not finite, he realized. It was an infinite place that kept pulling a man apart. Resigned, he offered to help her from the sled, but she hopped out on the other side.

"Lorenzo." He patted Flannigan before kneeling to unbuckle the harnessing. "And those other school boys. What were their names? James and Luken and that blond-headed kid."

"Funny. What could have possibly given you the idea that half the graduating class of boys is carrying a torch for me? Surely." She rolled her eyes, laughing at him, unaware of the doting man who stood right in front of her. Of course she had not noticed the others, either.

"I am telling you the truth." He worked one buckle free and circled around for another. "You are breaking hearts, Fiona, right and left. Think of the poor fellows, would you? It is all I am asking."

"No one is ever going to love me." She looked vulnerable in the thickening twilight, certain as she tucked her Bible into the crook of her arm. "I don't intend to let anyone close enough to try."

"What? Not even me?" Instead of working the harness free, he ambled closer. "I heard you and your girlfriends. It sounds like you've already let me far too close."

"*They* were talking about weddings and forever, not me." Her voice trembled. "I hope you don't think I told them—"

"No," he interrupted, saving her from having to say the words aloud. "We both agreed there would be no wedding. Just a long engagement."

"Yes." She didn't move away. She didn't look away. She couldn't. "I hope this will be a benefit for you, too. I hate to think that your staying here for me would hinder your dreams."

"I am exactly where I want to be. Trust that." His knuckles grazed her cheek tenderly. "You are wrong about my dreams, Fiona. The only ones I have are for you."

Chapter Fifteen

What was the man doing to her? He made it impossible to forget him. All night long he had snuck into her dreams like a bandit, out to steal her heart. *I could not make myself ride another step east, so I followed my heart back to you. I'm going to make sure you are never frightened like that again.*

All morning his velvet-coated promises and declarations drove out all other thoughts. Standing at the front of the classroom, she gripped her hands, trying in vain to find historical facts in her head. But all she could locate were Ian's startling confessions. *You are wrong about my dreams, Fiona. The only ones I have are for you.*

What did that mean? Surely she was not part of his dreams. No, that could not be right. He had meant that he wanted her happiness. As a friend might.

A friend. That's what she was to him. That was exactly what she wanted to be. And if disappointment whispered through her, she was determined to ignore it.

"Miss O'Rourke," the teacher scolded, her frown as severe as her tone. "I'm afraid you will have to study this lesson again."

"I'm sorry, Miss Lambert." Miserable, she hung her

head. She could not remember what she had learned about the battle of Gettysburg. There was nothing in her mind but Ian.

Lila grabbed hold of her hand and squeezed in sympathy.

"That is all, class. You may return to your seats." Miss Lambert laid her history book on her desk, watchful as the twelfth-grade students filed down the aisles, quietly so as not to disturb the others who were studying industriously.

Fiona slipped into her desk. She had never failed a lesson before. She wanted to blame Ian, but the fault was hers. She was the one who could not stop the images of him in the barn doing the evening chores, of how relaxed the horses and the cow were in his presence and how happy they seemed. She hardly recognized Flannigan, who no longer looked prairie-ward with longing in his eyes. Ian, who had walked her to the house and with one stare at her da, ensured that not one cruel word was spoken to her. Ian, who had driven her to school in the morning, helping her from the sled at the schoolyard, tipping his hat in goodbye to her like any courting man.

He was being polite, that was all. No need to read anything more into it. She stacked her books, hearing the school bell ring. Noise burst out around her. Books slammed shut, kids bounced up from their seats, shoes knelled against the floorboards. Conversations drowned out the last echoes of the bell. All she could think about was seeing Ian again. Knowing he would be waiting for her outside Miss Sims's shop was like a gift, one she couldn't wait for.

"Poor Lorenzo hasn't been the same since he met Ian." Scarlet leaned close, whispering as they made their way through the emptying classroom. "I think you broke his heart, Fee."

"Whose heart?" She wondered if Ian would be shivering in his too-thin coat.

"I think she did, too." Lila spoke up, all sympathy. "Maybe I can offer him a few kind words during caroling practice to soothe his wounded feelings."

"You certainly should." Earlee's wistfulness was that of a staunch romantic. "Lorenzo does look downcast today, poor dear."

"And it's all Fee's fault." Kate winked.

"What did I do?" she asked, hardly realizing she hadn't buttoned her coat yet. In fact, she couldn't remember fetching her coat from the hallway or walking through the schoolroom, or even getting up from her desk. The sunshine blinded her as she waltzed out into the winter afternoon, squinting against the brightness as she searched the roadway for him. Ridiculous, because she knew he wouldn't be there, but did that stop her from looking for him? Not one bit.

"There's no sense trying to talk to her," Scarlet said, chuckling warmly. "I talked Ma into making a cake for our party on Friday."

"Perfect. My stepmother is going to help me fix chicken and dumplings." Lila sounded excited. "Fiona, will you bring the biscuits?"

"Sure." She didn't realize how much she could miss Ian. It made no sense. It wasn't as if she cared for the man, right?

"My brother has agreed to come fetch me if the weather is bad, so I can come for sure," Kate commented happily.

"That's wonderful!" Earlee clasped her hands together prayerfully. "This might be our last celebration together.

Our sewing circle might break apart after graduation. You never know where life will take each one of us."

"I hadn't thought of it that way." Fiona sank into the snow, but it was more than her shoe sliding into the icy drift. "Our last sewing-circle Christmas party. That sounds so sad."

"Depressing," Scarlet agreed. "Which is why we do not have to think about it. Instead, it will be the best party we have ever had."

They parted ways—Scarlet and Lila headed off to the church for caroling practice, Kate climbed into her father's sleigh and Earlee walked away with six of her younger siblings. She did not have time to walk uptown today, for she was needed at home.

It was a beautiful day. The sun tossed diamonds onto the pristine snow, and she followed its sparkling trail. She was as cheerful as the lemony rays of sunshine, thinking of the tatted snowflakes she had finished and blued last night. They would be dry and perfect when she got home. Her gifts for her friends were done. Her parents did not celebrate Christmas with gifts, so she had all the presents she would need for the holiday—all but one.

Ian. Her thoughts looped back to him. All roads led inexorably to him. The church steeple rose above the cluster of trees and the tall storefronts, reminded her of how perfect yesterday after the church service had been. The looks they had shared across the sanctuary, how Ian had appeared different with worries and responsibilities lifted from his strapping shoulders. Of what he had told her about his family and his grandmother. She thought of the older woman, who had been best friends with her grandmother.

In her mind's eye she could see her own grandmother's kind face as she told of the McPhersons. Love, she realized, was the reason Ian was here—for his grandmother, and respect for what two girlfriends had shared long ago.

She turned onto the main street, snow tumbling off her shoes and onto the boardwalk. Perhaps, then, it was not so strange she and Ian felt such strong friendship for one another. Maybe she did not need to fight it so much.

"Good afternoon, Fiona," Cora Sims greeted from behind the front desk. "It has been a busy day. Let me finish up this sale, and I will be right with you. There is tea steeping on the stovetop. It will warm you right up."

"Thank you, Miss Sims." Fiona liked the older woman. Cora Sims had been her inspiration for her future life. The lady had come to town long ago and started her own dress shop. She had made a fine life for herself, sewing for others. Maybe, thanks to Ian's help, she could do the same one day.

What used to give her joy to think about now weighed her down. That future did not seem as bright. It was not only the prospect of leaving her friends, but something else. Something that hurt worse, and that made no sense.

Ian. She felt his presence as surely as the warmth from the stove. She unbuttoned her coat, searching for him through the wide display window. There he was across the street, confident and manly, tethering Flannigan to the hitching post. The big horse nudged the man's hand affectionately, as if wanting one last nose rub. Ian obviously agreed, his affection clear. He was a true horseman in a worn-thin coat. He had to be freezing, his teeth looked to be chattering, but he made no hurry to end his time with Flannigan to rush out of the cold.

"I'm pleased to see you, Fiona. I hope this means you have the basting done so soon?"

"Yes, Miss Sims. I worked most of the weekend on it." She opened her book bag and carefully withdrew the folded dress. "The collar was tricky, but I got it set just right. See what you think."

While the seamstress shook out the garment to study it, Fiona let her attention wander back to the street. Ian had left Flannigan's side and was lumbering up the steps onto the boardwalk, cane in hand. The sun brightened because he was near. Tenderness stirred within her, reverent and sweet. Tenderness she wanted to deny, but couldn't.

"This is excellent work, Fiona. Let me get your wages."

She blinked; for a second she had forgotten where she was. She nervously brushed a curl behind her ear. "Do you have any good heavy wool in stock? Something suitable for a winter coat?"

"Some new bolts came in on Friday's train." Cora tapped toward the front desk. "I put them out this morning. Just to your left, next to the buttons display."

It did not make any sense to spend so much money, but did that stop her from wandering over to the table? Not one bit. There was no looking or debating. A bolt of black wool stood out from all the others, and she snatched it without thought. The finest quality, judging from its weight. She didn't even ask Cora the price per yard.

"Will you hold this for me?" she asked. "I can come by after school tomorrow to pay for it."

"That would be fine." Cora smiled knowingly as she took the quality fabric and unrolled it with a thump onto the cutting counter. "Why don't I cut it for you now, and you can take it with you? That way you can get started on it tonight. Christmas is fast approaching. How many yards do you need?"

"Enough for a man's coat," she whispered, for the bell above the door jingled. Ian's uneven step tapped into the store, the sound meaningful to her. This was more than friendship she felt. Much more. Ignoring it or denying it would not change that fact.

"I've had a talk with your horse." He took off his hat, revealing a relaxed, happy smile. He must have gotten the job. "Flannigan would like you to drive him home."

"How thoughtful of him." She stepped away from the counter, hoping Ian would not notice the fabric. "What else did Flannigan say?"

"That he misses you. You used to spend your evenings in the barn."

"And he would like me to do that again, would he?"

"I believe so. I'm sure Riley would not mind at all, either." He held out his hands to warm them at the stove. "Or the cat. He has set his cap for you, I fear."

"Oh, you do not fool me one bit, McPherson."

"McPherson, is it? Again? You must be mad at me."

"Blaming all that on the animals. Yes, indeed. If you want me to know you wouldn't mind sharing the barn with me in the evening, then you could simply say so." She thanked the shop owner with a conspiratorial smile and tucked a brown-wrapped package into her book bag. "Thank you, Miss Sims. Have a good afternoon!"

"Goodbye, dear. Same to you." The sewing lady looked mighty pleased and gave him an approving smile. He had been getting a lot of those lately. Word had traveled about town he was here to marry the O'Rourke girl. Her hardships were no secret, nor could they be with the fading yellow bruise on her cheekbone.

Gentleness filled him. He resisted the need to pull her close and lay an arm around her shoulder. He wanted her step to remain light as she waltzed to the door. He opened it for her and followed her into the sunshine gracing the boardwalk.

"Did you get work?" She whirled around in a swirl of red gingham. "You look happy, so that must mean yes."

"Aye. I start in the morning. I'm afraid you will have to walk to school."

"I don't mind. I usually stop by Earlee's house so I can walk most of the way with her." She skipped down the steps, her twin braids flying behind her.

He would forever remember this picture of her with dark wisps curling around her heart-shaped face, her happiness contagious, her wholesome beauty.

"C'mon, Ian. I can't wait to drive." She glided across the street, one step ahead and all that was dear to him. Her dark hair gleamed blue-black, her porcelain skin blushed by the winter air.

How precious this time with her was, he realized as he followed her across the road. The bustle of town, the approaching whistle of the train, the too-slow beat of his pulse were too commonplace for this moment. When Fiona turned to him, he sensed more than tolerance in her manner. Perhaps more than friendship.

"I see you have had a very busy day without me." She touched his sleeve, nodding toward the sled's bed. "What do you have under the tarp?"

"Fence posts. When I went to repair the broken board in the corral, I decided it would do little good if the post was ready to fall down. So I stopped by the lumberyard."

"I'm sure Flannigan will be pleased. He will get to romp in the corral again. Right, boy?" Although she had drifted away from his side, a form of closeness remained. A tie Ian could not explain or prove, but he felt it.

Or he surely hoped he did. He worked the tether free, watching as Fiona ran her fingers through the horse's forelock. He enjoyed her musical laugh as the gelding tossed his head, preferring to have his nose stroked instead.

"All right, have your way, big fella." She obliged. "As long as you know I am boss when we drive home."

The gelding nickered low in his throat, perhaps a bit of a protest, and Ian felt hope as Fiona laughed again. She had the kind of spirit that she would be happy wherever her future took her.

"Did you hear that, Ian? I think he is planning on giving me some trouble." She didn't look worried, no, she looked like perfection. She was his dream come true.

Please, Lord, he prayed. *If it is Your will, let her know it one day. I am a patient man. I do not mind waiting.*

No answer came from above, but then, he did not expect one so soon. He took hold of the driving reins, for the gelding did have trouble glinting in his adoring eyes. He knew just how the horse felt.

"Aye, I think Flannigan is making plans." He helped her into the sled, something he wouldn't mind doing the rest of his life. "I guess you had best be making some plans of your own."

"You're going to leave me to deal with him if he runs away?"

"Don't think you can give over the reins to me when times get tough." He spread the lap blanket over her, tucking it in so she would be warm.

"Who else would I turn to, Ian?" She took the reins from him, but it felt as if she took something else. Likely it was his eternal devotion, for she already had his love. "There is no one else in this sled."

"You think I will rescue you whenever you need it, is that it?" He settled on the seat beside her, taking care to double the blanket over so that she had all of it. The thermometer in the tailor's store window said it was fifteen degrees below. "You know me too well, for I will always be here when you need me."

"I know." Deeper meaning layered her words and chased away every shadow. What she didn't say—perhaps what she couldn't—remained between them, a sweetness he felt soul deep.

"I care for you, too, lass." He tried to keep all the affection he felt from his voice, but he failed. It was too great to hide, too powerful to hold back. Like an avalanche it crashed through him.

Never in his life had there been a love like this. He laid an arm across the back of the seat and drew Fiona close against him. She did not shy away. She bowed her head, studying the reins for a moment as if she could find some answer there.

Flannigan broke the moment and darted into the street before Ian could know Fiona's reaction. Would she say the same, or would she turn away from him? The horse had impeccable timing, that was for sure.

"Tighten the reins more," he advised. "A little heavier bit will give you more control."

"I like going fast." She didn't draw up the reins but she didn't move away, either. The town's last block flew by in a blur and they raced toward the dazzling white prairie together, blessed by a winter-blue sky.

Storm clouds gathered at the horizon, but for this perfect moment it was a clear day.

Fiona loved driving. She loved the feel of Flannigan's strength telegraphing down the thick leather reins and into her hands. She liked being the one to direct the horse, to give him his head so he could run as fast as he wanted and she would feel the wind whipping through her hair.

"You are as bad as the gelding." Ian's hands closed

over hers. "You will have to slow him down or we will never make the turn."

"You're afraid I am going to crash your sled." She rather liked that his arms were around her, and she leaned into the curve of his chest. Never had she felt so safe and comforted. Nothing in her life had ever been like this. She was utterly secure and gently cherished.

This cannot be love, she told herself firmly. Sure, it was a great deal more than friendship, but she wasn't the kind of girl who lost her heart.

"I'm afraid you are going to tumble us into the ditch." He was laughing. "While you probably think that is nothing less than I deserve, that's how I broke my leg in the first place."

"In a sleigh accident?"

"No, going too fast. In a race." He tensed, every muscle, every tendon. Tightness snapped in his jaw. "You haven't been so wrong about me. I was once a desperate man."

It was hard to believe he would do something wrong. "What happened?"

"After selling off parcels of our land, I couldn't stand to do the same with our last quarter-section. Raising and training horses is an expensive endeavor, especially when a false rumor made my last customers panic. Owners pulled their thoroughbreds from my training stable, and I was left with bills I couldn't pay. That had been my hope to restore the family name—training winners for other men so I could bankroll the training of our champions."

"It was a gamble." She saw the cost. The wince of pain, and the weight of his failure. "You lost because of someone's cruel words about you?"

"Worse than that, afterward I took a bet. I know the Lord frowns on such things, but I didn't want to have to explain to my grandmother she would have to leave her home. The house Grandfather had built for her was filled with all the memories of their life together. So I bet the rest of my land, and all but a dozen horses, that I could win a cross-country race. Not a legal race, mind you, on the track. But a private one through the low country, dangerous to man and beast. It was funded by wealthy men. The chance to win so much money was something I could not turn down."

"You would have lost your family home anyway."

"That was my reasoning. My justification to do what I knew was wrong. But the lure of winning a fine amount of money was enough to make me saddle my best stallion and ride."

"And you fell?"

"The horse landed wrong on a jump over a fallen tree. He broke two legs and had to be put down. The cost of my foolishness." He pulled away, withdrawing his arm from her shoulders. Maybe it was because the sled had come to a stop. He studied the horizon, where the first blaze of sunset stained the encroaching clouds. "I splinted my leg, carved a pair of crutches and pressured men I knew for a job. I cleaned stalls day and night."

"On an injured leg?"

"I could not lie abed. Nana was ill, there were enough doctor bills without my adding to them. So I did what I had to do. I kept a roof over my grandmother's head and her needs met." He cleared his throat, battling something she could not see.

Flannigan nickered, tossing his head for attention, reminding her she held the reins still. They had reached the barn, she realized, but she could not move. Ian felt distant, as if he were miles away instead of beside her. She wanted to reach out to him, but she stayed motionless on the seat. "A lot of men would not have stayed in the first place. They would have fled their responsibilities."

He said nothing more, although his throat worked, as if he had more to say. He swept off his hat, knocking snow from the brim, but he could not hide his trembling. From cold, from the failure dogging him, perhaps from something more she could not see.

"Come on." He climbed out of the sled. "Flannigan isn't happy standing. It's too cold, and he's worked up a lather."

Fiona wasn't fooled. Whatever Ian's faults and the mistakes he had made, he had done them for the greatest reason of all—love. Respect filled her, slow and sweet and endlessly deep.

He lifted the blanket away from her and folded it so that she would not trip on its cumbersome length. When he gave her his hand, as he always did, as she knew he always would, a force swept through her. She loved him. She wished she could stop it, hold back her tenderness like a dam in high water, but she could not.

Chapter Sixteen

"Fiona! You daft girl! You are spilling water all over the floor."

Ma's shrill tone, full of fury, penetrated Fiona's thoughts. She realized she was kneeling on the kitchen floor, her hands wrist deep in suds. The edge of the washboard dug into her ribs.

"Staring off into nothing when you should be finishing the wash. You're lazier than ever, girl." Footsteps pounded from the table to the stove, and sizzling erupted when the cut potatoes hit the hot fry pan. "I do not approve of that man."

"I rather like him." She gripped a pair of her father's trousers in both hands and scoured them on the washboard.

"You say that now." Ma turned, spatula in hand. "Do not think you are so smart, missy. That is the way men are, pretending to be kind and good to you when they want something. Aye, they can sweet-talk you into believing they would do anything for you. All that matters is your happiness. Sound familiar?"

How did her mother know? Her strength faltered, the garment caught midstroke, and she skinned her knuckles on the corrugated washboard. A streak of blood stained her raw skin. "You and Da have been listening in—"

"Uh! As if I need to." Ma's laugh rang high and cruel. "I have walked in your shoes before. How else do you think I married your da?"

"I—" The garment in the tub was blurry, probably due to the effects of the soapy water.

"I was sixteen, and the man who came courting, the man my parents picked for me, was charming. Bringing me flowers and notions for my sewing. I was making a wedding ring quilt for my hope chest." Ma left the pan sizzling, pounding closer. "Oh, I fell heart and soul for the man who treated me like such a lady, who held doors for me and pledged his undying affection. Who wanted me to have all of my dreams."

Fiona wished the barbed words did not find their target, but they did. She kept wringing, and over the splash of the rinse water she heard the echo of Ian's promises. *I followed my heart back to you. The only dreams I have are for you. I care for you, lass.*

He had told her the truth. She would have known if he had been false. She plopped the trousers into the clothes basket and reached for a nearby towel. She would not listen to her mother: it was simply years of unhappiness that made her say terrible things.

"Don't believe me." Ma returned to the stove, stirring the potatoes harder than necessary. Several flew out of the pan and she left them to smoke. "You think your charming Mr. McPherson is a shining knight now, but mark my words. He is out for himself, as all men are."

Don't listen to her, Fee. She mopped up the last of the splashed water and scooped the clothes basket off the floor. Her parents were unhappy with the way Ian was changing things. Da was unhappy that he was no longer in complete control. That was all this was. Her mother's hurtful words could not be true. She unhooked her coat from the peg and slipped into it.

"Don't have anything to say, girl? I know what you are thinking. You think your man is nothing like your da. That's what I thought about *your* father, that he was not like mine." Ma shook her head, grown too hard with her disappointments in life to care about the hurt she was causing. "You might as well smarten up, girl. We are wasting time waiting for the wedding. Marry the boy. I am on pins and needles not knowing for sure if he will keep his word."

"I have never said I would marry Ian, and besides, he has paid the bank." All the proof she needed that her mother was not right. She grabbed the latch and tugged. The door squeaked open.

"No, he has not. He has only promised to. He went and got some fancy lawyer involved."

"Whatever Ian is doing, he is a fair man." She did not need to list all that he had done for her to prove it. It was one of the things she admired about him. Besides, he had said he didn't want the farm because of the high mortgage, the very reason Da could not easily sell it. "You shouldn't worry so, Ma."

"No man is fair. Can't you get that through your thick head? Forget this foolishness. Let us get on to the business of saving our home. I am not going to live out of the back of our wagon."

This was what twenty years of unhappiness and unkindness could do to a person, eroding away the tender places. She could not listen to any more; she wrestled down anger as she drew the door closed.

Ma's final words drifted out to her. "The moment he gets his name on the deed, he will change, and not for the better. All he wants is the land. So stop being difficult and marry him now—"

The door clicked shut and Fiona walked away with a heavy heart. Glad she was that Ian wanted her to spend the evenings with him in the barn. She might not be able to work on his coat, but she could make a pattern for it. Perhaps get measurements from his clothes, if she offered to wash them. Her step quickened as she hurried down the steps and plunged into the snowy path.

The glow from the faded sunset blessed the silent prairie with a rare light. She walked on lavender-hued snow toward the clothesline, breathing in the wonder of the prairie. The hush felt reverent, almost sacred, almost as if God was peering down from heaven through the ragged clouds. One star twinkled at the horizon's edge, a reminder that night was coming.

What was Ian doing? She caught sight of the sled, drawn up to the corral's gate. Perhaps he was inside taking care of Flannigan. She let the basket drop to the ground and dug a half-dozen wooden pins from the hanging bag. She clipped them to the top of her apron before shaking the wrinkles from the first garment she grabbed. Thinking of him made her worries lighter. She did not fret over Ma's words, because she trusted Ian. The safety and comfort she'd felt in his arms remained like a gift, one she had never guessed could be so wonderful.

She clipped up one pair of Da's trousers, and reached for another pair. The wind stirred around her in little swirls, and snowflakes lifted from the ground in a slow, circling waltz. It did feel as if heaven were nearer, she thought, as she reached for another garment to hang.

A rumbling disrupted the prairie's peace, angry tones skimming the darkening snow as if riding the wind. They came too softly at first to hear more than the rise and fall of baritone and tenor, but as she reached for another clothespin, the wind shifted to bring the words straight to her.

"—that is one point I won't budge on, O'Rourke. Fiona is—"

"—my daughter, and she stays and takes care of us. We are not as young as we used to be. That's the deal."

"No, that's not the deal I shook on."

"It is if you want the deed signed over to you. Isn't that what you want? Isn't the land the reason you are here?"

"Aye."

The clothespins slipped from her fingers and plinked to the ground. Night fell like a blanket over the land and over her shock.

She could not be hearing them right. There had to be a rational explanation.

"Good. I've spoken with the sheriff. He will be performing the ceremony at noon the day after Christmas. Agreed?"

The wind gusted, stealing Ian's answer. It didn't matter. She didn't need to hear him agree. She hadn't misunderstood. She had heard him loud and clear.

Isn't the land the reason you are here?

Aye. He'd answered with resignation, but he had answered with the truth. His first priority was the land—not her. It always had been. She had been too blind to see it. He had lied to her, and she had believed it.

She had loved him for it.

The first crack of pain struck like a blow. She grasped at the fallen pins, her fingers fumbling, her whole heart shattering one tiny piece at a time. The snow swirled whimsically at her feet, as if all were right with the world. Stars popped out like hope renewed, as she turned her back on the barn and the men there.

Maybe if she held herself very still inside the pain would stop. She managed to gather the last fallen clothespin and stood, feeling dizzy. The terrible truth would twirl away like a thousand crystal snowflakes and would be lost on the lonesome prairie. She could go back to believing in the cocoon of Ian's safe comfort and the hopeful love she felt for him.

A love he did not harbor for her. By rote, she grabbed another piece of laundry from the basket. The second crack of pain hit her like the strap cutting deep. For Ian, she was a means to an end, that was all. Just like her mother had said.

"Fiona! What are you doing, standing around like a loon? Get finished up there." Ma marched into sight. "I need help with supper."

"Yes, Ma." She clipped the last garment—Ma's Sunday dress—to the line. The cold did not touch her as she grabbed the empty basket and tromped toward the house. The darkness trailed her through the deep drifts, past the strap on the lean-to wall and into the house where more work waited.

I don't like the way you are doin' things. O'Rourke's words taunted him as he beat the ground with the ax. Chunks of frozen soil and sod spewed into the night. Sweat rolled down his face as he swung again. The leverage he had on the man was gone; the tables had turned. Nana had somehow found the money to pay the man his asking price. *Fiona is mine, and until you put a ring on her finger, you will not be letting her drive a horse or go running off with those snooty friends of hers.*

Oh, but he was in a temper. He drove the ax downward a final time. Flannigan's nicker reminded him he was not alone in the corral. He leaned on the ax handle, pulled a handkerchief out of his back denims pocket and swiped the sweat off his face. His breath rose like smoke in the dark. Overhead all but a few stars kept watch; a storm was moving in.

"Sorry, boy. Let me chain up one last post and after we get it moved, I will treat you to a nice long—" A shadow moved at the edge of his vision, a slim, willowy form in a familiar gray coat. "Fiona. It is too cold for you to be out."

"Oh, and it's not for you?" Her chin went up, the faint starlight finding her.

"Point taken." He leaned the ax handle against the pile of rotting posts he'd extracted. "Is that supper I smell?"

"Yes. When you didn't come in to eat, I set a plate aside for you." She stopped to pat Flannigan, and probably to feed him a treat, as the horse lapped her palm and crunched away. Sounded like a carrot.

"You are an industrious man. Some would wait until morning to start refencing." She held out a cloth-covered plate. "Smarter men might wait for spring."

"I never claimed to be a smart man." He took it, aware that while she was only a few steps from him, she felt a mile away. The plate's heat penetrated his leather gloves, proof she had taken care to heat the food well for the trip outside. Thoughtful she was; his chest felt wrenched apart.

If you want the land in your name, you will marry her. O'Rourke's demands rocked through him. He set the plate on the flat-topped fence post before he dropped it. *I'm back in charge now. I have your grandmother's money, and I am through waiting. That girl is a burden, and you will take over the cost of supporting her or find another ranch.*

With his financial position, no bank would give him a mortgage. Ian's stomach soured, hating his choices. "I

start my job in the morning, so if I want to get this re-
paired, then I have to work in the evenings."

"Repairing? No, that's replacing a board or two. You
are putting in a whole new fence." She crossed her arms
over her midsection, and with the wind whipping at her
skirts, she looked oddly alone and lost. "Are you bringing your horses out here from Kentucky, then?"

"Aye. I can sell one of them to pay for the rail costs.
But I would rather wait to see how much of my wages
I can save and pay for it that way." His hand trembled
as he tried to hold the plate steady and lifted the cloth.
The buttery scent of hot biscuits and the meaty fried salt
pork made his stomach growl, although he did not feel
hungry. He was speaking of his dreams, when he had
promised to protect hers. "In truth, I don't know how it
is going to work out."

"That is the problem with the future. You cannot see it
ahead of time." There was no greater beauty than Fiona
in the stardust. Wherever she moved, the light hurried
as if to illuminate her path. She climbed onto the remaining part of the fence and swung over to sit on the
top rail, and the starlight lovingly pearled her hair and
kissed her dear face.

Love for her filled every crack and hollow in him. He
wished that an answering love would show on her face.
Impossible, he knew, but maybe with time she would do
more than care for him. Looked like now that time had
run out, it was not to be.

He hardly tasted the biscuit or the butter melting on
his tongue. How did he tell her what his grandmother
had done? He took another bite, memorizing the way she
balanced like a lost princess on the barnyard fence. She
perched, straight-backed and regal, a spirit of dignity and
composure in gingham and braids.

"Will you be bringing out your grandmother, too? You must worry about her." Her question came gently, laced with understanding.

"Aye. I'm guilty for leaving her. If I bring her here, I fear she will be disappointed in the prospects." He cut into the slice of salt pork with his fork. "She was expecting a grand place."

"Tell me about her."

"She is absolute kindness. I cannot remember her ever speaking a harsh word." He missed Nana, but all things changed. He was no longer a boy riding home from school at a racing gallop to tell her of his perfect marks for the day and to share cookies and milk on the front veranda. "She managed all my childhood mistakes with patience. She comforted my grandfather when my father's gambling ways had shamed them and later when his investments went bust. When I lost what was left, she did not once think of herself. Her only concern was for me. Misplaced, aye, and what I did not deserve."

"You must love her beyond measure."

"She is in large part to blame for the man I am."

"So I see." Flannigan wandered over, nosing for more treats. She pulled a carrot from her coat pocket and broke it in half. The crack resounded in the forlorn yard, as if emphasizing the broken-down poverty of the place.

The wind stirred the tendrils that had escaped from her braids as she leaned her forehead against the horse's neck. He wished he knew what would become of them all—a used-up horseman, an old gelding and a Cinderella girl with no prince to save her.

"You should bring her here." She broke the silence between them. "You worry about her disappointment, but from what you have told me, she could never be disappointed in you. She loves you, and she is family. That is what matters."

"True." He wondered at the sorrow on her face, but there was no hint of it in her voice or in the way she dropped from the fence post with a hop. Her skirts swirled around her and her braids thumped against her back. He resisted the urge to draw her into his arms and hold her close, to keep her safe and snug against his chest.

Instead he watched her take the empty plate and utensils, the cloth and his dreams.

"Good night," she said, but it felt like goodbye.

She took the starlight with her. The night deepened, the shadows took over and the first flakes of snow tumbled from an unforgiving sky. A blast of brutal wind razored through his coat as if it were nothing; he was glad when the flash of light of a door opening told him Fiona had reached the warmth of the shanty.

The snowfall tumbled like a blanket from heaven, stealing away all sight of her.

She wrung the last drops of water from the fine wool fabric. The splashes and plunks of the droplets made a pleasant melody as she worked. She could not return cut fabric, and she didn't want to. There was nothing to be done but to continue on with the coat. The storm gusted against the eaves, echoing in the rafters inches above her head. Her attic bedroom might be small, but the heat radiating off the chimney stones kept her warm enough. But what of Ian? Was he still out there struggling to rebuild what he had lost?

She wanted to hate him for his deception, for the omission he had kept from her about buying the land anyway. She wanted a great many things as she hung the thick wool over a makeshift line. The fabric would be dry by morning and tomorrow she would work out a pattern for it. Maybe when she stopped by Miss Sims's store, she could ask the seamstress's advice.

You are a fool of the first water, Fiona O'Rourke. She wiped her damp hands on her apron. She had only herself to blame if her heart was broken. She had started to believe in stories and in schoolgirl fancies that had no place in a life like hers. She was not Meredith from a fine family or Lila with dreams to spare. She did not have Kate's optimism or Scarlet's indomitable ways. Stories did not fill her heart like they did Earlee's. She did not believe in storing away treasures in a hope chest or placing her trust in a man's love.

But hadn't she done that anyway—just a bit—without noticing it? She hefted the small buckets of rinse water and suds and carried them down the ladder. The splash of water and clink of the metal emphasized the emptiness of the kitchen, the barrenness of the home.

As she padded by the doorway, she caught sight of Da asleep in his chair. The empty bottle of whiskey reflected the single lamp's glow. Ma's rocking chair was empty. It was late; likely she had gone off to bed, but her hard words about men came alive in the kitchen again. Try as she might, she could not silence them. The memory kept rolling through her as if without end. All the kindness Ian had shown her, the promises he had made, the happiness he had given her.

He had not lied, not really. She was at fault, reading more into his goodness toward her and in wishing for what was out of her reach. Her friends, dear as they were to her, were wrong. God did not mean for her to have the kind of love and family that had always eluded her. God was surely watching over her, but what He wanted for her was a mystery, one she did not understand.

I'm trusting You, Lord. There has to be some good to come from this.

She unlatched the door and eased the buckets into the lean-to, to be dealt with during her morning chores. The storm blasted her with snow so that she was dusted white and her teeth chattered by the time she shut the door.

"Is that you, girl?" Da's shout was rusty with sleep and slurred from his drinking.

"Yes, sir." She crept into the fall of lamplight, stomach knotting over what he might say.

"Put some more coal on the fire. I'm gettin' cold." He rose from his chair, like an old man, one far past his prime. Sad it was he had wasted whatever had once been good in him, but that had been his choice. "I don't want you goin' to school in the morning, you hear? There's no sense to it anymore. You will be helping your ma with the housework from now on."

An angry gust slammed against the north wall of the room, shaking the window glass in its panes. Smoke puffed down the pipe and rattled the door. Without a word she knelt before the old potbelly, filled the scoop from the hod and opened the door handle with the hem of her apron. Heat and smoke made her eyes burn as she poured coal into the glowing embers.

Da said nothing more as he cracked open the seal on a new bottle. "What are you lookin' at?" he snarled.

"Good night." She closed the door, and it was like her fate sealing. When she stood, she felt light-headed and her knees were unsteady as she crossed the room. The cold deepened and the storm worsened. The howling wind filled the kitchen like a wild animal on the loose.

Ian was surely tucked in the barn by now. But that was little comfort as she climbed the ladder. Never before had she been so torn between what was right and what she wanted. She'd never known there were so many shades of gray between right and wrong. For if she ran with the few dollars that would be left in her savings after paying for Ian's coat, she would be without a job or anywhere to go. If she did not marry him, Ian would lose all he had and his grandmother's dreams—she did not fool herself by thinking her father would fairly return an old woman's money.

But how could she agree to marry a man who did not love her? A man who would marry her only because she came with a farm he wanted? Ian would always be kind to her, because that was the brand of man he was, but she could not be happy living her mother's life. At what cost did she refuse? Would the cost be greater if she accepted?

Worse, she did not want to spend twenty years of her life secretly in love with a man whose kindness to her was not affection, whose thoughtfulness was not devotion, whose heart would not be hers. It would be no happy ending, just a compromise, a business to gain land. Worse, she could not blame Ian, for he had the best excuse.

He had done it out of love.

Chapter Seventeen

At the toll of the schoolhouse bell, Fiona lifted her skirts higher and broke into a run. Snow blinded her, the icy flakes needled her face and the chilly air burned like fire in her chest. A hitch bit into her side, but she kept going. While she had been hurrying as fast as she could, it hadn't been quick enough. School had let out, and that meant in a few minutes' time, if she didn't reach the streets of town first, she would meet schoolchildren on their way home. She shut out images of kids asking her where she had been this morning and why she'd missed class. The notion of meeting Earlee on the road and having to explain, of seeing pity on her friend's face, made her miss a step.

She pushed harder until the houses on the edge of town appeared through the shroud of white. She didn't slow to a walk until her shoes hit the boardwalk and she was just another person hurrying about her errands. Safe in the crowds of Christmas shoppers, she wove her way to the bank, where wreaths hung festively from the impressive wood awning, and garlands added holiday cheer to the front windows. Cheer that was at odds with her.

"Fiona? Is that you?" A familiar voice broke above the rush and bustle of the busy street.

Earlee. Fiona stopped in her tracks, dread filling her. What was she going to say to her friend? Some things were too painful to speak of.

"I was so worried about you." Earlee tapped closer, all friendly concern. "Are you all right?"

"I am fine." *Fine* was a relative term, but it was all she could manage.

"What are you doing here in town, and not at school?" Earlee looked her over carefully and appeared relieved, perhaps that there were no fresh bruises. "Is everything okay at home?"

"Fine." There was that word again. It was *not* fine, but it was all she seemed able to say. "What are you doing in town?"

"Bea is ailing." Good-natured, Earlee rolled her eyes. "I have to stop and pick up some medicine. You haven't answered my question."

"I'm running errands for Ma."

"Is she feeling poorly?"

"No." Somehow she had to put a smile on her face and keep pretending she wasn't hurting. Maybe then she could convince herself. After all, falling in love with Ian wasn't the first foolish mistake she'd made, and life went on. Right?

"You *are* having trouble at home again." Earlee wrapped her in a brief hug, all sympathy, all caring. That was Earlee. A good friend through and through. "Is there something I can do?"

"No, I—" Her smile was faltering, no matter how she fought. "There's nothing. Really."

"I have today's homework assignments. Tomorrow we might have a quiz."

"I don't need them," she interrupted, too abruptly, too harshly, hating that she made her friend stare at her in surprise. "I'm sorry, I just—"

"It's okay. Tell me what is hurting you so."

I thought Ian was in love with me. I thought he was different from the men I know. I believed what he told me. I fell in love with him, and he only wanted the farm. Just like what happened to my ma. I'm afraid I will have the same life and as much unhappiness. She wanted to say all of that, but too many people were hurrying by with their Christmas shopping packages and seasonal cheer. Singing erupted down the street—the church caroling group. How could she speak of her private heartbreak where anyone could overhear?

"My parents think I don't need to finish school. That I need to stay home and learn how to be a wife." She sounded wooden to her ears, but at least her emotions did not show.

"Oh, Fee. I'm sorry." Earlee understood. "Being able to graduate meant so much to you."

"Yes, but there are other things to consider." Duty. What was right. What was merely being selfish. Once, she had been sure about those things. But her heart was involved now; she could not say Ian's dreams were more important than hers. She could not say her dreams were expendable, either.

"Is it Ian?"

"It's complicated." Fiona caught sight of a familiar face across the street. The sheriff must be keeping an eye on her for Da. Dismayed, she turned her back to him. "I'm sorry, I have to go. Ma will be waiting for me."

"I have to make haste, too. Where are you heading to next? I'll meet you there, and we can hurry home to-gether. We don't have to talk if you don't want to."

"Thanks. I really need a friend right now." She swallowed against the tightness in her throat. Those pesky emotions were troubling her again.

"I will always be here for you, Fee. You can count on me, right?"

"I know." What would she do without her friends? She let Earlee hug her one more time. With the closing verse of "O Come All Ye Faithful" accompanying them, Earlee broke off toward the dry-goods store. With one last wave goodbye, Fiona disappeared into the bank.

His thigh bone felt as if it had been hit by dynamite. He slid from Flannigan's broad back in the shadow of the barn, doing his level best to ignore the burning pain. Teeth gritted, he hauled the door open and led the horse inside. The day had been long, the work hard, but he was thankful for it. He had not expected to find a job so easily.

"I'm sorry it was a hard walk home, boy." He patted Flannigan's neck. The gelding lipped his hand, tired too. "I'll give you a good rubdown and treat you to some of Duchess's oats. You like warm mash?"

Horse ears flicked forward, pricked and eager. Answer enough.

"That's a good boy." He swiped off the snow gathered on the animal's mane and flanks. "I will make your bed up nice and thick for a good night's sleep. We must get up and do the same thing tomorrow."

A meow cried out from the beam overhead. Riley poked his nose over his gate. Duchess nickered low in her throat from some comfortable place inside her stall. The cow, chewing her cud, placidly leaned against her gate to see what all was going on. A welcoming committee of sorts and fine it was, but short one important person.

"It's late, sorry to bother you all." He half expected to

see Fiona lean down from the haymow with bits of grass in her hair, or to scowl at him for disturbing her in her secluded spot in that far stall. Aye, he knew it was late, she would most likely be abed, but that didn't stop his hope. He wanted to speak with her.

You should bring her here. Her advice about Nana had preoccupied him the day through. *From what you have told me, she could never be disappointed in you. She loves you, and she is family. That is what matters.*

Aye, family was what mattered to him. He had always remained fiercely loyal to the grandparents who had raised him when his own father had refused. Now was his time to take care of them, to repay them for all the wise lessons in horses and life he had learned at his grandfather's side and for the gentler teachings of his strong, ever kind nana. He unbuckled Flannigan's halter, removing the bit with care.

"And how am I to do that?" He voiced his concern to the horse, who swiveled his ears as if to listen intently. "If I do not marry Fiona, then I have failed, good and truly. I cannot bring my mares out here if I have no land for them. I cannot make my grandmother happy in her last days without knowing their legacy lives on. If I make the lass marry me, then I have my chance to rebuild. I know I can do it. I am not afraid of the work it will take."

Flannigan must have sensed his turmoil, because the big horse leaned into him, pressing his face against Ian's chest. An intimate, comforting gesture. Touched by the fellow's concern, he leaned his cheek against the horse's forehead, savoring the coarse scratchiness of the animal's forelock.

Perhaps it was the long hard day of physical work or that he was infinitely tired of fighting for someone else's dreams, but his defenses were down, his soul weary. He had failed Fiona, too. He wanted to blame his grandmother for interfering again, but what good could come of that? Every mistake he had made along the way smarted like deep, unhealed wounds. He had pushed himself to the limit, working to make things right and following where he thought the Lord was guiding him, but he was at a dead end. There would be no good solution, whatever he chose to do. He would lose his grandmother's faith in him, or he would ruin Fiona's chance for happiness.

How did he choose?

The past was good and truly gone. Maybe that was what God has been trying to tell him, closing all doors but this one and bringing him here to Fiona's sad life, the girl he had been destined to marry in his grandparents' dreams. Maybe, if the good Lord had led him here, then it was not the past he needed to build on, but a different future.

"I feel as if I am letting down those I have loved the most." He released Flannigan, but the horse didn't move away. With his liquid brown eyes and intent stare, he seemed to care a great deal about the outcome, too. "Maybe the best way to repay my grandparents' legacy of love is to do what I think is right."

Flannigan stomped his front hoof as if in agreement, as if to say it was truly time to let go, that no one should hold on to the past so tightly that he destroyed what is good in life and in his future. Sometimes a man had to follow the hardest path, no matter its cost.

"What a good friend you are, boy." He stroked the animal's feather-soft nose, warm with affection for the old boy. "You have not had an easy time. I know O'Rourke is a hard master to you, and you have not deserved it. A truer heart I have never met. You've the spirit of a champion, my friend."

In appreciation, the draft horse lipped Ian's hat brim, earning a chuckle. "Let's get you rubbed down, so I can fetch the mash I promised. How does that sound?"

Flannigan nodded enthusiastically and took off for his stall. His tail flicked, waiting while Ian hurried to open the gate. The cat pranced along the rafters overhead, and Riley leaned out for attention and perhaps to ask for mash, too.

This would be a good life, he decided, glancing around at the small barn, the handful of livestock and the memories of Fiona lingering here. Aye, the lass had changed him. His love for her drove him now as he clenched his jaw against the ever-present pain in his leg and kept his voice gentle as he rubbed down Flannigan until he was dry and warm. She was the reason he had the strength to make the hardest decision, the one best for them both.

The evenings were the worst, Fiona decided as she guided her needle through the thick fabric with a click of her thimble. Her chores were done, and with the weather taking an unusually brutal turn, her fingers went numb every time she tried sewing in the barn. She missed her animal friends and the sanctuary she once had found there, but it was gone now and the place a reminder of the cost she was to pay. She had not run; she had paid Miss Sims what she owed her, although she was sure if she explained the situation, the fair lady would have gladly taken back the fabric. No, sewing this coat was the right thing. Ian had sacrificed Duchess's foal for her, a foal Ian surely loved and wanted.

He should have his dreams. She pressed the seam flat with her fingers, careful of the pins holding the fabric, and memories of him filled her mind. How thrilling it had felt to gallop with him through the snow in the sled, and the joy that filled her when he had given her Flannigan's reins. Every smile, every chuckle, and the afternoon he had given her at the church. Even his promises that for a moment she feared were false—that he had come back to help her, that he cared about her dreams, all of it she knew he had meant.

The trouble was, some things mattered to him more. That was simply the way life was. She had fallen in love with him, and that love made her wish for what could never be. She was not going to marry Ian, but neither was she going to run from her problems.

The candle on her bureau chose that moment to flicker. The wind gusted again, blowing through the cracks in the wall, nearly dousing it. The flame writhed as if in pain, and she squinted, trying to see enough for her next stitch. Iciness crept through the floor and roof above, and the next gust extinguished the candle.

The night closed in on her, and the hopelessness that always chased her caught up. Without her dreams of running away to escape into, without her brother who had always lent a kind word of understanding, with only the present and this life stretching ahead of her forever, she had nothing to console her. She put down her work, pressed her face in her hands and breathed deep, fighting not to give in to it.

A rush of wind howled through the house, rattling the glass chimney of the lamp in the kitchen and ghosting up the ladder. She shivered, realizing she wasn't alone. An uneven gait padded on squeaky floorboards. The oven door creaked open.

Ian, home for the night. How was he? She had not seen him for days. She crept off the foot of the bed and along the floor, knowing which boards to avoid so she could move in silence. She stretched out on her stomach, easing up to peer over the edge of the doorway. The kitchen stretched out before her, black as a void except for the glow of orange lapping from the open oven door and onto the man seated before it.

He had drawn one of the chairs over to the heat, and, still coated in snow and ice, held his hands out to the warmth, rubbing to thaw them. The building fire tossed ever brighter light over the man, who remained in silhouette as he hunched toward the warmth. Cold radiated from him, but so did his strength and his goodness. He made no sound of discomfort, although he had to be frozen clean through.

More affection dawned within her, as wonderful and as blessed as Christmas morning. She eased into the safe shadows, hidden from his sight. Love for him bloomed fully, like grace falling into her life. It was a love never meant to be returned, she feared, but one that would always live inside her heart.

Chapter Eighteen

"Fiona! You made it." Lila greeted her in a warm hug before tugging her into the lovely parlor. "Look, everyone. She's here."

"We didn't think you were going to come." Scarlet bolted up from a chair and hugged her, too. "You look frozen clean through."

"Come sit in my seat." Earlee hopped off the edge of the couch. "It's closest to the fireplace."

"Things weren't going to be the same without you, Fee." Kate stood to hug her, as well.

"I had just made up my mind to drive out to fetch you." Meredith took her by the hands and led her to the seat Earlee had vacated. "We are all so glad you could come."

"I almost didn't." Fiona clutched her satchel and her book bag, both stiff with frost from the walk to town. Actually, it had been a run-walk, hurrying as fast as she could and hoping no one came riding after her. "My parents forbade me, but I couldn't stay away. I have missed you all so much."

"We have missed you, too," Scarlet and Kate chorused, and Earlee took her hand in silent agreement.

"I have had to sit at our desk all by myself. During

class I start scribbling a note to you on my slate, and realize you aren't there." Lila poured a cup of tea from the service on the coffee table. "School isn't the same without you, Fee."

Her throat burned, and she felt out of place, the outsider in this group where she had always belonged. She was no longer a schoolgirl like they were. Everything within her yearned to go back. If only it were possible.

"I know how you feel." Meredith took the bags from her and set them on the floor, near to the hearth, so they would thaw out. "Every day I have spent away from you all is a form of misery. Mama thinks she is doing right by sending me away to school, but I'm happiest when I am with my best friends."

"Remember how we all met?" Lila squeezed in to hand over the steaming china cup of sweet tea.

"In first-grade Sunday school." Earlee settled into a chair. "Remember? My ma had just left me there. I was the first little girl to arrive, and I was afraid to stay with Mrs. Hadly. Then Scarlet came marching up with her ma. You took one look at me and said—"

"—you are my friend," Scarlet finished, laughing. She settled on the cushion beside Fiona with a flourish. "I have always been forthright. It appalls Ma to this day. Anyway, the next kid to come along was Narcissa Bell. I didn't like the way she wrinkled her nose at me and said my dress was, what did she say?"

"'Common calico,'" Lila supplied as she lifted the china teapot and began refilling everyone's cups. "As I love calico and was wearing the new rosebud-sprigged dress my mother had lovingly made for me, I took great offense."

"And I told Narcissa she was *not* my friend."

"You were an excellent judge of character, even at six

years of age." Meredith stole a sugar cube from the service and handed the bowl to Fiona. "I can see you all arriving in your cute little dresses and Scarlet telling each one of you that you were her friend."

"It was the first time I was with children my own age." Fiona remembered how terrified she had been when Ma had left her at the bottom of the basement steps. "I couldn't make my feet move. I felt everyone looking at me. So when Scarlet strode forward and took my hand, I thought she was wonderful, that you were all so amazing for wanting me."

"Same thing with me," Earlee confessed. "Who would have thought that first Sunday-school class what, twelve years ago, would be the start of lifelong friendships?"

"One of God's great blessings," Kate agreed, and swiped a tear from the corner of her eye.

"Which is why I am not going back to Boston." Meredith's confession raised shocked comments from them all. "I have been utterly miserable there, and I haven't known what to do about it or how to make Mama understand. But listening to you all has made me realize something. I have never been happier since the day I walked into Sunday school almost five years ago and you all invited me to sit with you."

"Narcissa Bell and her group wanted you, too." Fiona sipped the steaming tea, but that wasn't what warmed her. Her friends and their memories together did. "Remember? You were a vision in that gown of yours. I've never seen anything prettier."

"Not even Narcissa had anything so nice," Earlee added. "What I remember was how you held your sisters' hands, like you were all close. And how Mrs. Hadly split you up by age. I could tell you and your sisters didn't like it, and that's how I knew you would fit in just fine with us, although we weren't so fancy."

"That's what I thought, too," Scarlet added.

"It's going to be fun to have you back in school," Kate said thoughtfully as she picked up her sewing. "But it comes at the same time we are losing Fiona."

"Maybe you can still come to our sewing circle?" Lila asked as she threaded her needle.

"I wish I could." She slid her cup and saucer onto the edge of the table and reached for her bag. She unfolded her work and settled it on her lap.

"That's beautiful." Earlee leaned forward to examine the fabric. "Is that something you're working on for Miss Sims?"

"No, it's a Christmas present. For Ian." She smoothed the lapel lovingly. The seam was sitting well, and she couldn't help being pleased with her work. "He will be bringing out his herd of mares soon, and I want him to have a warm riding coat. Something suited to the stature I'm sure his ranch will soon be."

"*His* ranch?" Scarlet's embroidery needle stilled. "Does this mean you will be marrying him for real?"

"And soon?" Meredith looked up from pinning a quilt block seam.

"No. Ian does not love me, so he shouldn't be forced to marry me. And you all know how I feel about marriage. I'm not going to be tethered down." She didn't believe in love, right? She was the girl who had never started sewing treasures for a hope chest. The last thing she would ever trust in was a man's love for her.

And if a tiny voice deep within her wanted to argue, she silenced it entirely.

"But you are in love with him." Earlee, ever the romantic, put down her crocheting.

"I don't intend to let any man own or dominate me, not even Ian." She ran her fingertips over the coat, remembering how Miss Sims had helped her with the pattern and had even cut it for her. How she had spent her evenings pinning the pieces, basting them and stitching each seam with care. She had fitted the collar and sleeves, imagining him astride one of his beautiful mares or training a young colt in the corral.

In truth, the reason she loved Ian was simple: he was not the kind of man to dominate a woman. But this was a celebration, and not a place for her disappointments, so she kept silent about them. "When are we going to exchange gifts? I am so excited for you all to see what I made for you."

"Oh, me, too!" Scarlet twisted around to tug a bag off the floor. "As is our tradition, I made something for each of our hope chests. Even Fiona's, although she refuses to have a real hope chest."

"That's okay, Fee. We will keep hoping for you when you are out of faith." Earlee put five equal-size gifts wrapped in newsprint in the center of the table.

"We will keep praying for you when you stop praying for yourself." Lila rescued five identical gifts wrapped in lovely wrapping paper and put them beside Earlee's.

"We want you to be happy," Kate added, gathering her gifts from her sewing basket.

"Even if you can't keep coming to our sewing circle, we will keep a place open for you. Just like we did for Meredith." Scarlet added five more gaily wrapped presents to the growing pile.

"We will be here for you, Fee." Meredith crossed the room to fetch her bag full of gifts. "Always and forever."

Fiona looked from one dear face to the other—her family, in all the ways that mattered. There were those pesky feelings again, making her far too vulnerable and trying to blur her vision. Touched by the amazing wealth of friendship, she saw for the first time the incredible richness of her life.

Ian knew the moment the sun set. The storm changed, the air turned reverent and the snowflakes floated through the air solemnly. Flannigan, warm in his stall, snorted, as if he could scent night's approach. Duchess cast an anxious gaze down the aisle, for this place was not home to her.

"We won't be here for much longer, so rest easy," he told his mare and gave the pitchfork a final turn. He had rented a two-room house north of town, closer to his job. A place Nana might like, and the owner did not mind if he improved on the fencing. A better place for his future than this broken-down farm of neglect and sadness. The cow patiently chewed at the fresh hay in her feeder. He patted her flank with his gloved hand, to slide behind her and out of the stall. "I'll be back to milk you, sweet girl."

The cow blinked her liquid-brown eyes in agreement, content with her dinner.

The cat, however, was not so pleased. He yowled underfoot.

"I've not forgotten you, you mop." Affectionate, he knelt to give the feline a fine scrub around the ears. The rusty, ardent purr was reward enough. "I'll get to the milking next."

He felt Fiona's presence before he heard her—the tug as if a door opened within him, the sweetness of first love, the brightness of hope stirring. The day was no longer ordinary. At the pad of her footsteps, he looked up to see her approaching the open barn door. Snowflakes danced around her as if glad to be with her. The twilight was perfect because she walked through it.

Flannigan nickered, perhaps in love with her, too. Not ashamed to show it, the gelding leaned hard until the wood gate dug into his flesh and stretched his long neck as far as he could go, craning to get a view of her. Riley, with a mouthful of hay, followed suit, and the cow gave a hopeful moo. Even Duchess in her corner stall offered a welcoming nicker and the cat raced the length of the barn as if eager for the privilege of curling around her ankles.

"Good evening to you, handsome boy. I'm glad to see you, too." She knelt, her hood shading her face, elegant in her thick woolen wraps.

Ian, eager to see the first glimpse of her face, knew he was standing in the aisle like one of the posts, still and staring, but did he care? No, not one bit. He would cherish all he could of this time left with her.

"McPherson. What are you doing here?" She straightened and although he could not see her face, he felt the sting of her glare. "I thought you would be at work."

"What? You are afraid I am like your father, unable to hold a job?" Tender, he saw what she thought of him; he could not help teasing her. "No. The mill closed at noon. It is Christmas Eve, after all."

"I didn't know you would be here." Her arms were full, and a bag hung from her shoulder, thick and heavy. "I just came in from town."

"Were you with your friends, like last week? At Lila's, is that her name?"

"Yes." She pulled back her hood, icy crystals tumbling from the fabric to rain down at her feet. Flecked with snow, she looked like a storybook princess, too beautiful to be real and too good to want to be with a man like him.

That didn't stop him from hoping.

"We had our own Christmas celebration. I got a lot of beautiful things for the hope chest I don't have." The lantern light found her, bathing her with its luminous glow. She tripped forward to lay her bundle and bag on the grain-barrel lid. "My tatted doilies and matching snowflake ornaments were very well received. Why don't I finish the chores? You have had a hard week, Ian."

"One I am grateful for. I have a good-paying job." He winced at the signs of exhaustion on her face—the shadows smudging the porcelain skin beneath her eyes, and the strain etched into her forehead. He shoved his hand in his pocket to resist the urge to try to smooth them away. All he wanted was to draw her into his arms and shelter her, hold her until she understood everything was going to be all right. "I will finish the barn work, lass. But first, there's something I want to give you."

"You mean, like a gift?"

"It *is* Christmas Eve." A dapper man would know what to say to win her heart. A smart man would know the right way to let her go. But as he was neither dapper nor smart, he pulled the train ticket from his coat pocket. "This is for you. Merry Christmas."

"I don't understand." She took the first-class permit, staring at it as if she didn't know how to read. "You want me to go and fetch your grandmother?"

"No, pretty girl." He cradled her chin in his palm, unable to hold back the tidal force of his affection. "This is to take you anywhere you want. I am not going to make you marry me. You are free to go."

"But the farm. Your grandmother paid my da—"

"That she did." He prayed she would never know how hard this was for him, all that he had given up for her. "Your father and I have come to final terms this afternoon and there will be no marriage. You need never worry about being forced to live your mother's life. You and Flannigan are free."

"Flannigan?" Her lower lip trembled; he rubbed the pad of his thumb along her plump bottom lip.

"He is yours. I paid your father for him."

"But your wages were to go for your mares." Instead of the joy he expected, her sorrow deepened, and the shadows swallowed her, as if she had lost the last bit of hope.

"What is wrong?" Her sadness splintered him into pieces. "You promised to take him with you. I heard you tell him so the day he tried to run away."

"But what about you, Ian?"

"My dreams have changed." If he had thought her beauty great before, it was nothing to her comeliness as the lantern light flared. He knew how that light felt, unable to let go, unable to keep her. "Some things in life are not to be, no matter how much you want them. If I can't have what I wish, then you will have your happiness."

He could not help it, he was a besotted man and he wanted her to feel—not just to know—how he cared for her. He leaned forward and brushed her mouth with his. Sweeter than Christmas candy, that kiss, and he savored it—savored her—before he moved away. The memory of it was the last he would have of her.

It took all his strength to withdraw his fingers from her chin, to step back and hitch up his dignity. No sense letting the girl know how foolish in love he was with her. "Go follow your dream, Fiona."

Chapter Nineteen

"What about your grandmother's money?" She could not think straight. The gentle bliss of Ian's kiss had muddled her mind, and she could not gather it enough to make sense of what he was saying. She only knew that her father would not let her go out of any sense of Christmas spirit. "I can't allow her to be swindled on my behalf. She was my grandmother's best friend, I know the value of that bond. I do not want to dishonor their friendship. She has paid for the property. Did my father sign over the deed to you?"

"No, he did not." The steely mask that Ian kept in place slid away, just a second's weakness, and she saw the truth and felt it settle in her soul. The bond between them remained, stronger than ever, and she caught his hand with hers, his so much larger and capable of accomplishing so much. She thought of the horses he had been destined to train, champions yet to be proven, and his gentle horseman's nature. He had sacrificed much for that future. She hated that it would be delayed again.

"There might be another farm? You have a good job. Is that what you are hoping for?"

"No. That road is no longer meant for me." His fingers twined through hers, locking them together, and that felt like destiny, too. "I sent a draft to Nana to reimburse her for the money. The original offer was for you, not the land. Do you remember?"

"But you wanted the land."

"No. I want you."

To have her dream, she finished for him. To take the ticket and leave town, she told her impossibly rising hopes. Not because he loved her. He did not mean he wanted her and he loved her and he felt an endless, abiding devotion, too. Her lips tingled, proof of his kiss—goodbye? Was that why he had kissed her? As a farewell gesture?

Of course, it had to be. She stared at the ticket in her hand. She was the one holding on to him. She was the one with lead feet, unable to move. Wasn't she the one who had fallen? And yet his grip tightened, his fingers clutching hers. As if he did not want to let go.

Hope lifted on wings within her. All the things he had done for her, all that he had said came back to her anew.

"Where did you get the money?"

"I sold my mares, all but Duchess." His throat worked, and his granite mask was back in place. Only the tic of tension in his set jaw revealed the cost of that decision.

"You sold your thoroughbreds? No. I don't believe it." She couldn't make her brain accept it. "You couldn't have. They mean everything to you."

"Not everything." Tender, those words, and layered with something more, something deeper. "I did it for you, Fiona."

"For me?" A terrible cracking rent through her, the last of her denial, the last of her old, useless beliefs she had been clinging to. That there were no noble men, that no man would love her, that she did not believe in love.

Those notions shattered like glass, their shards landing on the dirt at her feet, useless and impossible to pick up. Falsehoods she could no longer believe in.

"Midweek I sent a telegram to my friend, the one keeping what was left of my herd." No sorrow rang in the deep notes of his voice. Only peace. "Jack was happy to buy them."

What did she believe in? Ian. She believed in his noble heart, in his compassionate spirit and in the love polishing him in the lantern's coppery light.

"You have to get them back." She tore her hand from his, whirling away. "This isn't right, what you've done."

"What isn't right about it? It is the best thing for you."

"But what about you?" She had been prepared to care for her parents, find a job in town to help support them and do her share of the work forever, if it meant Ian could have his land. Was it too late to give him what he wanted most? What he deserved? "If you take Flannigan right now and hurry to town, you can make it before the depot closes. You can send a wire and get your mares back."

"Dear, sweet Fiona." He came to her, both comfort and might. No sorrow shadowed his gaze, for there was a greater emotion, one pure enough that nothing could mask it. "Do not be so upset for me. I am glad to do this. I have been able to pay the last of my grandparents' debts. My burden is lighter."

"But I could see them here, those beautiful horses like Duchess grazing in these perfect green fields, their coats of every color gleaming in the sunshine. And you—" Her breath hitched, betraying her sorrow for him. He might not be sad, but she was. "You were supposed to train them and prosper. I know you will be successful. I see you, Ian, all of you, your goodness and your gentleness. Horses love you. Look at Flannigan. He behaved terribly most of the time. He was afraid of men, all save my brother, and you came along and turned him into a kitten. Look at him. He adores you."

"The feeling is mutual."

For a moment it did not seem as if he were speaking of the horse. More hope rushed in, making her long for the impossible—a lifetime loving him.

"So you can go with good conscience now, lass. I will be well. My grandmother will be able to buy back her family jewelry. And you can have that little house somewhere with flowers all around it."

"I cannot go," she confessed. "I spent all but five dollars of my savings."

"On what?"

"Your Christmas gift." She broke away from him, the silence of the barn echoing like a great stillness. The animals had quieted, watching intently. Mally, sitting on a stall rail, did not blink. Not even his tail moved as she opened her bag to withdraw the finished garment. "It's the warmest fabric I could find. A riding coat, for working with your horses."

"The horses I do not have?"

"Yes."

"Ah, lass, but you have touched me. You have captured me heart and soul. How am I to let you go now?"

"Do you not want me to go? But you sold your horses so I can leave you. This train ticket—"

"No, my love. I want you to be free to choose." He brushed her cheeks with his thumb, and her tears glimmered on his glove. "Remember I said that a marriage between us always has been your decision and no other's?"

"I do. I choose you, Ian McPherson. You have made me believe in true love and noble men."

"And happily-ever-afters," he finished. Not sadness,

then, driving those tears, but the same poignant emotion driving him. He felt it when she laid her hand on his chest, her small hand over his heart. He loved her; the infinite gentleness he felt for her had no bounds, no ends, no reason.

Happiness roared through him, strong enough to drown out all his old losses, and he knew that the past was gone. There was a future to build, the only one that mattered, the one God had led him to. For surely it was God's presence gentle in the air above them, and in the proof of their love so strong. "I cannot give you a mansion full of fine things and servants."

"I would not want it if you could." In her perfect blue eyes, on her beloved face, her love shone for him. Unmistakable and the greatest gift he could imagine. The best Christmas gift on this holy night of love and saving grace. She smiled up at him, their hearts and souls as one. "A little house someday, with a happy family. All I want is for you to love me, Ian, and I will have the greatest of all riches."

"We will be very wealthy indeed." He drew her into the circle of his arms, where she was safe, where she would always be cherished and protected. "Marry me, Fiona. Be my treasured wife."

"It would be an honor."

Their kiss was perfection, as pure as the night. The winds stilled and the last flakes of snow tapered gently to the ground. Heavenly moonlight fell between the breaking clouds as if to bless the love of a worthy horseman and his gingham bride.

* * * * *

Dear Reader,

Welcome back to Angel Falls. This Montana town has become a beloved place to me, full of fond friends and new ones yet to meet. I hope you feel the same way. In this story, you will see familiar faces, like Cora and her nephews (from *A Blessed Season*) and new ones, like Fiona and her friends.

    Gingham Bride is a story I have been wanting to tell for a long time. It is a tale of how love comes to a girl who has not known it before and the good man who can win her heart. I hope you are touched by Fiona's journey, Ian's sacrifice for her and their discovery of the true riches God has blessed them with.

    Thank you for choosing *Gingham Bride*.

    Wishing you the best of blessings.

Merry Christmas,

Jillian Hart

HER PATCHWORK FAMILY

Lyn Cote

**To my fellow Love Inspired authors—
you are a blessing to me!**

Trust in the Lord, and do good.
—*Psalms* 37:3

Chapter One

Gettysburg, Pennsylvania
May 1867

Keeping to the line of fir trees rippling in the wind, Felicity Gabriel tiptoed to the rear of the dark clump of mourners at the memorial service. There she attempted to hide behind a bulky man. A strong gust tried to snatch away Felicity's Quaker bonnet and lift her gray skirt. She held on to the ribbons tied at her throat and pushed her skirt down. Ahead, she glimpsed the pastor holding on to his hat while reading from the Bible.

Her emotions hopped like crickets within her, distracting her from the familiar scriptures of victory over death. Then the man shielding her moved. She caught sight of the brand-new limestone marker. All that was left to show that Augustus Josiah Mueller had lived. Seeing Gus's cold stone marker with the dates 1846-1865 took her breath. She drew in damp air. *Gus.*

The war had lured Gus away and then cruelly abandoned him in an unmarked grave somewhere in Virginia. The cannons were all silent now, but when would the consequences of this war end—one generation? Two? More?

"Why are you here?" The voice Felicity had dreaded hearing snapped like the sharp tongue of a whip.

She looked at the mourners and murmured, "I'm here to show my respect to Gus, Agnes Mueller." Felicity lowered her eyes, not wanting to linger on the woman's red-rimmed, hate-filled eyes.

"I'm surprised that you had the gall to show your face here today." Each word was delivered like a blow.

"Agnes, please," Josiah Mueller pleaded, tugging at his wife's elbow.

"Our Gus is gone forever and we are left without consolation. And here you stand!" the woman shrilled, her voice rising.

There was a rustling in the crowd. Felicity knew there was nothing she could say or do that would comfort this woman who'd lost her only child. Or end her groundless grudge against Felicity. So she kept her eyes lowered, staring at the soggy ground wetting her shoes.

The tirade continued until the woman became incoherent and was led away, sobbing. As the mourners followed, many nodded to Felicity or touched her arm. They all knew the truth.

When everyone else had gone, Felicity approached the stone marker. Tears collected in her eyes. She knew it was human foolishness to speak words to a soul at a grave site, but she still whispered, "I'm leaving Pennsylvania, Gus, but I won't forget thee ever." And then removing her glove, she spit on her palm and pressed it—flat and firm against the cold stone.

Altoona, Illinois
September 1867

Amid the bustling Mississippi wharf, Ty Hawkins eased down onto the venerable raised chair. The chair was now his daily refuge where he got his shoes shined. Afterwards, he would catch a bite to eat at a nearby café. He rarely felt hungry these days even though he was several pounds lighter than he'd ever been as an adult. He would have liked to go home for lunch, sit on his shaded back porch and cool off. But he couldn't face home so soon again.

I'm home but I'm not home.

This dreadful fact brought a sharp pang around his rib; he rubbed it, trying to relieve the pain. *What am I going to do about Camie?*

Jack Toomey had shined shoes here as long as Ty had worn them. Ty smiled and returned Jack's friendly good day. The shoeshine man's dark face creased into a grin. "It's going to be another scorcher."

"'Fraid so, Jack."

"When is it going to realize it's fall?" As Jack blackened Ty's shoe, he gave him a long, penetrating look. He lowered his eyes. "Coming home's not easy. Takes time. Patience."

Jack seemed to be one of the few who understood Ty's suffering. The shoeshine man's sympathetic insight wrapped itself around Ty's vocal cords. Jack glanced up. Ty could only nod.

Jack's gaze dropped to Ty's shoes. "It'll get better. It wasn't easy going off to learn how to shoot people and it isn't easy to put down the rifle and come back."

Ty managed to grunt. No one said things like this to him. Everyone seemed to overlook how hard it was not to jump at any loud noise, or to walk out in the open without scanning his surroundings for people who wanted to kill him. Ty wondered for a moment what Jack would advise if Ty told him about Camie's dilemma.

The thought of discussing this private trouble with

someone other than family only showed how desperate he was becoming.

Two urchins had come up to a woman on the street begging. She turned from the wagon and stooped down so her face was level with the children's. Through the moving stream of people on the street, Ty watched the unusual woman. The ragged, grimy children—a little girl who held a younger boy by the hand—nodded. "What's she up to?" Ty muttered to Jack.

"She don't look like the kind who would hurt a child," Jack said, looking over his shoulder again as he continued polishing Ty's shoe.

The woman started to help the little girl up onto the wagon.

Then it happened.

A towheaded boy of about ten or eleven ran by the woman. He snatched her purse, throwing her off balance. With a shocked outcry, she let go of the girl's hand and fell to the dirt street. Ty leaped up to go to the lady's aid. He shoved his way through the crowd. As he reached her and offered her his hand, Hal Hogan, a town policeman, appeared from the other direction. Red-faced, Hogan had his beefy hand clamped on the thief's shoulder. The boy cursed and struggled to free himself in vain.

Ty helped the lady up. "Are you all right, miss?"

She ignored his question, turning toward the caught thief. She very obviously studied the child's smudged and angry red face.

Hogan handed her back her purse and said in his gravelly voice, "I usually would have to keep the purse as evidence but since I witnessed the theft that won't be necessary. Would you tell me how much money you are carrying, miss?"

The young woman hesitated, then said, "I think only

around five dollars." She looked into the thief's face and asked, "If thee needed money, why didn't thee just ask me? I would have given thee what I could."

The boy sneered at her and made a derisive noise.

Hogan shook the boy, growling, "Show respect, you." His expression and tone became polite as he said to her, "I saw the robbery and can handle this. No need for a lady like you to get involved in such sordid business." Hogan pulled the brim of his hat and dragged the boy away.

"Please wait!" the woman called after him and moved to pursue Hogan.

"Hey, lady!" the wagon driver demanded. "Are we going now or not? I've got other people who are waiting for me to get you delivered and come back to the station."

Ty had watched all this, his jaw tight from witnessing the theft and her fall. He touched the woman's sleeve.

She looked into his face, her large blue eyes worried. How could this woman say so much with only her eyes? This near-theft troubled her. Again, Ty nearly offered his protection, but why? The thief had been caught. He tightened his reserve and asked in a cool, polite tone, "May I help you up into the wagon?"

With one last glance in the direction where Hogan and the miscreant had disappeared, she nodded. "If thee would, please."

Then she gave him a smile that dazzled him. She was a pretty woman—until she smiled. Then she was an extraordinary beauty. Was it merely the high caliber of the smile that made the difference?

After he helped her up onto the buckboard seat, she murmured, "I thank thee." She was barely seated when the drayman slapped the reins over his team and with a jerk, the horses took off.

The lady waved her thanks once more and over her

shoulder sent him another sparkling smile. He found himself smiling in return, his heart lighter.

Dalton watched from the shadowy doorway across the busy road. One problem taken care of. That kid wouldn't be making trouble for him anymore. But he didn't like that woman in the gray bonnet. What was she talking to those two little beggars for? He'd been watching them for days, waiting till they were ready. He frowned. No use looking for trouble. As soon as Hogan had appeared and nabbed the kid, the two had disappeared. But they wouldn't go far and soon they'd be ready for the picking. He smiled. The dishonest life was good.

Felicity turned forward, distinctly unsettled. The two hungry children had been frightened away and the boy arrested. This was not how she had envisioned starting out here. Would she be able to find the little pair again? She sighed. Her eyes threatened to shut of their own accord. Traveling by train for miles and days had whittled her down to nothing. She forced her eyes wide open, stiffened her weary back and folded her hands in her lap.

What she needed was a long hot bath, a good night's sleep. But those would be hours away. "Just a few more miles to tote the weary load"—her mind sang the old slave lament. But that was deceiving. In spite of her fatigue, uncertainty and hope tugged at her like impatient children. Here in Illinois, her work, the work God had given her to help the children, would begin, not end. She had planned on arriving a month earlier, but her sister Verity had needed help after the delivery of her first son in Virginia. Felicity smiled, thinking of how proud Verity's husband, Matt, had been of his son.

Then the recent touch of the man's strong hand on her

arm intruded on her thoughts, the sensation lingering. She inhaled deeply. The man who'd leapt to her aid was not one to be taken lightly. And the red welt on his cheek could be nothing but the mark of a saber. A veteran like so many others. And with such sad eyes.

The wagon turned the corner. And there were the little girl and boy. The little girl was waving frantically, jumping up and down. "Lady! Lady!"

Felicity grabbed the reins. "Whoa!" The team halted, stomping, snorting and throwing back their heads. The drayman shouted at her for interfering with his driving. Thrilled to find the two so easily, she ignored him. She reached down with both hands and helped the children up. They crowded around her feet. The children were ragged, very thin, tanned by the sun and had tangled dark hair and solemn eyes.

She turned to the burly, whiskered driver and beamed. "I apologize and promise to make thee no more trouble."

The driver looked bemused. He shook his head and slapped the reins, starting off again for Number 14 Madison Boulevard. Madison Boulevard proved to be a long avenue with wide lawns and massive houses, which struck Felicity as mansions. Very soon, the wagon pulled up to a very large, three-story white house on a wide piece of land with oak and fir trees and bushes. Looking through the porte cochere on the side of the house, she glimpsed a carriage house at the back of the estate. The grounds were well tended but the house looked uninhabited with its shades and lace curtains drawn.

"Is this your house?" the little girl asked, sounding impressed and scared at the same time.

Felicity was experiencing the same reaction. She had known that Mildred Barney was a well-to-do woman, but Mildred had always come east for the abolition meetings and work. "Yes, my new house." Felicity tried not to feel intimidated by the home's quiet grandeur. This did not strike her as a neighborhood which would welcome an orphanage. *Indeed I have my work cut out for me.* "I've just come for the first time. Thee may get down now, children."

Within minutes, the silent driver had unloaded her trunk and valise and had carried both up to the front door. She paid him and tipped him generously for his trouble.

He looked down at his palm. "Unlock the door," he ordered gruffly, "and I'll carry that trunk upstairs for you."

As Felicity turned the large key in the keyhole, she hid her smile. She stepped inside, drawing the children after her. "Please just leave it here in the entryway. I don't know which room I will take as yet."

The drayman did as asked, pulled the brim of his hat politely and left.

Felicity stood a moment, turning on the spot, drinking in the graceful staircase, the gleaming dark oak woodwork, the obviously expensive wallpaper with its lavish design of pink cabbage roses and greenery. Her parents' parlor could have fit into this foyer. In this grand setting, she felt smaller, somehow overwhelmed and humbled. When God blessed one, He didn't stint.

"Miss?" The little girl tugged her skirt. "You said you'd give us food and a place to sleep tonight."

"I did indeed. Come let us find the kitchen." Felicity picked up the covered oak basket that she'd carried on her arm since leaving Gettysburg. In it were the last remnants of her provisions for the trip. She hoped it would be enough for the children.

"Hello," a woman hailed them from the shadowy end of the hall that must lead to the kitchen in the rear. "Who are you, please?"

When the woman came into the light, her appearance reduced Felicity to gawking. She was a tall, slender woman in a blue calico dress with a full white apron and red kerchief tied over her hair. Neat as a brand-new pin. She looked to be in her late twenties and had skin the color of coffee with much cream. Her smooth oval face reminded Felicity of drawings she'd seen of Egyptian queens. And her thick, black eyelashes were perfection. Felicity had been told that a housekeeper would stay until she came. But was this the housekeeper? She'd never seen a beautiful housekeeper before.

Felicity held out her hand, hoping the woman hadn't noticed her momentary preoccupation. "I am Felicity Gabriel. I've inherited this house."

The woman shook Felicity's hand, firm and quick. "I been expecting you, miss. Mrs. Barney's lawyer told me you would be coming any time now. I been keeping things ready for you. I'm the housekeeper, Vista."

Felicity listened to the woman's low musical voice with pleasure. Beautiful to both the eye and ear.

"Miss?" the little girl prompted, tugging on Felicity's skirt again.

"Vista, we have company for lunch." How would this very neatly starched and pressed woman deal with unkempt, ragged children in this elegant house? This was something she must be able to handle or there would have to be a change. Would she understand how to handle this situation?

The woman considered the children, tapping one finger to her cheek. "Why don't I bring lunch out onto the back porch? There be a shaded table there. Mrs. Barney liked to eat outside in the summer. And it's such a lovely September day." Then Vista nodded toward the door behind Felicity.

Felicity got the message. She was to take the children outside and around to the back porch. And so she did.

Vista met them in the back and greeted them beside the pump. "I don't allow anyone with dirty hands or a dirty face to eat at my table." Vista pointed to a white bar of soap and a white flour-sack towel, sitting on an overturned wooden box nearby. Then she began to pump water.

As the water splashed, Felicity slipped off her bonnet and gloves and tossed them onto the nearby back-porch steps. Setting an example, she lathered her hands with the soap, then handed the bar to the little girl. "Be sure to keep your eyes shut so the soap doesn't sting them," Felicity cautioned. After scrubbing her face and hands, she rinsed off in the cold water Vista was still pumping. And then, since she'd taken her own advice and shut her eyes, Vista put the towel into her hands.

When Felicity opened her eyes, she looked over to find that the girl was teaching the boy how to lather his hands and face. When they were done, she passed the towel to the children, who left dirty prints on it. The girl said, "I 'member washing up. He doesn't."

"Does thee?" Felicity resonated with the impact of that simple but telling sentence.

The girl nodded. "Can we eat now?"

Felicity wondered how she could persuade these waifs to stay. She sensed a deep caution in the girl, wise for her years. *Father, guide me.*

"Right now, chil'run." Vista led them to the small round table on the trellised porch, shaded by lavish, bright purple clematis. She went into the kitchen and returned with a cup of coffee, a plate piled high with slices of buttered bread and cheese and two glasses of milk on a tray. The minute she set the plate on the table, the little boy grabbed two slices of bread and shoved one into his mouth as deep as he could.

"Donnie, that's not good manners," the girl scolded.

"Sorry, miss, but he don't 'member eating at a table."

Felicity choked down her reaction. Was eating at a table another privilege she took for granted? "That's all right. I'm sure he will get used to it. What are thy names?"

"I'm Katy and he's Donnie."

Felicity gave them a smile. "Happy to meet thee, Katy. Now I will thank God for this food." She bowed her head. "Thank Thee, God, for food and friends."

After that, Vista was kept busy bringing out more bread and cheese. Finally, she murmured to Felicity that she didn't want the children to eat themselves sick.

After her last swallow of milk, Katy stood up. "Thanks for the eats, miss. We'll be back later to sleep."

"Where is thee going?" Felicity asked, rising to stop them.

"We got to go beg. Donnie's going to need shoes before the snow." The child glanced down at the little boy's bare, dirty feet.

"Does that mean thee doesn't have a home?" Felicity asked.

"No, miss, but I take care of Donnie." Katy took the boy's hand and began edging away.

"Would thee like a home?" Felicity blurted out.

Katy stopped and eyed her with suspicion. "What's the catch?"

"Catch?" Felicity echoed.

Vista spoke up. "The catch is that you got to be scrubbed clean to come inside. I know you chil'run can't help it, but you have to be scrubbed head to toe before you come in. No vermin allowed in any house I'm living in or cleaning up."

Vista's calm but firm pronouncement slightly embarrassed Felicity. But better to start as one plans to go. Katy glanced at Felicity, who nodded her agreement with Vista.

Katy glanced around and then pointed to the door mat. "What about out here? Could we sleep here on the porch?"

Felicity turned to Vista. After all, she was the one who would be cleaning and she was the one who'd brought up the issue of cleanliness.

"You can," Vista replied, "as long as the weather is warm like this, but if you stay till Donnie needs shoes, you will have to be clean to stay inside."

"You mean we could really stay here?" Katy asked with an appraising expression.

"That's why I've come—"

Vista cut Felicity off. "We got no chil'run and I need help with chores and such. The gardener has been away so the weeds have started getting thick. If I show you how to weed today, would you pull weeds, not my flowers?"

"And we might need errands run," Felicity added, catching on. These children had probably rarely known generosity which asked nothing in return. Better to draw them in slowly, gaining their trust. Vista was already proving to be an asset.

Katy nodded. "We got a deal. Where are them weeds?"

Felicity glanced at Vista and lifted one eyebrow, asking her to proceed.

"Over here. I have a garden patch that is choked with them. And I do not like pulling weeds."

Katy followed Vista down the steps and around the house with Donnie in tow. Relief whispered through Felicity. Vista had displayed a practical kindness and sensitivity that impressed Felicity. And the children were staying—at least for now.

Vista returned and Felicity helped her carry in the dishes. After waving Felicity to a chair at the kitchen table, Vista began to wash them. "I see you are planning to start the orphans' home right quick."

Sitting down after eating caused exhaustion to sweep through Felicity and she closed her eyes. "I want to give children who have no home a place, a safe place to grow up strong and good."

"That's why Mrs. Barney left you this house and all the money?" Vista glanced over her shoulder.

"Yes, she came to Pennsylvania and we worked together coordinating movement on the Underground Railroad. She was a wonderful woman. And she was certain that many children would be left orphaned by this dreadful war."

"And just generally, too?"

Felicity nodded, blinking her eyes to keep them open. "Will thee stay with me and help?"

Vista gave her a sidelong glance. "I got no plans to leave…yet."

So Vista was sizing her up, too. Felicity stretched her tight neck and sighed.

"I got a room ready for you upstairs, miss. Why don't you go on up and rest?"

Felicity sighed again—a habit she must overcome. "No, first I must walk back into town and speak to Mrs. Barney's lawyer."

Her hands in the wash basin, Vista frowned. "Well, first of all, if you going into town, you're not walking. The groom will hitch up the gig for you. But what do you need to talk to the lawyer about?"

"Why mustn't I walk into town?" Felicity asked, not answering the housekeeper's question.

"Mrs. Barney had a certain standing here. I know she wouldn't want you to walk to town," Vista replied firmly.

Felicity tried to think of a polite answer to this. Yes, Mrs. Barney had been a lady of generous means. But Felicity didn't ride where she could easily walk. But here and now, she was just too tired to argue.

"And the lawyer, Miss Felicity?" Vista asked again.

Clearly there was no putting anything past this woman. "There's a child who needs my help," Felicity answered. "And I'm going to need a lawyer in order to give it to him."

That evening Ty paced his library, wishing he were deaf. After four years of listening to cannon fire and bombs bursting in air, he should be. Unfortunately, he could still hear well enough to suffer each evening's ordeal. The rocking chair on the floor above him creaked in a steady but rapid rhythm. Every once in a while, Camie cried out as if someone had jabbed her with a needle.

No one should have to rock a seven-year-old girl to sleep. But if no one rocked her, Camie would stand by the door in her room and sob till she fell down with exhaustion. Then upon waking in the night as she always did, she would scream as if someone were scalding her.

Ty rubbed his face in time with the rocking chair. The sounds of the rapid rocking and Camie's sudden cries of terror shredded his nerves into quivering strings. He halted by the cold hearth and rested his head on the smooth, cool mantel. When would this nightly torture end? *Dear God, help my little daughter, help us.*

Finally, the rocking above slowed and quieted, then ceased, along with the outcries. Ty's tension eased. He slumped into the wing chair by the fireplace. His mother's light footsteps padded down the stairs. As always, she paused at the doorway to wish him good-night.

Tonight, however, she came in and sat down across from him. His mother, Louise Pierce Hawkins, perched on the tapestry seat, a small canary of a woman with silver strands liberally mixed into her faded blond hair. Her kind face showed her distress.

His heart beat faster. "Did something happen?" *Something worse than usual?*

She gazed at him. "Nothing out of the ordinary, unfortunately." She locked her hands together. "I'm becoming more and more concerned about our Camie."

Ty chewed his upper lip and frowned. He wanted to ask if she thought Camie needed…no, he didn't want to know.

"I don't think she's mentally unbalanced, son," she said, answering his unspoken question. "But nothing I do appears to help her get past her panic. In fact, I don't know why she has such fear or what exactly she is afraid of." She shook her head. "She fights sleep as if it were death itself."

Her face twisted with concern. "Whenever she feels herself slipping into sleep, she cries out to wake herself and hold…something at bay. I wish I knew what it was."

Ty could think of nothing to say, nothing that could end this nightly struggle. Guilt weighed on him. He hadn't been able to tell his mother the part he may have unwittingly played in making his daughter's night terrors worse.

Louise rested her head in her hand. "I confess I'm at my wits' end. God must send us help, an answer, someone who knows what to do."

His mother's strained, defeated tone alarmed him. "I

could hire someone to care for her. This is too much for you—"

"No." His mother's tone was firm, implacable. "Camie is a sweet, biddable child all day." She looked to the cold hearth as if seeking warmth, encouragement there. "It's just the falling asleep. She can't face the night."

His mother left out the other worrisome problem, which was that Camie would not look at him. Or suffer him to come near her. He clenched his jaw and then exhaled. "Mother, I appreciate all you do for Camie. Maybe we should do what Mrs. Crandall—"

Louise hissed with disapproval. "Ty, you know my opinion of that woman." She jerked her head as if warning someone away. "I try to be charitable, but I think much of the cause of this worrying behavior lies at her doorstep." She pressed her lips together.

Ty looked out into the night. The question of what to do hung unspoken and unanswered between them.

That evening, Felicity stood at the kitchen window, looking out at the two children huddled together on her back porch like stray puppies. She had been tempted to overrule Vista and let the children come inside without cleaning up first. But Felicity hoped Vista would become a part of her work here, and she didn't want to do anything that might upset the housekeeper.

By staying here and keeping the house safe and cared for after Mrs. Barney's death, Vista had proven herself to be honest and hardworking. It would be hard for a stranger to town like Felicity to replace Vista. Trust took time to forge.

And Vista was right. Basic cleanliness must be established for the benefit of all the children who would come here to live. Cleanliness was healthy. A home with children—Felicity hoped to have many children here in the future—must be a house with firm, sensible rules.

Felicity wiped the perspiration on her forehead with the back of her hand. It was a warm, humid night. Sleeping outside was probably more comfortable than sleeping inside. Still, homeless children sleeping on her porch grieved Felicity, causing a gnawing ache deep within.

Donnie snorted in his sleep and opened one eye. She realized he could see her through the window because he wiggled one of his little fingers as if waving to her. The boy, barely more than a toddler, hadn't spoken a word to anyone all day. Though nearly moved to tears, she grinned and wiggled her little finger back at him. The child closed his eyes and fell back to sleep.

Felicity sighed. And then reminded herself that she must stop this new habit. Sighing sounded lonely and a bit sad, pensive even. She caught herself just before she did it again.

Dear Father, please bring me children, the lost ones, the ones that the evil lion Satan wishes to devour. Give me strength and wisdom to carry out the work Thee has given me. I will depend on Thy promise from Psalm 37. I will trust in Thee and do good.

Felicity turned from the window to go upstairs before she remembered one more request.

And Father, please give me the courage I will need in court tomorrow so that I may right the wrong committed against a child—a wrong that has been committed in my name.

Chapter Two

The next morning after breakfast with Katy and Donnie on the back porch, Felicity stood in the kitchen. The heat and the humidity were already growing uncomfortable. How could the calendar say September when it felt like July?

While the children pulled weeds, Felicity and Vista discussed the grocery list. Underneath these routine concerns lurked apprehension over what she would be facing in town today. Felicity glanced at the kitchen wall clock. She needed to get busy and set off for town. The lawyer had told her to be in court at 9:00 a.m. The coming test tightened her mid-section. She was pitting herself against the powers of this world.

"What are you children doing here?" A strident female voice flew through the open window, followed by squeals of pain.

Felicity burst through the back door and sailed over the grass toward the woman, her heart outracing her feet. "Stop! Let them go!"

A tall, slender, very well-dressed woman had Katy and Donnie each by an ear. The sight sent anger rushing through Felicity like a hot spring.

The woman was brought up short and glared at Felicity. "These children can't possibly belong here. This is a respectable neighborhood."

Pulling them from the woman's grasp, Felicity drew the children to her. "Katy and Donnie are my guests." She gasped for air, trying to catch her breath after running in the sultry air.

"Guests?" The woman's eyes narrowed as they took in every detail of Felicity's attire and face. "Who are you?"

"I am Felicity Gabriel. Who is thee, please?" Standing very straight, Felicity offered her hand, which was ignored—a sting that tried Felicity's temper.

"Thee?" the woman snapped, her face crimping up. "Are you some kind of Quaker?"

"There is only one kind of Quaker that I know of." Taking another sip of the humid air, Felicity tried to keep her irritation out of her tone. "And yes, I am a member of the Society of Friends."

"Well, I am a God-fearing Christian and this is a respectable neighborhood. We don't want riffraff from the riverfront here."

Felicity could think of nothing Christian to say to this so she merely looked at the woman. She knew she wasn't to judge others, but...

"Why are these children *here* on Madison Boulevard?" The woman pointed at the ground as though it were sacred ground that Katy and Donnie were not worthy to walk upon.

Felicity gripped her spiraling temper with both hands. "They are here because they had no one to feed them and nowhere to sleep," she replied in an even tone. "They are doing a few jobs for me in return for food and shelter."

"You are not from around here," the woman said, her attractive face reddening like a bull about to charge.

"So you don't know that we keep the river rats and their spawn down at the wharf. We don't let them roam through town—"

Felicity gritted her teeth. "I met Katy and Donnie at the wharf and invited them home because they are hungry and homeless orphans. I hope to invite many more to come here." Felicity quoted, "'Pure religion and undefiled before God and the Father is this, To visit the fatherless and widows in their affliction.' So since thee is a God-fearing Christian, I would think thee would be pleased."

The woman leaned forward as if trying to either read Felicity's mind or intimidate her. "Are you telling me that you're starting an orphanage here?"

Felicity's forced smile thinned. Her hold on her temper was slipping, slipping. "I think 'orphans' home' and 'orphanage' are unpleasant titles. They sound so institutional and unkind. This will be the Barney Home for Children. I am going to welcome homeless children into this house and make sure they are kept warm and well fed. So yes, thee can expect to see many more children here in the future."

The woman began making a sound that reminded Felicity of a dog growling at trespassers. "The law won't let you disrupt our quiet neighborhood with an orphanage."

Churning with righteous indignation, Felicity patted the children's backs, trying to reassure them, and felt their spines sticking out, no padding of fat over the knobby vertebrae. This woman saw only their bare feet and ragged clothing, not their need. *Father, help me make her see these children with Thine eyes.*

"Mrs. Barney's lawyer has already checked all the legalities of this charitable work which that good woman requested in her will. She asked me to carry it out in her stead." Felicity took another breath of the sultry air. "I am breaking no laws. I don't know why thee assumes that a small number of orphans will disrupt—"

The woman raised her chin another notch. "We don't want beggars and sneak thieves living among us."

"Neither do I." Felicity gazed at the woman, trying to reach the soul behind all the vainglory. "Thee hasn't introduced thyself. I'd love to talk to thee about my plans—"

"I am Mrs. Thornton Crandall," she interrupted, "and I am uninterested in your plans to despoil our good neighborhood."

Mrs. Crandall turned, lifted her skirts as if the ground had been defiled by Katy and Donnie and marched off. The kitchen door behind Felicity opened. She glanced over her shoulder toward the sound.

Vista gave her a wry smile. "I see you met Mrs. Crandall, one of the leading ladies in Altoona society."

Stirred as if she'd just fought hand-to-hand in the opening battle of war, Felicity shook her head. She tried to return Vista's smile and failed. How could this woman look at these children and not be moved to pity?

Katy tugged Felicity's skirt. "Miss, was you telling the truth? Are you going to take in children that don't have homes?"

"Yes." Felicity gentled her voice and stooped down. "Katy, would thee and Donnie like to come live here?" With the back of one hand, she touched the little girl's soft cheek.

Katy looked back and forth between Felicity and Vista. "I'll think on it, miss."

"Yes, please do, Katy. We would be so happy to have thee and Donnie with us." Rising, Felicity squeezed her shoulder. "Now I must get into town. Please do whatever Vista tells thee and I'll be back by lunch."

I hope.

* * *

Ty walked into the stark, whitewashed courtroom with its polished oak floors as the bailiff declared, "All rise. Judge Tyrone Hawkins presiding." Ty settled himself on the high platform in the judge's seat and looked out over the sparsely filled courtroom. And there she was.

The woman with blue eyes he'd seen arrive in town the day before whose purse had been stolen was sitting on one of the spectator's benches. A tingle of recognition coursed through him. Hadn't anyone told her that she need not suffer coming to court? He never liked to see ladies in court. It was such a rough setting and often the defendants used coarse language.

No doubt she'd come out of a sense of duty. He tried not to stare in her direction, but she kept drawing his tired, gritty eyes. In this stark setting, she glowed, the only appealing face present.

The first dreary case began and then another, and another. Finally, the boy who'd snatched the newcomer's purse was ready to be heard, making his plea. The boy was marched into the room by Hogan, the arresting officer. Ty wondered if there was any hope for this lawless child. He hated this part of adjudicating the law. He could not believe that children should be treated as adults by the courts. But what was he to do? The law was the law.

One of the prominent lawyers in town, John Remington, with his silver hair and imposing presence, rose and approached the bench. "I am defending young Tucker Stout."

The young, already portly prosecuting attorney looked back and forth between the defendant and Remington, his mouth open in disbelief. Ty felt himself goggling at Remington. Surprise crashed through him, making him even more aware of his bone-deep fatigue. Months of little sleep was wearing him down, making him vulnerable. "Did I hear you right?"

"Yes, I am defending Tucker Stout." The elder lawyer continued in his distinctive, deep voice, glancing over his shoulder. "Miss Felicity Gabriel has hired me to act as his counsel."

Still unsettled, Ty looked to the woman. She responded with a half smile. Even her subdued smile had the power to dazzle him.

The prosecuting attorney blurted out what Ty was thinking, "But she's the plaintiff. Hers was the purse stolen."

Remington nodded. "She is aware of that. But she is anxious, in light of the defendant's tender age, that his rights be protected." Remington paused and then added as if in explanation of such odd behavior, "She's a Quaker."

Ty sat back and studied the woman, who sat so deceptively prim in his courtroom. A Quaker. Well, that explained the situation somewhat. He'd met a few Quakers. They spoke strangely and didn't fight in war. Peculiar people.

Loose jowled, Hogan snorted where he sat on the prosecution side of the courtroom. Ty drew himself up. He'd lost control at home—he wouldn't also lose control of his courtroom. "Very well. Bailiff, please read the charges against the defendant."

The bailiff did and Ty asked, "How does your client plead, Mr. Remington?"

"We plead not guilty."

"And you realize that I witnessed the purse-snatching myself?" Ty responded dryly. Was this woman trying to play him and the other men in this room for fools?

"Yes, but Miss Gabriel believes that the boy is too young to be held to adult legal standards of behavior."

"What Miss Gabriel believes may be true, but not in the sight of the laws of Illinois," Ty retorted, antagonized at having to defend what he did not believe.

The lady suddenly rose. "God does not hold children accountable for their sins until they reach the age of reason. Are the laws of Illinois higher than God's?"

The question silenced the courtroom. Every eye turned to the woman who looked completely at ease under the intense scrutiny. Ty chewed the inside of his cheek. *Does she expect special treatment because she is a woman?*

"Females," Hogan grunted, breaking the silence.

"Miss," Ty said curtly, "you are not allowed to speak in court without permission. You must let your counsel do the talking."

She nodded and sat down without dispute, giving him an apologetic little smile. He found he had no defenses against her smiles. They beckoned him to sit beside her and be at ease.

"Your Honor," Remington spoke up, "Miss Gabriel has asked me if I might have a word with you in your chamber during a short recess."

"What is this?" the prosecutor asked, rearing up.

"You'll be included, of course." Remington bowed to the man whose face had reddened.

Ty passed a hand over his forehead. After falling asleep last night, Camie had cried out with nightmares twice more, keeping the whole house up. He closed his eyes for just a moment, then opened them. He couldn't let the situation at home interfere with his work. Though the headache was making his right eyelid jump, he forced himself to act with magisterial calm. "Very well. The court stands adjourned while I meet with counsel in my chambers."

He rose and so did everyone else. His black judge's robe swirling out behind him, he strode into his paneled chambers just behind the courtroom and sat behind his oak desk, waiting for the attorneys to knock. The bailiff let them in and the two men sat down facing him. "Remington, what's this all about?" Ty asked without preamble, able at last to release some of his spleen.

"Miss Gabriel is Mildred Barney's heir. She has inherited the Barney house and all the Barneys' considerable estate."

The prosecutor let out a low whistle.

Remington nodded. "Miss Gabriel is also following Mrs. Barney's instructions and turning her house into a private orphanage which the Barney money will support."

Ty lifted his eyebrows. His mother-in-law would love that. He studied Remington, thinking of Miss Gabriel's pretty face. He shook his head, resisting. Pretty or not, he had to judge this case fairly. "The boy is guilty. What can I do but sentence him to jail time?"

"This isn't his first arrest," the prosecutor was quick to add.

"We know that." Remington folded his hands in front of himself. "Miss Gabriel would like you to dismiss charges so that she can take the boy with her to the orphanage."

The prosecutor made a sound of derision. "And how long would he stay there? Till her back's turned and then he'd just go back across the river to St. Louis, picking pockets and snatching more purses. Women are idealistic but we men must be realistic. The kid is from bad blood. He'll never be anything but what he is."

Ty didn't like the sentiment the prosecutor expressed

but he suspected that the man was right. If he released the boy, he wouldn't stay at the orphanage. Like a wild horse, Tucker Stout had never been broken to bridle. And at eleven or twelve, it might already be too late to salvage the boy. Weighed down by this unhappy thought, Ty rose. This signaled the end of the conference.

The attorneys left to meet him on the other side of the wall back in the courtroom. By his desk, Ty waited, chewing the inside of his cheek, giving them time to reach their places. Then he strode back into court and took the judgment seat.

Remington waived the boy's right to a jury and the trial was brief, proceeding just as Ty had expected. When they reached the time for sentencing, he looked out at the few people sitting in the benches of the courtroom.

Miss Gabriel's head was bowed as if she were in prayer. Her smile still glowed within him, a tiny ember of warmth. He hated to disappoint her. He opened his mouth to sentence the boy to a month in the county jail.

"I am sentencing Tucker Stout to six months' probation," he said, surprising himself. "The conditions of probation are that he live and work at the new orphans' home under Miss Felicity Gabriel's supervision. If Tucker leaves Miss Gabriel's house and refuses to follow her orders, he will be sent to jail for a year."

The prosecutor gawked at him. Hogan balked with a loud "What?"

Miss Gabriel rose, beaming at him. Her unparalleled smile brightened the whole of the sad room where no one ever found cheer, least of all Ty. The ember she'd sparked flared inside him. "Will you accept this responsibility, Miss Gabriel?"

"Of course!" she beamed.

Ty caught himself just before he returned her brilliant smile.

He struck his gavel once, unusually hard. "Case closed. Bailiff, please announce the next case."

Outside, under the sweltering noonday sun, Felicity gripped the lawyer's hand. "I cannot thank thee enough, John Remington."

The lawyer shook her hand. "Good luck," he said, eyeing Tucker. "The judge was kind to you, young man." He tipped his hat and was gone.

The intriguing face of the judge popped into her mind. So the man she'd seen in town that first day was a judge. A judge who could show mercy as well as justice. And a man who looked worn down by some secret pain.

Felicity shook off her thoughts and turned to Tucker. "We need to get home in time for lunch."

Tucker looked like he wanted to say something rude. But he shrugged and got in step with her. They walked in silence down the busy, noisy street. "Does thee have parents?" she asked.

"Everybody's got parents. Somewhere." The boy didn't even bother to look her way.

"A good point." People kept turning to look at them. Felicity resisted the urge to lift her chin. She hoped in the coming weeks that people would become accustomed to the sight of her walking beside uncared-for children. "Are thy parents living?"

He shrugged again. "Might be. Don't know. Don't care."

Felicity had spoken to souls scarred like this before. At this tender age, Tucker had given up on people. "How old is thee?"

"Old enough."

Felicity gave up questioning him. If this one ever opened up, he would do it in his time and in his way. "I am from Pennsylvania. I am the middle daughter of seven sisters. I grew up on a farm near Gettysburg."

Tucker kicked a stone and ignored her.

Felicity was glad to see home ahead—until she noted that Mrs. Crandall was coming toward them. *Oh, dear.* Could they get into the house before she reached them? "Two children have already come to my home, Katy and Donnie. They are deciding whether or not they want to stay with me."

"Oh, goody."

"But thee will be staying." Felicity walked faster. "Or thee will be in jail."

Tucker snorted. "Been there before. Be there again."

"The question is, does thee want to go there again?"

He gave her a sidelong glance. "I don't have much use for do-gooders."

Felicity knew what he meant. She'd met many do-gooders who lorded their superiority over those they "ministered" to. Many of these, she would gladly have kicked. She knew that wasn't a Christian thought but it was the truth.

As she and Tucker turned up her front walk, Mrs. Crandall bustled up to her. "I see you have brought another undesirable into our neighborhood. If you go forward with this orphanage, no decent person in town will have a thing to do with you."

Felicity's first inclination was to give this woman a talking to about Christian charity. She settled on, "I'm afraid I'm very busy right now, Mrs. Crandall. Could we discuss this later?" *Or when thee has had a change of heart?*

The woman turned and huffed away.

The back of Felicity's neck was unusually tense. She began to lead the boy toward the back door. He surprised her by saying, "That lady's right, you know."

Struggling to quench the aggravation burning inside, Felicity paused and then fixed her gaze on Tucker's face. "I doubt what she said is true. If it is, then I don't think much of the decent people in this town. Now let's get our hands washed and sit down to lunch. I think thee will find that Vista's food is worth the effort to stay and do what is expected of thee."

"I'll let you know."

Felicity hid her smile at his unexpected savoir faire. And then the moment of lightness was gone. What a world this was where boys became cynics before they even began to shave. She led Tucker to the pump and handed him the soap. He made a face of sincere distaste, but began lathering his hands.

For a moment, she lingered on the memory of the judge's sad drooping mouth, troubled dark eyes. It was a strong face with eyes that didn't flinch from meeting hers.

He also had that lean look many veterans had. Too many hardtack meals and days of travel, and then the ordeal of battle after battle. How did a good man put aside his rifle and sword and go back to life, put the war behind him? Her mourning for Gus, a dark chilling wave of loss, welled up and swelled, tightening her stays.

Felicity almost sighed, but stopped herself. *Father, bless Judge Hawkins and keep Tucker here while Thee works Thy will upon him.* Felicity decided to keep mum on the topic of Mrs. Thornton Crandall. She was certain that the Lord had heard quite enough already about Mrs. Crandall from others.

* * *

The next afternoon Felicity tried to slip away and walk to town, but was caught by Vista and the groom. The groom drove the half mile into town and helped her down at the clothing store on Merchants Street. How could she persuade them that she should walk?

Inside the door of the large well-appointed store, a man in a crisp dark suit greeted her. "Hello, miss, I am Robert Baker, the proprietor. May I help you?"

She smiled. "Thank thee, friend. I need clothing for children and I'm afraid I have never bought much before."

The man smothered his obvious surprise and asked, "What are the ages and gender of the children, please, miss?"

She pulled a list out of her reticule. "I will need an assortment of clothing for boys and girls of all ages."

The salesman looked confused.

"I should tell thee—"

"Are you here buying clothing for those orphans of yours?" A lady with a jarring voice bustled up to them.

Felicity didn't appreciate the sound of the question. Worse, there was only one way this woman could have heard of Felicity's plans for the Barney house—by listening to gossip. Disapproval ground inside her. However, Felicity gagged it down. She smiled hopefully. "Yes, I am. Would thee advise me on clothing for children?"

"No, I would not. I live on Madison Boulevard. I, along with many of your neighbors, don't want an orphanage in our neighborhood."

"Thee doesn't like children?" Felicity asked, her spirit suddenly simmering, bubbling with displeasure.

"We don't need riffraff from the wharf infesting our lovely avenue."

"I am truly sorry thee has that opinion. How does thee know of my work here?"

"Mrs. Thornton Crandall is one of my best friends. She told me all about your despoiling the Barney mansion." The woman brushed past her. "And she is going to do something to stop you!" The woman departed with a slam of the door.

If God be for me, who can be against me? Still prickling with outrage over the gossip being spread, Felicity looked at the proprietor. She calmed herself. "Would thee show me some clothing now?"

The man stood looking back and forth between the woman's retreating form and Felicity with her long list in hand.

Well, Robert Baker, does thee want my business?

Finally, he bowed. "Don't orphanages usually order a large quantity of uniforms—one for boys and one for girls?" The man led her down the aisle.

"I considered that and rejected it. It's like marking the children as odd, different from other children. Being orphaned is bad enough without being branded. Doesn't thee think?"

He nodded. "But it is less expensive—"

"Funds from Mrs. Barney's estate are more than adequate."

"Follow me, miss. We'll look at my selection for girls first, if you please."

She followed him down the neat aisle of folded shirts for men over to the girls' section. Felicity was relieved to discover that the man was not about to lose her as a customer, just because her children's home had evidently ruffled a few fancy ostrich feathers in town. With any luck, Felicity would be rewarding the man's decision by becoming one of his best customers, ordering more chil-

dren's clothes than he could possibly keep in stock for
the many children she planned to care for.

Felicity's eyes opened wide. By the scant moonlight,
she distinguished the gray outlines of the furniture in
her room. What had wakened her? She listened. The
house was quiet. Still, something had roused her. She rose
and donned her blue-sprigged wrapper and slippers. She
slipped down the hall and peeked into the room where
a very clean Katy and Donnie should have been sleeping in the high four-poster bed. Except that they were
sleeping on the rag rug *beside* the bed. The forlorn sight
wrenched her heart.

She nearly stepped into the room to lift them onto the
bed. Then she halted. They would adjust eventually. She
would never forget the image of the two of them with
tightly shut eyes and agonized expressions sitting in the
heaping soap-suds, neck-high tub of water on the back
porch. Vista, singing under her breath, had ruthlessly
scrubbed them with a soft brush. Such beautiful children.

Felicity turned away to the room across the hall and
found the bed where Tucker should have been sleeping—
it was empty. Her heart tumbled down. If the boy had run
away—a year in jail. She hurried down the stairs and out
the front door, looking up and down the dark street. Just
turning the corner ahead was Tucker. No! She kicked off
her slippers and picked up her skirts and ran.

Within seconds, she was at the corner and around it.
The boy didn't hear her. He was walking, head down
and hands in his pockets. She put on speed. Just before
she reached him, he turned. She clamped a hand on his
shoulder.

"Tucker," she said, her heart beating wildly, her breath
coming fast. "Why are thee out here?"

His expression showed his shock. Before he could say a word, a man came around the corner ahead of them. Felicity's heart began doing strange antics. It sank to her knees and then leaped into her throat. The fact that she was outside barefoot and in her night clothing hit her like a wet mop in the face. This could spawn gossip for years to come.

The man walked toward them, head down and hands in his pockets just like Tucker. She saw it was the judge. She wished she could become invisible.

"Turn around and start walking normal," Tucker whispered and did what he'd just told her to do.

Felicity hurried to follow his example. The two of them walked, her hand on the boy's shoulder. Every moment she expected to hear the judge call for her to stop. And since she couldn't lie, what possible explanation could she give to explain why they were out in the night?

Tucker and she came to their house at last. When they came to her abandoned slippers, they paused as she slipped her feet into them. Then they walked up the flagstone path and through the front door. Felicity had never been so grateful to hear her door close behind her. Either the judge had not seen them or he had chosen to be merciful again and behave as if he had not seen them. And she must make certain that Tucker's night wandering ended now.

Tucker tried to go on, but she squeezed his shoulder and led him down the hall to the moonlit kitchen. "Sit down at the table." When he made no move to obey, she added, "Please."

The boy sank into the chair. She sat down across from him. He would not meet her gaze. "Tucker…" What could she say? He knew he should be upstairs in bed. So she just sat, letting her tight, serrated worry flow out. She prayed, waiting for the Inner Light to lead her.

"Are we going to sit here all night?" the boy finally snapped.

She stared into his eyes. "That's up to thee."

"What's that supposed to mean?" The boy's tone showed plainly that he didn't hold her in any respect, probably held no adult in respect. The defiant eyes that returned her gaze told her much more than she wanted to deal with tonight.

It grieved her. "Tucker Stout, I don't understand what took thee out of thy comfortable bed in a comfortable home—"

"I like being on my own. I don't like people interfering with me, see?" His brows drew together.

"I must on the whole agree with thee." Peace began trickling through her, soothing her rasped nerves. "I also like being on my own. And I don't like interference of any kind either. So we have that in common. What interference are thee expecting from me?"

The boy snorted. "You'll be telling me to wash my hands and do this and do that and say grace at the table and don't pick my nose—"

The last forced a chuckle from her. Her good humor surged back. "Does thee do that often?"

Rebellious, Tucker made as if to rise. She pressed a hand over his and said, "Sit, please."

He stared and then capitulated, scowling.

"May I ask thee a question?" She waited for his permission.

Finally, he realized that she wasn't going to speak until he granted her the opportunity. "Okay, ask me."

"If thee runs away and is caught and sent to jail, won't

they tell thee to wash thy hands, and do this and don't do that?"

He stared at her.

"I would think that Vista and I would be preferable to jail guards." She folded her hands in front of her on the table and waited. Would he accept this simple truth?

He lifted one shoulder and demanded, "So what do you want me to say, lady?"

"Nothing, really. I will ask for no promise from thee. And I am not going to tie thee to thy bed. Or bolt thy door and window shut. And this is the last time I will come after thee. Thee must decide for thyself which to choose—this home or jail."

Tucker looked at her as if she were speaking in ancient Greek.

Felicity rose. "I will bid thee good-night. Will thee turn the lock on the back door, please? Thank thee." She walked up the stairs without a backward glance. *Oh, Father above, heal this wounded heart. Only Thee can. I cannot.*

In her room again, she took off her robe and slippers and sank onto the side of her bed, still praying. Forcing herself to have faith, she lay down again, trying not to listen for Tucker's footsteps on the stair. Her final thought was not about Tucker but about Judge Hawkins. What was he doing out well after midnight? And had he seen her with Tucker? And if he had, what would he do?

Chapter Three

After a too-short, two-block walk, Felicity strode up the Hawkins' front stone pathway. Her every step tightened her anxiety. She mounted the steps. And before she could turn tail, she sounded the brass knocker on the door twice politely. The judge's troubled eyes had haunted her for several days, etching her heart with sympathy. What beset the judge? Did God have work of mercy for her to do at this home?

Even if the answer had been no, she couldn't have stayed away. She'd stewed for hours till she'd come up with a reasonable excuse to visit him at his home, where she might glimpse a hint of what tortured his eyes. So here she was with deep apprehension—deep, gnawing apprehension.

While she waited, golden twilight wrapped around her with its heavy humidity. She took out a handkerchief and blotted the perspiration from her face. Why did women have to smother themselves with gloves, high shoes and hats even in summer?

Drawing in the hot, moist air, she resisted the urge to pluck the bonnet from her head and tear off her gloves. She needed all her "armor" to meet Tyrone Hawkins face to face without a courtroom of people looking on. Her hand again tingled with his remembered touch that first day at the wharf…

The door opened, revealing a dainty older woman with silvered blond hair.

Felicity smiled, uneasiness over the unsolicited visit skating up her spine. "Is Tyrone Hawkins at home, please?"

The woman looked her over thoroughly. "Yes, my son is home. Won't you step in?"

This gave Felicity another jolt. The judge's mother had answered the door herself? The judge lived on Madison Boulevard in a home nearly as large as the house she had inherited. These types of estates needed staff to maintain. Wondering at this discrepancy, Felicity crossed the threshold. She followed the woman through a long hallway out onto the shaded back porch. "Ty, we have company."

He was already rising from his wicker chair. "Miss…"

Though her heart was fluttering against her breastbone, she said, "I am Felicity Gabriel." She offered him her hand, a fresh wave of awareness of his deep sadness flowing through her. "We met yesterday in court?"

"I remembered your name," he said, taking her fingers, not her full hand, as if holding himself at a distance. "However, I didn't expect to see you here this evening." He bowed formally. His words and expression warned her away as if he'd thrown up an arm to fend her off.

Grateful for the excuse to turn from his intense, unwelcoming gaze, Felicity offered her hand to his mother.

"My mother, Louise Hawkins."

"Louise Hawkins, I am pleased to meet thee," Felicity greeted her. His mother's eyebrows rose at her Plain Speech but Felicity was used to this and made no comment.

"Won't you sit down, Miss Gabriel?" Louise invited.

The woman watched Felicity as if she were an exhibit in a sideshow. Had Louise Hawkins heard gossip about her, too?

Looking anywhere but at the tall, brooding man and the rudely inquisitive woman, Felicity noted a little girl with long dark braids, sitting far from the adults, rocking in a child's rocker. She held a rag doll and was sucking her thumb.

Felicity sat down in the white wicker chair that her hostess had indicated, which put her opposite Tyrone and beside Louise. Why hadn't he introduced the little girl?

"What can I do for you, Miss Gabriel?" Ty Hawkins's brusque voice snapped Felicity back to the fabricated purpose for this visit.

"I have come to thank thee for letting me take Tucker Stout to my home."

"No need to thank me. Prison isn't the place for children." He didn't look her in the eye, but focused on a point over her shoulder.

"Indeed." She resisted the temptation to lower her eyes. *I have nothing to be ashamed of.*

Her disobedient eyes went over his face again, noting the dark gray puddles beneath his eyes and the vertical lines in his face were so pinched and somber. She sealed her lips to keep from asking him plainly what was wrong.

From the corner of her eye, Felicity noted that the little girl had stopped rocking and was listening to the conversation. Her intense brown eyes studied Felicity with an unnatural solemnity in one so very young. Felicity smiled bravely, trying to shove off the oppressive gloom of these three. "Still, I wished to thank thee."

He made a dismissive gesture. "No doubt some, many of my colleagues, would not agree with my giving a miscreant into another person's hands as in Tucker's case."

Felicity nodded, drawing up her strength. She glanced sideways at the little girl and saw so much pain in the little girl's face—unmistakable unhappiness. The child's misery thumped Felicity in her midsection. She tore her gaze back to the judge. "I wonder if thee has followed the career of Mary Carpenter."

Ty raised an eyebrow. "I'm sorry, I'm not acquainted with the lady."

"Just fifteen years ago in England, she wrote *Reformatory Schools for the Children of the Perishing and Dangerous Classes, and for Juvenile Offenders*. Mary Carpenter said good free day schools and reformatory schools were urgently needed."

As she spoke, Felicity realized the child had her chair turned away so she couldn't see her father. The child looked only to her. Felicity's unmanageable heart contracted.

"We have good free day schools here in Altoona," Louise said with a touch of irritation in her tone.

Felicity turned and smiled though she could sense that they wanted her to leave. The little girl was still watching Felicity with an unnerving intentness. For a child with a family and a home to look so forlorn, so lost, was unnatural. Felicity wanted to gather the child into her arms and hold her, comfort her. "Louise Hawkins, I'm sure Altoona has excellent day schools. But what of a reformatory school for young ones like Tucker Stout who have no parents and who fall afoul of the law?"

"I thought you were just here to start an orphanage—" Tyrone began, sounding unaccountably frustrated.

"I prefer to call it a children's home," Felicity interrupted, yet smiled to soften her words. "A place where children will be loved and cared for."

"You got a home for children?" the little girl asked. Both her father and grandmother jerked and swung around to look at the child.

Felicity smiled. "Yes, I do. Hello, I'm Felicity Gabriel. What is thy name?"

The little girl tilted her head to one side. "My name's Camie."

"Hello, Camie." Impulsively, Felicity offered the child her hand.

Looking uncertain, Camie rose, still clutching the doll and sucking her thumb.

Felicity kept her hand out, open palm up as if offering it to a cautious stray. Camie edged closer and closer to her, keeping as far away from Tyrone as possible. *Oh, dear. A troubled child. A troubled man. And a gulf between them.* Felicity sensed the father and grandmother tensing. Were they afraid that the child would do something abnormal? Camie finally reached Felicity and took her hand. "Do you like little girls, too?"

"Little girls and boys. I want them to be well cared for, loved and happy like I was when I was a child." Felicity leaned forward and smoothed the moist tendrils around the child's face.

Camie tilted her head again like a little sparrow and then lifted her arms in silent appeal. Felicity gathered the little girl onto her lap and kissed the top of her head.

Camie nestled against her, hiding her face against Felicity's gray bodice. Though the added body heat was unpleasant, Felicity smoothed her palm over Camie's back, trying to soothe the tense child.

When Felicity looked up, she was shocked to see tears in Tyrone's eyes. Louise was dabbing her eyes with a handkerchief. Why was this a matter for tears?

Something was very wrong here—something had happened to this family and something needed to be done to help them. Felicity did not want to ask for an explanation in front of the child, or pry.

The four of them sat in silence for many minutes. The child's stiffness didn't leave completely, but the little girl did rest against her. Stroking Camie and crooning whispered words, Felicity watched Tyrone master himself, bury his reaction. She longed to smooth his worried forehead and speak comforting words to him also.

Finally, Louise broke their silence as oppressive as the summerlike heat, "I think setting up an orphan—I mean a children's home—is admirable." Louise's voice had softened. "I had heard that Mildred had left her estate to someone in the east."

Felicity nodded. "Perhaps thee would like to help the work she wanted me to carry out."

The softly spoken suggestion appeared to surprise Louise. Tyrone sat forward, staring at Felicity, hawklike.

Felicity continued stroking Camie's back and said, "I have a housekeeper and a groom. I will of course hire staff as necessary, but I would like to have men and women from the community volunteer to help out. So often in children's homes, the children are kept clean, fed and schooled. But who is there to rock them and read them stories? Teach them how to play games? Would thee be interested in such work?" She included Tyrone in her glance.

"I never thought of that," Louise said.

"My mother helps me with my daughter." Tyrone's face had frozen into harsh, forbidding lines that didn't seem to fit him. "Camie's mother passed away while I was at war." His anguish came through his words. And yet she sensed immediately that this wasn't just the grief over losing his wife. Something had been added to that grief.

"I'm very sorry to hear of your loss." She squeezed Camie, reiterating her sympathy. "Perhaps Camie would like to visit and play with our first little girl, Katy, some afternoon?"

Tyrone looked away.

"Perhaps," Louise replied, looking at her son with uncertainty.

Felicity hoped that this lady didn't deem her granddaughter too good to play with Katy. Her welcome here had been cordial enough, yet the sense that she was treading on just a skim of ice kept her cautious. "I think it's time I left." Felicity stroked Camie's cheek and looked into her eyes. "I have to go now. I have a little boy and girl at home to put to bed."

Camie sat up. The sudden look of alarm on the little girl's face was startling. Felicity almost asked what was the matter but checked herself. *At this point, these people are just acquaintances. I must not pry or meddle.*

The kind of do-gooders that Tucker mistrusted were people who thought their good intentions allowed them to stick their long pointy noses into other people's private lives, to trample the feelings of those who needed help, wielding their "good" deeds like weapons. Felicity did not want to be like that. Ever.

She urged Camie, who was trying to cling to her, to slip down and then she rose. "I will see thee again, Camie."

"I'll walk you to the front," Tyrone said gruffly.

Felicity accepted this with a nod. "Good night, Louise, Camie." She couldn't stop herself from cupping the little girl's cheek. "I hope to see thee again soon." Tyrone followed her down the steps of the back porch and around to the front walk. There, Felicity turned and offered him her hand. A mistake. When he took it, in spite of her sheer summer glove, her awareness of him multiplied.

"I saw you out with Tucker Stout the other night," he said in a harsh tone. His unexpected, unwelcome words rolled up her sensitivity to him like a window shade, snapping it shut. Recalling that she had been in night-dress at the time, Felicity felt herself blush.

"Maybe I should come over and impress on him why he shouldn't run away."

Looking at him sideways, she glimpsed his face, which had turned a dull red. Perhaps he was regretting causing her embarrassment.

Felicity pulled together her composure. "I thank thee but I think that he has decided to stay with me for the duration."

"I hope so."

"I do, too." Felicity withdrew her hand. "Thank thee, Tyrone Hawkins. I am glad I met thy mother and thy sweet daughter. Thee has been blessed."

His face contorted with some unspoken pain, then he bowed. "Good evening."

Felicity started off toward home, feeling his gaze on her back. Behind her, Camie cried out with shrill panic from an open window in the judge's house. Felicity halted in midstep, her heart fluttering wildly. She forced herself to go forward. She had come here suspecting that there was a need, but she'd had no idea how deep, how grave a need. *Heavenly Father, what is amiss in that house?*

Ty walked back into the house. Dread settled over him again like a shroud. The Quaker's visit had been equally beneficial and upsetting. It had done Camie good yet highlighted how cruelly broken his family remained. His mother must have taken Camie upstairs to get ready for bed. The nightly ordeal had begun. Now Camie's cries were most likely heard all down the block. The Quaker had heard them—as she walked away. He'd noted her stiffening. What did the neighbors think? Did they think that he was abusing his little girl?

He stopped beside the stairs in the foyer and clutched the finial on the bottom railing. His emotions churned, threatening to spill over. He pressed his mouth to his fist. He'd go up if that would help, but his presence only made it worse.

He recalled his amazement when watching Camie go to Felicity and ask to sit in her lap. What did this Quaker have that drew hurt children to her?

Drew him to her?

He shook off this thought. *Nonsense.*

Now he regretted letting Felicity know that he had seen her outside in nightdress, no doubt chasing Tucker Stout. She was quite an unusual woman, willing to be caught in dishabille in order to help a child. And she was able to draw Camie in a way no other person had in his memory. Maybe it would do Camie good to pay a visit to the little girl at Miss Gabriel's children's home. Camie screamed again, a serrated blade through his soul. Something had to be done. The situation had become unbearable—for all of them.

After putting Katy and Donnie to bed with a story and a prayer for the night, Felicity walked out to the back porch. She couldn't go to sleep with her nerves tangled and snared by unanswered questions about all she had observed and felt at the Hawkins' home. In any event, she couldn't stay within walls in the heavy summery heat. Barefoot, gloveless and hatless at last, she enjoyed the feel of the smooth hardwood under her soles and the air on her skin. She found Vista watching the sun, a molten ball of gold, lowering behind the maple trees along the alley. Vista sat fanning herself and holding a locket that hung around her neck.

Felicity hadn't noticed the locket before. She hesitated to intrude on Vista's privacy. Finally, she murmured, "May I speak with thee?"

Vista looked up, startled, and slipped the locket back out of sight. She studied Felicity and then nodded.

Felicity sat down on the wooden loveseat, leaning forward with her hands planted just behind her. She stared out at the sunset and wondered about the locket Vista felt the need to hide.

Felicity took herself fully in hand. "Of all things, I abhor gossip. But sometimes information is necessary. I would not want to say or do anything out of ignorance that might cause hurt or harm. Will thee give me some information?"

Vista made no response. Felicity waited, images of the sad little girl niggling her. Finally, Vista said, "Go ahead."

"This evening I went to thank Tyrone Hawkins—"

"You mean Judge Hawkins?"

"Yes, the judge. Friends don't use titles. We think they separate people and feed pride."

"More than titles separate people around here."

Felicity thought this over, Mrs. Thornton Crandall's anger-twisted face coming to mind. "I was disturbed by my visit at the judge's home." *More than disturbed.* She pursed her lips. "Something is very wrong there. The little girl…"

Felicity couldn't go on, couldn't divulge the distress she'd witnessed. Her throat dammed up. Cicadas and a carriage going down the street alone broke the silence of evening.

"There is trouble in that house." Vista's voice was solemn. "That stuck-up Mrs. Crandall is Camie's grandmother. Camie lost her mother and Mrs. Crandall took care of that child till the judge came home from war."

Felicity waited for more, but none came. "I thank thee." She certainly would not have to worry about Vista gossiping about matters at the children's home.

Felicity rose and went into the house. Poor Camie had fallen into the hands of Mrs. Crandall. And had Camie's mother taken after her own mother? *Poor Camie. Lord, show me if Thee wants me to help this child and show me how. Please.*

In midmorning two days later, even though her feet itched to walk off her lingering restlessness, Felicity ventured into town in the old carriage. In an act of faith, she had purchased new clothing for more orphans. Now she set out to find more children to wear those clothes. Flashes of memory—Camie's wan face, her alarming outcries, the judge's grim expression—circled in her mind like a train on a track.

With his drooping gray mustache and matching eyes, the groom let her down near the hectic wharf. "Miss Gabriel, you shouldn't be down here by yourself. I should stay with you."

This restriction of her freedom of movement chafed Felicity. Still, she smiled up at the man's lined face. "I will not be alone. I always try to tread as close as I can to the Lord. Thee need not come back. I will walk home—"

"No, you won't," the man said, huffing. "Mrs. Barney wouldn't like that at all, miss. Not at all. In an hour,

I will drive back into town and wait for you by the post office over yonder."

Felicity shook her head. "Very well, Abel Yawkey. I will do as thee wishes." *For now.* "At the post office in an hour." She consulted the watch pendant that was pinned to her collar.

She turned and headed down the less than clean streets near the wharf. The Mississippi River was the major trade route, transporting goods from the center of the nation down to the Gulf and thence to the world. She threaded her way through the steady stream of people going to and from the barges, but the loud voices and sounds of river traffic did nothing to cheer her. Camie's cries for help echoed in her mind.

And the judge's pain-lined face would not leave her.

Felicity walked and walked but did not see any children like the ones she had already taken home. Wondering if she should have come in the afternoon, she halted near where she had met Katy and Donnie on her first day in town.

"You in trouble, miss?" a deep voice asked.

She turned her head and looked into an older black man's deeply lined face, lifted in a kind smile. "I am looking for needy children."

"I'm Jack Toomey, Miss Gabriel. I saw you arrive in town a few days ago."

"And thee already knows my name?" Felicity offered him her hand. She wasn't pleased to hear that gossip had spread this far. But that wasn't this man's fault.

Shaking her hand, Jack matched her grin and raised it a few notches. "Yes, miss. This town isn't as little as it was when I was a boy. But it's still small enough that information spreads pretty quick."

Felicity drew in a deep breath. "And what do the people of Altoona say of me?" From the corner of her eye, she glimpsed the policeman who had nabbed Tucker watching her talk to Jack Toomey. What was his name?

Jack rubbed his clean-shaven chin and ignored her question. His gaze was assessing. "You be a Quaker, right?"

"Yes, I am a member of the Society of Friends." Hogan, that was the man's name.

"The Quakers were friends to black people who were in bondage for a long time."

"Yes, we voted against slavery in our Pennsylvania Friend's Assembly in 1758." Hogan was watching her closely. Did he resent her actions to help Tucker?

"Did you know that Altoona was a stop on the Underground Railroad?"

"Yes, in fact, the house I inherited from Mildred Barney was one of those stops. There is a concealed room in the attic."

Jack laughed. "No doubt Sister Vista told you about that. She made use of it herself."

Felicity nodded. She filed away that bit of Vista's history and returned to her object for the day. She gazed at the foot and horse traffic.

"You be looking for more children for that orphans' home of yours?"

"Yes, I am. So far I have only three. Does thee know of any children who need a home?"

"You willing to take in black children?" he asked.

"Of course."

Jack smiled broadly. "I think there are a few children our church has been feeding and trying to find permanent homes for."

"Excellent. Would thee please bring them to Mildred Barney's house?"

"I surely will." Jack bobbed his head. "And if you go along the wharf, you might find a few more homeless children. I saw some begging this morning at the back of the bakery for stale bread."

"Thank thee, Jack Toomey. I will look forward to receiving those children." Felicity waved and walked along the quay. Men with bulging muscles wrestled large sacks and wooden crates onto and off barges. Passengers from a riverboat were filing down a walkway onto shore. Then two little boys ran from a side street and began begging there. A shabby older man followed them out of the alley and looked around in what struck Felicity as a furtive manner.

She paused and observed him until he blended into the jostling crowd. Then she focused on the two boys. Both towheaded blonds, they looked to be around eight to ten years. It was hard to estimate age accurately since lack of proper food always slowed or stunted growth not only of the body but also of the mind. After the passengers had all passed by, Felicity approached them. "Good day, children."

They both looked up, their blue eyes alert and wary, without the innocence of childhood. Then they looked around as if fearing someone. The boys' faces were grimy and their clothing tattered. The sight twisted her heart. How could people just pass them by? But then times were hard after the war. And in any season some people had little pity to spare for others.

"My name is Felicity Gabriel and I have a home for children who don't have a family. Would thee like to visit my home and see if thee would like to stay?"

They stared at her, no comprehension in their eyes, only suspicion.

She smiled. "I have three children who have decided

to stay with me, a little girl and her brother and another older lad. Would thee—"

"What do we got to do for you?" the older of the two asked, casting a nervous glance over his shoulder.

Their distrust grieved Felicity but no doubt it had been learned the hard way. She looked in the direction of the boy's glance but saw nothing worrying. "Thee must only follow the house rules. I am a Quaker and this is the kind of work we do. We are honor-bound to help others."

"Would a visit include lunch?" the older one asked, scrutinizing her.

"Yes, indeed it would. If thee will come with me—" she paused to look at her pendant watch "—my carriage is waiting near the post office." She turned and walked away without looking back, letting the two decide whether to come along or not.

When she reached Abel Yawkey, he got down and helped her into the carriage. The two boys climbed in after her, still looking guarded and edgy.

Felicity was delighted but hid it. She must present a calm presence before the distrustful children. But her spirit lifted, which she desperately needed after being haunted by the tormented eyes of little Camie Hawkins—and of her father.

Felicity and the children ate on the back porch. Vista had enforced her clean-hands-and-face rule, and then served a delicious lunch of Welsh rarebit. The new boys, Butch and Willie, had eaten three helpings and helped finish off a dozen large oatmeal cookies.

Felicity had introduced the new children to Katy, Donnie and Tucker. For just a moment, she had the notion that the boys knew Tucker. But Tucker had shown no evidence of this. At first, there was only silence at the table.

But after the new children had eaten their first helping, they started eyeing the others already in her care. Would these two stay for more than just lunch?

Vista came out and put down another dish of melted cheddar cheese on toast and said, "Miss Felicity, will you come into the kitchen a moment?"

"If you will excuse me, children." Felicity left her napkin beside her plate. Inside, she looked to Vista questioningly.

"I called you in to give the new chil'run a chance to talk to Katy and Tucker. They will trust what they say more than what you or me say."

Felicity beamed at Vista. "How wise thee are."

Vista shrugged. "I don't know if I'm wise, I just know how it feels…"

Felicity looked into Vista's eyes, waiting. But the lovely housekeeper left the rest of her sentence unsaid, making Felicity wonder again about the locket. She perceived its outline under Vista's demure collar but still did not ask. After a few minutes, the two women carried out more milk to the children.

"Well," Felicity said as brightly as she could, "are thee two staying or returning to the wharf?"

The boys looked to each other and then to Tucker.

Felicity was glad she was watching closely or she might have missed what came next. Tucker gave the slightest nod.

Butch and Willie turned their gazes up to her. "We'll give it a try, lady."

"You supposed to call her Miss Felicity," Katy prompted. Vista had insisted that the children follow her example.

"Miss Felicity," the two said in unison, and Tucker nodded in approval.

Felicity's awareness zoomed. It was clear that Tucker

and these children knew each other. How? Just because they had all lived on the streets? Felicity decided not to let herself be caught napping. She must be as gentle as a dove but wise as a serpent.

Later, Felicity looked out the window at the two new boys who—in between digging in the dirt for fun—were weeding the side garden. Then she looked back down at her sketch of needed alterations to Mrs. Barney's house to make it into a home for many children.

Turning her mind to the issue at hand, Felicity smiled at the builder. The man said, "I'd have to see if any of the interior walls are load-bearing before I start taking them down."

"Yes, I don't want to bring the roof down on our heads." Felicity grinned, trying to lighten the exchange. The builder seemed to be brooding on something. "I also want thee to make an outside staircase on each side of the house in case of fire. I need the children to be able to get out safely."

"Outside staircases?" He looked at her sketch and grimaced. "That will give a very odd appearance to this house."

"With so many more children than in a usual family home, we must take extra precautions. And I want to add a small room off the kitchen where the children will bathe. I'd like an indoor pump and stove in that room."

He looked dubious. "This is a lot of work. And I have other jobs—"

Whether due to his hesitance to work for a woman or something else, she would have none of it. *My children can't wait just because thee doesn't want to bother getting the work done.* "I suggest that thee hire more help."

He rubbed the side of his nose. "These projects change

the whole appearance of this house. I hate to take such a lovely dwelling and—"

Oh, that's what this is about. More consequences of Mrs. Crandall's gossip. "A house filled with healthy, joyful children is what I think is beautiful. Now if thee cannot take on this work immediately, I will contact another builder."

The door knocker sounded.

"I need the work." The builder added cryptically, "And I don't care what anybody says. Your money spends just like everyone else's."

Felicity flushed with annoyance over the implied criticism. A person would think she had proposed to establish a house of ill repute on Madison Boulevard. She heard muted voices in the foyer and rose.

He rose, too, rotating his hat brim in both hands. "I'll go up and take measurements."

Felicity offered him her hand, hearing Vista greeting someone at the door. "I think thee will do an excellent job."

As he started up the steps, Felicity moved toward the open door. Louise Hawkins and Camie stood at her threshold. Vista slipped away to the kitchen.

Felicity's breath caught in her throat. She hadn't expected them so soon. Again, it struck her how slight Camie was. She spoke like a child who should be in school but looked barely five years of age. Instantly, Felicity was on her guard. This was a fragile child. *Father, make me sensitive.* "Louise Hawkins and Camie, I'm delighted to see thee."

"We thought we would take you up on your invitation and come and visit," Louise said, her nervous gaze roving here and there as if fearing this was a trap.

"Hello," Camie said, looking up at Felicity.

Felicity stooped down, frantically trying to think what to do with this brittle child. "If thee will follow me, we will go to the kitchen. Vista is there and two of our children are helping her bake cookies." Not giving them time to refuse, Felicity led the way through the hall to the kitchen.

Katy was draped with a white kitchen cloth around her neck as a full apron. Standing on the chair, she had both hands in a small bowl of cookie dough. Donnie was sitting in the chair beside her and rolling dough on the table with cheery good humor. The sight melted Felicity's heart like butter on toast. Just days ago, these had been waifs. Both children stopped and gawked at the newcomers.

"Katy and Donnie, a new friend, Camie Hawkins, has come to visit," Felicity announced with a smile, hoping that the children would be welcoming. "And Camie has brought her grandmother with her." Felicity leaned over, looking into Camie's eyes. "Would thee like to help bake cookies?"

Her thumb in her mouth, Camie turned to look up at her grandmother.

"Would you like to help, Camie?" Louise asked with a slight tremor in her voice.

Camie looked to Donnie and Katy and shook her head, gazing down and pressing against her grandmother's skirts.

Felicity tried to think of what to say. Maybe trying to put Camie with other children had been a mistake. Outside, someone was shouting. Felicity tried to identify whom.

"It's not hard," Katy piped up. "You'd prob'bly be good at it. You got hair ribbons."

Felicity did not understand this connection, but caught the hint of longing in Katy's voice. She promised herself she'd buy ribbons on her next trip to town. She had been raised without ribbons but immediately saw their allure for Katy. As she was pondering where to purchase them, Felicity thought she heard shouting outside.

"If you don't want to help, you could sit and watch," Vista invited. "I'm baking in the outside oven. It's too hot to cook inside on a scorcher like this."

Louise raised one eyebrow, no doubt over Vista's forwardness in speaking up. However, she nodded in agreement. "Camie, would you like to sit down and watch the cookie making?"

Camie pressed herself into her grandmother's skirt. "You sit," she muttered.

"I think I'll sit down and help, too," the grandmother announced. She took off her gray bonnet and black lace gloves and put them on the bench by the back door. "Show me what I can do, Vista. And Miss Gabriel, why don't you show Camie where she can sit to watch this? I hope we're going to get to sample the cookies when they are done."

Heartened by the grandmother's attempt at sounding merry, Felicity led Camie by the hand to a free chair. "Here, Camie, thee may sit here."

"You." Camie pushed Felicity toward the chair.

Though the shouting outdoors was becoming much louder, Felicity didn't hesitate; she sat down. Camie climbed up on her lap. Felicity caught the flicker of some strong emotion on Louise's face and wondered again about this little girl and her family. The demeanor of both the judge and his mother made it clear that they viewed Camie's attraction to Felicity with surprise and uncertainty. Felicity rejoiced silently for Camie's taking to her.

She asked for some dough and began rolling it into

small balls, hoping Camie would venture to help. Then the front door brass knocker was hit in an angry tattoo, making them all jump.

Oh, dear, what now?

Chapter Four

The insistent and irksome sound plucked Felicity from her chair. Camie clung to her, so she swung the child into her arms. As the pounding became frantic, Felicity rushed down the hall and threw wide the door.

"You! Are you that Quaker?" demanded a fashionably dressed young woman of about thirty, not wearing either a coming-to-visit hat or gloves.

"I am a member of the Society—"

"What do you mean, letting children behave like that?" The woman's voice rose shrilly.

Felicity stared at the young woman. "What children? Behaving how?"

The pretty, dark-haired woman grabbed Felicity's elbow, dragged her down the steps and ran, pulling her around to the side of the house. There the two new boys, Butch and Willie, were throwing clods of dirt from the side garden toward a peculiarly dressed little boy on the line between the two yards.

"Look at that!" The woman's face was red. "Your little ruffians are attacking my son, Percy!"

The outfit Percy was wearing appalled Felicity. Topped by a wide-brimmed straw hat, Percy wore a white ruffled shirt with a large round collar, blue knickers, white knee stockings and shined shoes that were fastened by straps, not laces. Why would anyone dress a boy in ruffles—and *white* ruffles to boot? Felicity gawked at the poor boy.

"He started it!" Butch declared as he lobbed another mud ball at Percy. It streaked the boy's cheek and knocked his hat cockeyed.

Tucker came charging out of the carriage house, looking angry and ready to fight.

"We don't want your kind in our neighborhood!" Percy yelled. He aimed and threw a small rock, hitting Butch on the forehead.

Felicity rushed forward and interposed herself between her boys and Percy. Then Tucker placed himself between Felicity and Percy. His unexpected protectiveness caught Felicity around the heart. Abel, limping with arthritis, was also coming to her aid.

But she kept to her main concern. "Butch, is thee all right?" Camie still on her hip, Felicity bent down and took the boy's chin in her hand. She examined him, turning his face back and forth. "Thee will come in and I'll take care of that before a bump starts."

"You keep away, pretty boy," Tucker jeered. "Or you'll have a fight—"

The woman shrieked and began shouting, "We don't want your riffraff here starting trouble—"

At the word *riffraff* Felicity turned on the woman, her anger shooting out like bright lights of fireworks. "*Thee* started this trouble! Thee has poisoned thy son— thy innocent child—against defenseless orphans! No child would say, 'We don't want your kind' on his own. How dare thee put the blame for this on my boys! If thy son cannot play peaceably with others, I suggest thee take him inside." Felicity stretched out her hand. "Come, Butch, I must see to thy injury."

Garbled words issued from the woman's mouth, "Effrontery…gall…undisciplined." Then she marched to her son, grabbed his hand and headed into their house next door, Percy squawking all the way.

With Willie at her heels, Felicity took Butch's hand and hurried him to the back porch, her anger still pounding within. Tucker followed them. Looking disgruntled, Abel met them on the way in.

Vista was there with a silver knife. "This will take care of that bump before it gets bigger." She pressed the knife against the spot where an angry red bump was rising.

Felicity wondered at this home remedy which was completely new to her, but said nothing. Butch was not fighting Vista so it must not be hurting him.

"I see," Vista said, "that you met our neighbor Mrs. Eldon Partridge."

Felicity glanced at Mrs. Partridge's house and tried to extinguish the molten lava bubbling in her stomach.

"You best calm down. Pretty soon," Vista remarked, "you're going to start letting off steam like an engine."

Felicity couldn't help herself—she laughed.

Louise Hawkins stood in the doorway between the kitchen and the back porch. "Camie?" she asked in a strained voice.

Felicity had momentarily forgotten that Camie was still on her hip. She looked down into Camie's face, hoping that the scene had not frightened the child. "Is thee all right, Camie?"

"I don't like Percy." Camie smiled. "And you didn't let Percy hurt the boy." She snuggled her face into Felicity's blouse.

"Don't worry, Braids," Tucker said, tugging one of Camie's long dark braids. "We know how to fight."

This brought a smile to Felicity. "Thank thee, Tucker."

"No thanks needed. I'm the oldest, see?"

"Yeah," Willie said. "Tucker watches out for the littler kids." Butch nodded. This comment gave Felicity another hint. Filing this away for future use, Felicity looked over Camie's head to the grandmother, who was wiping her eyes yet trying to reassure Felicity with an approving smile. Felicity tucked the child closer. *Dear Father, help me help this troubled family.*

After Butch's bump had settled down to more of a red welt, Butch and Willie asked to go back outside.

"I will let thee go outside but thee must not throw mud, stones or anything else, or call anyone names, please."

"That fancy boy started it all," Willie insisted with a dark, stubborn look.

"I do not doubt that to be true," Felicity said. "However, I always try to get along with my neighbors. And I expect thee to do the same. If anyone else comes to stir up trouble, I want thee to promise to run to me or to Vista or Abel Yawkey in the carriage house. Will thee do that? Please?"

"Butch and me ain't sissies," Willie said with his lower lip stuck out. "We ain't gonna run from a fight."

Felicity didn't know quite how to deal with this. She'd grown up among sisters and the peculiarities of the male gender had always puzzled her. However, experience with her childhood friend Gus had taught her this attitude was the prevailing one with males. "Would thee call out to one of us before thee defends thyself?"

Butch and Willie considered this. "We'll try," Butch answered.

"I thank thee. Thee may go outside and finish thy weeding."

The boys didn't look delighted by this prospect, but went out. Felicity suddenly felt very tired. She sighed and instantly, silently scolded herself. *No more sighing. Especially not in front of the children.* Children, even children who were being raised by their own good families, were a handful. She would have to pray for enough energy to keep up with these new boys and Tucker.

The memory of that little signal that had passed between Butch and Willie and Tucker niggled at her. Also the way Tucker had come to their defense against Percy. How, exactly, did the boys know each other? And how would that affect her success in helping them? And, perhaps most important of all, would other town children be poisoned by their parents' prejudices against her orphans?

That evening, Ty walked up the steps to his house. Despite the continued heat, he was in a gray wintry mood and so tired he could have fallen asleep standing up. Years of soldiering had given him the ability to plod on even when his whole body wanted only to collapse, unconscious. Yet the thought of suffering through another night hearing his daughter scream had the power to make him halt on the top step. *My little girl is suffering. I can't help her. And she hates the sight of me.*

If there were anywhere else he could go, he'd be sorely tempted to turn tail and flee.

His mother opened the door. "Come in, son."

Her tone and expression weren't easy to read. Still, he recognized something was different about her face. He studied her, not moving. "What's wrong?" *Not more bad news. Please.*

"Nothing is wrong, son. I just hope you won't be

upset." Stepping out onto the porch, she knotted her hands together.

"Upset?" he repeated, apprehension chugging through his veins.

"Yes, well—" Louise took a deep breath "—I left Camie with Miss Felicity at her children's home."

Shock shot through him icy cold. "You what?"

"This morning Camie kept asking to go visit Miss Felicity, so I finally gave in by afternoon. She has never asked to visit anyone else. We walked over and were invited inside to help make cookies." His mother seemed to run out of words and just stood looking at him.

"And?" What dreadful scene had Camie enacted there?

His mother drew in more air. "After a while, Felicity said it was time for Katy and Donnie to take their naps. Somehow, Camie managed to go up the stairs with Miss Felicity as she was helping the children to lie down. When the Quaker came back, she said that Camie insisted on taking a nap with the two orphans."

Ty just stared at his mother, waiting for the worst to come.

"I didn't think you'd like it so I went up to get Camie. And…she was already asleep beside Katy." Louise looked into his eyes. "You know she never gets enough sleep. She fell asleep *without fussing* at all. At all. Not a peep." Louise smiled suddenly, wiping a tear from her eye with the heel of her hand.

Ty could not think of a single word to say to this unbelievable news. He sank onto the top step. Lack of sleep must be dulling his mind.

His mother came farther out onto the porch and sat beside him, gazing into his face. "Miss Felicity didn't seem to see anything out of order and asked me to feel free to leave Camie for her nap."

Ty tried to fit all this news into his numb mind. "Isn't it past naptime now?"

"She suggested I leave Camie to nap and then play with Katy—"

"Katy? Who is this Katy?" Ty hated how he sounded cranky, like an old man with rheumatism.

"Katy is an orphan girl who has a little brother, Donnie. Camie took a liking to her. Anyway, Ty, Miss Felicity invited us to supper tonight."

Camie had taken a liking to another child?

"Supper?" he asked.

"Yes. I accepted. We're expected—" she looked back into the house "—in fifteen minutes." She clasped her hands together even tighter and looked at him in unmistakable appeal.

He dragged himself upright. "Then we better start now or we'll be late."

Eyeing him, Louise rose, got her hat and gloves from the foyer. They covered the two blocks in silence. Ty repeatedly went over his mother's report about Camie with the Quaker and Katy. He walked up to the front door and sounded the knocker. A little boy opened the door. "Who are you?" he asked.

"Hello, Willie," Louise said, "this is my son, Judge Hawkins. Ty, this is Willie." The boy gawked at him, looking ready to run. It stung Ty. Why did children always behave as if he were about to harm them? His hand started to cover his scar but he lowered it.

Miss Gabriel walked up the hallway, smiling radiantly. "Please, let's walk around to the rear of the house. It's so warm this evening that we will eat our meal on the back porch. We'll be finished before the mosquitoes come out in force."

"How is our Camie?" his mother asked.

"I hope she behaved," Ty added as he doffed his hat, trying not to be snared by the woman's infectious smile.

"Oh, Camie is a delight. After the nap, she played with Katy and Donnie, and helped set the table."

A delight? His daughter had taken a nap and played? Yes, but all this had taken place in the daylight. Night was different. Dreadfully different. How was he going to get her home tonight without a scene? As soon as it started getting dark, Camie sank into her fear. At the thought of trying to carry home a screaming Camie, Ty's stomach roiled with nausea.

As they walked past the side bow window, Felicity glanced at him. "Did thee think thee should be concerned about Camie? She's quite safe with us."

Neither he nor his mother replied. He racked his brain for a reasonable reply. Finally, he came up with the completely inadequate, "Camie is shy."

"Really?" The Quaker paused and gave him a quizzical look. "In that case, I'm happy that she took to Katy. They have been chattering and playing with Camie's doll as happy as can be."

As happy as can be? They had reached the back porch. She led them up the steps to the long white-clothed table there. The handsome housekeeper rang a bell. The sound of footsteps heralded the haste of children all through the house.

The boy who had opened the door for them veered around Ty and went to the chair that Felicity was indicating. Then came a little girl leading both a toddler and his Camie by the hand. This must be Katy. She led them to their seats, eyeing him all the while.

His daughter glanced up once and then lowered her gaze. Of course, not even here would she look at him. Her continued rejection of him carved another notch in his mangled heart.

Finally, Tucker, the lad he'd sentenced to serve probation here, climbed the steps, also staring and giving him a wide berth. Ty kept a tight lid on his reactions to this assembly and its varied reactions to him. He was definitely getting tired of being viewed by children as a leper, a dangerous one to boot, especially by his own blood.

Soon they were all seated and Miss Gabriel had said grace. The housekeeper passed around broiled beefsteaks, tomato-and-lettuce salad and light biscuits. Ty began to eat, watching the children tuck into their food.

"Katy," the Quaker said, after introducing Vista to him, "will thee tuck Donnie's napkin into his shirt neck?"

Katy did as she was asked. Then she pointed to Ty. "What happened to your face?"

Ty kept his irritation to himself. The child meant no harm.

Felicity frowned. "Katy, thee should not make comments about a person's appearance. It causes the person to feel uncomfortable. Camie's father was in the war. Isn't that where thee got the mark on thy cheek, Tyrone?"

"Yes. I know it's not pretty but there's not much I can do about it." He watched Camie for any reaction. But as usual, she would not look his way. He fought the urge to cover the scar with his hand.

"It will not be so noticeable with time," the Quaker said. "Time heals all wounds."

Ty wished that were so. He began eating, trying to appear unconcerned while his stomach knotted and reknotted itself. In contrast, the children all were eating quickly and heartily.

"Children, remember what I told thee," Felicity said in a gentle tone. "Thee don't have to rush thy eating. Chew thy food and thy stomach will thank thee. And thee may have seconds, even thirds of everything. But please chew the first helping. Will thee?"

All the heads bobbed. Ty noted that even Tucker slowed up. Ty looked at Felicity and she smiled at him, momentarily transfixing him once more. He turned his gaze to his plate, hoping her marked effect on him had passed unnoticed.

"Did thee have a productive day, Tyrone Hawkins?" Felicity asked.

He didn't look at her. "I suppose so. Just the usual." He chewed the food, trying to enjoy it. Yet he was sick with dread over the scene his daughter would most certainly create when they tried to go home to put her to bed.

"We were so happy that Camie came to visit us, weren't we, children?" Miss Felicity asked.

Katy nodded so hard her braids jumped. "I like Camie. Does she belong to you, mister?"

"Yes, she is my daughter." He glanced at the thin girl.

"She's nice. And she talks polite and pretty. She let me play with her dolly."

"I'm glad that she met with your approval," Ty said.

Felicity beamed at him. "Louise, I hope thee will visit us again soon with Camie. I am hoping that my children will make friends with the other children in town."

Ty thought this was probably unlikely to happen. As it was, he was sure that he and his mother would hear a lot of negative comments about letting his daughter associate with "riffraff."

Tucker snorted, giving a similar opinion to Ty's.

The image of Felicity, barefoot in nightdress, walking beside Tucker in the moonlight flashed through Ty's mind. He hadn't decided yet whether or not the fact that this woman was prepared to go to any length to help Tucker—even public embarrassment—was good or not. An idealist with this kind of fervor wouldn't let well enough alone. That much he did realize. He tried to take a deep breath; his chest was tight with apprehension.

"What church does thee attend, Louise?" Felicity asked.

"We've always attended the Altoona Bible Church on Church Street," Louise replied, slicing another bit of beef.

"I asked Vista and she said there is no Friends Meetinghouse here. So I think we'll all visit thy church this Sunday."

"Church?" Tucker's head snapped up. "I ain't goin' to no church."

Tense, Ty barked, "You'll do as you are—"

"Tucker," Felicity interrupted, "while thee is with me, thee will go to church on Sunday and also school when it begins again. Thee children will receive food, clothing, shelter and love from me, Vista and Abel, but thee must do what we say. That is how a family works. The guardians or parents provide what the children need. The guardians in turn are obeyed because they are older and know what is best for the children. That is how I was raised. Wasn't thee, Tyrone?"

"Yes, I was." He wondered at the way she took time to explain this to a child who probably had never been provided for by his family.

"You mean you're going to be like our ma?" Katy asked.

"Yes, unless some other good family would like to adopt thee as their daughter—"

"I ain't leavin' Donnie," Katy said, standing up, nearly upsetting her chair.

Felicity held out a hand. "Katy, I would never separate thee and thy little brother. Never. I give thee my solemn promise. Come here and I will give it to thee."

Ty watched, uncertain of what Felicity was up to.

Katy came around the table and stood face to face with the sitting Felicity.

"Now, when a person makes a promise she will never break, this is the way it's done. First, spit into thy hand like this." She demonstrated. "And then press it to mine." The little girl followed the Quaker's example. The two pressed palms.

Ty recalled doing this type of childish ritual with his boyhood friends. It wasn't something he thought girls did. Again it revealed how different this woman was from the usual, different from Virginia. He shoved the thought away.

"Now I have given thee my promise. I will never separate thee and Donnie—"

"Except when he gets too big to sleep with the girls. Then he's got to sleep with the boys," Vista said as she brought in another platter of beef.

Katy looked uncertain about this. But then Donnie spoke for the first time. "I a boy." He pointed to himself and began chewing again.

"Yes," Felicity said, clapping her hands together, "thee is a boy and a boy who can speak."

Camie smiled at Donnie and then looked to Tucker. "And Tucker is the biggest and he doesn't let anyone hurt us."

"That's right, Braids. You don't need to be afraid here."

Ty felt tears smart in his eyes. He couldn't ever recall seeing Camie smile. The thought sliced his heart in two. And how had she decided to trust a boy he'd almost sent to prison? The dinner went on. The children tucked away a considerable amount of food. The little girl and his daughter were the only children who spoke, usually answering some question from Felicity. The boys just ate, each keeping a distrustful eye on him. What did they expect that he would do? Grab one of them and drag him off to jail? In any event, his traitorous eyes would not obey him; they continually drifted to Felicity's reddish-blond hair and expressive face.

After dinner, the adults sat on the back porch, fanning themselves and watching the children trying to catch fireflies. Ty found himself captivated by Felicity's lively mind. They discussed the recent amendments to the Constitution, the state of the still-rebellious South and the latest news. Was there any topic she couldn't converse about intelligently? Diverted, he couldn't recall ever having such a conversation with Virginia, or any other woman.

Finally the mosquitoes drove them inside. Fine but heavy cloth with weighted hems hung over every open window. The pleasant interlude must come to an end. Ty nodded toward his mother, signaling that it was time for them to leave. His whole body stiffened. How would Camie react?

Louise turned to Felicity. "Thank you for entertaining Camie today. And for a lovely supper." Then she turned to Camie. "Come now. It's time we got you home to bed."

His daughter's face shouted her panic. She turned, raced down the hall and pounded up the stairs. He ran after her, his heart thumping. "Camie! Camie!"

Felicity came up right behind him. His heart thudding, he paused at the top of the stairs, not knowing where his daughter had run. His worst fear had come true. There would be a scene here tonight.

"Let's try Katy's room." Felicity passed him.

He followed her to a closed door. She tapped on it. "Camie, dear, it's Felicity. May I come in please?"

No answer.

Ty held on to his frustration, unwilling to let this stranger know how bad things might become.

"Camie, dear, thee can come and visit Katy tomorrow. Tyrone, thee will let Camie come visit tomorrow, won't thee?"

"Yes," he snapped, "of course, Camie can come if you invite her." In the war, he had seen men so distraught that they had torn out their hair. He felt himself nearing this disaster point.

"Camie, dear, I'm opening the door now. Thee will always be welcome here. And thee knows that I like children and I protect them. Thee saw that today." Felicity entered slowly, peering around the door. "Camie," she called in a soft sweet voice. "Camie."

Ty waited in the hall, powerless to act and burning with embarrassment and frustration.

Felicity kept calling his daughter. Finally, she came out to him. "She's not in this room. I think perhaps it might be best if thee went down and kept thy mother company and let me look for Camie."

He couldn't stop himself from making a sound of irritation.

She touched his sleeve. "Camie is a good little girl, but remember, she was born into a war just like most of these other children. It affects us and them in unusual ways."

His heart throbbed with the agony only a father of a child with "problems" could know. What could he say to this woman who was offering him understanding? Nothing. He nodded brusquely and went back downstairs, his chin nearly touching his chest.

Many minutes later, Felicity walked quietly down the

steps. Camie was hidden within the folds of her gray skirt. Ty met them at the bottom of the stairs near the front door. His mother waited behind him, uneasy.

"I told Camie I would ask thee if thee would let her spend the night with Katy." Felicity looked him in the eye, appealing to him to allow this.

He couldn't. He couldn't subject this household—this kind woman—to the ordeal of getting Camie to sleep. "I'm sorry, but Camie must come with me. It's time to go home."

Camie clung to Felicity. Ty was forced to pry her fingers from Felicity's skirt. He swung her up into his arms. Camie began fighting him and screaming, "No! No!"

He tried to thank his hostess but was forced to carry his hysterical child outside. He ran the two blocks home. His child's screaming ripped him apart. Humiliated, he glimpsed people peering out their windows at the disturbance.

When he reached home, his taut nerves ruptured, flying apart. He climbed the stairs two at a time, set Camie in her room and slammed the door. He slid down to the floor and put his head in his hands.

Memories from the war flooded his mind—brutal bloodshed, staggering grief, crushing fear. Images too ghastly for a human to believe flickered in his mind. Bodies mutilated, faces unrecognizable. He tried to force the memories out. But cannons exploded in his ears. Black smoke billowed from rifles. Men fell around him.

Joining the mayhem of their outcries, Camie's hysterical screams stabbed him over and over. She began kicking the door, pummeling his body. His mother hovered at the top of the stairs. He wanted to say something to her, reassure her, but he couldn't. Would the horror never end? Would he never have peace?

I can't take any more. I can't. Oh, God, please, help.

He didn't know how long he'd stayed there like that, sitting on the floor, drenched in despair, unable to speak or move. Finally, his mother came to him and handed him a cup. "It's a chamomile tea with a few drops of laudanum. Drink it. Don't argue."

He looked up at her and realized that the house was quiet and very dark. His daughter must have finally given in to exhaustion. How could he have become senseless to Camie's screaming? Fearing for his state of mind, he sipped the bitter tea which would bring sleep. Finally, he managed to rise. He again longed to reassure his mother but he was empty, as empty as the cup he handed his mother.

"Go to sleep now, son. We will talk in the morning. We will pray tonight and tomorrow come up with some way to help our little Camie."

Without hope, he nodded and trudged the few steps to his door. Inside, he sat on the edge of his bed. Then without undressing, he collapsed and slept.

Moonlight glowed faint at the window. Ty realized that he was on his bed and still in his clothes. Then it all came rushing back—his daughter's hysteria at leaving Felicity's home. But he couldn't have left Camie there and put the kind woman through Camie's night terrors. He sat up. His guilt prodded him to go and reassure himself that his child was sleeping peacefully at last.

He crept out of his room and opened the door stealthily, fraction by fraction. He tiptoed into the room and looked down, expecting her to be crumpled on the floor right inside the door. She wasn't. She wasn't in her bed, under her bed, in her dressing room.

Thin and flat with fatigue, he felt his heart begin to

pound. The sensation nearly nauseated him. He had experienced this reaction before when pushed past endurance.

He forced himself to go over the room once more. Then he searched the entire house, all the way to the basement. Finally he hurried outside to the yard. He didn't find her.

Camie had run away.

Pressing the heel of his hand to his pounding right temple, he considered what he should do. The only place he could think that she had gone was to the Barney house. She had wanted to stay there and must have gone back. If she wasn't there…

He walked down the moonlit street, trying to keep his footsteps as quiet as possible. When unable to sleep, he had taken to walking at night and had mastered how to move without disturbing anyone in the quiet dark houses with their windows open to let in any faint breeze.

He reached the Barney house and stood on the porch. Now that he was here, he didn't quite know how to proceed. Waking a maiden lady in the middle of the night was not appropriate. Then he recalled Felicity pursuing Tucker Stout in her wrapper, barefoot. She wasn't like other ladies. He knocked softly and waited. He was about to knock again when the door opened.

There she stood in her wrapper and slippers. The very light blue cotton caught the low light, gleaming. And he sensed the same beckoning quality as always from her. Somehow she drew him as a fire on a cold night.

"Tyrone, I've been dozing by the door, waiting for you." She let him in and motioned toward a rocking chair that had been stationed at the base of the staircase, barely visible. Her voice was low and so gentle.

"Is Camie here?" The words cost him. His eyes burned. His head ached. His body cried out for undisturbed sleep. He wanted to lay his head on this woman's shoulder and find ease and peace, just as his daughter had.

"Yes, I didn't hear her come in, but I always get up at least once a night to check on the children. I found her at the foot of the bed with Katy and Donnie. She must have crawled in through one of the open windows in the parlor." She paused. He thought she must be looking at him, but the foyer was so dark he doubted she could actually see his face. The two of them were only shadows here.

His knees weakened with sudden relief. He stumbled over to the stairs and sat down, needing to put space between them. Weakened as he was, the urge to reach for her was nearly overwhelming.

"Has thee come to take her home?"

Something in her voice alerted him. "You don't think I should?"

"No, I don't. Please let us talk."

He heard her sit and the rocker begin to creak. "I'm just so tired," he said at last with his elbows on his knees, his hands hanging down limp.

"I said earlier that the war has left its mark on these little children. We do not know what they have suffered through, even if it was only to be separated from a parent. And thy wife died while thee were away, I would guess."

"Yes." The word was so low it scoured his throat.

"For some reason thee or I do not understand, Camie feels safe here. I do not think for a moment that she has anything to fear in thy home. I cannot believe that thee would hurt thy daughter in any way."

It was odd to sit here in almost total darkness speaking to a woman he barely knew about something he had not discussed with anyone but his mother. But her gentle words soothed the knot that was his heart.

"Perhaps if thy daughter is allowed to stay here, she will be able to get past her fears. Of course, if thee wants thy child home with thee, I would do nothing to prevent thee from carrying her home this night."

The darkness shielded him, freed him to speak plain truth. "I'm too tired to think."

"Why doesn't thee ask thy mother to come over during the day tomorrow and visit Camie? Let us see how Camie feels after being allowed to stay here for the night."

He knew he should go get Camie and carry her home. What would people say when they heard that he had left his only child at an orphans' home?

He didn't care.

He recalled how happy Camie had been at dinner. "I should have left her here instead of carrying her home. She…she hates the night."

"Ah." Felicity sounded as if this explained much to her.

"My mother and I try to be kind and loving and patient with her, but she fights sleep every night…and screams if she feels herself falling asleep." He passed a hand over his forehead, trying to rub away the strain.

"I see."

"We've tried letting her cry herself to sleep. That doesn't work so my mother rocks her to sleep every night and Camie screams…" Tears were barreling up through him, ready to spout past his self-control. He clamped his mouth shut, damming up his words and tears.

A hand came through the darkness and rested on his arm. "Thee has been carrying a heavy burden, friend."

Her touch comforted him. But what if Camie never wanted him? He folded a hand over his mouth to hold back words that had collected in his throat. All those years so far away, he'd imagined his little girl on his lap. He'd planned to read her fairy tales by the fire and in summer, push her in a swing in the backyard. Those thoughts of home and a little girl had sustained him through the unimaginable chaos and slaughter.

"I will pray that the God who loves us will show us the way to help thy little one. She is so dear. Such a lovely, sweet child. A blessing to thee surely. I always have taken God at His word. He says to trust Him and do good. We cannot heal Camie, but God and our love can."

Her kind, uncondemning words spoken in the dark soothed him like no others. He rose, his exhausted body aching, but with hope and peace flickering like a candle flame inside him. "I will go home now. My mother will come tomorrow. Thank you for your understanding."

"My understanding is limited, friend. But our God is not. Do not despair. Jesus said, 'Suffer the little children to come unto me and forbid them not, for of such is the kingdom of heaven.' We must trust God and do good. He will not fail us."

He forced himself to walk away from her comforting presence. He had often heard the scriptures she quoted, but for the first time they meant something real. Felt true. Somehow this young woman, this Miss Felicity Gabriel, was different from any other woman he'd met. Her smile dazzled him. Love flowed from her. Why should it surprise him that Camie had been drawn to her? She had drawn him, too.

What would tomorrow bring for them all? Would his sweet little girl ever run to him, asking him to swing her up into his arms?

Or would she remain lost to him—alienated—forever?

Chapter Five

Felicity and the children were still at breakfast at the long table on the back porch when Louise Hawkins ventured up the sidewalk.

"No!" Camie cried out and jumped from her chair. "I won't go home!" Camie tried to flee inside but was intercepted by Vista at the kitchen door.

Felicity leapt up and hurried to Camie, who was struggling with Vista. She lifted the girl in her arms. "Camie, thee is not being polite. Thy grandmother has just dropped by for a cup of coffee and to bid thee good morning." Felicity turned to Louise, who had paused on the first step. "Isn't that so, Louise Hawkins?"

"Yes, why, yes. I just stopped to chat with you and see how Camie is enjoying her visit with Katy."

Felicity nodded at the grandmother, who wore a bright smile that contrasted with her tired, worried eyes.

Louise came to the table and pulled out an empty chair. "Vista, I recall what excellent coffee you always make."

"I'll get you a cup right quick, ma'am." Vista nodded and turned back to the kitchen.

Camie still didn't let go of Felicity. This told Felicity

that some adult had treated her unfairly or capriciously in the past. Children who were lied to or cheated found it hard to trust. What kind of person had Camie's mother been? Felicity sat back down with Camie on her lap. Felicity hoped that Alice Crandall's daughter had been nothing like her.

And then she glimpsed something next door that ignited worry in her stomach. The pretty, dark-haired woman was standing in her backyard. Why was her neighbor staring at them?

"You act like a baby," Butch said to Camie with obvious disgust.

"Leave the little kid alone," Tucker said.

Felicity frowned at Butch, but Tucker's protection of Camie raised her spirits. Yet Camie was acting like a baby. What had happened when she was actually a baby? What had given her night terrors? Could Felicity hit upon a polite way of finding the answer to this question from Camie's grandmother?

"Camie's just a little girl," Tucker said. "Braids, don't worry. You're safe here. You heard Miss Felicity stand up for Butch yesterday." Felicity let this pass. Tucker's protective impulse intrigued her. What did it stem from? She thought of the boys she'd grown up with. Who had acted like Tucker and why? A possible answer glimmered in her mind. But she would wait for the right time to test her theory.

Vista delivered a cup of coffee to Louise. The somber lady smiled her thanks and sat quietly sipping.

Felicity tried to give no outward reaction to her neighbor, who was now pacing outside her back door and glaring at Felicity.

"What do I got to do today?" Tucker asked in a sour tone.

"I think that Abel wants thee in the barn and carriage

house again today, Tucker. Thee appears to have a gift of working with horses."

Tucker shrugged.

"We don't got to weed some more today, do we?" Willie asked in the same tone as Tucker.

"I'm afraid so. Vista wants thee to pull the weeds and grass in between the cobblestones in the path around the house." She added brightly, "But soon all of thee won't have as many chores to do. School began weeks ago. In a few days, thee will all be attending school, and only doing chores when thee comes home. After supper, thee will do thy homework and then go to bed."

Willie and Butch and Tucker all exchanged glances loaded with disbelief, resentment and rebellion. Felicity found herself sighing again. She had always loved school, but then she had never lived on the streets. She patted Camie and pulled the little girl's plate and fork to her, nudging Camie to start eating scrambled eggs again.

"Do I get to go to school, too?" Katy asked, looking pleased rather than irritated.

"How old is thee?" Felicity asked, watching the woman next door prop her hands on her hips and behave as if she were about to storm over. *Oh, dear.*

"I'm seven years old, Miss Felicity. Donnie's four."

A seven-year-old forced to care and provide for a four-year-old. For a moment, Felicity could not speak. Even though she had known this already, hearing their tender ages struck her deeply. Her heart hurt. She pressed a hand over it.

"Katy, I believe that you will be able to attend school then." Louise was carrying on the conversation for Felicity. "But Donnie will have to stay home and help Vista and Abel."

Katy fired up. "But—"

"Don't sass," Tucker barked. "No kid four years old can go to school. Any sap knows that." Then Tucker halted, looking shocked at his own outburst.

"I here," Donnie announced. "Here." And he pointed to the floor. "Katy school." He pointed at his big sister.

Felicity smiled. Donnie had already adapted to having a home. No doubt the younger the child, the easier that would be accomplished. She looked at Tucker. Had he ever gone to school? Should she keep him home and tutor him? She didn't know the answer to that. But she knew enough not to ask here and now.

She looked next door again, and was relieved to see her neighbor storm into her house and slam her back door. What was the fuss all about? Felicity's stomach jiggled with unsettled nerves.

"I've never been to school but I could go with you, Katy," Camie said from her place on Felicity's lap. "I'm seven, too."

"You could?" Katy's troubled face cleared. "That would be nice. We could go together."

Camie nodded vigorously and grinned at Katy.

Felicity called down the blessings from heaven on Katy, this sweet little girl who was somehow reaching Camie's troubled heart. Felicity sipped her hot coffee, hiding her joy though her mouth quivered with the desire to grin. *Thank thee, Father of the fatherless.*

But why hadn't Camie been sent to school this year and last year?

Soon the children finished eating. Hands, as usual, in his pockets, Tucker headed toward the carriage house. Willie and Butch grumbled their way to the sidewalk to pull weeds. Katy and Camie helped Vista gather the dishes and then followed like chicks behind a mother hen into the kitchen to help dry them.

Felicity told Donnie that he could get his box of blocks and play. Abel had bought them from a cabinet maker in town who made children's blocks from odd remnants of wood. Donnie beamed at her and hurried to his box at the other end of the porch.

Her family had encouraged her as well as her sisters to let the Light lead them to their life's work. And for a woman who had never meant to marry and have children, Felicity felt she wasn't doing too badly at starting to understand how to keep children busy.

She turned to Louise. "Camie spent the night and we had no trouble with her except once."

The grandmother pressed her lips together. "Did she cry out?"

"Just once. I went and talked to her a few minutes. Then she settled back down and fell asleep again."

"She fell asleep again?" Louise echoed softly as if not quite believing this. "What a miracle. Miss Gabriel, you don't know how this has worried my son and me. Made our lives miserable. I can't even keep any live-in help. No one can bear the nightly—" the woman shuddered "—ruckus. I just have a woman who comes in to clean every day."

That explained why Louise had opened the door when Felicity visited. "I don't want to pry but why hasn't Camie been to school?"

Louise shook her head. "My son stayed in the army for almost a year after the war. There was so much that still needed to be done. I wasn't able to take charge of Camie till he came home. Mrs. Crandall insisted Camie stay in her care."

"Mrs. Crandall didn't send her to school?"

Louise looked pained. "She said that Camie would be

tutored at home when the time was right. And that education for a girl wasn't that important."

Felicity reached a hand toward Louise's but before she could say another word of comfort, an angry voice assailed her from behind. She turned and swallowed a barely suppressed groan.

"What is my granddaughter doing in this…" Mrs. Crandall seemed to be unable to say the words.

"Children's home," Felicity offered.

She ignored this. "Louise Hawkins, what do you mean to be sitting here with this, this…interloper? Who wants to spoil our lovely boulevard with baseborn children no one wants—"

Baseborn children? Felicity reared up. "No one is going to slander innocent children, poor orphans with no one to protect—"

Mrs. Crandall turned her back on Felicity. "Louise—"

Louise rose, stiff with obvious disapproval. "Alice, I will not let you barge in here and tell me what to do with Camie. You've done enough harm to that poor child."

Felicity was worried that Camie might hear this exchange. She was just about to go to Camie and take her farther into the house when Vista slammed both kitchen windows shut.

Felicity turned back to the two women who were now quarreling in loud voices, nearly shouting.

Alice Crandall accused, "Your son never treated my Virginia right—"

"Your daughter was a conniving, spoiled little girl!" Louise snapped back. "There was a war on! How was my son supposed to stay here and cater to her every wish?"

"He didn't need to enlist when my daughter was expecting their first child! He could have waited—"

"Waited to be drafted?" Louise actually shook her

fist. "My son would never do such a cowardly thing! His country needed every able-bodied man and he volunteered!"

"He was needed here." Alice leaned forward, red-faced. "My poor, sweet Virginia needed him! My daughter died and your son lives! And he made the last years of Virginia's young life a misery!"

Felicity couldn't believe the harsh words that were being used like swords between these two well-dressed, genteel ladies.

"I will not speak ill of the dead," Louise said, standing with hands fisted. "But why did your daughter think that a whole nation of wives could do without their husbands as long as *she* had hers at home under her dainty thumb?"

Alice Crandall looked as if she had swallowed the wrong way. She turned an alarming bright scarlet.

Felicity was just about to call Vista for help when a familiar voice spoke up. "Miss Gabriel, sorry to bust in on things here, but I got those children we talked about the other day."

Felicity looked past the two women and there was Jack who shined shoes down near the wharf. She popped up from her seat, grateful for his arrival. "Jack! Welcome to the Barney Home for Children! Who has thee brought for me?"

Four children, two girls and two boys, ranging in age from around three to eight, clustered around Jack. Felicity grinned. None of these children would fail Vista's test for cleanliness. They were all scrubbed and dressed in faded but ironed and starched clothing. Their eyes were big and they stared at the two older women who had been shouting. A young woman probably around fourteen stood just behind Jack, glancing at the women and then away.

"Our church wouldn't be bringing them to you but

times are hard. We're barely able to feed our children," Jack apologized, his hat in his hand.

"I am delighted that thee has brought them." Felicity went down the steps and stooped down to be at eye level with the newcomers. "Children, I'm so happy that thee have come. We have been waiting for thee to arrive. Now tell me thy names." She looked at the eldest child.

Jack nudged the child's shoulder. "Speak right up. This lady likes children."

"I am Eugene, ma'am."

"Welcome, Eugene." Felicity shook his small hand.

Each of the other children said their names bashfully: Dee Dee, Violet and Johnny.

"Do you," Alice Crandall demanded in a fire-and-brimstone pulpit voice, "plan to mix black and white children?"

Felicity should have been able to predict how this woman would react. "Orphans come in all colors, Alice Crandall."

The woman responded with a loud huffing sound. "I will not tolerate this. I am going directly to my lawyer. I will not allow my only grandchild to be dropped off at an orphanage. If her father no longer wants her—"

This was the final pebble that released the avalanche. Outrage shot through Felicity like flames. From the little she'd seen of this woman, she imagined that Alice Crandall was responsible for much of Camie's fear.

"Thee is wrong," Felicity declared, facing the woman, "Tyrone Hawkins is just allowing Camie to visit the other children here. I don't know why that should upset thee."

Sniffing loudly, Alice Crandall marched down the steps and off toward the street.

As Felicity turned back to Jack, she realized that once again, her neighbor next door was peering out. Felicity guessed that her neighbor was responsible for this horrible scene. She must have been the one who had gone to Alice to tell her that she'd seen Camie at breakfast here. Felicity sighed and then scolded herself for it.

"Miss Gabriel, I thought that I would bring my granddaughter Midge along," Jack said, gesturing toward the young woman with the children. "She has been seeking work and is very good with children."

"Wonderful! Can she start now?"

Jack looked to Midge, who stepped forward and replied, "Yes, ma'am. Thank you, ma'am." The very pretty girl beamed and curtsied.

Felicity smiled in return. "Thee may call me—"

"You will call her Miss Felicity," Vista interrupted from the kitchen doorway, "even if she is a Quaker and doesn't want us to use *miss*."

Felicity shook her head. "And thee will call Vista miss, also. And the children and I will call thee Miss Midge. If one of us must be miss, then all of us will be miss."

Grinning, Midge bobbed another curtsey. Vista chuckled, shaking her head.

"Also, Jack, though the children will all have chores, we will need a day maid and two laundresses. Will thee send women thee recommend to do the work?"

Agreeing to this, Jack told the children to be good, shook Felicity's hand, and left to go to work.

Felicity sent the youngest boy to play with Donnie. She let Vista take Midge into the kitchen with the other children to get them set with chores for the day.

When it was just the two of them again, Felicity turned to Louise. "Thee may stay as long as thee wishes today. I hope that Tyrone will come this evening and we can discuss Camie and what is best for her."

Louise nodded and sighed long.

Felicity resisted the urge to join her. Alice Crandall was a problem, all right. And Felicity's spying neighbor, too. Felicity had expected some difficulty starting an orphan home. Evil always tried to stop good work. But could this unfriendly situation be changed for the better?

The shadows of twilight were about to be swallowed by night when Ty walked up to the Barney house. A visit at the end of the day from his mother-in-law's lawyer necessitated he discuss his daughter with Felicity. Alice Crandall was the most troublesome woman he had ever known. Why hadn't he seen that before he'd married Virginia? *She hid her true face because she wanted me to marry her daughter.* This thought was a boulder on his heart and lungs.

Then he thought of Felicity. To be honest with himself, Ty was drawn here just as his daughter had been. In a harsh world, Miss Gabriel seemed to beckon all the brokenhearted to her peaceful oasis. But would he disturb his daughter by coming here? He didn't want to upset the small progress they'd made.

Passing by the side bow window, he found that he'd guessed right about where Miss Gabriel would be. She and her housekeeper were sitting on the back porch, fanning themselves. Ty resisted the urge to tug at his stiff white collar. When would the cooling west winds of autumn finally arrive?

"Tyrone Hawkins," Felicity said, welcoming him with one of her irresistible smiles, "I was hoping thee would stop by this evening. Would thee like to go up and look in on Camie?"

"Is she…is she asleep?" He almost didn't want to ask. In fact, despite what his mother had reported to him over supper, he had been surprised to walk up Madison Boulevard and not hear Camie's screams.

"Of course. The children had a busy day. They weeded, dried dishes, played tag, jumped rope." Felicity smiled. "They nearly fell asleep in their baths."

"Baths?"

"Yes, we set up the large tub here on the porch and pull down the canvas shades. The girls go in first because for some reason," Felicity wrinkled her nose and gave him one of her teasing smiles, "they don't seem to get as dirty as the boys do. I find that freshly bathed children settle down more easily to sleep in warm weather."

"And it keeps the sheets cleaner longer," Vista commented.

Felicity chuckled.

The sound loosed something inside him. The back of his neck relaxed a degree and it didn't hurt to draw breath. How could this woman affect him the way she did? Her smiles and laughter released his somber mood like uncapping a bottle of warm sarsaparilla. A smile tugged at one corner of his mouth.

Felicity rose. "Let's take a walk." She came to him. He automatically offered her his arm. She refused it with a smile, but nodded toward the alley.

A wise choice. The two of them could speak more privately walking down the tree-lined alley. He thought of what nasty gossip would spread if she had accepted his gallantry and he'd been seen walking with this woman on his arm. Again, he found he didn't care very much.

He tried to tame his rampant thoughts about Camie, about this woman's marked effect on her—on him—to begin a coherent discussion. He gave up and said what he really didn't want to say. "You really didn't have any trouble getting Camie to sleep?"

She glanced up at him. "No, she followed Katy right to bed. I spoke with thy mother this morning. She was quite candid about Camie's night terrors. I have seen other children like Camie at an orphanage in Pennsylvania. I often helped the matrons get the orphans to bed at night. Some of them fought sleep or had nightmares that woke them up and frightened them."

Other children? "What did you do for these children?" He found himself walking closer and closer to her. Was it true? Was his Camie not alone in these disturbing fears?

"The head matron had worked with children for years. She said that calm, consistent care helped the most. And when the children wished, letting them talk about their nightmares and fear. And being sympathetic and reassuring."

"That worked?" he asked, gazing at her slender, graceful neck.

"It did for the children that I was caring for."

Her calm tone and reassurance nearly unmanned him to tears. He swallowed a sob threatening to break forth. For months and months, he and his mother had tried to help Camie get past her fear of sleep. Now for the first time, he had hope that Camie would come through this and in time be just a normal little girl. Was that possible?

Felicity paused and glanced up at him. "May I ask thee a few questions? Personal questions?"

He tensed. *No, I don't want to answer any questions.* He had hit bottom last night and they knew it. Still, answering her questions was the least he could do for the woman who had given him so much. "Yes," he said, mustering his nerve.

"When her mother died, how old was Camie?" The deep concern for his daughter radiated with each word.

This woman's essence, her spirit, seemed always to be reaching out, offering help where needed.

"Around five years old." Thoughts of Virginia made him see the difference between the two women. Felicity had the honesty and compassion that Virginia lacked.

"Do you think that Camie was a witness to her death?" Felicity asked.

Their footsteps crunched on the cinder-paved alley. Ty wanted to hide from shame. He was the father. He should have protected his child. He made himself reply. "Yes, her grandmother insisted she be at her mother's bedside."

Felicity nodded. "I'm sure that thy mother told thee about Alice Crandall's visit—"

"My mother-in-law's lawyer visited me today." This admission ignited the acid in his stomach.

Felicity halted and gazed up at him. "What did her lawyer say?" Her pale skin glowed in the dim light.

"If I leave her in your care, Mrs. Crandall will try to gain custody of my daughter." His voice shook, exposing his turbulent outrage.

Worry moved over Felicity's pretty face and then disappeared. "I doubt that her suit will succeed."

"Why?" The sky had turned nearly charcoal. Daylight was slipping away but he could still see her radiance—it drew him, soothed him, stirred him.

"It is very hard, isn't it, to sever a parent's right to a child? No doubt thy mother-in-law merely wants to make as much trouble for thee and me as she is able."

"Experience has taught me that is her usual goal," he muttered, old insults stirring inside. "In everything." Yet overshadowing his anger, he sensed a fine thread of trust forming between Felicity and him.

"It is sad but true. Some people delight in causing strife and stirring up contention. Since our first meeting, I have been praying for Alice. But I sense that the walls around her heart are thick and towering." Felicity shook her head in obvious sadness. An invisible warmth flowed from her to him.

How did this woman care so much? This world was so filled with grief, pain and cruelty. He sucked in air, keeping his unruly emotions under strict control.

She looked up at him. "Do you mean to leave Camie with me until she is better, recovered from these night terrors?"

In the near darkness, he gazed down into her glistening blue eyes. Inside, he heard a preview of all the squawking and criticism he would get for doing what she proposed.

"People will think it odd that thee have given thy daughter into my care," Felicity spelled out for him as if he might not know what she was really saying.

"I know they will." Unable to stop himself, he took her hand. "But I must do what is best for Camie." *I must make up for the harm I may have done her.* He longed to tell this woman all about it, about his disastrous marriage to Virginia, the war and how badly he'd handled coming home to Camie.

Felicity squeezed his hand. "I hope that I can help her, and thee has my promise that I will do whatever lies within my power to put these night terrors behind her and return home to thee."

Help had come at last. Ty drew her hand to his lips and kissed it. As soon as he did this, shock went through him in waves.

Felicity looked startled and gently pulled her hand from his. She turned and began walking again.

He could have kicked himself around the block a few times. Many eligible widows in town had already cast lures toward him. He had deftly kept himself from giving any woman any reason to hope that he would marry again. After his marriage, he wasn't interested in starting a romantic relationship with anyone. And certainly this fine woman was only interested in his daughter and her orphans. What had come over him? "I beg your pardon."

"I have been wondering," she said. "Does thee play baseball?"

The question took him so by surprise that it forced a chuckle from him. "What?"

She paused and looked up at him, so earnest in the pale last glimmer of day. "I know that soldiers played baseball during their days of waiting between marches and battles. I think it is an excellent game. Would thee believe that I have swung a bat a few times?"

He chuckled again, the sensation releasing his pent-up tension. What an unusual woman. "About you, Miss Gabriel, I would believe anything."

She grinned. "I was quite a tomboy as a girl."

He grinned in return, his mood suddenly lighter still. "Yes, miss, I have played baseball. Why do you ask?"

"I think it would be beneficial if the town children and my children played together and got to know each other. And I think baseball would be a good game to start with. What does thee think?"

What did he think? He thought most parents wouldn't want their children associating with orphans. Hating to disappoint her, he clasped his hands behind him and said in a repressive tone, "There is a deep stigma attached to being an orphan."

"I know. It is hard to believe that people somehow hold a child accountable for being orphaned. I do not understand such illogical thinking."

"It's hard," he agreed, suddenly sorry he had no chance of changing this for her.

"My mother told me she thought it was somehow related to people's fears of dying and leaving their own children orphaned. She said orphans remind them that the same thing could happen to their dear children."

He gave a sound of reluctant recognition. "That sounds logically illogical." The woman beside him unconsciously beckoned him to come closer.

"And people tend to think that people are poor because of laziness when that often isn't true." Felicity sighed. "Thy mother-in-law called my children baseborn, a wicked thing to say of any child. How is a child responsible for having been born out of wedlock?"

He'd had these same thoughts over the years. He wished there was some way to shield her from the realities of this world. But what could one man or woman do against such irrational prejudices?

"Will thee come and help the boys and girls learn to play baseball? And will thee invite children of thy friends to join in our games? I will prepare the lawn near the alley with bases and I've already bought several bats and balls." She looked up into his face expectantly.

In spite of his honest intention to the contrary, they had drawn closer as the darkness had grown. For once, she wasn't wearing her plain bonnet. Now moonlight illuminated her lovely face surrounded by strawberry curls that refused to stay pulled back into her severe bun. His fingers tingled with the imagined feeling of those vibrant, reddish-golden curls. Her blue eyes revealed her open soul of kindness and charity. How did she manage the bravery it took to confront and try to change the ways of their miserable, often cruel world?

"I don't seem to be able to refuse you," he murmured,

his hands straying up to those tempting curls. He let his fingers comb through them, which caused him to brush her soft cheek. He sprang to life inside as if he'd just connected with sunlight. He was suddenly awake, so very awake. The short inches between them crackled with awareness. He lowered his face toward her mouth.

She took a step back and turned away. "I'm so happy to hear thee say that. Thee will do such good for these children." She turned quickly around, heading back toward the Barney house.

He would have thought his touch had not affected her, but her voice quavered just enough to tell him she had not remained unmoved.

He took a deep, steady breath. He had nearly kissed her, and out in the common view. The shock of this vibrated through him. He would have to be very careful, very. Tonight he'd been drawn against all logic toward her. This woman was obviously devoting her life to the care of others. And he still cringed at the thought of remarriage. His course was clear. No more weakening to her innocent allure.

"Look." She pointed toward her neighbor's house. "That little boy tugs at my heart. He looks so lonely."

Ty followed her direction and glimpsed Percy Partridge standing in his window, looking out. The child's form was backlit by candlelight. Ty watched as the child was pulled from the window and the light went out.

"Poor boy," Felicity murmured. "He never gets to have any fun. He just stares out the windows at our boys playing."

Just then, an outrageous idea burst into Ty's mind. An idea that would allow him to help Felicity in her mission, and give back a small measure of what she'd given him. It was outrageous, yes—but why not?

* * *

Felicity waited until the next evening to carry out her plan. She had asked Tucker to help her set up the baseball field. All the other children were doing chores or playing on the back porch under the watchful eyes of Vista and Midge.

Felicity's memory tried to take her back to her walk with Ty. No doubt Ty was merely being appreciative of her help. But the sensations she'd experienced walking beside him, was still experiencing... She clamped down on the memory and turned her mind back to the matter at hand. She had been doing a lot of thinking about how to approach Tucker, how to get at the truth. She had finally decided just to talk to him alone.

"Here is the piece of paper that will be our guide to carving out bases in the grass," Felicity said, showing him, "and we will need to dig shallow base lines for the runners to follow to each base."

"I don't know what you're talking about," Tucker said with irritation. He held two hoes in hand.

"Look." With the point of one hoe, she traced in the dirt a rough diamond. "Here is the baseball diamond with its four bases." She gestured to each of the four points of the diamond. "The pitcher throws the ball from here to home plate. The batter tries to hit the ball. If he succeeds, he tries to make it to first base before he's tagged with the ball. How long has thee known Butch and Willie?"

"A couple of years—" Tucker stopped and his head reared up. "I don't know what you mean. I never seen them before you brought them home."

She had taken him by surprise as she'd planned. Still, she kept her voice and expression neutral. "Lying is quite unnecessary, Tucker. I guessed that thee three knew each other the first time I saw thee together. How does thee know Willie and Butch?"

"I told you. I just met them here when you walked them into the yard." He propped his hands on his hips and glared at her.

"Very well." She would have to try to get more of the truth from Tucker on a different topic. "Let's begin digging up the sod for the bases. I'll have to ask Ty Hawkins about what to use for bases. It seems to me that wood might be slippery."

Tucker eyed her, but took the hoe and began disturbing the sod for home plate. Felicity walked to what would be second base and began cutting through the thick green sod, too. Tucker's fondness toward Camie must have a root. What could it be? She worked in silence for a time, then went over to comment on Tucker's progress. "Very good. How much younger was thy sister?"

This time the ploy of the unexpected question did not work. Tucker merely glared at her and turned away. Nonetheless, she glimpsed a flicker of something in his eyes, something like pain. This added weight to her belief that Tucker had had a little sister. No doubt a little sister he had lost.

Felicity ached for him, for all the children this world judged sullied, tainted by death and poverty and irresponsible parents.

"Hey!" a voice hailed her. "Hey! Is this the orphanage?"

Felicity turned toward the boulevard and saw a man climbing down from a farm wagon. Waiting on the buckboard seat, a crushed-looking woman in a threadbare dress and bonnet looked after the man.

"What can I do for thee?"

"I just drove into town to do business and somebody

told me there was an orphanage here now. I'm looking for a couple of boys—strong ones." The man eyed Tucker. "This boy looks about right. I need someone who knows how to work. Boy, get any stuff you got. We'll take you, and lady, you got another one just about like him?"

Felicity was flabbergasted. Tucker just stared at the man who spit tobacco out the side of his mouth.

"Well, get moving, boy. I don't give orders twice. You'll mind or you'll be sorry."

"I'm afraid that thee misunderstands what Barney Home for Children is. We take in children—"

"Lady, I don't have time for a lot of folderol. Now I'm ready to take this boy off your hands. What's the problem?"

Felicity drew herself up and looked the unpleasant man in the eye. "There is no problem. Tucker is not going with thee."

"What?" The man took a step toward her menacingly.

She didn't flinch. "Nor any other child here. I will only allow orphans to be adopted by loving families who want children, not unpaid workers. In case thee hasn't heard, slavery has been outlawed."

The man glowered at her, but Tucker moved the hoe so that it became a weapon. "You better clear out, mister," Tucker said. "Miss Felicity isn't a woman to mess with."

The man cursed, turned and stormed back to his wagon. He drove away without a backward glance.

The man's curses set her teeth on sharp edge. "Thank thee, Tucker."

"I can't stand bullies," he said. "But that's what got me into trouble in the first place."

Still seething over the man's effrontery, Felicity contemplated asking him what he meant by those cryptic words. But decided to let it pass. For now.

They both turned back to their work. Shock and outrage at the man's attitude consumed her for a time, giving way to misgivings about Tucker, Butch and Willie.

She couldn't think of why she should be filled with such uncertainty. Why shouldn't the three homeless boys know each other from life down on the wharf? But why would Tucker lie about it? She shook her head, unable to put a name to her fear.

Bright and early on an October Saturday morning, Tyrone Hawkins showed up at her back porch, dressed in a casual shirt and trousers for the first baseball practice. It was the first time Felicity had seen him without a formal suit or judge's robes. But the biggest change in him was due to his cheerful expression. The sight had quickened her pulse.

She stuttered her good morning and introduced the children to Ty. Camie came to her and buried her face in Felicity's skirts. She decided it best not to comment on this.

The main reason for baseball was to bring together the town children and her orphans. Yet Tyrone had come alone. She murmured a question to Tyrone about the possibility of other children coming. He merely shrugged, but a smile lingered in his eyes. What did that mean? And why was she suddenly breathless?

Soon she had all the children outside, and Tyrone was showing Tucker how to hold a bat. Then movement caught Felicity's eye. She turned to see a man walking from her neighbor's yard to hers, clasping hands with a little boy on each side of him.

"Partridge!" Tyrone greeted him. "I see you brought Ernest as well as Percy."

Felicity goggled at the sight. Percy in her yard? And

he looking decidedly different. No ruffles or knickers. He was dressed in plain pants and a dark shirt, as was the other child.

"Miss Gabriel, may I introduce you to my old friend, Eldon Partridge, his son Percy and his nephew Ernest Brown."

Felicity greeted them, still not quite believing her eyes. And then from the alley came another friend of Tyrone's and his son and daughter. Felicity was introduced to them and then the batting practice started.

Thrilled by success, she moved away and sat in the shade of an oak tree with Donnie and Camie. The rest of the children were lined up, waiting for their turn at bat and calling encouragement to the other children as they tried to master how to hold the bat. Donnie was watching raptly. Every once in a while, Camie would chance a glance at her father. Felicity fought the urge to do the same. She sat with her back against the broad trunk and praised God for Tyrone Hawkins.

After a while she looked up and noticed that Percy's mother was standing at the line of bushes that partially separated the two yards. Concern tempered Felicity's elation. She pondered for a few minutes and then rose. *Lord, make me a peacemaker.*

Chapter Six

Felicity ventured toward Mrs. Partridge. Camie trailed after her, hurrying to catch her hand. Donnie didn't move; he was concentrating on the baseball lesson.

"Mrs. Partridge," Felicity said, using the title *Mrs.* because she didn't know the woman's first name. "I am happy to see that thy son is going to learn baseball—"

"You're happy, are you?" Mrs. Partridge snapped. "You are a meddlesome intruder in our town. You've caused trouble from the day you arrived."

Felicity stared at the woman, disbelieving her ears.

"Don't you say mean things about Miss Felicity," Camie declared, stepping away from the shelter of Felicity's skirt. "She loves children and protects them. Percy is a bad boy—"

Felicity stooped down and drew Camie to her. "Thank thee, Camie, but thee must not scold an adult. It is not polite."

"See!" Mrs. Partridge said as if to an audience. "You have alienated this child from her own home and are teaching her to be impudent."

Felicity rose and faced the woman. "Camie is visiting here for a while. Pray, what business is that of thine?"

The woman stepped forward. "Meddler! Old maid!"

Felicity looked into the woman's eyes and saw tears. Her anger dissolved like sugar in warm water. She chose to ignore the other impolite epithet. Why was it rude to call a woman unmarried? Bachelor was an honorable title. "I am very sorry that thee is so upset, but what have I done to meddle in thy affairs?"

"My Percy is a delicate child." The woman began wiping away tears. "He can't play with other boys. He'll get hurt." The woman glared fiercely. "And what's wrong with how I dress Percy? That's how Queen Victoria dresses her sons!" With this parting shot, Mrs. Partridge whirled away and ran, weeping, into her home.

Stunned, Felicity watched her go. She stopped herself from following. Her father had always told her not to try to reason with unreasonable people. Had someone, perhaps Ty, said something about Percy's clothing? She turned, drawing Camie back with her to Donnie. They sat down again on the dry grass and watched Katy come up for her lesson in batting. Felicity felt drained. Who might appear next? Did Alice Crandall hate baseball?

"You can hit the ball, Katy!" Camie called to her friend.

Felicity stroked Camie's hair and then kissed the top of Donnie's head. In only a few weeks, she had gained ten children, children who were now getting enough food, clothing and love. This was worth any unpleasantness from her neighbors. God would have to take care of the rest of the town. And what they thought of her and her work.

"Miss Gabriel," the builder called to her from the back porch, "I've come with the plans for you to approve!"

She'd known she wouldn't be left in peace. Suppressing a sigh, she rose. "Camie, will you stay here and keep Donnie safe while I go in with the builder?"

Camie nodded and moved closer to the little boy, her eyes not straying from the batting practice. Felicity felt herself smiling broadly. This was the first time that Camie had not clung to her at a parting. Felicity hurried to the builder, eager for the renovations. Mildred Barney would have been so happy today.

Dalton stood down the alley concealed by a grouping of fir trees. He'd come to see the Quaker's orphan home for himself. As he watched the judge teaching the kids some game with a ball and stick, anger rose in him like steam in a kettle. Not only had she nabbed Tucker, but Willie and Butch, too, three of his best boys. He'd have to put a stop to this. Then he recalled something he'd heard from his crony on this side of the river. The Quaker had taken in the judge's daughter. His anger turned to glee. He knew just what to do to ruin this Quaker and get her run out of town.

A week later, Ty timed his visit after what he thought would be bedtime at the Barney house. His mother had told him that Felicity wanted to discuss some matter with him, so here he was. Against his better judgment. Miss Felicity Gabriel threatened his ability to show a bland face to the world. That had been very important once. But Miss Gabriel demanded honesty. She demanded action. What would she want from him this time?

Vista let him inside. "Miss Felicity is upstairs putting your child to bed with Katy and Donnie."

He would have liked to watch his child go to sleep but kept this to himself. If Camie was able to lie down and go to sleep without any distress, he didn't want to do anything that would upset that. "I'll wait, then. Miss Gabriel said she had something she wanted to discuss with me."

"You come and sit out on the porch. This cool north wind has tamed the mosquitoes. They aren't busy tonight." Vista led him through the hall. "I'll go let Miss Felicity know that you're here."

He considered cautioning her not to let his daughter know. Vista must have guessed this. "Don't worry," she said, walking away. "I won't upset your little girl."

Choking down the humiliation of others knowing he was unwanted by his own blood, he sat on the wooden loveseat. He leaned forward, his hands hanging between his knees. The sound of crickets heralded the first touch of fall. Of course, there would be many more hot days when Indian summer came, but autumn was whispering its coming tonight. He tried to swallow down the bitterness on his tongue, bitterness which had come with the destruction of all his hopes about what life could be after the war.

"Tyrone Hawkins," Felicity greeted him as she walked onto the porch, "I'm so happy thee has come."

He rose and lost himself in her bright eager eyes. "I wish you'd call me Ty. I've always hated Tyrone." The words were out of his mouth before he knew it.

"As thee wishes. Please sit." She sat on a chair across from him. "The cooler temperature is lovely, isn't it?"

He did not want to discuss the weather. "Why aren't you married?" He was shocked by his rude, personal question. What had gotten into him?

She chuckled. "I am not interested in marriage. I know that makes me odd, a spinster by choice. But I want to devote my life to bettering the lives of children. That is my calling from God. And that brings me to something I wish to discuss with thee…if I may?"

"That's why I came. What's on your mind?" He took himself firmly in hand. Why was it that this woman provoked words and actions from him that no one else did or ever had?

"When we first met," she began eagerly, "we discussed the fact that Illinois law makes no distinction between lawbreakers over the age of reason and those younger."

He nodded.

"I think the laws must be changed."

He stared at her. *Just like that?* "Change the laws?"

She nodded decidedly. "Yes, how does one go about changing a law in Illinois?"

He sat back and studied her. How did she muster such pluck? And what did she want him to do in order to change these laws? He quelled the childish urge to fidget. "I suppose the first step would be to write to the state senator and representative for our district in the state legislature."

"I was thinking that might be the way to start. Every state is different and I know nothing of Illinois law. You do and I was hoping…" She paused and caught her lower lip with her teeth like a girl.

"Yes?" he asked, charmed by her sudden shyness.

"I was hoping that *thee* would write the letter."

His eyes widened. "Me?"

"Yes, I will of course write one. But men in government rarely pay attention to women, unfortunately. If thee, a judge, would write the letter, it would have to be taken seriously. Doesn't thee think so?"

He couldn't argue with her logic. Her letter would be dismissed as mere feminine sentiment. His would be read and considered seriously. He nodded. But was that all?

"And perhaps thee could encourage the county prosecutor and thy other law friends and acquaintances to send letters, too?"

He grinned. Did this woman ever stop? "Aren't you busy enough with the children here? Too busy to set in motion a task like this?"

Her brows rose quizzically. "I have an interest in all children. And I don't think that treating children as adults in court makes good sense. What does a child sent to prison learn except how to improve his criminal skills? In 1813 in England, Elizabeth Fry visited Newgate Prison and found three hundred women and children living in appalling conditions."

Ty sat back, watching her light up like the dawn. This woman was nothing like his wife, who had never cared about anything except the latest *Godey's Lady's* fashion plates.

"That was the beginning of prison reform in England," she said, her voice gaining intensity. "And our own Dorothea Dix has worked most of her life to improve living conditions for the mentally ill here and abroad, not to mention her work during the war for our wounded at President Lincoln's request."

He held up both hands in surrender, trying not to chuckle like a pleased lad. Trying not to reach out and brush her soft, tempting cheek. He pushed down these odd reactions. "I will write the letter and I will see if I can persuade my colleagues to do likewise." After the way she'd taken Camie in, how could he refuse her anything? "Anything else? Do you want me to run for governor or senator?"

She laughed. "I thank thee. Truly. And also I owe thee thanks for thy batting lessons on Saturday. The children were thrilled. They keep asking me when thee will come.

They are so eager for this Saturday." In spite of her cheery words, her face took on a somber cast.

Her change of mood deflated his momentary happiness. "What's wrong?"

She looked up, her expression arrested. "I was happy to see thee did not come alone. I was so grateful for thy persuading four fathers to bring their children here last Saturday. But I fear Mrs. Partridge was very vexed. I hope I didn't sow seeds of discord between a husband and wife."

"I don't think you sparked Mrs. Partridge's dislike of your work. My mother-in-law did that. Partridge is an old friend. He and I served together in the war. He feels his absence in his son's early life keenly. He has been upset with his wife and how she refuses to let Percy be a boy. He just couldn't figure out how to change things."

"I see." She remained still, head down, probably deep in thought. Probably wondering how to help Martha Partridge, who would like to box Felicity's ears if she could and still look the lady. He shook his head, admiring Felicity.

"How…how is Camie doing?" he forced himself to ask, his throat swelling, constricting his airway.

Felicity looked up. "She is doing better, sleeping and eating well. She is very attached to Katy and to me. I try to encourage her to spend most of her time with Katy. But she will be playing with Katy and stop and come to find me. I think she needs to know that I am here for her, and I won't leave her. I hope that soon she will begin to feel safe." She gazed at him as though trying to read his heart.

Regret dragged like a rough, heavy sack over his raw, ragged soul. He must let her know some of what had caused Camie's problems. "When she…when Camie was born," he began, "I wasn't here. And I was only able to

visit twice on furlough. Both times she was still a baby."
He drew in air, fighting his feeling of failure. He had not
been able to be the father he had wanted to be. The war,
the terrible war. His hand itched to cover his scar which
he felt certain must be part of the reason he frightened
his child. "You said the other day that the war had affected these children."

"Yes, it is a dreadful weight they all carry. Katy's father was killed in the war and her mother died about a
year ago. The two of them had no family. A woman took
them in for a while, but mistreated Donnie so Katy took
him and ran away. Can thee imagine a seven-year-old
trying to provide for herself and her little brother? The
thought hurts my heart." She pressed her fist over her
breastbone as if she were indeed in pain.

He felt a sympathetic pain with her. "Do you think that
Camie will ever be able to come home?" he spoke, rushing his words, almost panting as if he'd been sprinting.

She smiled. "Yes, I do think she will want to come
back to thee and Louise. We must give her time to heal. I
hope that thee and thy mother will visit here every day. I
think that will help Camie begin to see thee as friends of
mine and of all the children here. The other children let
your daughter know how much they enjoyed thy coming
and teaching them baseball. Actions like these will begin
to build a bridge between thee and thy daughter. I hope."

He nearly shouted at her to stop, stop giving him hope.
This pushed him to his feet. Suddenly he wanted to run
down the street, to escape. He didn't want to hope. That
way lay the possibility of being hurt more. If he had chosen a wife wisely and not just based on how pretty she
was, this all might have been avoided.

He turned his back to Felicity who'd become his guide,
his hopeful link to his daughter, and said, "I will trust

you. Do you think she's asleep? I'd like to look in on her." He put distance between himself and this disquieting woman.

"Come." She motioned to him. "We'll go up together. We'll peek in on her." She led him inside and up the steps to the second floor. She held her index finger in front of her lips and then opened the door to one of the bedrooms. Ty noted that the deconstruction of walls had begun farther down the hall.

Felicity turned and waved him in.

He stepped silently into the room. On a high bed, his daughter slept on one side of Katy with Donnie on the other side. Instantly, he saw how much more comforting sleeping with two other children would be to a frightened little girl. He tiptoed over to Camie and gazed down at her. Love for his only child poured from him. Suddenly he was able to draw an easy breath. She was happy at last. She was sharing a bed in an orphans' home, but she was happy.

He glanced toward Felicity, who stood at the foot of the bed. Her head was bowed and he was certain she was praying for him and Camie. He tried not to notice what a lovely picture she made in prayer. She was a woman dedicated to children, not a woman who wanted a husband. And evidently God listened to this woman. *Thank God for Felicity Gabriel.*

Felicity couldn't get last night's conversation with Ty out of her mind. In a starched white apron, she stood in the warm, clean kitchen, kneading bread dough beside Vista, who baked eight loaves twice a week. Felicity rolled and folded the soft, pliant dough. The dread issue of registering the children for school had become the next hurdle. Today, Felicity was discovering if any of the children knew their letters or numbers so she would be able to discuss the learning level of each child with the town teachers. She hoped they would welcome her children.

"Miss Felicity," Camie said, "see? I made a flower." The children, sitting around the table had been given dough to form into whatever shapes they wanted.

Felicity looked over her shoulder. "Is it a daisy? A pretty one?"

"Yes." Camie glowed.

Felicity gazed at the child. Ty had asked her why she wasn't married. Why?

"Snake," Donnie said, pointing at his long curve of dough. "Snake."

"And a very fine snake, too," Felicity said, enjoying the yeasty scent of the dough. Images from her conversation with Ty the night before kept coming to mind. He'd grinned when she'd suggested he persuade his colleagues to write letters, too.

"Katy, it's your turn," Felicity prompted. "How high can you count?"

"To twenty." Katy did so, holding up fingers one by one for each number.

Camie knew how to count to ten but nothing else. Felicity wondered again about Alice Crandall and her daughter. A child of seven in a good home should know her letters and numbers by sight and Camie did not. "Very good, Katy."

Last night had meant so much to her. Being able to discuss weighty matters with a man had been a treat. Most men thought women unable to discuss politics, but Ty Hawkins had taken it in stride.

Vista spoke up briskly. "Now, children, the bread is ready for its first rising. You leave your dough and I'll cover it with a moist cloth. You all go out and wash your hands and play in the backyard."

Felicity took off her apron, hung it on a peg and headed outside, too. She ambled toward the carriage house. It was a perfect day—bright sunshine, blue sky, white puffy clouds.

Still, she felt the burden of concern. When Ty had gazed at his sleeping child, he had worn such a look of defeat and pain. She inhaled, filling her lungs, trying to temper the weight of her concern for them. She must focus on today's chore. She still needed to find out if Tucker knew his letters and numbers. And she would broach the subject of school with him. She wanted him to get an education but doubted he would agree. Praying, she approached him where he sat talking to Abel. Both of them rose.

"Abel, I'd like to walk with Tucker for a bit."

Abel bobbed his head. "He's been doing good work."

Felicity smiled. "I have no doubt." She motioned and Tucker followed her into the alley.

This was where Ty had walked beside her not long ago—where he had kissed her hand. The spot his lips had touched still tingled at the memory. She covered it with her other hand. She cleared her throat. "I will get right to it. Tucker, does thee know thy letters?"

"You mean the alphabet?"

"Yes."

"Yeah, I know them when I see them."

She paused at the sandy edge of the alleyway. This near the river, sand was generously mixed in the soil. "Will thee trace an *A* for me in the sand?"

Tucker gave her a disgusted look and stooped and traced an *A* in the dirt.

"Now a *Q*, please."

Tucker traced a *Q*.

"Can thee read words?" She started walking again.

She heard Katy and Camie's voices. Suddenly she heard again Ty's words: *I will trust you.* For some reason, her spirits lifted every time she thought of her conversation with Ty last night.

"Some." Tucker walked alongside her, his hands stuffed in his pockets.

"Numbers?" she asked. Overhead, geese honked, flying south. She shaded her eyes and looked up. The seasons were changing. How long would Camie stay with her? How could she reunite her with her family?

"I can count to a hundred and I know what numbers look like." Tucker also gazed up at the migrating flock.

"Good." She paused again. "Does thee want to go to school, Tucker?"

"No."

She recalled that this was the exact place where she was certain Ty had almost taken her in his arms. Turning away, she blushed warmly. "Very well." She headed toward the house, away from these dangerous memories. After a few steps, she glanced back and noticed Tucker had not moved. "Tucker?"

"That's it? I say no and you say okay?" He sounded almost miffed with her.

She faced him, suppressing a smile. This boy never liked it when she didn't react as he expected. But then he had often surprised her, too, as with his protectiveness of the younger children, especially Camie. "Tucker, I want very much for thee to get an education. But I think it will be best if I tutor thee at home this year. Thee will need to catch up."

"So you think you'll make me go to school next year?" His tone was belligerent.

She chuckled. "No, I think I will *allow* thee to go to school next year, if that is what thee wants."

He stared at her, obviously disbelieving. "I can't figure you out. What's your game?"

There it was again, his distrust. Would she ever be able to shatter his hard shell of suspicion? "My game is helping children who need help. That is my only game." She waved for him to go back to Abel. He turned and went back to the horses he loved. She hoped that she had planted seeds that might bloom in the future.

Ty's face came to mind again. She hoped she was planting seeds of reconciliation for this good man and his child. Her honesty also scolded her. Was she starting to have more than friendly feelings for Ty? She pursed her lips. That would not do. She must cultivate only camaraderie with Ty, nothing more. Of course that was the right plan. Still, she couldn't forget the way he looked at her sometimes—as if she were a beautiful woman. No man, not even Gus, had ever looked at her quite that way.

Dalton stood, looking out the grimy window in the warehouse loft. Murky dawn was leaking out from darkness. His head hurt from imbibing too much last night. He rubbed his throbbing temples. That reminded him of his other headache. He'd been too busy to take care of matters with that interfering Quaker across the river. He'd worked it all out and his plan would work.

He walked over to one of the lumps on the floor and kicked it. The girl of about twelve got up, rubbing her side and glaring.

"Make the morning gruel, girl, and get the rest of the brats up. Time's a-wasting." *Time's almost up for you, Quaker.*

* * *

On the next Monday morning, Felicity walked up to the white clapboard primary schoolhouse only three blocks from home to enroll the children. Would Alice Crandall's vile gossip make this a difficult day? *Father, I don't want these children hurt. Protect their hearts today.*

Behind her, like a parade, all the children except for Donnie and Tucker walked in a double row. Camie and Katy were holding hands. Felicity's nerves were taut. And she had the strange feeling that someone was following her. But every time she looked around, she saw no one. Just nerves, no doubt. And, of course, the repeated experience of having Alice Crandall coming out of nowhere to scold and accuse her caused her an unsettled stomach.

On the school grounds, children were calling to each other, playing on the swings and jumping rope. Several large burr oaks, whose ruffled leaves were turning bronze, surrounded the school yard. Her children eyed the town children and vice versa. The town children started whispering and pointing. Felicity moved quickly to set the right tone.

This school, for children from first grade through fourth, had two rooms and two teachers. The women, wearing severe black dresses and dour expressions, were standing outside the school door, one on each side. Felicity marched up to the one who looked older. "Good day, I am Felicity Gabriel. I've come to register my children for school."

The woman with gray at her temples looked at her and then the children. No doubt the mix of children of different colors was what made her raise one eyebrow.

The teacher with a disapproving twist to her mouth asked, "Are you that Quaker who has started an orphans' home?"

"I prefer to call it a children's home." Felicity beamed at her, ready to object to any prejudice with the invincible cheerfulness she'd learned from her mother. "Who can help me register the children?"

The two grim teachers scowled back and forth. "This school is for the children of residents of this town," the older one said.

Felicity replied, "Yes, and these children are residents of this town."

"But they don't have parents," the younger teacher pointed out, her lower lip dipping down farther in more disapproval.

"No, but now they have me," Felicity said with a touch of steel in her tone. "I am here to register these children for school. Which of thee will handle this?"

The two teachers exchanged glances and then the older one said, "Follow me, please."

Shrugging off the insistent feelings of someone watching her, Felicity waved the children to follow her inside the schoolhouse. In a few minutes, the children's names had been registered and they had been divided between the two teachers. When Katy and Camie were assigned to the same class, Felicity was relieved and grateful. The children were curtly dismissed to the school yard to play.

Just as Felicity started to leave, the older teacher said sourly, "You know, in this school we don't spare the rod and spoil the child."

Felicity raised her chin. "All my children are very well behaved. So I must let thee know that I will not allow my children to be mistreated in any way just because they have suffered the misfortune of losing their parents."

At the door, the younger teacher, her thin face sinking into critical lines, commented, "I see that it's true. Judge Hawkins has abandoned his own daughter."

Felicity stared at the uncharitable woman and had to fight her natural heated reaction to this provocative statement. She gave a tight smile. "Camie is visiting with me. The war affected all the children in this town. And indeed, in this nation, in one way or another. Ty Hawkins is a fine man and is doing the best he can for his daughter. I hope none of thee will make the mistake of trying to cause Camie to feel unwelcome here. Or to make her feel that her father does not have the right to do whatever he thinks best for his child. Ty Hawkins would not appreciate it."

Without another word but with a cheery wave to the children, she marched away. A block from school, she glanced over her shoulder but still saw no one. She heard the school bell ringing and said a prayer. The two unwelcoming teachers had not given her any confidence in their ability to nurture her children as well as teach them. And she couldn't shake the feeling that someone was very curious about her and her movements. She headed for home, resisting the urge to look over her shoulder again.

Felicity woke suddenly in the dark.

"Help! Help!"

She bolted from her bed.

She heard the sound of someone falling downstairs, loud bumping and grunts and groans.

"Stop!" a voice yelled. And then a yelp of pain. A little girl screamed. A crash and glass breaking.

Hand trembling, Felicity lit a candle and ran barefoot into the dark hall. Now she recognized the shouting. It was Tucker's voice. She ran down the stairs toward the sounds.

"What's happening?" she called out.

"Miss Felicity! Help!" Camie shrieked.

Felicity raced into the dining room. A man, his face covered with a cloth bag, was swinging a chair at the cracked bow window. Tucker gripped the back of the man's jacket. The intruder swung around and hit Tucker in the head with the chair. The boy fell.

Felicity screamed.

The man swung the chair at her, hitting her on the side of the head, knocking the candle from her hand. She bumped against the walnut buffet. And then fell hard onto the oak floor.

More glass breaking. The candle rolled against the long sheers at the bow window. They burst into flame, lighting the room suddenly. The intruder scrambled out the shattered bow window.

Tucker jumped up. At the window, he yelled, "Abel! Get your gun! Abel!"

Felicity rolled to her feet. Dazed, she looked around for something to fight the fire with. She ran into the hall, picked up the needlepoint rug and raced to the burning wall. She began beating the flames with the rug.

"The children! Tucker! Go get the children and Midge out of their beds!" she ordered. "Get them outside! Fire!" she shrieked out the window. "Fire!"

A gun discharged. A man cursed. Another gunshot.

Felicity beat at the fire. The wallpaper burst into red-orange flames. Sparks and ash flew around her head. Then Vista was there beside her beating the flames, too. Outside, people began appearing at the bow window. The cry of "Fire! Fire!" burst out from everywhere, echoing, echoing.

Felicity began coughing with the smoke. Then Vista turned and struck her back with a rug. Felicity dropped to the floor, coughing, coughing. The front door burst open.

Felicity could feel the pounding of feet through the floor. She tried to speak, but only coughed violently, retching.

"Get Miss Felicity outside!" Vista shouted. "She's been burned!" Then Vista began coughing, too, staggering forward.

Light-headed, Felicity felt herself being dragged by her wrists. She wanted to get up, but the hands dragging her were stronger than she. When the hands dropped her, she lay on the chill dew-dampened grass. By the light of the fire, she saw that a man was working the pump in the backyard. A bucket brigade had been formed. She lay gasping for air.

"Are you all right?"

Felicity looked up and recognized Mrs. Partridge. "Chil...dren! Children?" She tried to get up.

Mrs. Partridge pushed her down. "The children and their nurse all got out safely. I counted them. See?" The woman pointed toward the sidewalk, where the children stood huddled around Midge and Vista. "The big boy got them all down the stairs. He carried the littlest one."

"Thank God," Felicity breathed and then went into another coughing fit.

Mrs. Partridge helped Felicity rest her head in her lap. Lying on her side, Felicity gazed at the men who were putting out the fire.

Then a man loomed over her. It was Ty Hawkins. "Felicity, are you all right?" he asked, concern etched all over his face.

"She needs the doctor," Vista said. "She got burned."

At these words, Felicity suddenly felt searing pain on her shoulders.

"Here. This will help." Someone poured several buckets of cold water over her back, drenching her. She began shivering uncontrollably.

"We should get her inside," Mrs. Partridge said. "She will catch her death of cold out here soaked and lying on this damp ground."

Ty Hawkins lifted her into his arms. She knew she should protest that she was able to walk. But was she? Chilled to her marrow, she began shuddering, unable to stop. Ty carried her up to her room. "The house?" she managed to stutter.

"Looks like just the dining room was damaged. Now don't worry." He laid her on her bed and was gone. Vista and Mrs. Partridge came in. Together they stripped off her drenched gown and helped her into a dry one. When the cloth touched her shoulders, Felicity nearly cried out.

She began weeping. She didn't want to, yet she couldn't stem the tears. The door opened and Camie ran in. "I want Miss Felicity!"

Felicity opened her arms and the little girl nearly knocked her backward. She felt as if Camie were trying to bore her way into Felicity for shelter.

"He tried to take me," Camie said, crying. "The bad man tried to take me away."

Felicity looked up and found her shock reflected in the faces of the other two women. "The man with the sack over his head?"

"Yes!" Camie's voice rose shrilly. "Tucker came. He fought the bad man."

Stunned, Felicity looked to Vista. "Please get the judge."

Ty paused at the door. Looking wilted, Felicity was sitting on the side of her bed with Camie in her lap. Her fresh gown was tucked modestly around her. The doctor was carefully applying ointment to her slender red and blistered shoulders. Still, her pale skin glowed in the candlelight. Her frailty struck him. She was such a forceful woman that one forgot how delicate she was. Anger stirred in him. Who had done this?

He cleared his throat. "Vista said that someone tried to *take* Camie?"

Felicity looked so tired, crushed. He fought the urge to gather her into his arms. "Bring in Tucker, please. He knows."

Ty turned and found Tucker at the head of the stairs. Ty motioned to him. The boy showed evidence of a violent struggle. One eye was swollen shut. His lower lip was swollen and bleeding, and he limped. Just inside the bedroom door, Ty rested a hand on the boy's shoulder. "Tell Miss Gabriel and me what happened, please."

The doctor was packing his black bag, frowning and listening, too. Vista was securing Felicity's gown in place.

"I heard a sound. It woke me up. I run down the stairs to this floor where the girls and Miss Felicity sleep. Seen that man was carrying Camie away. I had to stop him any way I could. I ran and bumped into him. He fell down the last two steps to the front door. Camie screamed then. I think she was still asleep when he got her at first. But falling woke her."

Ty tried to keep back the anger but couldn't. He slammed his open hand against the door. "What man?"

Tucker jumped at the sound. Felicity began to shiver again. Camie whimpered.

"I'm sorry. I just can't believe that someone would come here and try to kidnap my daughter," Ty protested.

"I suppose I just made it all up!" Tucker glared at him.

"I saw the man—" Felicity began.

"I know." Ty fought for control. "I know. I believe that what took place happened just as you told me, Tucker. It's just that this kind of thing doesn't happen on this side of the river. St. Louis maybe, but Altoona?"

"It seems unusual," Felicity murmured.

"You got any enemies?" Tucker shot him a strange look.

Ty rubbed his taut forehead, unable to think.

"I mean, you're a judge," Tucker continued. "Did you make somebody mad at you? Somebody that ain't scared to break the law?"

Ty held up both hands as if surrendering. "I can't make sense of this." From the corner of his eye, he saw Felicity begin to slide off the bed toward the floor. He ran to her and lifted her onto the bed. "Vista," he called softly, "come help me, please."

Vista hurried over and helped him lay the lady down on her side, pulling up the covers. Camie clung to Felicity and Vista said to leave the child. The three of them walked out into the hall with the doctor who said he'd be back after breakfast. Ty hung back, not wanting to leave Felicity or his daughter.

"The doctor give her something for the pain," Vista explained to Ty. "That's why she just let go like that. And it was a good idea, too." She looked up at Ty. "Some men helped Abel nail up wood over the broken window. I think you two best come down with me and check to see if everybody's gone home."

Ty nodded and so did Tucker. Abel stood at the bottom of the stairs with a shotgun in his arms. "I shot twice but I missed him. How's our lady doin'?"

"The doctor treated her burns and gave her something to put her to sleep," Vista answered. The stunned-looking children all sat on the floor in the foyer. The housekeeper looked to him. "I'd feel better if you and Abel spent the night in the house."

"Already thought of that," Abel said. "I'm going to settle myself right here on the floor. Nobody else is getting in here tonight."

"Where's Miss Felicity?" Katy asked.

"She's asleep upstairs." Vista held out her hand. "You and Donnie come spend the rest of tonight with me. Camie is sleeping with Miss Felicity." The little girl and her brother followed Vista toward the back of the house.

The boys looked up at him. Tucker spoke up, "The boys and me sleep on the third floor. You should come up there, probably. There's a chair you can sit on. I wish you had a gun."

"I do." Ty patted his belt where a pistol was concealed under his jacket.

"Good," Tucker said and led them up the stairs to the third floor. There Ty saw that the boys were sleeping on pallets on the floor.

"Miss Felicity is getting us beds," Tucker said as if Ty had disparaged the pallets. "They just ain't got here yet."

Ty nodded. "Go to sleep, boys. I will sit in the rocker by the door with my gun. No one will get into this house again tonight. Now settle down."

As Tucker moved away, Ty reached out and grabbed his shoulder again. "Well done, Tucker. Well done."

Tucker shrugged and went to a pile of blankets. The other boys got between their covers, too. A couple of them whispered for a time and then fell asleep.

Wide-awake, Ty sat in the rocker, his loaded pistol on his lap. A loaded pistol in his heart, primed and ready to protect or avenge. His mind buzzed with thoughts and feelings. Why had someone tried to steal his child? And who was the culprit?

Ty burned with outrage and fury. Someone had tried to take his daughter. Why? Then the image of Felicity fighting the fire and then lying on the grass limp and in-jured sliced his hot anger like iced razors. *I will find out who's responsible and he will suffer the consequences.*

Chapter Seven

Felicity woke and moaned. For a few seconds, she was
disoriented. Why was she in such pain? Then a whirring
string of images from the night before spun through her
mind. She groaned and tried to move. Tears formed in
her eyes. *Dear Father, why did this happen? And what
will happen now?*

The skin of her shoulders and upper back still burned
and felt as if it had shrunk at least one size. She moved
inch by inch and finally sat up on the side of the bed.
Suddenly she recalled that Camie had slept with her. She
looked around for the little girl, but she was alone.

Someone tapped on her door.

"Come in," she said, her voice lower than usual. She
found she couldn't breathe easily, as if she were fighting
for air. She coughed.

Ty Hawkins peered around the door. "You're awake
then?"

She nodded. She wanted to greet him but couldn't
catch her breath. The pull to go to him worked on her
powerfully.

"I'm going home now. I have to get dressed and get to
court," he said, sounding apologetic.

Felicity gazed at him, recalling how he had lifted her last night and carried her here, holding her within his strong arms. Such comfort. In spite of her not being dressed for male company, she wished he would come in. Such comfort. She grappled with persistent tremors, no doubt an aftereffect of last night's violence. "How is Camie?"

The mention of his daughter appeared to strike him with unusual force. His whole face tightened into grim lines. "She's fine and is down in the kitchen finishing oatmeal for breakfast. Your housekeeper asked me to tell you that you don't have to come down. As soon as she gets the children off to school, she'll come up and help you dress."

"I should be able to get up by—" She paused, realizing she did not want to move. Searing pain held her captive.

She tried to take a deep breath and coughed painfully instead. Finally she was able to speak. "Does thee have any idea what happened last night? Why would someone try to take away thy daughter?" Her heart pounded, making her weaker. But she wouldn't let herself sink onto the sheets again.

"No, I don't know why this has happened. I must go. I'm due in court in an hour. I will return this evening. Abel is going to take the children to school and bring them home. They won't be allowed to go anywhere without someone with them. You stay here and rest." Ty looked as if he wanted to say more. But he only shook his head and left.

Though Felicity tried to ignore it, his leaving chilled her. She cautiously eased herself to her feet. She had been worried that she wouldn't be able to stand without the dizziness of last night. But except for her painful shoulders, she felt fine. Well, maybe not fine, but as close to normal as possible after all that had taken place last night. Her weakness and helplessness chafed her.

She drew her light blue wrapper from a peg near the door. The thought that she had run downstairs in only her nightgown and been carried outside like that gave her pause. But in the midst of all the drama and commotion, probably no one had taken much notice.

As she tried to slide the wrapper onto her shoulders, her body rebelled at this usually easy but now intricate set of movements. She found she really couldn't tolerate any added weight, not even a layer of light cotton, on her blistered skin.

Vista knocked once and walked inside with a cup of coffee. "The judge said you were awake. You can't put that on." Vista took the wrapper and hung it back on the peg. "Now you need to rest." She shooed Felicity back to bed and gave her the cup.

Sitting down on the bedside, Felicity tried to take a deep breath and failed, coughing again. She pressed a hand to her neckline. "Thank thee for the coffee. I don't want to be shut up in this room all day. But what can I wear? My shoulders are most painful."

"I been thinking." Vista looked around the room. "I know where Mrs. Barney's niece's party dresses are packed away. I'm going to find one and let you wear that."

"A party dress?"

"Her party dresses were cut low and didn't have much sleeves."

"Oh!" Felicity put her hand to her mouth in surprise. In the past, when in the city, she had glimpsed these kinds of dresses. In the evening, ladies had turned out in low-cut silk and satin gowns. "Oh, no. I couldn't wear anything like that."

Vista just shook her head and left, saying over her shoulder, "I'll be right back."

Setting down the hot coffee, Felicity went to the dressing room and drew out her simple everyday gray dress. She found, however, that even contemplating trying to lift this on bested her. Every movement tormented her tight, burning shoulders. Her already low spirits sank to the cellar.

Vista came in with several dresses over her arm. "Now don't argue. Everyone will know why you're wearing this. And if I know anything, that brass knocker is going to be busy today. You want everyone to see you in that nightgown?"

Felicity gaped at Vista. But before she knew it, Vista had helped her freshen up, even brushing her hair and pinning it up for the day. Then in the face of Felicity's misgivings, Vista helped her don the least embellished dress, a gown of light blue silk with cap sleeves that gathered into a thin soft band around her upper arms.

Feeling nearly naked, Felicity was glad that she'd had the mirror in the room taken down and put at the end of the hall. *I will not look at myself.* "I want to see how bad the damage is downstairs."

Vista helped her down the hall and steps. Felicity halted as she viewed the smoke-blackened ceiling and walls in the hall and dining room. She kept telling herself that it could have been so much worse. Yet it was bad enough. She blinked away tears. "Did the smoke penetrate the rest of the house?"

"Except for the dining room, the downstairs only suffered a little ash and smoke. We can be thankful that it wasn't worse, and be thankful that today is warm and we can open the windows to get rid of the foul burned odor."

Felicity nodded. Vista led her to the kitchen, where

she poured Felicity another cup of coffee. Soon, sitting very still, Felicity was nibbling buttery scrambled eggs and golden toast with red raspberry jam for her breakfast. She had held it at bay, but now her main concern crashed over her. "How were the children this morning?" *How was Camie?*

"They were upset, of course. But Tucker told them not to worry, that he and Abel would make sure that no one got in here again." Vista looked her in the eye. "The judge's little girl was quiet but she seemed to believe Tucker. I mean, he saved her last night, didn't he?"

The confusion and terror of last night slashed ice shards through Felicity again. Fighting to keep rising panic at bay, she sipped her reviving coffee. She leaned her head into her hand. "I can't believe it. I saw it with my own eyes and I still can't believe it. Why would—"

The front door knocker sounded, sharp and loud, twice. Vista took off her apron. "I told you how it would be. I'll make your excuses to whoever it is."

Felicity closed her eyes. She didn't want to see anyone today and was glad that Vista was here to keep her from curious eyes. She made herself finish her eggs and toast. She savored the last few swallows of Vista's good coffee.

The doctor followed Vista into the kitchen. "I am here to check on your burns, Miss Gabriel."

Felicity smiled and offered her hand to the doctor. She was surprised to find that even that simple movement caused her scorched skin to pull and hurt. Vista came inside with a basin of water, a bar of soap and a towel.

"Thank you. Vista knows I like to treat my patients with clean hands. Now let me see if I can't make you more comfortable." He looked at her burns. "Very little evidence of infection. Excellent. Now I'll apply another treatment of this herbal ointment."

As he applied the ointment, Felicity drew in air bit by bit. But when she thanked him, it was genuine. The ointment made the skin easier to move and soothed the burn.

"I may not be able to come back until tomorrow. If there is a turn for the worse—redness and sign of infection—send for me. Otherwise, I made up a quantity of this ointment and will leave it with your good housekeeper." He turned to Vista. "Apply the ointment every four hours and before bedtime."

"I will, Doctor. I'll make sure she takes care of herself and doesn't try to do too much today." Vista fixed Felicity with a stern look that would have made her laugh if she weren't sick with worry over the safety over her children—and Ty Hawkins's daughter.

After leaving Felicity, Ty strode the few blocks to town to go about his job. He couldn't shake the anger that had consumed him since last night. How was he going to protect Camie and Felicity? And who had tried to take his child? It made no sense.

He jogged up the steps into the courthouse, heading for his chamber. He was hailed by Lyman Kidwell, the chief of police. "Judge Hawkins!"

Ty paused, turning to face the man who was commandingly tall and silver-haired, with a gruff voice that announced that he stood for no nonsense. "I need to talk to you, Judge."

Ty stared at him, his jaw tight. "I was going to come see you over the midday break. What have you found out?"

"Let's go to your chamber. I'll let you know how the investigation is going."

They hurried to Ty's office. Ty unlocked the door, led Kidwell in, and settled behind his desk.

Kidwell sat, facing him. "Now I have my officer's notes from when he interviewed witnesses after the fire last night. I want to hear what you make of this."

Ty couldn't sit, but paced behind his desk. "I am astounded that something like this has happened in our town. And I can't imagine why someone tried to kidnap my daughter. If it weren't for—"

"Kidnap your daughter?" Kidwell snapped. "No one mentioned that to me."

Ty's dour expression settled into harder lines. "Yes, I couldn't believe it at first myself. But my daughter told me that a man was carrying her away and that Tucker Stout knocked him down the steps."

Kidwell's frown consumed his whole face. "My patrolman was told that some thief broke into the house and attacked Miss Gabriel and a fire started."

"That's probably how it appeared to everyone. But I talked to my daughter, Miss Gabriel and Tucker. They all said the business started with a man trying to carry off my daughter."

"Why didn't you tell the patrol officer that?" Kidwell asked.

"He didn't talk to me. I was busy trying to soothe my hysterical daughter. And I carried Miss Gabriel up to her room. She suffered burns, you know."

"Why would anyone try to steal your daughter?"

Ty gave Kidwell a sour look, worry and anger twisting and tangling around his lungs. "I wish I knew."

Kidwell studied him. "Are you sure the intruder didn't just take your daughter because she was the first one he came to?"

"No, Camie was in a room with a little girl and her brother. The intruder could have just as easily taken them. He targeted my daughter."

"It's hard to believe someone would bother a house full of orphans in any case." Kidwell stared at Ty. "Can you think of anyone who has it in for you?"

"You mean besides all the men I've sentenced to prison?" Ty said in an arch tone. "Tucker Stout asked me that last night."

The police chief's eyebrows peaked. "That boy you sentenced to probation at the orphans' home?"

"Yes, and evidently he's the boy who prevented the kidnapper from getting away with my daughter."

Kidwell again scrutinized him for a few silent moments. "I need to ask you. Why is your daughter living there?"

"My daughter suffers what Miss Gabriel calls 'night terrors.' She says it's common among children who have lost one or both parents. My daughter, for whatever reason, feels safe at Miss Gabriel's."

"Even after last night's attempted kidnapping and fire?" Kidwell's tone became harsh.

"After the ordeal last night, she turned to Miss Gabriel and wouldn't be parted from her." The image of his daughter clutching Felicity both comforted him and ripped up his peace.

"You say the Quaker calls what ails your girl 'night terrors?'"

Ty forced himself to speak with measured tones as he revealed facts he wanted no one to know. "Miss Gabriel has worked with other orphans and says this is not uncommon. I am grateful to her for the loving kindness and understanding she has showed to my child. And I won't rest until whoever broke in last night is behind bars." He realized he was clenching his teeth.

Kidwell rose. "I'm with you on that one hundred percent. I'll give this information to my patrol officers and my captain. They'll comb the town and talk to everyone. Someone must have some information. I understand that the intruder wore a sack over his head?"

"That's what I'm told," Ty said.

Kidwell looked sour. "We'll do our best."

"I know you will." Ty rose and the two shook hands. Kidwell left, muttering under his breath.

In the chief of police's wake, Ty's law clerk entered. The serious young man handed Ty the court agenda for the day. Ty sank back into his chair, ignoring the piece of paper in front of him. Just when he'd thought he'd been given a way to help his daughter heal, *this* had to happen.

Propping his elbows on his desk, he folded his hands in front of his mouth. Who wanted to kidnap his daughter? Would his mother-in-law go to such lengths? Was there a criminal whom he'd sentenced who was now free and coming after him and his family for revenge? He scrubbed both hands over his tired face.

The law clerk knocked. It was time for court. He rose, donned his black robe and headed down the hall to the courtroom. He heard case after case as exhaustion threatened to overwhelm him. At the end of the day, as he was trying to focus on the petty thief in front of him, Felicity Gabriel's face, blackened by soot, and her charred night dress and red, blistered shoulders haunted him. How could he keep Camie, Miss Gabriel and her household safe?

He stared at the man, mentally putting a sack over his head as the man made his excuses.

"I seen the error of my ways, Your Honor," the defendant said. "I won't never touch nobody's property again."

Ty wished he could believe the man but this was just another offense in a long list of his thefts. Yet the defendant wasn't violent—

Hogan strode into court and headed right for Ty. "Your Honor," he said, handing him a folded piece of paper. Ty read the note, stiffened, and nodded to Hogan, hiding the sudden increase in his breathing. "The defendant is found guilty and will serve the maximum sentence. I hope this time is the last time I see the defendant in my court. Court is adjourned for the day." Ty sounded his gavel and rose.

In his chamber, he flung off his robe. Outside, Hogan waited for him and the two of them headed to the police station.

Ty's heart thudded, pounded. "What have you found out?"

Kidwell rose. "We got lucky. One of the street vendors, an older widow who sells notions to riverboat passengers, remembered a black man who was asking about where the Barney house was not long ago. She was able to give us a good description. We found him loading grain onto a barge."

"Is he in custody?"

Nodding, Kidwell rose and grabbed a large brass key off a peg on the wall. Ty hurried after him to the two-cell jail that had been erected less than a decade ago. One cell had two men Ty recognized as men he'd sentenced. The other cell held a tall black man who looked like he could lift the jail with one hand. His eyes were wary.

"Judge, have you ever seen this man before?" Kidwell asked.

"No." Ty shook his head.

"One of my officers has gone to get Miss Gabriel to see if she can identify him," Kidwell said with Hogan hovering at his elbow.

Ty swung around and glared at Kidwell. "You know she was burned last night. And I don't think a lady should have to come to a place like this, especially when she's indisposed."

"I'm sorry," Kidwell said, "but she must tell us if this is the man. Hogan, go and see if Miss Gabriel's carriage is outside."

"I'll go, too," Ty said. "I want to make sure that she's fit enough to come into the jail." Ty didn't wait for the police chief to reply.

Outside, he saw the old black carriage that had been Mildred Barney's approaching the jail. He waved to Abel and the man drove up to him. The blinds on the carriage windows were pulled so no one could see inside.

"Did Miss Gabriel come?" Ty asked Abel.

"Yes," Abel replied, "but I told her I won't let her step foot out of this carriage. Vista had to dress her in an evening gown because she couldn't bear cloth on her shoulders—"

"Ty Hawkins, is that thee?" Felicity's voice from the interior of the carriage interrupted.

"Miss Gabriel," Ty said, stepping to the carriage door. He glimpsed her pale face as she parted the shade. Her woebegone expression tugged at his heart.

"Ty, I don't think I can identify the man from last night." Her voice quavered.

Ty reached inside and grasped her ungloved hand. "I'll go in and talk to the chief of police."

It didn't take long for Ty to convince Kidwell to bring the prisoner in chains outside. Ty hovered near the carriage window. "Here's the suspect, Miss Gabriel."

From the barely parted curtains, Felicity gazed at the large man whose hands and feet were manacled. Four policemen hovered around him. Why had they insisted she come here? She knew she wouldn't be able to identify the man who had invaded her house and who had tried to make off with Camie.

One of the policemen forced the suspect to look toward where she sat at the carriage window. She was immediately struck by the prisoner's large, dark eyes. Fear, pain, humiliation and sorrow flashed from him to her like sharp darts of suffering. But she saw no guilt or defiance.

If she said, "This cannot be the man. He is sad, not guilty," the policemen would pay little attention to her. They would dismiss her view as woman's intuition or sentimentality. Indeed, men usually dismissed what women said in serious situations such as this. So she would not reveal what she had read in the man's eyes. But dissatisfaction with this made her restless.

She looked to Ty. "I'm sorry, but I can't identify this man as the intruder from last night. It was dark. The man had a sack over his head and everything happened so fast."

"Well," the police chief asked, "is this man about the right size?"

"This man appears larger than the intruder, but I cannot be certain. Perhaps Tucker would be able to give thee more of a description."

"Were the man's hands white or black?" Hogan asked.

She shook her head. "I didn't pay any attention to his hands. My focus was trying to get Camie from him. And then he hit me. I fell and the fire started." These few words brought it all back, the horror, the terror of last night. She looked away, shaken.

Ty moved closer to her window as if shielding her. "Miss Gabriel must go home now. I can see that this is upsetting her and she's been through enough."

The police chief thanked her. The men shoved and dragged the prisoner back into the jail. It grieved Felicity to see him handled so roughly. As if he heard her thought, the prisoner turned for one more glance toward her. She read his appeal as if it had been printed on the air. The spirit within her stirred. Was the Inner Light leading her? Telling her she was right about his innocence?

"Miss Gabriel, are you going directly home?" Ty asked her.

"Yes, would thee like to ride with me?" she asked in turn. "Camie will be home from school. Vista and Tucker went to walk them home. I left thy dear mother in the house, expecting the children."

"Much obliged." He opened the carriage door and climbed inside. As he took his seat opposite her, the carriage swayed. Abel called to the team and the carriage moved forward. "I'm sorry you were subjected to that. But the police chief had to ask you. It's routine."

Felicity nodded, holding her lower lip with her teeth to keep from saying what she was thinking. Then she felt herself blush at the thought of how much her low-cut dress was revealing to this man. "I'm not attired as I would like. I've never worn such a revealing dress."

Until now, he hadn't noticed anything but her pained expression and red, blistered shoulders. But now he realized she was wearing a blue dress that made her eyes look otherworldly. He caught himself and tried to speak calmly. "Your costume is attractive. How are your shoulders?"

She shuddered. "Painful, but it could have been so much worse. I'm grateful that only the dining room was damaged and Camie wasn't taken." Then she looked at him, hesitating. "Thee is not intending to take Camie home, is thee?"

"No. But neither can I sleep at your house like I did

last night. I have been trying to think of a way to protect you—the children, as well as my daughter."

Ty realized he was staring at the gold-red curls that clustered around her face. He quickly looked away. He was looking at her far too much and with far too much interest. It had to stop.

Ty helped Felicity down from the carriage and insisted she take his arm. Out in the daylight, the sight of her red and blistered shoulders added more fuel to his anger. Whoever had done this would be caught and punished. He considered the black man the chief had in custody. Could anyone actually identify the man with a sack over his head, seen in a dark and chaotic situation? Ty shook his head.

"Miss Felicity!" Camie came running out the door and down the porch steps. Her grandmother was right behind her. "Miss Felicity, thee wasn't here when I got home!"

Felicity stooped to greet Camie, looking pained.

Ty interposed himself between them and caught Camie. She struggled against him. "I want Miss Felicity!"

"You must touch her carefully. She was burned last night, remember? You don't want to hurt her, do you?" Ty set her down.

"That's right, dear," Louise said. "We need to take care of Miss Felicity until she is all better."

Camie edged over and offered her hand. "Come, Miss Felicity, I'll walk thee inside. That's a pretty dress you—I mean thee—has on."

Ty was struck by Camie's new use of Felicity's Quaker words. Was this a good sign or a bad one?

"Thank thee, Camie. How was school today?"

Camie began to skip, drawing Felicity along, Ty and

his mother in their wake. "We are learning to spell. I spelled cat *c-a-t,* rat *r-a-t,* sat *s-a-t,* mat—"

A familiar yet unwelcome voice cut in. "It's about time you were home!" His mother-in-law was marching toward them from the street. "And you're here, Tyrone. Excellent. I wanted to speak to you. After last night, neither of you can possibly keep little Camille here. It isn't safe—"

Vista interrupted from the front steps. "Miss Felicity, you got company. It's the mayor."

Felicity looked up, her eyes and mouth wide with surprise. "What? Why?"

Ty stifled a grin. Why, indeed? The mayor always wanted to be in on everything. And he could talk a man's leg off and then start on his arms.

Vista didn't bother to answer her. "Come along. The quicker you listen to his condolences, the quicker he'll leave."

His mother-in-law snapped something about undisciplined servants. And was ignored.

Vista urged Felicity inside to the parlor opposite the wrecked dining room. Ty let his mother-in-law precede him. Of course, as usual Alice Crandall wouldn't leave till she gave each of them an excessive headache. His mother stayed by his side. He noted that his daughter clung to Felicity's hand and regarded her maternal grandmother with fearful distrust and caution. He simmered with irritation and injustice. Alice Crandall would never take responsibility for what she'd done to contribute to Camie's night terrors. Never.

The mayor hadn't stayed in the parlor. He was looking over the fire-damaged dining room and making a tsk-tsk sound and shaking his head. He turned and took both of Felicity's hands in his. "My dear young woman, I am so grieved that this has happened to Mildred Barney's house. I'm Mayor Wallace Law. I have come to offer my sympathy at this calamity and to promise you that nothing like this will happen again. No, indeed. Nothing like this has ever happened on Madison Boulevard."

Mrs. Crandall snapped, "Not till this Quaker moved here and brought riffraff—"

Ty raised his voice, speaking over his mother-in-law's diatribe. "Miss Gabriel needs to sit down. As you can see, Mayor, she has suffered injury." Ty gently took Felicity's arm and led her to a chair near the hearth.

His mother-in-law snapped her fingers as if calling a dog, and demanded that Camie come and give her a kiss in greeting.

Her head down, Camie waited till Felicity was seated and then took her hand again and stood beside her chair. Ty noted that she kept the chair and Miss Gabriel between her and her grandmother. His mother hovered nearby as if backing up Felicity.

Mrs. Crandall snapped her fingers again but was ignored. "Disobedience," she said. "I would not tolerate that in my home."

Ty wanted to snap his fingers in front of his mother-in-law's face and then order her from the room.

Still tsk-tsking, Mayor Law followed them and took the seat across from Felicity. Ty stood on the other side of Felicity's chair, shielding his daughter from Mrs. Crandall.

"I will not stay any longer than necessary," the mayor promised.

Ty hid a sudden smile at this prevarication.

But before the mayor could get rolling, he was interrupted. Another knock on the door and Vista sailed past the doorway to the parlor. She ushered another man in.

"Miss Felicity, this is the newspaper editor, Mr. Mac Sharp."

Ty should have expected Sharp to come calling. He moved closer to Felicity, a spark of temper igniting in his stomach.

Felicity stammered a welcome and cast Ty a glance, which he thought meant she wanted him to help her get rid of all these people. He nodded his agreement.

The newsman sat down across from her and scrutinized her.

Felicity blushed. "I'm not dressed as I usually am. My shoulders are too tender…" She trailed off, sounding embarrassed.

Ty's inner bonfire intensified. He glanced at the mantel clock and began tracking the second hand.

Mr. Sharp licked his pencil and asked, "Who do you think started the fire? Do you think it was one of your disgruntled neighbors?"

"Of course not!" Mrs. Crandall announced, glaring at the newspaperman.

Felicity stared at Sharp, openmouthed.

"Why would you say that, Sharp?" the mayor demanded. "No one on Madison Boulevard would commit such a dreadful act."

The editor gave Mayor Law a sharp look. Ty did, too, as he kept an eye on the clock. Soon he would clear this crowded room.

"I'm certain none of my neighbors did anything of the sort," Felicity spoke up. "In fact, the men and women of Madison Boulevard turned out to fight the fire last night."

Vista entered with only one cup of coffee on a silver tray. "Miss Felicity is right. The neighbors come out with their fire buckets, even before the volunteer fire department arrived."

Felicity accepted the cup of dark coffee. Ty noticed that Vista served no one else, no doubt emphasizing the point that they should all leave sooner rather than later. His mother-in-law was seething at this slight. Ty watched the clock. Time was nearly up.

"Then who do you think started the fire?" Sharp asked as if Felicity knew the answer but was hiding the truth.

Ty spoke up, trying to let Felicity just sip her coffee. "It was more than—"

The brass knocker sounded again. Ty tensed, heat rolling through him. *More* visitors. Vista ushered in Eldon Partridge from next door.

Felicity offered him her hand, appearing harassed.

Sharp ignored Partridge. "I've been hearing all kinds of rumors today. Like one of your neighbors tried to burn you out. Like a band of river rats came to steal you blind."

Felicity covered her eyes with her hands.

Ty could no longer stand to see her in such a state. "Miss Felicity is indisposed. If you gentlemen want to argue, you'll have to leave. She's not well," he said.

"That's right," Vista agreed, bustling into the room. "It's time for her medicine."

Both men apologized but neither looked ready to leave. Sharp glared at Ty. "The free press has a right to get the facts for the people."

Ty snapped, "If you want the facts, talk to Vista. She isn't in pain and she fought the fire, too."

Felicity reached up and squeezed Ty's hand in a wordless appeal. "Mr. Sharp, I will tell thee what I know of last night and then I must ask thee to leave. I must spend time reassuring the children."

After Felicity gave her succinct account, she looked up at Ty. "Will thee see our visitors to the door?"

Gladly. A real pleasure. Ty helped her up.

"Miss Gabriel," Partridge said, "I was going to discuss something with you, but I will consult with Ty, if that's all right with you."

Ty wondered what Partridge wanted.

"Ty Hawkins, I would appreciate it if thee would act for me with my neighbor." Felicity rose and offered her hand to Camie.

"Why hasn't my granddaughter come and greeted her loving grandmamma?" Mrs. Crandall demanded in a false sweet tone as Camie took Felicity's hand. "It's plain to see that living with riffraff—"

Felicity's face flushed red, glaring at the woman.

Ty knew why. His mother-in-law had called her orphans riffraff twice now. And he could see that like a cannon, Felicity had reared back, ready to fire.

"Alice Crandall, if thee were a loving grandmamma, thy granddaughter would have run to thee, not hid from thee. I do not know what thee has done to alienate thy grandchild, but I will not let thee trouble Camie here. If thee would like to try to improve thy relationship with her—"

At this, Mrs. Crandall stormed out of the house, slamming the door behind her. Ty nearly rubbed his hands together in satisfaction.

Sharp raised both eyebrows and the mayor looked stunned. Partridge grinned and tried to hide it.

Sharp narrowed his eyes on Felicity. "How many orphans do you house here?"

"Mr. Sharp," Vista said, "I baked those sugar cookies you like today. I can tell you all about Miss Felicity's orphans and you can meet them in the kitchen. They're having after-school cookies and milk." Vista held out her hand. "Camie, child, you come with me. Katy is missing you. And Miss Felicity got to lie down."

Camie allowed herself to be drawn away with many backward glances. Felicity looked ready to drop. The brass knocker sounded again and she moaned.

Ty took command. "Partridge, answer the door, please. And, Mayor, I think Miss Gabriel must have quiet."

"Of course, of course." Mayor Law headed for the door with Partridge.

Ty led Felicity to the stairs and began helping her to climb them. He tried not to notice how close he wanted to be to her. Given any pretext, he would take her into his arms and carry her up the stairs.

Felicity tried to push him away. "I should be able to go to my room without assistance—"

"No, you just think you should," the doctor said as he followed after them. "I've come to have a look at your burns before I go home."

Disappointed, Ty let the doctor accompany Felicity up to her room. He was about to follow and ask if he could bring her anything when he heard a familiar—and very unexpected—voice at the front door.

Chapter Eight

"Jack," Ty greeted the man, "what brings you here?"

With his hat in his hand, Jack nodded politely. "I come for two things. The first is because of my granddaughter Midge and the four children I brought here to Miss Gabriel. After what happened in this house last night, I am frankly wondering if it's safe to leave them here." He glanced toward the smoke-blackened hallway ceiling.

Ty looked into the familiar face and honest brown eyes. Before he could reply, Partridge broke in, "I came because I'm worried about Miss Gabriel and the children, too."

"Why don't we go into the parlor and talk? It's empty now." Ty led the other two into the tastefully decorated rose-and-ivory room. They sat as if forming a triangle—Jack stiffly on the ornate loveseat, Ty and Eldon on the tapestry wing chairs by the fire.

"What I heard is some man broke in and attacked Miss Gabriel and a fire broke out." Jack looked stern.

Ty took in the lingering odor of acrid smoke. "The police chief and I don't want this generally known, but a man did break in. He tried to carry off my daughter. Tucker Stout heard him and tackled him on the stairs.

There was a struggle in the dining room. The candle Miss Gabriel was carrying was knocked from her hand and started the fire."

"He tried to kidnap your daughter? And Miss Gabriel fought with the man?" Partridge asked, sounding aghast.

Rubbing his chin, Jack spoke up. "I know a Quaker's not supposed to fight, but I can see her fighting somebody trying to take your daughter."

"Why would someone want to kidnap your daughter?" Partridge asked.

Shrugging, Ty shook his head. "I'm a judge. I deal with criminals. This might be the fruit of an old grudge." He leaned forward on his elbows, recalling the horror of last night, hearing the fire bell ringing to call the volunteers and neighbors to help. The sight of the flames as he'd run toward the house had taken him back to the war again. The horror shuddered through him.

"My wife told me that Virginia's mother is trying to get custody of your daughter." Partridge looked pained, as if the words he'd said were refuse he didn't want to look at.

"Alice Crandall is a…troublesome woman," Ty conceded, choosing his words with care. The muted sound of children's voices filtered into the room. "But I don't see her hiring some thug to come and steal Camie from me."

"Yes, sir, that doesn't make sense," Jack agreed. "I mean, where could she hide the child? It would get out that she had her."

Ty assessed Jack in a new light. He'd always just been the affable shoeshine man at the wharf. They'd never sat in a formal parlor together, having a serious discussion.

"Well, then?" Jack looked from Ty to Partridge and back again. "Should I take my granddaughter and the children home?"

"No." Ty was suddenly sure of this. He edged forward on his chair. "We can't let whoever did this get away with destroying Miss Gabriel's work. Mildred Barney was a fine woman and she wanted this house to be used for good after her death."

Partridge agreed, nodding soberly. "That's why I came over. I wanted to know if you wanted me to take a turn guarding the house at night. I know you stayed last night along with Abel, but that will start talk if you do it again."

Ty's face twisted with aggravation. "Yes, there's never a shortage of gossip."

"I'd come and so would some of the men from our congregation," Jack offered. "Some of them are veterans. All of us hunt, so we got guns."

"I can round up the rest of the men in this neighborhood. I'm sure they don't want anything like this happening again," Partridge said.

Ty rubbed his hands together. He wanted to do the protecting here by himself, but that wasn't feasible. He couldn't stay here every night on guard and work at the courts during the day. "I can't do it alone," he admitted, almost surprised to hear the words out loud. "If we could get together another eleven men, we could each take a four-to five-hour sentry duty one night a week."

"That makes sense," Jack said, nodding several times. "I'm sure the men at my church would be more than willing. We take care of our own. Not only are my Midge and Vista living here, but Eugene, Dee Dee, Violet and Johnny have been orphaned or abandoned and we want them kept safe. Black children mean as much to God as white children do."

Ty looked up. "You won't find me disagreeing with you."

"Of course, a child's a child," Partridge said.

"I just wanted that to be clear," Jack said. "Some people don't think our children are as important."

Ty smiled suddenly and sat back more at ease. "Well, I'd warn them not to say that in front of Miss Felicity Gabriel."

The three men chuckled at this.

Partridge rose and so did Jack. "Ty, I'll organize the men in the neighborhood and set the night up into two watches."

Both men shook Ty's hand with extra firmness and turned to leave.

"Wait," Ty said. "Jack, you said you had a second question."

Jack turned back. "Yes, sir, I heard that the police have arrested a black man and he's going to be charged for this crime. Is that right?"

"Yes, I'm afraid it is." Ty pictured the large man who now sat in jail. "Miss Gabriel was unable to identify him as the culprit."

Jack looked down and then up again. "They'll have to release him if they don't have enough evidence to hold him, won't they, sir?"

Ty nodded, but dissatisfaction wrinkled his forehead. "Jack, I may be forced to rule that the man is a material witness and keep him in custody."

Jack soberly met his eyes. "You mean for his own protection?"

Feeling sour, Ty nodded.

"Yes," Partridge said in a harsh tone, "there are a lot of people who don't wait for evidence. We don't want any lynchings here."

Ty looked into Jack's eyes. "Tell the people in your congregation that I won't let *any* man be railroaded in my court. But jail may be the safest place for this man until the case is solved."

"Thank you, Judge." Jack put on his hat again and he and Partridge left.

Ty stood in the empty room, listening to the sounds of the children's voices from the other room. The smell of burned wood hung in the air. Above him, he heard someone moving. Was it Felicity?

His mind went back to the sound of the fire bell and his mother shouting for him to get up. The alarm had ripped through him like barbed wire. He'd run all the way here. When the fire had finally been quenched, he'd been faced with the spectacle of Felicity lying on the grass in her charred nightgown. His hands clenched.

He experienced the phantom memory of her light, soft weight in his arms. He passed a hand over his eyes, trying to banish the memory from his mind.

Then another thought bobbed up in his mind. It had been with him since last night but he hadn't been able to act fully on it. He took a deep breath. He shouldn't put it off any longer.

He walked past the wrecked dining room. Someone had removed the furniture and done a better job of covering the missing window—probably Felicity's builder. He found Vista preparing food in the kitchen. The children were playing a game of tag in the backyard under the watchful eye of Jack's granddaughter.

"Vista, where's Tucker?" he asked.

She glanced up from the huge bowl where she was peeling pounds of potatoes. "Look for him with Abel. Tucker spends most of his time in the carriage house and stable."

"Much obliged." Ty walked out the door and made his way around the children playing in the yard. Hearing his daughter laugh filled him with great joy and great sadness. He still dreamed of picking her up and tickling her into squeals of laughter. But that pleasure had not been permitted him yet. Would it ever?

He approached the carriage house and saw that Abel sat smoking a pipe in an old rocking chair propped against the carriage-house wall. Tucker was perched on a bale of hay, whittling. "Abel." Ty nodded to him and then turned to the boy. "Tucker, I came to thank you for what you did last night. You saved my daughter from being kidnapped." He offered Tucker his hand.

Tucker went on whittling as if he hadn't heard what Ty said.

"Tucker," Abel ordered, "Miss Gabriel wants you children to have good manners. Now stand up and shake the judge's hand. Learn to be a man."

Tucker looked up, flushing at Abel's words and glaring at Ty. But he took Ty's hand and shook it. "I didn't do it for you. I did it for Camie."

"She's a sweet little thing," Abel said. "She brings us a snack sometimes when we're working. Sit a spell, Judge." Abel motioned toward the hay bale. Ty lowered himself next to Tucker, who sat frowning as he whittled.

"I see Jack and Mr. Partridge come by," Abel continued.

Ty explained the night watch that would start tonight. He was aware that the boy was listening even though he didn't act as if he heard a word.

Ty burned with sudden shame around his tight white collar. He would never have believed that Tucker would do something heroic. And that revealed that he really had deemed Tucker riffraff, just like his mother-in-law. He gave Tucker the same covert attention Tucker was giving him.

"Last night Tuck yelled for me to get my gun," Abel said. "I got off a couple of shots at the man."

"It's an important quality of leadership to be able to keep one's mind clear in a time of trouble," Ty commented.

Tucker shot him a nasty glance. "Think I'm going to be a leader somewheres?"

Abel remonstrated with the boy, telling him not to be disrespectful. "Tucker is already a good leader here with the littler boys," he said to Ty.

Ty was near enough that he caught Tucker whisper to himself in reply, "I tried that once and look what it got me."

Ty nearly asked Tucker what he meant, but stopped himself from commenting. He rolled the boy's words around in his mind. What had Tucker tried to do that had gone badly for him? And where?

Ty wasn't going to make the same mistake twice. He wasn't going to ignore clues and hints about Tucker and the other orphans here. Someone had it in for them. And it was Ty's job to keep them safe.

Ty couldn't blame the boy for being sarcastic in light of what most people believed of him. Again, Ty promised himself not to make the mistake of underestimating a child merely because he had no family and probably stole to survive. This prejudice against Tucker Stout and the other orphans was a shame to all of Altoona. And Miss Felicity Gabriel was a lesson to them all.

The doctor approached them. "Tucker? Miss Gabriel wants me to ask if you were injured in the fight last night."

"I'm fine." Tucker hunched up his shoulder. "I've had worse."

"You're able to move all your joints then?" the doctor asked.

"I'm fine," Tucker said, sounding nettled.

The doctor took the boy's chin in his hand and looked over his bruised face. "Any ringing in your ears?"

"No."

The doctor released Tucker's chin. "If anything starts bothering you, do Miss Gabriel and me a favor and let us know before it gets so bad you can't hide it. I like to get an occasional full night's rest. I'll be going now. Oh, Tucker, Miss Gabriel wants to see you in her room."

"I need to talk to her, too," Ty said. "I'll come along."

Tucker cast him an irritated glance, shoved his hands in his pockets and started off fast. Ty hurried to keep up.

"Tucker!" Camie called.

Ty watched his daughter run away from a game of tag and head toward the boy. She reached Tucker and walked alongside of him, chattering away. Envy instantly consumed Ty, who fell back so he wouldn't spoil his daughter's happy mood.

Tucker pulled one of her braids. She laughed and ran back toward the game again. And then Tucker turned and sent him an accusing look.

It hit Ty like a gavel in the face. The look told him loud and plain that Tucker thought he must be a cruel parent to have a daughter so frightened of him. Words of self-justification jumbled in his throat and mouth. He held them back.

He had proved the old saying, "Marry in haste, repent at leisure," true. He'd been so afraid that some other lucky young man would snap up Virginia Crandall. He recalled the few words of caution his mother and Mildred Barney, her good friend, had spoken—and which he had ignored.

It was only right that he pay for his mistake, but why did his innocent child have to pay, too?

Tucker had preceded him up the stairs to Felicity's bedroom. Ty reached the doorway, but he hung back. Tucker had paused halfway between the door and the bed. The lady lay on her stomach. The silk party gown she had worn had evidently been put away. She now wore a light white gown with only two loose narrow straps to hold it up on her shoulders. Her skin was as red as before but the blisters had all shrunk. He hoped the ointment the doctor had administered was helping with the pain. He reached up and knocked at the door, hesitant to disturb her.

"Is that thee, Tucker?" she asked, sounding as though she had very little energy. "Please come where I can see thee." Tucker moved forward, nearer her face.

Felicity held out a hand. "Tucker, what with my burns and everything else, I haven't been able to express how thankful I am to thee for protecting our little Camie."

"You don't need to thank me, miss." Tucker squeezed her hand and let it go. "I owed you and besides, I wouldn't let *him* take…any kid." Tucker stiffened. "I mean, somebody breaks in, he can't be up to any good, right?"

Felicity studied Tucker's bruised face, as Ty did.

Ty's pulse sped up. It was obvious that the boy had almost said something, revealed something he hadn't wanted them to notice.

She reached for the boy's hand again, but Tucker was looking away. "Tucker, after last night," Felicity said, "thee doesn't have to hang thy head anymore. Thee proved that thee are a fine boy and will become a fine man."

Tucker snorted with derision, looking away.

"Take my hand again, Tucker," Felicity prompted.

He finally accepted it, but with a grimace.

"Thee is a good person, Tucker. Never doubt that. Thee heard a sound and acted with great presence of mind. Many others might have given in to panic and hidden. Thee did not."

"I like Camie. She's a good little kid."

The boy's words took Ty by surprise. Ty ached physically, not from the fire last night, but from the emotions and energy he'd expended over the past twenty-four hours. The boy's heartfelt words pierced his unusually vulnerable heart. *My little girl. I could have lost her.*

Felicity smiled. "Yes, Camie is sweet. And thee is a fine boy." Her eyelids tried to drift down. "Thee may go now. I am falling asleep. The good doctor says that I must stay abed and heal."

"The judge is here," Tucker said, nodding toward the door.

"Tyrone Hawkins?" She turned her head slightly.

"Yes, it's me. I'm sorry to bother you in your boudoir. But I have to tell you some important news."

Tucker passed him without a glance on his way out the door.

Ty approached the bed. "I just wanted you to know that Jack Toomey and Eldon Partridge are setting up a night watch on your house, starting tonight."

"Does thee think that is necessary?" Her voice was thin and faint.

Her unusual frailty worried him. "Yes, we all agreed that you and the children need added protection. Now go to sleep. Heal. You have nothing to worry about." He began moving away from her.

"Tucker," she murmured, "I think... Tucker." And she was asleep.

He turned and saw Tucker, whom he'd thought had

left, just disappearing from the doorway. What had she been about to tell him about the boy? And why did Ty have the distinct impression that Tucker knew more about last night than he was telling?

Ty took one last glance at Felicity. Even as she lay there in agony, unadorned beauty still radiated from her. He was determined to do everything he could to protect her and the children. And he was becoming more and more convinced that Tucker held the key to Felicity's safety and happiness.

From the bushes in the alley, Dalton watched the judge walk over to the back porch of the house next to the Quaker's place. It pleased him to see the damage that he'd brought to the house, the boarded-up window and the blackened side of the house. But it did not please him to see that Ty and the neighbor were talking with the black shoe-shiner from down at the wharf. All three were glancing over at the burned house. Then Tucker came out of the back door.

I should have wrung his neck last night. *Dalton's hands fisted.* If he'd been able to snatch the judge's kid, the Quaker would have been run out of town. And then everything would be back the way it should be. *Lousy do-gooders, making it hard for a man to make a dishonest livin'. I'll get you yet, Quaker. And Tuck. I got ideas. Plenty of them.*

Days later, Felicity woke in the night. She froze, her heart pounding. What had wakened her? She heard voices. She rose from her bed and went to the window. Parting the curtains, by moonlight she saw two men in her front yard.

Both carried what looked to be rifles. They shook

hands and one walked away. The other moved into the shadows around her house. She went back to her bed and sat. Her back still burned, but it was healing without infection. And except for the itching, this was a true boon.

But she didn't like the fact that her home and her children had to be guarded like this. Where would this all end? And how did God want it to end? Was she to be doing something more than she was?

Felicity wondered about the poor man still in custody for the attempted kidnapping. The police chief wasn't happy with her or Tucker since neither of them would say that the prisoner was the kidnapper.

The man had no money for a lawyer and the police chief refused to release him, saying that the man was a material witness in an investigation. The chief was certain the man was the guilty party. The prisoner was the perfect scapegoat—a stranger and black.

Felicity would send Midge with a basket of food for him and try to think of some way to help. She was afraid that if she merely paid his bail or had her lawyer defend him, he might be set free only to suffer abuse outside the jail. Until he could be cleared, he was safer where he was.

Would she ever get used to men patrolling around her house every night? *I would much rather depend on thee, Lord. But sometimes Thee uses human hands to carry out Thy protection.*

Felicity attempted to lie back down and sleep, but she could not stop her mind, and her thoughts—of the fire, of Camie and of Ty—kept her up until dawn.

On Saturday morning, ready for baseball practice, Felicity strolled out into the perfect early November, Indian-summer day. Indian summer, that last breath of summer before winter, had lasted for over a week. At least, that's what Vista and Abel had been happily commenting on for days. Weeks had passed since the fire. Her shoulders had healed and she was feeling herself again. And Thanksgiving would soon be here.

The days fit for baseball were drawing to a close. But today would be perfect for it. Ty and the others should be here soon. She tried to quell her anticipation of seeing Ty again.

Thoughts of Ty brought thoughts of Camie. Felicity had prayed and thought and prayed, and knew no more about who had tried to kidnap Camie than she had the night Tucker had saved her. She didn't know why God had not pointed out who the would-be kidnapper was yet. But she was certain justice would be done—as long as she prevented injustice from being done.

Midge had visited the prisoner still in custody, taking extra food. The man had refused to give his name, much to the police chief's irritation. And the man never said anything to Midge except for "Thank you, miss." What was he hiding?

The bright sun warmed her face, distracting her thoughts. Donnie and Johnny, who'd become best friends over the past few weeks, ran to catch up with her at the tree where they usually sat. Soon everyone had arrived and Felicity, with Donnie and Johnny, settled in to watch another ball practice.

Baseball practice had attracted more and more children so that today, after a time of practice, they might have enough numbers to play a ball game. Eldon Partridge and Ty had the children in parallel lines and were having them practice catching and throwing the ball between the two lines. The sight filled Felicity with deep satisfaction.

"Hi!" Donnie called out, "Hi, lady."

Felicity turned to see who Donnie was waving at. Eldon Partridge's wife was approaching them. Felicity grimaced inwardly, dreading the woman's arrival. "Good morning," she said as cheerfully as she could manage.

"Good morning. I wonder…may I watch the baseball practice with you?"

Of all the words that might have come from this woman's lips, Felicity could not have anticipated these. "Of course! Thee is always welcome here."

"I'm Martha Partridge. My husband says that you don't use titles like 'Mrs'."

"Friends do not."

Martha Partridge had brought a thin cushion, which she put on the grass. She sat, carefully arranging her skirts. She smiled. "I haven't sat on grass for so long."

Felicity imagined that to be correct. The woman didn't seem like the type to enjoy watching sporting events.

Still, Martha watched the children tossing the balls back and forth. And Felicity did likewise. Finally, Martha cleared her throat. "Percy truly enjoys this new game."

"Baseball is a good game for teaching many skills and sportsmanship. How to win or lose like a gentleman or—" Felicity grinned "—a lady."

"I was never allowed to run and play with the boys." Martha sounded wistful. "Mother didn't want me to be what she called a hoyden."

"I'm sorry," Felicity said sincerely and then covered her mouth with one hand in embarrassment.

Martha chuckled. "I am sorry, too."

Felicity smiled. "My parents let me run and play. My best friend was a boy on the next farm. He was always getting us into trouble." Memories of childhood days with Gus tugged at her heart. The limestone grave marker set for him in the Pennsylvania cemetery also pulled at her heart. If only she had been able to love him the way he'd wanted her to—romantically. When would thoughts of him not bring regret?

"You were fortunate." The lady looked down and plucked a blade of grass. "I was wrong to take such a negative attitude toward…"

"My work here with children?"

Martha nodded.

"Would you mind if I asked thee why thee has had a change of heart?"

The woman bent her head and plucked another blade of grass. The children playing ball were calling to each other with eager voices. "The night of the fire, I woke and all I could think of was the chance that the children might be hurt. Or die. It made me think. Children are children. I didn't want anything to happen to Percy or to your children."

Felicity rested a hand on Martha's, truly touched. "Yes, children are precious gifts from God."

Martha looked up, smiling. "And Percy, my son, is so much happier. He used to hate to go to school. I didn't know that the other boys made fun of his clothes. Why didn't he say something?"

"Boys don't like to talk about such things. They think they must handle it themselves. They don't want to be thought…" Felicity's voice faltered.

"Tied to mama's apron strings?" Martha finished for her and shook her head, grinning.

The throwing practice ended. Both women turned toward the game. Ty was calling everyone to count off to form two teams. Some of the children were dancing up and down with excitement. This would be the first time they tried to play a game.

There were many strikes, outs and foul balls chased.

Sitting near Felicity, Johnny yelled encouragement. "Hey, Eugene, hit that ball!" Eugene missed and Johnny groaned.

"Katy, hit ball! Hit ball!" Donnie's face glowed with excitement. He hopped up. Felicity noticed that the child was no longer thin. His toothpick legs had filled out and were now sturdy. He jumped up and down like a healthy, happy boy. Tears of joy filled her eyes.

"What's wrong?" Martha asked.

Felicity shook her head, unable to speak.

Katy managed to hit the ball so that it bounced a few times. But she ran as fast as she could. And with all the fumbling by the other team, she made it to first base.

Donnie screeched and jumped up and down. Johnny joined in. Felicity realized that she had risen, too. Martha stood beside her, grinning. Felicity suddenly thought that in some indefinable way, her best childhood friend Gus was there with her, jumping up and down, cheering her on. Tears flowed down her face. She turned her head to hide these.

Gus had been her best friend. But now Ty was the one working beside her, helping these children. She wiped away her tears with her fingertips. Ty had become her champion.

Breathing in the crisp autumn air the week before Thanksgiving, Ty walked from the courthouse to the Barney house. The cases against petty thieves and drunks had petered out early. At only a half hour after the luncheon break, he'd adjourned court. He drew in the clean, fresh air and lengthened his strides. As soon as he'd taken off his judge's robe, he'd known whom he wanted to talk to—Felicity Gabriel.

The two of them had been so busy with work, with

baseball, with children, that they hadn't had a moment to do anything concrete about her campaign to change Illinois law. He knew when he announced the purpose for his visit this afternoon, she would spend precious time with him—uninterrupted. The children were all still at school and the house would be quiet.

He found himself smiling. Last night when he left, Camie had said good-night to him without being told to for the very first time. He had read about people who had their hearts warmed. Now he knew that sensation was real. He'd walked home last night, his heart no longer aching. Hope had taken root there. Someday his daughter would let him swing her up into his arms and squeal with happiness.

Hearing the scrape of rakes dragging leaves into piles, he turned up the path to the Barney House. He was greeted by a sudden spate of industrious hammering. Then a sawing sounded. So much for a quiet house. Instead of just repairing what the fire had damaged, Felicity had decided to go ahead and enlarge the dining room. He grinned, waved at the carpenters at work and walked around them to the back door.

"Come in!" Vista called when he knocked.

Ty stepped into the warm kitchen. "I didn't want to make you come to the front door. Is Miss Gabriel at home?"

"She's in her den. Midge has taken the little boys for a walk. And the new maid is busy cleaning." Vista held up her hands, covered with bread dough and flour. "Would you mind showing yourself in, Judge?"

"Not at all." He passed Vista and walked down the freshly scrubbed and painted hall. The outside wall with the bow window had been replaced by a canvas partition, keeping out the wind and the sawdust as the carpenters worked, and muffling the sounds of hammers and saws.

Ty sauntered to the den on the opposite side of the staircase. He halted at its open door. Felicity was bent over papers on her desk. In this rare private moment, he let himself gaze at her. Though she always dressed in modest gray without any lace or intricate tucking, she couldn't hide the fact that she was a very pretty young woman. How had she stayed single? The answer of course was that she had probably turned down proposals. He liked that; he didn't like that.

"Felicity." Her given name was off his tongue before he could call it back.

She glanced up and one of those blazing smiles burst over her face.

He walked in, feeling the pull toward her and for once, not resisting it. "Do you think we might actually have an uninterrupted conversation?" he teased.

The smile sparkled now, bathing him with the warmth of sunshine. He moved to the chair next to her, not across from her. He wanted nothing between them today. "I came to go over the rough draft of my letter to the senators and representatives in the state legislature. I wanted to know what you might want me to add. The legislators are back in session for two weeks."

She glowed in the dim afternoon sunlight. "Wonderful. What shall we—"

The sound of heavy footfalls stopped her. She looked past Ty. The builder appeared at the door. "Miss, I'm going to have to drive to the lumber yard to see if our order for more quarter-sawn oak for the floors and trim has been finished."

"Excellent," Felicity said. The man hurried away.

Ty thought about closing the door, but of course that

would be most improper. The subtle scent of roses came to him from the lady. He drew it in. "I wrote a rough draft last night. I need some information that I know you must have—" he grinned at her "—committed to memory."

"Indeed?" Her glimmering smile turned mischievous.

He loved that quality in her—as if she still retained some of the fresh joy of childhood. He pulled a few folded pages from his pocket. He smoothed them out and then sat back and began reading, "Dear Senator, I am the justice of the peace for Altoona. Prior to the war, I acted as a circuit court judge. As I go about my duties, I am often powerless to rule in a manner I think best for delinquent children under the age of reason…" He read to the end.

"That is an excellent letter, Ty." She reached for it and their hands touched. Neither of them moved. The air around them became charged. He closed his hand over hers. The letter fluttered to the desk and Ty could hardly breathe.

Extricating her hand, Felicity picked up the dropped letter and gazed at it. Within seconds, her prim façade had been put back into place.

He took a deep breath, trying to reestablish their usual rapport. It wasn't easy. "I was thinking that it might be advisable to prick their vanity."

"Vanity?" She gave him a measuring look.

He was careful to sit up straight again, not lean toward her. "Yes, I thought we might mention what is being done in other states and even England. I think that our state representatives won't want to be thought backward."

"Ah." She nodded, grinning.

He loved the quick intelligence she always showed. "So why don't you tell me more about those women you've mentioned? I can't remember their names."

"Mary Carpenter and Elizabeth Fry." A sudden extra-bright shaft of sunlight gleamed on her wayward curls, which had pulled free of her plain, tight bun. Ty tried to look away.

"You said we should include our own Dorothea Dix. So the representatives will have a precedent for action. The problem, of course, is that special treatment for children will necessitate the raising of funds through taxes for—what did you call them?"

"Reformatories." She tapped the end of her ink pen against her lips as if prodding her thoughts.

Silence settled between them, quiet and companionable, nothing like any moment he'd ever spent with Virginia, who had always been playing one of three parts: injured party, trusting maiden or her most accomplished role, shrew. He pulled his mind back to the present, recalling the very first time Felicity had come to his house. His daughter had sensed Felicity's sincere goodness and had gone to her willingly. *I should have realized then how special this woman is.*

Felicity continued tapping the pen tip against her soft lips.

Ty leaned forward, fascinated by her perfectly shaped mouth. Fascinated by this woman whose every thought was to help others. Such a tender heart he'd rarely known. "Felicity," he whispered. Her eyes connected with his as if she could not look away. His hand drifted up and he brushed her cheek. Once. Twice.

His mouth was dry. He cupped her chin with his open palm. He waited, expecting her to pull away or shake her head. Yet she stayed still, very still, watching. He leaned closer, closer. He couldn't breathe. He pressed his lips to hers. Soft. Exhilarating. Heavenly.

The front door banged open. They jerked apart. "Miss! Miss!" The familiar voice of Donnie echoed in the hall and was joined by Johnny's. "Miss Fesisity! Miss Fesisity!"

Ty leapt up just before the two little boys shot into the room. They crowded around Felicity. "We got peppermints! The man at the store gave us peppermints!"

Midge hovered in the doorway and curtsied. "We were walking through town and the man at the general store came out and gave the boys each a peppermint drop."

Both boys thought that this was the signal to stick out their tongues streaked with red. "See?" Donnie helpfully pointed to his tongue.

Felicity shook with laughter. "Peppermint tongues! How sweet!" She clapped her hands.

Giggling, Midge captured two wrists, one from each of the sticky-handed boys, and shepherded them out. Donnie turned back. With his free hand, he waved at Ty. "Hi!"

Ty waved back at him, unable to do more than that. He was still reeling from the kiss he had bestowed upon Felicity, unsure what to do or say next. When he finally looked back at her, he noted the pink rising up in her pale face. He took every ounce of strength he had not to lean over and kiss the beautiful Felicity again.

Chapter Nine

If possible, Felicity could have shrunk to the size of a white button mushroom. She had just let Tyrone Hawkins kiss her. No one had ever kissed her before. At twelve, Gus had tried and been sternly rebuked. And he'd never tried again—even when he proposed marriage. *What was I thinking?* Felicity realized that she was trembling.

She sat down in her chair and folded her hands to keep him from seeing them shake. The rigid wood of her desk chair forced her to sit up straight, reassuring her that she was still a mature and intelligent woman, a woman of strict principles. A woman who never planned to marry and did not engage in flirtation.

Felicity tried to still her inner mutiny and draw breath normally. "Your suggestions are very apt. I will write you a list of reformers here and abroad, and what measures other states and England are taking toward dealing with youthful offenders."

"Fine. Excellent," he said, sounding distracted. Flustered. He sat down where he had been before the boys— so fortunately—interrupted them. "And I've already made a list of everyone in Illinois who might be influential or favorably disposed toward these changes."

Reading the signs of his own discomfiture, she hoped that he was just as shocked as she. If so, this…amazing, astonishing kiss, no, this lapse of decorum wouldn't be repeated. Even as she thought these words, she felt her face increase in temperature. Her face must be bright crimson now. But she could not be sorry. *I have been kissed by a wonderful man.*

Both of them kept their focus studiously on the list of names he was showing her. But before Felicity's eyes, the letters jigged up and down. She couldn't stop her inner shaking, the heady sensation.

Then she heard a door slam with unusual vehemence. She rose. *What now?* "Please, thee must excuse me. I don't allow door slamming in the house." He rose out of courtesy. She reached the door and halted there. "Jack, I didn't know you were here."

The older man came up the hall toward her, looking upset. "Miss Gabriel, I dropped by to give a message to Vista."

"Oh?" Felicity tried to read more from his somber expression.

"I didn't think I was doing anything wrong." He stopped and stood, bending his hat with both hands.

"What has happened, Jack?" she asked. "I heard a door slam."

"That was Vista. I give her the message and she just turned and ran into her room and slammed the door."

"What kind of message was this, Jack?" Felicity asked, her mind whirling with possibilities.

Jack did more damage to his cloth hat. "You see, I been meaning to go down to the jail and visit the man who they say started your fire." He nodded toward the opposite side of the house where the carpenters still pounded nails and sawed boards. "But with one thing and another, I didn't get there till today."

"Why did you want to visit him?" Ty asked.

Jack looked over at him. "Hello, Judge, sorry I didn't see you there. I went because I thought he might need help. Our congregation doesn't have much money but we'd try to help, you know. And my granddaughter Midge told me he wasn't a rough man, but a polite one. So I went to see him." Jack pursed his lips and then said, "The man told me his name and asked me if I knew a woman of color by the name of Vista."

"Vista?" Felicity parroted Jack, tingling with unpleasant surprise.

"Yes, miss. I didn't want to disappoint the man. So I came straight here and talked to Vista in the kitchen. I told her that this man wanted to see her. That's why he came to Altoona and asked for the Barney house. He said that he'd heard that she was working for Mrs. Barney. When I told Vista his name, I was afraid she'd faint. I took her arm but she pulled away and ran into her room and slammed the door."

When Jack fell silent, Felicity stared at him. Vista had run away and slammed her door?

"The man gave you his name?" Ty asked. "He wouldn't give it to the police. Why would he give it to you?"

Jack began to rotate his hat brim within his hands. "He said he been waiting for them to let him go. He didn't want to be known to have been in jail before he got to talk to Vista again."

Felicity questioned, "What did thee think of this man, Jack?"

"I think he's an honest man, miss."

Felicity nodded thoughtfully. "I am of the same opinion. When I saw him that day he appeared frightened and sad, not defiant and guilty."

"You can tell if a man's guilty by just looking at him?" Ty said skeptically.

"Not always. But much can be read from a man's stance and in his eyes," Felicity replied.

Ty didn't look as if he believed this, but she couldn't let that sway her.

"Perhaps I should go to Vista." Felicity looked to Jack for advice.

"That's why I came to get you, miss." Jack stopped mangling his hat.

Felicity nodded decisively. "Do not worry, Jack. Thee has done right, not wrong. I thank thee." She turned to Ty.

The full force of his effect on her gusted against her like a blast of wind. She clung to her self-control. "I must bid thee good day, Tyrone."

"I understand." He paused, looking confused. "I will take what we have worked on and I'll bring another draft. May I?"

"Please. I am very pleased with our progress and thy support." She knew she should offer him her hand, but she couldn't risk that. Touching him might undo her.

Ty hesitated, glancing at Jack and Felicity. Then he excused himself.

"Miss, the prisoner told me I could tell you his name, as well as Vista."

She heard Ty close the front door behind him. "What is his name?" she asked, shrugging away her sudden sense of loss.

"Charles Scott." Jack bobbed his head, donned his hat and departed without another word.

Felicity stood alone in her den, listening to the voices of Donnie and Johnny, who must have gone outside to play. This day had dawned like any other. Nonetheless, it had turned into an extraordinary day. Tyrone Hawkins had kissed her.

Felicity gripped the edge of the pocket door to steady herself. Center herself. She closed her eyes and prayed, "Holy Spirit, guide me. Show me the way Thee wants me to go." She whispered that to herself several times. A measure of composure returned.

Her first inclination was to go to Vista and try to talk to her. But she hadn't lived with Vista these past months without realizing that her housekeeper was an intensely private woman. No, she would let Vista come out when she felt she could face others again.

Felicity walked to the kitchen. Midge was just finishing shaping the yeast dough into six loaves of bread. "Midge, thee is taking over the kitchen while Vista is indisposed?"

"Yes, miss. I thought I better." The young woman looked confused and worried.

Felicity patted her shoulder. "We will not bother Vista. When they come home, I will watch the children. Does thee think thee can go on with preparing supper?"

"Yes, miss. We're just having the soup here in the pots and bread."

Felicity nodded her thanks and patted Midge's shoulder once more. "We will do what is in our power and let God take care of the rest."

Midge assented to this and began putting the loaves in the buttered pans.

Felicity walked to the back door and went outside to give Donnie and Johnny a few moments of attention.

Ty's unbelievable kiss lingered on her lips. She fought the urge to touch them—as if touching them would make the kiss feel real. *Ty Hawkins kissed me.* And this had opened a door to completely new and radical feelings. She glanced at the window of Vista's room.

Yet in spite of this lightness, her heart was heavy for Vista. What had driven her into her room?

The next morning a subdued Vista came out of her room and cooked breakfast and went about her duties. She offered no explanation for her absence the day before. And uncertain what was best, Felicity asked for none. What had brought about this marked change? Should Felicity intervene or continue to give Vista her privacy?

Vista appeared to have retreated within herself. She went about her duties but no smile touched her mouth or eyes. Even the children became serious in her presence. They were no doubt accustomed to her giving them orders and urging them to eat more. Her silence had communicated itself to the children, who went quietly off to school without the usual last-minute hectic rush to find papers and books.

Felicity walked to her den and sat at her desk. Her mind was quickly overwhelmed with the memory of Ty's kiss here in this room just a day ago. She pressed fingertips to her mouth. She felt the touch of his lips on hers. Closing her eyes, she savored the remembrance. If one was going to get only one kiss in a lifetime, was it better or worse that the kiss had the power to shake, tempt her?

She rose without any answer. *I can't sit here. I have work to do.* She marched to the hall tree in the foyer and put on her bonnet and gloves. She let herself out the door and crept down the steps—she wanted to walk to town, not be driven by Abel. With a wave to the carpenters, she scurried down the street. Soon she was approaching the jail, a place she didn't really want to go. But if

Vista refused to reveal why she was upset, perhaps the prisoner would.

She stepped inside and approached the desk where a man sat, reading the morning newspaper. "Good morning."

The young officer dropped the paper to the desk and sprang to his feet. "Ma'am, what may I do for you?"

"I've come to visit a prisoner. The man who is accused of burning the Barney house. If thee pleases."

"You're that Quaker woman."

She nodded.

He stared at her as if trying to make up his mind.

"Prisoners may receive visitors, may they not?" she asked.

"Yeah, I mean, yes, ma'am." Still, he made no move to take her to the man.

"Will thee please take me to the prisoner?" She looked around at the barred windows and row of rifles hung on the wall.

"Ladies don't usually come to the jail," the young man stammered.

"No doubt thee is correct, but I am a lady who does unusual things." She smiled. "Please."

Shaking his head, he reached for a large ring with two keys. He waved her to precede him through the door to the inner hall, the keys clanking. "Now, ma'am, you can't give the prisoner anything we haven't looked at first. And you can't touch him. You just got to stand outside the cell. And I got to stand back and watch you."

"As thee wishes," she agreed. This was her first visit to a jail, though her father had gone to the nearby jail whenever he could to minister to the prisoners. She was pleased to see that everything here was clean and neat.

"Hey, you, stand up," the jailer called out. "This lady is visiting you, so watch your manners."

The prisoner rose from the bare cot where he sat. He approached the bars with caution.

"Good morning to thee." She greeted him with what she hoped was a warm smile.

"You're the lady Midge told me about." Holding the bar with both hands, he studied her.

She lowered her voice to almost a whisper. "I hear that thee came to town to visit someone who lives at my house."

He nodded.

"Can thee tell me anything else?" she asked.

He gripped the bars more tightly. "No, ma'am. This is a private matter."

She nodded. "I will send Midge again with more food. Does thee need anything else?"

"No, ma'am, I thank you," he said.

Felicity bubbled with unasked questions. But here in front of this guard, she didn't feel comfortable in trying to pry from this man what he did not want known. She bid him farewell and allowed herself to be escorted out to the office area.

The police chief walked in, halting at sight of her. "Miss Gabriel?"

She nodded and offered him her hand. And hoped he wouldn't ask her any questions.

"What brings you here, miss? Did you finally decide that our prisoner is the one who broke into your house?"

"No, I did not. I do not think I will ever be able to make that identification. I just came to see him for myself now that I am better. I must bid thee good day." She smiled and walked out, thankful that gentlemen could not insist on answers from ladies. She walked briskly down the wooden sidewalk, wondering at this new puzzle.

Puzzles, secrets and plots. These were not what she had expected in this new place. But since no one would tell her what they knew, she had to make do with what she had and start unraveling the mysteries. Or the children might suffer. Or Vista.

That afternoon she sat at the kitchen table with Tucker and a pile of books. A savory stew simmered in two large pots on the nearby wood stove. Tucker was reading aloud about the writing of the Declaration of Independence. Usually Vista would have been there, busy making cookies or something else for the children for after school. Her absence was louder, more prominent than her presence had been.

Tucker stopped, looked up at her and muttered, "Is Vista going to be all right?"

His question took her by surprise. She took a chance and laid her hand on his sleeve. "I hope so."

"What upset her?" he asked, still keeping his voice low.

"I don't know. Sometimes people have…secrets, troubles from the past. And sometimes something happens to stir everything up." A totally inept reply.

Tucker nodded solemnly. "I like Vista."

Felicity smiled. "I do, too. Now let's discuss what thee has just read."

The boy made a face. "What do I need to know this stuff for?"

"Someday thee will be a grown man and thee will vote. Thee must know the history of how our nation was established."

Tucker began punching the point of his pencil through

the paper he had been practicing his penmanship on. "You should send me away."

This pronouncement shocked Felicity into gaping silence.

Tucker looked up. "More trouble will come. As long as I'm here."

"Will thee tell me what thee means?" she said.

He shook his head and began reading aloud about Thomas Jefferson.

Secrets, troubles from the past, puzzles and plots. Her mind hummed like a beehive in spring. She placed a hand on each side of her head as if holding in all the questions, buzzing within. *Lord, reveal whatever I need to know for the safety of the children Thee has put into my care.*

As Ty left the courthouse, he noted it was one of those austere November days. He had stayed away from Felicity for a few days—since the kiss. As much as he tried to put it behind him, he couldn't. Thoughts of Felicity plagued him in every undisciplined moment. Though he knew it impossible, he wanted her to be closer. But he wasn't a good candidate for marriage. And she had made it plain by her reaction that she was not going to kiss him again.

Still, when court had adjourned early, he hadn't been able to keep his feet from heading straight for her door. Around her large yard, the maple trees were already bare. Fragile bronze leaves flew from oak trees with every gust of wind. The harvest had been nearly finished outside of town. Wagons rumbled into town every day carrying grain in fifty-pound bags to be shipped south on barges.

At the Barney house, the children were playing in

their new winter coats. Soon, snow would come and the baseball games would turn to sledding parties and snowball fights.

He approached the back door. Nearby, his mother was teaching three girls a rhyme while they swung a long rope in circles. Dee Dee was jumping. The neighborhood girls chanted, "Mabel, Mabel, set the table. Do it fast as you are able."

He paused, watching the children, looking for his daughter. He found Camie with Tucker, who was evidently helping her practice swinging the bat. He had his arms around her and was helping her hold up the heavy bat. Tucker glanced around and saw him. "Hey, Judge, come here."

Ty didn't appreciate the less than respectful tone, but decided not to take offense. Tucker had shown his true colors the night Camie had nearly been abducted. "What can I do for you, son?"

"These bats are too heavy for the little kids," Tucker said.

Ty nodded. "I've noticed that, too."

"Well, what are you going to do about it?" Tuck asked.

"What do you think I should do?" Ty countered.

"Get one of those carpenters—" Tucker pointed toward the workman busy at the side of the house "—to make us a few lighter, shorter ones."

"Yes, please," Camie added.

Once again, Camie had spoken to him. This still had the power to stop him. For a moment, he couldn't speak. "I'll do that, children."

He turned and walked toward the carpenters. His little girl was speaking to him. He snapped a tight control on his emotions. He couldn't let on that inside, he was dancing a highland jig. And Felicity Gabriel was the one who'd brought about this change. How could he not want to be near her?

That evening, Ty had been invited to stay for dinner on the chilly back porch along with his mother. The canvas curtains had been pulled down and tied. Though the night wind had calmed, it reminded Ty that the dining room must be finished soon, before the harsher winds of early winter blew in. After serving the two little boys on either side of him, he helped himself and then passed the heaping bowl of mashed potatoes to Felicity. He took special care not to touch her hand.

"I like mashed potatoes," Johnny told him.

"I must agree," Ty said. Johnny and his friend Donnie always made their preference for his company clear. They liked to sit one on either side of him. After months of feeling as if he were a monster in the eyes of his daughter and other children, this was healing something raw inside him. Of course, he would never admit it aloud but the admiration and approval in their eyes was a rare blessing.

Camie had taken to sitting near his mother and he could see that this was lifting her spirits, too. Was it possible that his child would soon be healed and come home?

He owed such a debt to Felicity. He tried to keep his eyes from drifting toward her, but he might as well try to change the way the wind chose to blow. He made himself look down at his plate.

"Ty," Felicity addressed him, "has thee made any progress in persuading more influential men to write about changing laws governing juveniles?"

He turned to her. "Yes, the mayor and several on the town council will write letters. Also several other attorneys around the state."

"Excellent." She beamed at him.

He nodded and looked away from her vivid smile, afraid he might express more than he wished with his eyes. This woman didn't miss much.

"What kind of laws?" Tucker asked.

"Ty, why doesn't thee answer that?" Felicity said.

"Tucker, Miss Gabriel and I agree that children under the age of reason should not be held to the same standard and suffer the same punishments as adults." Ty kept his gaze on the boy, not letting it drift to Felicity.

"What would that mean? Kids could do anything and not be put in jail?" Tucker asked.

"No, but if a child fell afoul of the law, he wouldn't be sent to an adult prison. There should be a place where the young have a chance to change for the better."

"You mean like this place?" the boy asked.

"Yes, something like this," Ty replied, helping Donnie to another biscuit. "According to Miss Gabriel, they are called reformatories."

Eyes downcast, Tucker stirred his mashed potatoes. "That's a good idea. Is there one of those places anywhere close?"

"Why do you ask that?" Ty paused with his fork in midair.

"I think that's where I should go," Tucker said. "You know, a place like that. Away from here."

"No, Tucker, I don't want you to go," Camie objected.

Tucker reached over and tugged one of her braids. "Don't get excited, Braids." Camie appeared pleased by his teasing.

Ty looked to Felicity.

She mouthed, "Later."

He nodded and asked Eugene what he'd learned in

school that day, though what he really wanted to do was press Tucker for more. Ty suspected Tucker thought he should leave because he was attracting danger. And if that was the case, Ty was no longer sure he wanted the boy anywhere near his daughter, yet how to protect the boy from himself?

Felicity led Ty to her den that evening after supper. She knew she should not be bringing him back to the very place where they had kissed. But she did want to discuss the letters to legislators and the hope of a reformatory in Illinois.

I will keep a polite distance.

"What is behind Tucker Stout wanting to leave this place?" Ty asked without any preamble.

She stared into Tyrone's dark eyes. A mistake. She sat down behind her desk, making sure that her spine did not touch the chair. "I don't know. This is the second time that he has said that he should go somewhere else."

Ty sat down. "Do you think it has something to do with that night?"

She knew exactly what he meant. "He has said that we would be safer if he weren't here."

"Troubling," Ty said.

"I think—I may be wrong, but I think he knew the man who broke in." Felicity straightened the papers on her desk.

Ty captured her attention with his fierce stare. "Why do you say that?"

"Just a feeling. But I know children and I've gotten to know Tucker. He's carrying some heavy load, some burden." She shook her head, dissatisfied with her own reply.

"I don't discount your intuition. You've shown great

insight and wisdom, especially with Camie. Did you hear her talk to me tonight?" Ty's faced glowed with happiness.

Felicity had to repress the inclination to reach for his hand. *This man is dangerous to me, dangerous to my calling.*

He glanced away and reached into his pocket. "Here is the list of men. I sent each a letter, outlining what the problem is as we see it and the advances being made elsewhere, and appealed for their support."

She took the list and read the dozen names there. "Thank thee, Tyrone Hawkins. Thee is a good man." He smiled at her and before she could do a thing to stop it, her attraction to him overpowered her.

As if drawn by an unseen string, she rose and moved toward him. He rose also. Both of them moved forward inch by inch. Felicity couldn't deny the thrumming of her pulse. He was going to kiss her again. And she was going to let him. But at the last minute, he stepped back, breaking their connection. "If you don't mind, I think I'll go spend time with Camie. I can never thank you enough for all you have done for her."

She hid her chagrin—chagrin at herself and him. "It has been my joy to help Camie. I hope that someday she will wish to go home and just visit here."

He bowed and left her so quickly that she stood where she was, pondering what had just happened.

She had intended to stick to their easy friendship. What had that to do with her wanting to hold his hand and moving toward him? For what? An embrace, a second kiss? *What's happening to me? I've never felt this pull toward a man before.*

Then she heard the door open and rapid footsteps coming up the hallway toward her. She pulled herself together. To her immense surprise and dismay, Alice Crandall appeared in her doorway.

"Good evening, Miss Gabriel. I saw through the window that you were here in your office. I didn't want to disturb your staff so I let myself in."

Felicity tried to read the woman's elegant face. All she gleaned was a smooth façade. Felicity was certain Alice had come up with another ploy to get her own way. Suddenly she felt so very tired. But politeness dictated her response. "Won't thee have a seat and tell me what has brought thee here tonight?"

Ty came back from supervising the children washing up in the kitchen, and headed for Felicity's office. He wanted to take leave of her. It was a school night and Midge was getting the children to bed. As he came up the hall, he heard a familiar and unpleasant voice in the den.

"I think it's time you heard my side of the story, my late daughter's side of the story."

He stopped at the bottom of the staircase in the foyer. Her side? He almost turned away, not wanting to eavesdrop. But then he thought Felicity might be glad to have someone help her show Alice to the door.

"What story is thee talking about, Alice?"

"My daughter Virginia was a beautiful girl and she had the most delicate nature. I always took great pains to shelter her from the storms of life. She wasn't strong, you see."

If Virginia didn't get her way, she was strong enough to throw tantrums for hours that could be heard a block away. Ty fumed in silence.

"So many men courted her. She could have married ten times over, but she chose Tyrone Hawkins, her one true love."

Virginia's one true love was herself. Ty began chewing the inside of his cheek, a habit that living with Virginia had caused.

"Alas, she chose the wrong man," Alice complained.

"Indeed?" Felicity commented, sounding unconvinced.

Just try to pull black wool over this woman's eyes, Alice. Ty rested a hand on the staircase railing.

"Tyrone didn't seem to understand my daughter's fragile condition. Then the war started. Virginia had just miscarried. I nearly lost her that time."

"I am very sorry to hear that," Felicity said sincerely.

"Tyrone didn't care at all," Alice moaned. "He enlisted as soon as she was able to leave her bed. Virginia begged him on her knees not to leave her when she needed him so."

Ty remembered that awful scene. Virginia had enacted it in front of a roomful of Alice's cronies. In steamy waves, anger began rising in him.

"As a Friend, I do not participate in or support any war. But this war had a moral aspect. Slavery was what broke our nation apart—"

"I have no interest in politics," Alice interrupted. "I only know that my frail daughter needed her husband and he left her. She wept for weeks and would barely eat a morsel. And then Virginia found herself with child. She wrote to Tyrone telling him he must come home or she might not make it through the pregnancy."

Ty was blazing now. He remembered those tactics all too well. If Virginia didn't get her way, she'd starve herself and then go out in public and faint. *She should have taken to the stage.*

"Then Ty finally came home on furlough," Alice said. "I thought he'd see the state Virginia was in, but no, he did not. He went back to war."

"I don't believe that soldiers are allowed to quit the army for that reason," Felicity said, sounding unimpressed.

"We have friends in the state house and the U.S. Congress. We could have arranged an honorable discharge for him," Alice insisted.

Both Alice and Virginia had lived in a dream world of their own. Facts and reality were not allowed. Facts and reality were expected to obey their whims. Ty gripped the carved walnut finial on the railing until his knuckles were white.

"I sincerely doubt that," Felicity said, putting his thoughts into words. "And I doubt that any man would want one under those circumstances."

"You are a cold woman," Alice snapped. "I saw that from the first time we met. No one will ever make me believe that Tyrone Hawkins's callousness wasn't the cause of my daughter's decline. I have said it before and I'll say it again. Tyrone Hawkins killed my daughter."

"That is a serious charge," Felicity said. "What I want to know is why Camie is so afraid of the night. Can thee tell me?"

"It doesn't lie with me," Alice said. "She was never pampered and spoiled at my house. After her mother died, I put her in the care of a nurse. And I told her not to coddle the child. That only feeds a child's disobedient nature." Alice huffed loudly. "If Camille wanted to cry herself to sleep every night, that was her choice. In time, she would have learned that those tactics don't work in my house. So I've come tonight to appeal to your better nature. My granddaughter needs discipline and I can give her that. Her father killed my daughter, and he and his mother have ruined that child."

Ty realized he was gripping the finial so tightly that

soon he would snap it from the railing. He heard a chair pushed back in haste.

"I am very glad that thee has come to give me thy side of the story, Alice Crandall," Felicity said, her voice loud and firm. "It is plain to me that thee would do anything, say anything, to get what thee wants. And from what thee has said, thy daughter was the same. I am very sorry that thee lost thy daughter. Nevertheless, no power on earth would prompt me to give even a stray cat into your care."

A second chair was shoved back and hit the den wall. Ty took a step forward, then halted.

"You are a woman without conduct," Alice accused. "I will do whatever I can to ruin you and this orphanage. I will have my granddaughter back."

"No, thee will not," Felicity said.

His mother-in-law shouted a vile epithet and then charged out of the den. She saw him in the foyer and cursed him, too. "You killed my daughter!" Then she stepped out and slammed the door so hard that the glass in the windows rattled.

Ty hurried into the den. Felicity was flushed and shaking with obvious outrage. He threw his arms around her and pulled her to him. "There, there, don't let her upset you."

"That woman," she said. She shuddered in his arms. "I'm so sorry for you, Ty, and for Camie. That awful woman."

Her warm sympathy and outrage on his family's behalf overwhelmed his good sense. He stroked her hair and cradled her in his arms. "Alice is not important. And Virginia is gone."

"Someone like Alice Crandall, entrenched in her own self will, can be dangerous." Felicity lay her head in the crook of his neck. "I couldn't believe what she was saying to me, obviously misrepresenting the facts. She must have no conscience left."

She doesn't. Ty kissed Felicity's cheek.

"I can't imagine living with someone like Virginia." Felicity looked into his eyes. "I know I shouldn't speak ill of the dead, but how could she torture thee just because there was a war on?"

"It doesn't matter now." *Because you are here. And you are nothing like Virginia.* He tucked her closer within his embrace.

Felicity suddenly broke from his arms. "Thee shouldn't be holding me."

Had she even noticed he had kissed her? Part of him wanted to take her into his arms and kiss her until she could think of nothing but kissing him back. Another part ordered him to stand back. Alice Crandall's visit had not changed their circumstances. Just because Felicity turned to him and he had turned to her in a moment of stress meant nothing.

The sound of many footsteps forced Ty to distance himself further from Felicity. The children crowded in the doorway. "Story time! It's time to read us a bedtime story!"

She smiled at them. "Have you all brushed your teeth?"

Nodding, the children grinned. They scampered toward the stairs and clattered up them.

Ty took a deep breath. "My mother and I will be leaving then, too."

"I bid thee good-night."

He didn't look at her as he left the room. His mother was donning her hat and gloves in the foyer. He took his hat and coat off a peg and offered her his arm. Although he heard Felicity's soft footsteps behind him, he did not turn around.

I will not be ruled by my ephemeral emotions. He just had to convince himself of that—and soon.

A few weeks later, the cutting winds of December had come. Felicity donned a sweater and heavy shawl, and walked between Camie and Tucker on their way to town. Camie was skipping and Tucker kept trying to hide his smile.

Camie had been kept home for the morning because Felicity felt it would do her relationship with her father some good if Camie saw Ty in his respected role as judge. Tucker was going to get new shoes today. His old ones were on the verge of falling apart. And he was the last of the children to get his pair.

"We got a late start this morning, so Tucker, we'll stop at Mr. Baker's store for your shoes first. Then you can take them home and I'll take Camie to the courthouse so she can see what her father does every day."

Tucker looked around Felicity. "Braids, don't you know what your dad does?"

Camie stopped skipping and gripped Felicity's hand tighter. "No."

"Of course not," Felicity said. "She's been too young to go to court and see her father. She wouldn't have understood."

"I wouldn't have understood," Camie parroted.

"I guess." Tucker began to whistle and kick a pebble along.

Felicity tried not to let her spirits take flight just because she was going to see Ty again. See the man who had kissed her—who might kiss her again. Caution whispered in her ear but she refused to let it tamper with her bliss.

Felicity reveled in the bright, cheery sunshine and disregarded the sharp wind, reciting Browning to herself. "God's in His Heaven; All's right with the world." What could go wrong on a day like today?

Chapter Ten

Felicity led Camie up the steps of the courthouse, hoping this outing would be another bridge between Camie and her father.

"This is a big place," Camie said, staring up at the ornate building topped with a dome.

"Yes, and it is also a very serious place. We must not talk and we must sit very quietly." In spite of her cautious words, Felicity tried to keep her rising anticipation in check. "Thy father will be the most important man in this courtroom."

"He will?" Camie said, sounding awed.

"Yes. Thy father holds a very important position." She was smiling, not only with her mouth but with all of her. "He is the one who decides who is guilty of breaking the law and who is not. And he is the one who decides what must be done to persuade people to do right, not wrong."

"Oh," Camie said.

Felicity was going to be free to sit and watch Ty and no one would think it unseemly of her.

Felicity squeezed Camie's hand to reassure her. "He is a very wise and good man." Camie looked puzzled at this.

As they walked to the courtroom, Camie looked

around her and kept up with Felicity. The bailiff looked surprised to see her with a little girl. But she merely nodded her greeting and led Camie to a seat in the visitor's area. Felicity had timed their visit just right. At the end of the midmorning recess, the court was now about to resume. The bailiff called everyone to rise. Ty entered and took the judgment seat.

He looked startled to see them, but an irresistible smile spread over his face. Every bit of Felicity wanted to rise from the hard bench and go to him. Instead, she smiled and bent to whisper to Camie why everyone had risen as her father entered.

The court proceedings were quiet and few. Though Felicity was certain that most all the conversation was far above Camie's understanding, the little girl watched with evident fascination.

When the lunch recess was announced, Felicity led Camie to her father. "Good day, Ty. As thee can see, I brought thy daughter along so that she could see where thee works. And know what an important man her father is." She beamed at him, flushed with pleasure.

"I don't know how important I am," Ty replied, sounding uncomfortable with her words. But he smiled, too, his face lifting into happy curves. "Hello, Camie. Why aren't you in school?"

"Miss Felicity said that I could stay home this morning. She said that she wanted me to learn something else." Camie spoke up without hesitation, though she still clung to Felicity's hand.

"And what was that?" Ty stooped down.

"She was teaching me about what you do. That you decide who's done right and who's done wrong."

"Well, I'm impressed, Camie. Well done." Ty's voice

betrayed how deeply this simple exchange was affecting him.

"I wonder if Camie might see thy office." Felicity glowed with satisfaction over Camie speaking to Ty.

"Would you like to see my office, Camie?"

Camie nodded vigorously.

Ty offered her his hand. Camie took it. And Felicity rejoiced on. Despite all the unanswered questions about the fire and near-kidnapping plaguing her present life, she saw that progress with reuniting Camie and her father had been made. Perhaps by Christmas, Camie would be home with her father and grandmother, where she belonged. A touch of sadness trickled into Felicity's mood. She banished it as unworthy.

With evident pride, Ty showed off his daughter to the county prosecutor, and several law clerks. Camie sat in the big chair at his desk and asked many questions about the room.

Finally, Felicity excused them. "I must get Camie to school. Her lunch is there and she wants to eat with Katy."

Ty walked them down the steps of the courthouse, and paused. He took one of her hands and one of Camie's. "Thank you for coming."

Felicity read the gratitude in his dark eyes. She nodded, suddenly unable to speak.

"I…" Ty started.

A colleague hailed him to go to lunch. Ty hesitated, then squeezed her hand. "Thank you. Thank you for everything." He kissed Camie's forehead and then hurried away.

Felicity felt warm and cozy inside. Her hand quivered from his touch. She understood his hesitation here in public. That made it hard for a man to put his feelings into words. She hummed to herself as she and Camie walked down the cobbled streets, the cold wind hurrying them along, but it could not touch her inner glow. At the school, Felicity explained to Camie's teacher where they had spent the morning. At the teacher's request, she promised she would ask Tyrone if a few of the older students might visit the court and observe how a court worked. This conversation was not lost on Camie, who looked proud that her father was someone who impressed her teacher.

When Felicity reached home, she walked up the steps and into the foyer where she took off her bonnet and gloves. She entered the warm, welcoming kitchen, hoping that Vista would be feeling better today.

Still subdued, Vista looked up but said nothing.

"Am I in time for the noon meal?" Felicity asked, her happiness tempered by her friend's sad look.

"I see Abel coming." Vista nodded toward the back windows. "And Midge is at the pump washing Donnie and Johnny's hands. They been playing in the last piles of leaves all morning."

"Excellent." Reassured by Vista's being able to perform her usual routine, Felicity went to the back door. She opened it to welcome Abel and the others into the kitchen. Now that the dining room was enclosed, they usually took their meals there. But when the children were at school and there were only the few of them, they sat in the cozy, warm kitchen. "Abel, isn't Tucker coming to eat?"

"He never come back from goin' to the store with you," Abel replied, looking surprised.

Felicity halted where she stood, Tucker's words suddenly ringing in her mind: "You should send me away— more trouble will come as long as I'm here."

A feeling of dread stole over her as she sent up a silent

prayer for Tucker's safety—she knew instantly something was very, very wrong.

Had he run away to protect her and the children?

By the time the children had returned from school, Felicity's nerves were fraying. She could remain idle no longer. She had to find Tucker.

He had been so happy to have new shoes for the coming winter. He'd been so proud of them. Why would he run away? She was in the foyer when someone sounded the brass knocker. She opened the door and there stood Ty. Relief washed through her. Help had come. "Ty, I'm so—"

"I have bad news for you," Ty said in a cheerless tone, his expression shuttered.

"Tucker," she breathed. "He's been hurt."

"No." Ty wouldn't meet her eyes. "He's back in jail."

Felicity gaped at him. Her ears filled with a humming.

Ty took her arm. "Here, sit down on the steps. You look faint."

She sat on the hard step and looked up into his face, so full of concern for her. "What has happened?"

Ty's face twisted with displeasure. "I'd give anything not to have to tell you this. Tucker snatched another purse. Just like he did to you."

"No." She knew this could not have happened. "No."

"The facts are very straightforward," Ty said gently. "Hogan was there again and nabbed him. I'm very sor—"

"Hogan was there? Isn't that odd?" she asked.

"No, Hogan's beat is the wharf and that's where this happened."

Felicity rose, her pulse racing. "Where is Tucker?"

"He's in jail, as I said. And since he has violated the

terms of his probation, he will be sent to the state prison as soon as possible to serve his year sentence."

"Tucker did not steal anything." As she spoke these words, the truth of them glowed within her. "I must call on Mrs. Barney's lawyer."

Ty caught her sleeve. "Felicity, that will do no good. Tucker will come before me tomorrow. He'll be asked what his plea is." His voice begged for her to understand. "But no matter the outcome, I must go through with the terms of my previous sentencing. He has broken his probation by stealing—"

Felicity looked into Ty's troubled eyes and knew without a doubt that he was wrong. "I absolutely refuse to believe this. Tucker is not the same boy he was when he came to me over three months ago. He has changed."

Ty shook his head, looking miserable. "Old habits die hard."

"Why would he steal?" she asked, sizzling with sudden irritation. "We had just been to Baker's to buy new shoes. He has everything he could need or want. This doesn't make sense, Ty." *Can't thee see that?*

They stared at one another. Felicity read sorrowful disbelief in his face. She ached over it. "Ty, thee can't tell me that thee thinks the boy who saved thy daughter would do this?"

He flung out both hands. "How can I argue with the facts? Hogan brought him in and gave a full account of what he saw."

Felicity stood straighter. "Then Hogan is lying."

Ty couldn't believe his ears. Felicity had always been so much more logical than most women. This unexpected irrational thinking snapped him like the end of a whip.

"That doesn't make sense," he said, trying not to let his disappointment show in his voice.

"Did anyone else see this purse-snatching?" she demanded.

"Yes, the man who lost his purse came to the station with Hogan and preferred charges." Did she think that he was happy about this failure? He tried to soften his tone. "There is no doubt of Tucker's guilt—"

"Yes, there is doubt," she insisted. "Tucker told both thee and me that he should leave this place for our safety. And we know that someone tried to steal thy daughter from this house. Something isn't right here in Altoona. Not right at all."

Fuming silently, Ty folded his arms and shook his head. Why couldn't she accept the facts? "No. There is no proof of any connection between—"

"Miss Felicity!" Camie ran into the hall. "Miss Vista says that Tucker isn't home. Where did he go? Oh, hello."

His daughter had just greeted him. He wanted to pick her up, but was afraid to take any action that might upset her. Then the full impact of Tucker's dilemma hit him. A cold brick settled in Ty's stomach. Camie loved Tucker. *And I must send him to prison for a year.*

Felicity glanced into his eyes. "Camie, there has been a misunderstanding—"

"There has been no misunderstanding." Aggravation with Felicity's denial unraveled his nerves. Didn't she know that he would have given anything not to have to be the one telling his daughter this? But even when sad or hurtful, truth and reality must be faced.

Felicity gripped his sleeve. "No," she whispered.

Putting off the inevitable never won anything but more unhappiness. As he had this morning in his courtroom, Ty stooped down to speak to his only child. "I'm afraid that your friend Tucker tried to steal something. He won't be coming back here."

Camie stared at him openmouthed. "Not ever again?"

Her crestfallen expression cut him in two. "He may come back but it will be a long time. He has to go to jail."

"But Tucker is a good boy. He wouldn't steal," Camie insisted and looked up. "That's right, isn't it, Miss Felicity? We're good children and we wouldn't do anything like that."

"I believe so," Felicity admitted.

"Camie, I don't want to send Tucker to jail—" Ty said.

"No! I don't want Tucker to be in jail." Camie's voice was rising shrilly. "Miss Felicity, I want Tucker back!"

"I will do my best—" Felicity began.

Camie turned to him. "You're the judge. You tell those people at the jail that Tucker is good. Miss Felicity said you decide who has done right and who had done wrong. You can tell them."

He tried to reach for Camie.

She pulled away. "Tell them!"

"That's not the way it works," he said, knowing that his words were futile. How could he make his little girl understand the complexities of the law?

Felicity knelt down beside him. "Camie, dear, it looks bad for Tucker now. But we must have faith that we can prove that he is innocent. Now go and stay with Midge. I must go talk to my lawyer so he can help Tucker."

Camie looked to him again. "But you said my daddy was the judge and he decided."

"I will do everything I can to prove that Tucker is a good boy." Felicity patted her shoulder.

Camie looked into her father's eyes. Her face and voice turned hard with accusation. "Why isn't my daddy in jail? He killed my mama."

Ty couldn't swallow. Shock riveted him to the floor.

"Camie," Felicity objected, "that isn't true. Thy father didn't kill thy mother. She died of influenza, a disease. Thy grandmother Louise told me that."

"My other grandma told me." Camie's face was turning a dark red. "She said my papa killed my mama. She told me."

Ty clenched his fists, holding in a shout of rage. *That woman.*

Felicity folded Camie into her arms. "Camie, people say things like that when they are angry or upset. But when thy mother died, thy father was far away at the war. He couldn't have had anything to do with thy mother's dying." She stroked Camie's cheek.

Camie's eyes filled with tears. "I want Tucker back. He protects me. Not even the bad man hurt me. Tucker stopped him. Tucker's my friend." She turned and shouted at Ty, "He's not bad!" With that, Camie whirled around and pelted toward the kitchen.

His daughter's footsteps echoed within his heart. Ty stood rooted to the floor. He knew his wife and Alice had portrayed him in a bad light, but he'd never thought that Camie would take Alice Crandall's vitriol literally. He had always blamed himself for upsetting Camie his first night home. He arrived late on a stormy night. In the midst of thunder and lightning, he'd bent over her bed. She had wakened and screamed.

I always thought it was the scar on my cheek. But it wasn't that alone. It was Virginia getting revenge on me through her mother. Virginia—petty, willful and cruel to the end and beyond. He felt nauseated at the thought that his daughter had screamed each night because she thought he was going to kill her in her sleep. *Dear God, help.*

"Ty, I'm so very sorry this has happened," Felicity

said, touching his sleeve. "But I think Camie has the right of it. Tucker did not steal that man's purse."

Ty stared at the floor. Why couldn't Felicity understand that cruel reality had to be faced? With a harsh edge to his voice, he said, "Hogan reported what he saw and I have a man willing to testify that Tucker stole his purse. What am I supposed to do in the face of such evidence?"

"They must be lying," Felicity stated. "I know Tucker. I know that the boy I walked to town and bought shoes for had no reason to steal and had no intention of doing so. Will thee help me find out what is wrong?"

Her insistence on denying the facts turned his stomach to curdled milk. "I am the judge. I cannot take any interest in this or any case beyond what is presented by counsel before me in a court session."

"Then I will have to find out the truth myself." She tightened her grip on his sleeve. "I will do what I can to calm thy daughter and help her see that thee is only doing thy duty."

He tried to pull together a smile and failed. Tugging free, he walked out the door and down the stone path. Why did this have to happen just when he was beginning to have hope that Camie might come home?

"Ty," Felicity called after him, "don't forget—'Trust in the Lord and do good. And evildoers will be cut down like grass.' Don't despair."

He kept walking. He couldn't swallow her reassurance. He'd wanted Tucker to break away from evil, hoped he would. But evidently the habit of theft had been too powerful for the boy to break.

Why had he thought that leaving Camie here was a good idea? It had just shoved another wedge between them. He recalled Camie repeating Alice's vicious words and he was instantly filled with rage. When would he ever stop paying—or worse, when would Camie stop paying—for his poor choice of a wife?

In her bedroom later, Felicity rocked Camie, patting her back and crooning a wordless melody softly. This was the first time that Camie had been afraid of going to sleep with Katy and Donnie. And Felicity couldn't blame the little girl. Felicity herself wished someone was there to hold her and soothe her fears. She forced the memory of Ty's strong arms from her mind.

"I want Tucker to come home," Camie whispered, her throat raw from weeping.

"Tucker will come home." Felicity rocked her.

"But my father says he's going to make Tucker stay in jail." Camie touched Felicity's cheek. The little girl's eyes were red from crying.

"Everybody makes a mistake from time to time." Felicity kissed the small hand. "Thy father has been misled, lied to. I will do everything in my power to show him that. Thy father is a good man. He will change his mind."

"My father isn't a good man," Camie said.

"Camie, I'm sorry to have to say this." Felicity stiffened inside with harsh outrage. "But thy grandmother Alice is not a person thee should listen to. She does not always tell the truth."

"Grandma Crandall is a fibber?" Camie nestled closer.

"She thinks she—" Felicity found herself at a loss for words to explain a twisted mind to a little child. "Camie, some people a person can trust. Others cannot be trusted. I am afraid that thy grandmother Alice is a person who cannot be trusted. I'm sorry to say that, but it would be wrong for me to let thee believe her lies."

"Can I trust my Grandma Louise?" the little girl asked, looking up.

"Yes, thee can trust her." Felicity hugged her tighter. "She tells the truth. She loves thee very much and thy father does, too."

"I want Tucker to come home." Camie yawned.

"Camie, I have always followed a promise of God. I trust in God and do good. Thee must trust God to take care of Tucker, too."

Camie sat up. Katy was standing in the doorway. "Camie, can you come to bed now? Donnie is worried about you."

Camie glanced up at Felicity seriously. "I better go to bed. Donnie is a little boy and needs his sleep."

Felicity nodded and let Camie slip from her lap. Katy held out a hand and the two girls walked away together. Doubt assailed Felicity. She was going to do her part. But digging into sin to expose the truth was always dangerous. She would have to follow her own advice and trust God to do the rest. But would Ty be able to do the same?

The next day, wearing her warmest shawl, Felicity stood outside the cell in the jail. Tucker wouldn't meet her eyes.

"Tucker, I wish thee would tell me what really happened yesterday. I know thee didn't steal any purse."

"The cop nabbed me, okay?" Tucker shrugged. "Forget me. I'm just unlucky."

"Camie is heartbroken." Felicity rested her hand on a bar.

Tucker hunched up a shoulder.

"Will thee tell me the truth?"

Tucker snorted. "The truth is what the cop says, right?"

Felicity glanced into the other cell and saw that Charles Scott was listening to them. Felicity knew that neither this boy nor this man deserved to be in custody.

Yet how to prove that? "I have hired a lawyer for thy arraignment today. And I will be there."

The officer arrived to take Tucker to court, effectively ending their conversation. With a sigh, she followed them to the courthouse, her mind spinning wildly, trying to come up with a way to break through the wall of lies someone had constructed around Tucker.

She seated herself behind her lawyer, John Remington, and prayed as Tucker pleaded guilty. Looking unusually forbidding, Ty sat in the judgment seat. After the bailiff read Tucker Stout's previous sentence and the terms of probation, Ty asked Tucker, "Do you have any explanation for what has happened?"

Tucker shrugged.

"Your Honor," the prosecuting attorney said, "the man Tucker stole from is here in court and ready to testify."

Felicity followed the prosecutor's gesture and looked at the man he was indicating. Felicity's mind began to buzz. Where had she seen this man before? And then everything clicked into place in her mind.

She had to speak to Willie and Butch. They knew Tucker from before, no matter what they all said. And Felicity knew in her heart that those two boys held the key to saving Tucker.

The next morning, Felicity sent all the children to school except for Willie and Butch. In the foyer, she drew on her gray wool shawl, gloves and bonnet. Vista stood beside her doing the same while Willie and Butch waited.

Fear bubbled within her. Today she was going to do something very risky, perilous even. If there were any other way to make the men in this town see reason, she would not be forced to this extreme action. But she had finally questioned the truth out of Willie and Butch.

Now she must put this knowledge into action so that the truth could be made visible to all. *Father, protect me and Vista—but more important, protect the children.*

"Now boys, thee knows what I want thee to do?" *What I'm forced to ask thee to do, so thee and the rest of the children will be safe.* So much was dependent on her success today. Surely God would be in this with her.

The boys looked at her warily. "Yeah."

"You mean 'Yes, Miss Felicity,' don't you?" Vista scolded.

This note of normalcy eased Felicity's tight worry one tiny notch. "Thee two are the only ones who can help me show the truth about what really happened to Tucker."

"Yeah, but—" Willie began and then corrected himself, "Miss Felicity, we don't want to go back to St. Louis. We like it here."

"Thee will not go back there. Ever again," Felicity said with an assurance she didn't feel. "And the danger that has hung over both thy heads and Tucker's will be done with, broken." *Lord, let these words be true.*

"Okay, we'll do it then, Miss Felicity," Willie said with evident resolution. Still, both boys looked scared and worried.

Felicity smoothed her dress, preparing to go into the battle for truth and justice. "Now start out and Vista and I will follow thee. Don't look back and try to behave as naturally as thee can."

Willie and Butch walked outside and headed for town. When they reached the corner, Felicity nodded to Vista. The two women started out, following the boys at a discreet distance. As Felicity watched the boys, she questioned her plan. Was she putting their lives in danger? What if something went wrong? Regardless, it was too late to turn back now. All she could do was stay on her guard—and pray. For all of them.

* * *

From the bushes near the house, Camie watched Willie and Butch leave home and head in the opposite direction from school. And more troubling, she saw that Miss Felicity and Miss Vista were walking to town, too. Camie had dawdled on the way to school with Katy, feeling that something was very wrong. Did it have to do with Tucker? Was Miss Felicity taking Butch and Willie to see Tucker? This had made her decision. She wanted to visit Tucker. She turned to Katy. "I forgot something. I'll catch up with you."

When Katy was around the corner, Camie turned toward town, following Miss Felicity. Camie sensed something important was happening. Worry tingled through her. She walked near the full bushes that edged most yards in case she had to hide, but Miss Felicity didn't look back.

Heart thumping, Felicity was praying as hard as she could. The sharp wind flapped her bonnet ribbons while she hovered near enough to hear but not be seen, Willie and Butch would make contact with the man she'd seen in court yesterday. They had said they knew where the man they called Dalton would be, somewhere here around the wharf.

As planned, Vista would hover farther behind in case she needed to run for help. Felicity wished that she could have turned to Ty, but Ty refused to consider that Hogan might not be honest. And neither would her lawyer. So she must depend on God.

Drawing in cold air, she wondered if she had the courage to confront the men responsible for such evil. The Lord had said it would be better for a man who corrupted little ones to have a millstone tied around his neck and to be cast into the sea. *Dear Lord, protect me, Vista and these children. Let us catch the evil ones in the act. Then Ty will believe me.*

Soon, deep in the noisy, busy wharf area, Felicity and Vista hung back farther. Willie and Butch were looking for Dalton. Felicity glimpsed Hogan and turned to look at a street vendor's wares, hiding behind her bonnet brim. Willie and Butch walked up to Hogan and within a few minutes, Hogan nodded with a satisfied smile and waved them toward the wharf. Then he turned and went the opposite direction.

Felicity turned to Vista, gave her a nod, and walked in the same direction that the boys had gone. She tried to look nonchalant, smiling and nodding at acquaintances. The quay was stacked with all sorts of boxes and huge cloth bags of grain. The workers were calling to each other and singing a work song. The wharf was crowded with people who weren't aware of the drama taking place.

Willie and Butch slipped into an alley and then inside a shack that was shielded by bags of grain piled high, ready to be shipped.

Her heart beating was so loud, Felicity wondered why even in this tumult no one heard it. She drew near to the ill-fitting shack door. Immediately she knew that her intuition had been accurate. She heard a rough voice saying, "You seen what happened to Tucker, did ya? He'll do a year in jail for crossin' me. I'm going to go back to St. Louee today and I'll take you boys with me. And you better tell the others there not to cross me or—"

A muffled outcry came from behind Felicity. She whirled around and found Hogan with a hand clamped over Vista's mouth as he held her tightly. "Get inside, Quaker," he ordered in a low tone. "I've had enough of your interfering."

Struck mute, Felicity could not have cried out if she tried. But would she have been heard anyway? And she and Vista were hidden from sight by the bags of grain piled high all around them.

"Move," Hogan ordered. "Or else I snap her neck."

Felicity walked into the shack, shrieking silent prayers for help to come. Now.

Camie had followed Miss Felicity and Miss Vista all the way to the wharf. The women hadn't looked back once. Everything was so noisy and busy. People pushed past her. Then she heard what sounded like Miss Vista shriek with hurt, like the time she had caught her finger when shutting a kitchen drawer. Camie hurried around a pile of bags. She glimpsed a man pushing Miss Vista into a bad-looking place.

Camie couldn't move. She couldn't cry out. What was happening? She couldn't catch her breath. She closed her eyes. What should she do?

She needed to find out if Miss Vista and Felicity were being hurt. Creeping around the big piles of bags, she was able to get near enough to the shack to catch some of what a man inside was saying: "…toss her in the river…tired of Quaker meddling…losing me money."

Toss her in the river? Icy fear inside, Camie turned and zigzagged through the high piles of wares and workers carrying big sacks. She ran right into a man.

"Aren't you the judge's daughter?" he asked, taking her shoulder in his hand.

Camie looked up. It was the nice man Jack who had brought Eugene and the other children to Miss Felicity's home. "Yes, please, I need help." She grabbed his big hand. "Please."

"What's the problem?" Jack demanded. "I seen Miss Felicity and Miss Vista going this way."

"A man grabbed Miss Vista and had his hand over her mouth. I heard him say he was going to toss the Quaker in the river." Camie's words rushed out. Would this man believe her? "Something's wrong. Please, what should I do?"

Jack looked around. "You say a man forced Vista in there?"

Camie nodded, silently calling help, help!

"I seen you yesterday going to court with Miss Gabriel. Your daddy's there now. Go get him. Now. I'll keep watch here in case they take the ladies away."

Camie spun around and started running. She ignored everything around her till she saw the stairs of the big courthouse. She ran up and inside. She knew right where the courtroom was. A man tried to stop her but she ran around him and with both hands, pushed open the door.

She saw her father in that high seat and headed straight for him. "Papa! I need you! The man's going to hurt Miss Felicity and Miss Vista! Help me!" Gasping for air, she ran around hands that tried to stop her. Her father met her at the front of the court.

"Camie, what is it?"

"Papa!" She threw her arms around his waist and looked up at his face. "Someone is going to throw Miss Felicity in the river! I heard him say it. Jack told me to come and get you! Help! Please! *Help!*"

Horrified, Ty gazed down at his terrified daughter. "Someone's going to hurt Miss Felicity and Jack told you to come and get me?"

"Yes!" Camie began to tug him to go. Tears were streaming from her eyes. "Yes!"

Coming out of shock, Ty didn't know what had happened but Jack would. "Court's adjourned!" He took his daughter's hand. "Take me to Jack!"

As they ran out of the courthouse, Camie clung to his hand. Ty tried to ask more questions but his daughter would do nothing but run. Soon, she slowed and turned to him. She pressed her index finger to her lips, telling him to be quiet.

As they came around a pile of grain sacks, Jack rose. He held his finger up just as Camie had. The concern on Jack's lined face punched Ty in the gut. Something was wrong, very wrong. *Dear Heaven.* He pushed Camie behind him. "Stay," he whispered.

"I been listenin'," Jack whispered. "And your little girl's right. Something's going on in that shack. I heard voices and sounds of someone in pain. Your girl said Vista is inside. And I seen Miss Felicity go this way first."

A steel band snapped around Ty's lungs. "How many men inside?"

Jack held up two fingers.

"There's two of us," Ty stated.

Jack nodded.

"I'll go in first." Ty turned his head. "Camie, stay here." Then he started forward, kicked down the flimsy door and rushed in. In the dim light, he saw that Hogan— *Hogan*—was tying Felicity's hands behind her back.

Hogan shouted and another man wheeled around—the man who'd testified against Tucker.

Ty didn't hesitate. He slammed his fist into Hogan's jaw. The man went down, but reared up. He swung at Ty. He missed. Ty barreled into him and bashed his fist into Hogan's eye. The man yelped. Then Ty hit him with an uppercut and a left hook. Hogan staggered and fell, unconscious.

Ty swung around to see about the other man but found that Jack had knocked him unconscious, too. Ty moved to Felicity and pulled out his pocketknife to cut her bonds. She ripped the dirty gag out of her mouth and threw her arms around his neck. "Thank God thee came. I was praying."

Jack had taken care of Vista's bonds and she was rubbing her wrists as she wept. Jack wrapped his arm around her and helped her up.

"How did this all come about?" Ty asked, fresh shock crashing over him.

"I think we better get these two tied up and taken in first, don't you, Judge?" Jack suggested.

Ty nodded. "You're right."

Then Jack squinted. "Boys, is that you? Willie and Butch?"

Ty looked over and found the two boys cowering in the corner of the littered, dirty shack. "Boys, are you all right? Did anyone hurt you?"

"No, we're okay," Willie said, his lower lip trembling.

"Now that you're here," Butch added. "We were afraid Hogan and Dalton were going to throw Miss Felicity in the river. And make us go back to St. Louis."

"I don't understand any of this, but first things first." Ty pulled a length of rope from the floor that had been used to tie the women.

But before he could tie Hogan's hands, the man reared up and punched Ty right on the jaw. Lights flashed in front of Tyrone's eyes. He felt weightless as he fell.

Chapter Eleven

"I don't care how ridiculous it sounds!" His head still throbbing, Ty shouted at the chief of police in the jail's office. The small room was crowded with everyone who had been in the shack on the quay. With his hands tied behind his back, Dalton looked downward while Jack still gripped his arm.

"Hogan tried to kidnap Miss Gabriel and knocked me unconscious," Ty declared, anger at himself rising, searing inside. "Then he took off. You need to get your men on the street to catch him. He can just jump a boat and be gone down river!"

"You're not making any sense," police chief Kidwell retorted. "You come in here with that Quaker woman and the man Tucker Stout robbed with his hands tied up—"

"Tucker didn't rob anyone," Ty objected, clenching his fists. "I tell you Hogan and this man are working together. They are the ones who should be in jail."

Showing signs of rough treatment, Felicity held up both her hands. "Please let us sit down and start at the beginning. But first, this man needs to be taken into custody." She pointed to Dalton. "He took my housekeeper and me against our wills and tied us up. He threatened us with harm, even murder. And we will both swear out a complaint against him."

Kidwell didn't look happy about this.

"Are you going to believe this crazy woman?" Dalton demanded. "I didn't do nothing."

Ty fought the urge to backhand the liar.

"I'm another eyewitness along with the judge, Miss Gabriel," Jack spoke up. "He tied up both the ladies."

"Yes," Camie, who was clinging to Felicity's hand, agreed. "He's a bad man."

Still looking disgusted, Kidwell motioned to another officer. "Put him in a cell."

"Not with Tucker!" Felicity cried out. "He might try to hurt the boy!"

Ty chafed at these delays. Why didn't Kidwell get it?

"Put the boy in with the black prisoner and put this man in the other cell alone." The officer did as he was told. "Now, Miss Gabriel, will you please explain to me what has happened?"

Felicity sat down in the chair that Kidwell showed her to. She pulled Camie onto her lap and motioned for Willie and Butch to come in and stand by Jack and Ty. "This isn't going to be easy to sort out."

"It isn't?" Kidwell heaved himself onto the chair behind his desk.

"No. Has thee read the book *Oliver Twist*?"

Kidwell looked startled. "My wife read it to our children. What has that got to do with this?"

Felicity took a deep breath. "The man the other officer has just taken to a cell is a man like Fagan."

Kidwell's eyebrows rose. "He's corrupting children? Teaching them to steal for him?"

Ty paced, trying to keep a cap on his furious, billowing rage.

"Yes, and evidently Hogan has been working with him," Felicity added.

"That's a serious charge." Kidwell looked at her with narrowed eyes.

"If I couldn't prove the charge, I wouldn't make it." Felicity lifted her chin.

"Will you please take action?" Ty demanded, his fury pushing him. "Hogan is a dishonest cop. He's been working with Dalton. I didn't believe it either till I saw it with my own eyes."

Kidwell threw up his hands. "What are all these children doing here?"

Ty's anger was a pot about to boil over. He clenched and reclenched his hands. The urge to choke sense into Kidwell threatened to overpower him.

Felicity put a hand on Kidwell's desk. "I know it's hard to believe that a long-respected policeman has been two-faced. But please dispatch officers to catch Hogan. From what the boys have told me, Dalton allows children who steal for him to live in a St. Louis warehouse. I'm afraid Hogan may go there and hurt or take the children away with him. They could testify against him and Dalton. I fear for those children." Her voice faltered. "Please, don't delay."

Felicity's simple, direct words appeared to work. Kidwell rose and began barking orders to the other officers in the station.

"And thee should talk to these boys and Tucker," Felicity said.

"Let's do that right now," Kidwell said.

Ty took Felicity's arm and helped her walk back to the cells. As they approached, he saw that Dalton was talking in low, harsh tones to Tucker.

"Shut up, Dalton!" Kidwell roared. "You're finished."

Then he unlocked the door of the cell where Tucker and the black prisoner were.

Felicity spoke up, "Tucker, was this man Dalton the one who tried to kidnap Camie?"

Dalton growled a curse and a warning.

"Yeah," Tucker declared, glaring at the man in the other cell. "I recognized him that night—even with a sack over his head."

Dalton shook the bars with his hands, promising to pay back Tucker for this.

Kidwell barked, "Shut up or I'll have you gagged. Come on out, you two." Kidwell motioned to them. Both Tucker and Charles hesitated.

"It's all right, Tucker," Felicity said. "We know the truth. And we need your help. Hogan is at large and he might go across the river and hurt the other children. Will thee show the police chief where they are? He wants to see to their safety."

Dalton cursed Felicity and tried to reach her through the bars.

Ty wished he could get his hands around the man's throat.

Kidwell roared, "Somebody manacle his hands behind his back and gag him!"

Dalton's face hardened and he turned his back on them, still muttering to himself.

Tucker slowly approached Felicity, pausing in the opening. "You know everything?"

Felicity hugged him. "Yes, Hogan and this man were caught in the act." She turned and gestured toward the two boys. "Willie and Butch helped me."

Tucker let out a gust of a sigh. And then he leaned his head against the bars. "It's over then?"

Ty spoke up. "Yes, it is. I'm very sorry we doubted you."

Tucker shrugged. "Dalton and Hogan knew how to work things. That day Miss Felicity come to town, they set me up to get caught purse-snatching as a warning to me."

"A warning?" Kidwell asked.

"Yeah, Dalton would get drunk and beat the kids. I stopped him and so they set me up."

At this Ty wished he and Jack had beat on Hogan and Dalton a bit longer.

"It's over now," Felicity repeated. "Will thee go with the police chief? He has children of his own and doesn't want anything to happen to thy friends across the river."

"Hogan might go there but he might not. He knows that I know where they are," Tucker said.

Charles Scott stepped out of the cell, looking around like he couldn't believe what had just happened.

"Before you leave," Kidwell said to the man as he led them back to the office, "I'd like to know what your name is and why you were asking about the Barney Home."

No one answered. Ty looked at the troubled faces around him. Finally, the man replied, "I'm Charles Scott, sir. And I thought I knew someone who lived at this woman's house." He pointed to Felicity.

"You knew this woman lived at the Barney house?" Kidwell asked.

"Yes, sir, she was pointed out to me. And I..."

"And you?" Kidwell stared at Scott.

"I followed her one day, trying to see what kind of woman she was, sir." Scott wouldn't look anyone in the eye.

Felicity looked thoughtful. "Was that the day I took the children to school?"

"Yes, ma'am, I apologize."

Felicity gazed at him. "That's all right, Charles Scott. No harm was done."

Ty realized that Vista had not come with them to the cell area. And she was no longer in the police office. Why had she disappeared rather than face this man?

"Mr. Scott," Jack said, "you should come home with me. We'll get things straightened out soon."

Kidwell apologized to Charles and thanked Jack. The two of them left.

"Please take Tucker across now," Felicity urged. "I'm sure he can show thee the place and convince the children to come here. I want them to be safe and cared for at my home."

Kidwell sucked in air. "This is bad business. I hate to think that adults would corrupt or hurt children. I have five myself."

Felicity nodded solemnly. "It grieves my heart, too." She pulled Tucker into another quick hug.

Relief weakened Ty and he leaned against the wall. When he'd seen Felicity tied up and gagged, scorching anger had rushed through him. Now, in the pit of his stomach, a chunk of ice hardened and radiated icy waves, freezing him. Would Felicity ever forgive him for thinking she was just another emotional woman? *I was a fool. A fool not to believe Felicity.*

Ty entered the court, still reeling from the day's astounding events. Since court rarely convened after dark, it was odd to see the candles in wall sconces lit. But with December came the early darkness. And today, reconvening court was necessary in the cause of justice, justice that had been denied. Ty's own incompetence left a sour taste in his mouth. *Why didn't I suspect Hogan?*

The prosecutor was at his place, looking stunned. John

Remington, the defense lawyer, appeared startled but pleased. Tucker Stout sat beside him.

"I think we can take care of this legality fairly quickly," Ty began. "Mr. Remington?"

"Your Honor, in light of facts which I can enter into the record, I ask that my client be released back into the custody of Miss Gabriel."

"Does the prosecutor have any objection to this?" Ty asked.

"No, Your Honor." The portly prosecutor looked stunned, but his words came out calm and clear. "Though the facts, which will become apparent in a subsequent trial, are still unfinished, we feel confident that Tucker Stout should be in Miss Gabriel's custody."

"Granted. This court stands adjourned." Ty rapped his gavel and watched as Felicity sprang to her feet and clapped her hands. The chunk of ice in his midsection had almost rendered him numb. There was a breach between him and Felicity. How could that be healed? He stopped in his office, shed his black robe and then set out to do what he must to protect the children and the ladies at the Barney Home. Hogan remained at large.

After bedtime that evening, Felicity opened her front door. Ty stood there. She recalled the moment he'd kicked down the shack's door and burst in to save her. For a second, her arms rose of their own accord, as if to wrap around his neck.

Interrupting this, her neighbor Eldon Partridge, who stood just behind Ty, said, "Miss Gabriel, we are going to start patrolling your house again until Hogan is arrested."

She swallowed and clasped her hands together so they wouldn't reach for Ty again. "Does thee feel that is necessary?" She wished that Ty would say something. A disagreement lay between them. She wanted to tell him that she understood. But for some reason, she found she couldn't speak of this. Men took the protection of females very seriously. And Ty must be regretting his not believing her. She tried to form the right words.

"We do think it's necessary," Eldon insisted. "Two men will keep watch, one front and one back, all night. We've just let everyone know to start up the same schedule."

"But it's so much colder now," she cautioned. "I will leave the front and back doors unlocked so the men can come in out of the cold," Felicity said, looking to Ty, hoping he would speak to her.

"I don't think that is advisable," Ty said grimly, not looking into her eyes.

"Most of us have served in the army," Eldon reminded her. "We can handle four hours of cold. Now don't you women worry. You're protected." The man actually saluted her. Then grinned.

Felicity tried to think of more to say, but could only say, "Thank thee." Ty was already turning away, so she shut the door, trying to ignore the feeling of being rejected by Ty. She stood for a moment in the foyer, looking up the grand staircase. The house had finally settled down for the night, hours later than usual. All the children save Tucker were in their beds sleeping—safe.

Felicity couldn't recall ever feeling like this before. It was hard to find words to describe all the turmoil and emotions that she was experiencing—shock, sadness, joy, vindication, fear, exhaustion. She'd wanted Ty to fold her in his arms, warm the chill she couldn't shake. Rubbing her chilled arms, she made her way down the hall to the warm kitchen and found Vista sitting there.

"Good." Vista rose. "I was hoping you'd come here. I

can't settle down. Too much…too much." She shook her head. The kettle on the stove whistled. She turned to it. "I got the pot ready for chamomile tea. That might help us calm down."

Felicity couldn't speak. Too many words clamored to be spoken. She sank into the nearest chair and watched Vista prepare the tea. Finally, a large cup was set before her. She sighed. "Thanks."

Vista sat across from her. "I keep going over in my mind what all happened today." She shook her head again. "I can't believe it. I can't believe we followed the boys and put ourselves into such jeopardy."

"I knew it was dangerous." Felicity sipped the hot tea laced with honey. "But I couldn't get Ty to believe that Hogan had dirty hands. It was the only way to break Ty's confidence in Hogan. We had to catch him and Dalton in the act of doing what they were to the children. I know it was risky." Felicity laid her hand over Vista's. "But we had to do it. Or the children would suffer. Ours and others."

Vista nodded. "I know. It's just that it's hard. It's hard to think that two men would use children like that. I've seen a lot of evil in this life so it shouldn't shock me. But it does."

Felicity agreed, nodding her head.

"Miss Felicity?" an unexpected voice called.

Felicity turned to see Camie in her nightgown, rubbing her eyes. "Camie, what is it?"

"I woke up. I can't get back to sleep. I'm scared. What if that bad man comes here?"

What if that bad man comes here? Felicity opened her arms wide and Camie climbed onto her lap. "Thee doesn't need to be afraid. Men are patrolling around the house like they did before. No bad man will be able to get inside."

Camie clutched her. "Good." But the child still looked fretful.

"What is it, Camie? Thee can tell me."

"I keep thinking about my papa. Why did my grandma say such bad things about him? He's not a bad man. He fought that real bad man today and saved you and Miss Vista."

"Your father is a good man," Vista agreed.

Suddenly hot around her prim collar, Felicity was glad Alice Crandall wasn't here right now. If she were, Felicity wouldn't have been answerable for what she might say to the self-centered, coldhearted woman. Felicity couldn't ever recall wanting to box someone's ears before. Keeping tight control on her words, Felicity said, "Camie, as I told thee, unfortunately thy grandmother Alice is not a person who can be believed."

Camie nestled closer and whimpered. "When my papa came home from the war, I was so afraid. Grandma Alice said he killed my mama and he would kill me, too. And so I was afraid to go to sleep 'cause my mama went to sleep and never got up."

No child should ever have to live with such fear. And this little one had been terrorized her whole young life. Had her mother, Virginia, spared one thought for her precious child?

"Evil," Vista murmured. "Evil."

"Camie, once and for all," Felicity said, tightening her hold on Camie, "thy father is a good man. He did not kill thy mother. Thee must let thy father know that thee is glad he came home from the war."

Camie looked up into Felicity's face and touched her

cheek. "When I ran to him for help, he came right away. I believe you. My papa is a good man."

Felicity drew in a deep breath, holding in how much Camie's gentle touch meant to her. "Good. Thee were very brave to do what thee did." She kissed Camie's cheek. "I should scold thee for following us, but in the end, thee did what God had planned. Now thee is a brave, big girl so thee can walk upstairs and put thyself to bed again. I must not baby thee."

"I can go by myself." Camie slid from her lap, but turned back for one more hug. "I'll go see that Donnie is covered up. Sometimes he gets uncovered and gets cold."

Felicity smoothed back Camie's dark hair, smiling. "That would be a good thing to do. We must take care of the littler children."

Camie waved to Vista and left the kitchen. The two women listened to her footsteps fade away.

"How could a woman be so evil?" Felicity asked, resting her head on one hand. In that moment, Alice Crandall's malice oppressed even her spirit.

"It's bad, all right. Alice Crandall is a captive of sin. A slave of sin."

Felicity shook her head. Why did people do evil? She'd never understood the desire to hurt others.

"I been a slave of sin, too," Vista murmured.

Startled, Felicity looked up. "What?" Vista had never revealed anything about her life.

"Charles Scott came looking for me and I wouldn't go to him." Vista traced the rim of her cup with one fingertip and then she pulled out the locket she wore under her collar. "Mrs. Barney give this to me and told me to hope for the future. I have hid this locket, hid from hoping. I never thought I'd see Charles again."

"Thee *does* know Charles Scott, then?" Felicity

smoothed a wrinkle in the starched tablecloth, giving Vista some space to speak freely.

Vista nodded with a moody expression. "I didn't want to look him in the face."

Felicity sipped her hot tea, trying to find a way to help Vista free herself from whatever weighed on her. "Why didn't thee want to see Charles?"

"Because seeing him would bring it all back on me." Vista's voice became vehement. "All the slave days of my life. All the sorrow. I felt like I was suffocating all over again. It's hard—" Vista clenched her hand "—so hard to think of the past."

"Were thee in love with Charles?" Felicity was startled by Vista's sudden flare-up and her own audacity in asking these plain questions. But who knew when this very private woman would open again?

Vista nodded slowly. "We were childhood sweethearts."

This phrase echoed inside Felicity. "Childhood sweethearts," she whispered.

"When I was around fifteen, Charles wanted to marry me." Then Vista fell silent.

Memories of Gus Mueller's proposal before he went off to war played through Felicity's mind. "Thee didn't want to marry him?"

Vista stared down into her cup. "It wasn't that. I *wanted* to marry him. But as I got older, I just couldn't bear being a slave. It was like being smothered alive. Being a slave made it impossible to simply marry Charles and settle down to life together."

Felicity thought deeply on Vista's words.

Shivering suddenly, Vista took a sip and then put down her cup. "How could I marry him if I could be taken from him at any time? My mother said I should find whatever happiness I could. That life was short anyway. But I wasn't like her. I wanted my life to be *mine*." Vista wrapped both hands around her cup. "And I was a pretty girl, a very pretty girl, and that's not good if you're a slave."

Felicity said nothing. What was there to say about such things? "Thee ran away and came here?"

Vista nodded. "Mrs. Barney hid me for a long time. Finally, the slave-catchers gave up and left. She smuggled me out of town. Then, in new clothing, I come back with a new name and a story to tell of living near Beardstown, Illinois." Vista sighed. "She hired me as her housekeeper. Her former one had just retired. I was happy here. I didn't let myself think about the past—it just made me sad. So I taught myself *not* to remember."

Felicity squeezed Vista's hand, glad Vista had trusted her, confided in her. "I don't know what it feels like to be a slave. But I understand wanting to be free. I was fortunate to come from a family that didn't deem girls as less than boys. I am one of seven sisters and we all have been blessed with a mission to live for. After I volunteered at an orphanage, I knew I wanted to devote my life to children."

Vista gave her a small smile. "I didn't have any mission for my life. I just wanted to be free. And I didn't want to remember."

"That's understandable," Felicity said.

Vista looked away. "But it made me a coward. I should have been brave and gone to see Charles."

"None of us can be brave all the time." Felicity touched Vista's wrist.

"You're brave all the time," Vista said.

Felicity shook her head, smiling sadly. "I was afraid this morning. And I'm afraid now. I'm afraid Hogan will try to hurt the children in St. Louis or try to pay me back."

Vista looked into Felicity's eyes. "You ask me if I loved Charles. What about the judge? Do you love him?"

Hearing the words out loud stung Felicity. "I don't plan to marry," she said without even thinking about it.

"Planning is different than feeling, different than being," Vista observed. "I think the judge wants to make up with you. I think he's sweet on you."

Felicity said nothing. Her mouth had betrayed her once and she wouldn't let it do that again. Marry? No. That wasn't the plan for her life. If she married, her first loyalty would have to be to her husband, children and their home. No time for orphans in that life.

Ty's face lingered in her mind. But that should mean nothing. She closed her eyes and held back tears.

Felicity awoke with a start, lifting her head from her arms folded on the kitchen table. Someone was knocking hard on the door. She'd sat up waiting for Tucker's return and she had fallen asleep sitting in the kitchen at the table. Stiff and groggy, she rose. Vista came out of her room off the kitchen. "Didn't you go to bed last night? You said you were when I left you."

Felicity stretched her spine and tried to wake completely. "I'm fine," she muttered.

"Not if you slept at the table all night. I'll go get it." Vista seemed herself again as she bustled out of the kitchen.

Felicity went to the sink and from the bucket there, splashed some water onto her face. She heard loud exclamations coming from the foyer. She turned and hurried there.

Charles Scott had come. He'd lifted Vista off the floor

and was holding her tightly. Then Vista kissed Charles. And though she knew she should, Felicity found she couldn't look away, couldn't hold back a wide smile.

Jack remained in the doorway, looking pleased with himself, too.

Felicity waited till Vista finally ordered Charles to put her down. Then Felicity went forward, beaming. "Charles Scott, I'm so glad to see thee."

Charles bowed slightly. "Ma'am, I spent the night at Jack's house. But before I left town, I wanted to try once more to see Vista."

Felicity studied Vista's face. She looked happy but shamed and uncertain, too. "Vista, why doesn't thee take Charles to the parlor? Thee will have privacy there."

Vista nodded. Not looking at Charles, she led him by the hand.

"I'll be leaving now," Jack said.

Felicity went forward, her hands out. "Thank thee for thy help yesterday. Thee showed great courage."

Jack smiled and bowed himself out. Felicity had barely gotten halfway up the steps and the brass knocker sounded again.

She opened the door and there stood the police chief with a crowd of ragged children and a beaming Tucker.

"Miss Gabriel, Tucker and I did go over to St. Louis on the ferry late yesterday," Kidwell said. "We found these children in that warehouse. Tucker explained everything to them and they came with me. The police chief in St. Louis has his men searching for Hogan, too. He said I could leave these children at the orphanage in St. Louis, but I figured they belonged with you. We got back so late that they spent the night in my house."

Felicity looked at all the grimy, frightened faces lifted toward hers. Her heart expanded with love for these little ones. How could she have doubted her calling, even for a second? She opened her arms wide. "Welcome, children. Welcome to thy new home."

The new children had been scrubbed mercilessly clean in the new bathing room off the kitchen with its indoor pump and stove for heating water. Felicity had sent Midge to town to buy more clothing. The number of children had doubled overnight. Twenty children now lived in the Barney house. The bedrooms were filling up and Felicity was grateful for the larger dining room. All day Camie and Katy had shown the newcomers how things were done here. Katy was quite the little leader.

Now sitting around the dining room table after supper, the new children clustered together and eyed her with uncertainty. Felicity wished she had slept more last night and thought longingly of bedtime.

The brass knocker sounded. The new children looked apprehensive. Felicity went to the door. She opened it to a huge evergreen tree filling the doorway. "Hello, Miss Felicity!" Jack called from somewhere on the other side of the tree. "The men in my church thought you could use a Christmas tree. We went out on a member's farm and cut this one down for you."

"Come in!" Sudden gaiety zipped through Felicity. *A Christmas tree!* The children were clapping and calling out in excitement.

After some consultation, it was decided that the tree should be set up in the grand foyer where it was visible from the dining room table and the parlor, but away from the warmth of the fireplaces in both rooms. Jack and Charles then set the tree in a bucket of water and braced it with rocks and blocks of wood to stand straight.

Soon the children and Felicity sat around the table,

some stringing popcorn and others stringing cranberries. Vista and Charles were in the kitchen baking gingerbread cookies to hang with ribbons on the tree. The fragrance of nutmeg, ginger and cinnamon wafted through the house. A few snowflakes drifted by the windows. All was happy inside.

Outside, however, Hogan was still at large, so two men would be patrolling again tonight, a pebble in Felicity's shoe. Over and over, she glanced at the window with a sense that she was watching, waiting for something, someone.

The brass knocker sounded. When Felicity made to rise, Tucker hopped up. "I'll get it."

Felicity had to smile. Tucker was a different boy. The burden of worry had been lifted from him. Willie and Butch showed the same new confidence. They encouraged the new children who were beginning to smile a little.

"It's the judge!" Tucker announced. "And his mother, Mrs. Hawkins."

The new children shrank visibly. Tucker reassured them, saying, "He's okay. He's the one who punched Hogan."

"Thank you, Tucker," Louise said as she took off her bonnet, smoothed her hair before the mirror on the hall tree and then entered the dining room. "Jack stopped to tell us that he had delivered your Christmas tree. We brought some red and white Christmas candles and candleholders. My, the tree is a magnificent one."

"Hello, Grandma Louise," Camie greeted her. "I'm stringing cranberries for the tree. Hi, Papa."

Ty followed Louise in, carrying a wooden box. Camie hopped up, kissed Louise and hugged her father. Felicity couldn't ignore Ty's response to this spontaneous affection. She glanced away, not wishing to embarrass him. She realized she was disappointed that she couldn't show him the same gratitude for rescuing her. But that would be most improper.

After exchanging greetings, Ty set the box on the table and lifted the lid. "I'll go ahead and start clipping the holders onto the boughs."

"Can I help?" Tucker asked.

"Sure." Ty and the boy went to the tree and began clipping the small candleholders on the branches, fiddling with the candles so that they would stand straight and not burn nearby boughs.

Felicity couldn't take her eyes from the two of them, working so well together, all antagonism gone. When the job was done, Tucker and Ty returned to the dining room.

"When is Camie going home?" Tucker asked out of the clear blue.

Felicity held her breath. This was something she had wondered about but had not had the courage to bring it up. Now, taking her cue from Tucker, she turned to Camie. "When does thee want to return home?"

Silence. Camie stopped stringing cranberries and looked around the table. "Do I have to go home?"

"Well, yeah," Tucker replied. "This is a home for kids who don't got family. But you have a dad and a grandma right here." He motioned toward them.

Felicity prayed silently for reconciliation.

Camie started kicking the rungs of her chair with her heels. "I didn't think about that."

"We'd like to have you come home," Louise said, her voice strained. "I know it's hard to leave Katy and Donnie, but you would still see them every day at school, and you could visit here, too. And they could visit you at our house."

"I could come home," Camie said, "but I would miss sleeping with Katy. I don't like sleeping alone."

"Maybe you could stay. You don't got a mother," Katy added. "You're half orphan. Does that count?"

"I want Miss Felicity to be my mother," Camie said.

Felicity shimmered with surprise.

"That makes sense," Tucker said with a grin. "I think your pa should marry Miss Felicity. I think he's sweet on her."

Felicity's face warmed. "Tucker, this is not—"

"Yes, I agree," Louise said, grinning. "My son is sweet on Miss Felicity. And I think she would make a wonderful mother for Camie."

Refusing to look at Louise or Ty, Felicity cleared her throat. "I am the mother here. This is my place to care for children."

"But why couldn't you take care of the children here in the daytime and then come home with me in the evening?" Camie asked, picking up the large needle and beginning to string cranberries again.

"That makes sense," Katy agreed.

Felicity shook her head, blushing furiously. "No, children, no husband would want a wife who did that. If I were a married woman, I would have to devote myself to my own home. I would have no time to care for the children here."

"I don't know about that," Vista said, coming in with a plate of gingerbread men, Charles following her. "Charles and I have decided to marry and I don't know why we couldn't live here and be house parents, do you? And Midge and her cousin who's going to start after the New Year will be here, too. If your husband hired help at your place, you wouldn't have much work to do at home."

Felicity was completely flustered. Why didn't Ty say

something? "This is a most improper conversation. I made a decision long ago that my calling is to care for orphans and children who are being mistreated—"

"I think that's an admirable goal," Louise said. "But I don't think that should prevent you from marrying my son."

Ty spoke up at last, an amused look on his face. "I think that this is something Miss Felicity and I should discuss privately." He rose. "Will you come with me into the den, please?"

Felicity stared at him as if she'd never seen him before. But courtesy dictated that she at least refuse the man in private.

Once inside the den, Ty closed the pocket door. Felicity felt his gaze upon her. Her nerves began to hop. "Ty, I'm so sorry—"

Pulling her close, Ty silenced her with a kiss.

She gasped for air. "Ty, please—"

He kissed her again, more insistently. This man had given her her first kiss here in this very room. But that tender touch was nothing like the kiss he was giving her now. His arms clasped her to him and his lips persuaded hers to part.

"Felicity," he whispered.

She felt each syllable as his lips touched hers. She trembled against him, against her will. "Ty," she murmured breathlessly, "thee mustn't kiss me."

He gazed down into her eyes, grinning. "Don't you like my kisses?"

That put her in a quandary. In all honesty, she did like his kisses. She had often wondered why a woman would let a man kiss her—she was getting the full explanation for that here and now. But it wasn't proper for her to encourage him. "Ty, I will not marry. I have a mission—"

He interrupted her again with a kiss, pulling her even closer to him. She tried to think but her mind was dancing, reeling.

"I'm sorry," he murmured next to her ear. "When you said that Hogan was dishonest and lying, I should have believed you. Don't hold that against me. Please."

"Of course I won't." Felicity tried to step out of Ty's embrace but found she was backed up against the desk and had nowhere to go.

"Felicity, until Camie spoke up tonight, I thought we could never be together. I've behaved so foolishly."

Felicity tried to interrupt and was ignored again.

"Now I realize I can't face that empty house without you. Camie loves you and needs you. I need you and I love you."

"Thee loves me?"

Ty kissed her nose. "Yes, doesn't *thee* love me?" he teased, using her plain speech.

"That's beside the point."

"I will hire a full-time housekeeper again and have a maid and laundress at our home." He lifted and kissed one of her hands. "You will be free to spend your days here at the orphanage. I don't see why you can't do both." He kissed her other hand. "We'll work together to protect orphans and get the Illinois laws for juveniles changed. I'll be a help to you. I promise." He squeezed her hands. "Your mission will become ours."

Felicity felt herself weakening. "Ty, thee is so persuasive. But I already refused to marry my childhood sweetheart, Gus, because I'd committed myself and my life to my mission. He went off to war and died. His mother blames me for her losing him and any possibility of a grandchild. How can I have turned down Gus, my best friend, only to accept thee? Can a sensible person change her whole life plan just because of love?"

Ty chuckled. "You have always talked sensibly, Miss Gabriel. But those are the silliest words I've ever heard from your lips. People change and grow. You will not dishonor Gus's memory by pursuing your own happiness." He reached up to touch a strand of her hair. "I never knew real love till I met you. Love changes everything. You of all people should know that. See what love has done for Tucker and Camie? See how Vista glows now that Charles has come back into her life? How can you say that love shouldn't change anything? It changes everything—and for the good."

She looked at him, openmouthed. *Love. These three abide—faith, hope and love—but the greatest of these is love. How could I be so foolish?*

She rested her cheek against his shirt. "Truly will we work together for the children?"

"Yes, a thousand times, yes. And we will make a home for the children here and for our children in my house. I will do everything in my power to help you." Ty looked down and stroked her hair. "Do you love me, Felicity Gabriel?"

The past fell away and Felicity smiled. "I do, Ty. And I will marry thee."

Epilogue

Hogan had not been seen since the day he was exposed for what he was. With Charles living on the premises, the Barney house was no longer guarded by the men of the neighborhood. They had a lovely Christmas, and today, the afternoon of the first day of 1868 in the parlor of the Barney house, Felicity in a new dark blue dress with white cuffs and collar faced Ty in his best suit and said, "I do." Ty echoed her promise of lifelong devotion, and kissed her so sweetly, he brought grateful tears to her eyes.

Then Vista, wearing a lovely new red dress, faced Charles in a new black suit. The pastors from both Jack's church and Ty's officiated at the two weddings. After the wedding, neighbors and friends of Felicity and Ty's and from Vista's church sat around the large dining-room table and sipped punch and nibbled the beautiful white cake that Martha Partridge had baked and decorated herself. The shared friendship and shared joy of this day enfolded Felicity in a blissful cloud.

Surrounded by the general gaiety, Felicity looked around. A shy but beaming Vista came to her and whispered, "Is it time for us to toss our bouquets? The children keep asking."

Felicity nodded. Both of them carried bouquets of pine-cones and short pine boughs, and holly with red berries. They walked to the front porch. All the young women and even little girls gathered below them on the walk, calling for the bouquets, their breath floating white in the chill air.

Felicity watched Vista turn her back and toss the bouquet. When Midge caught Vista's bouquet, everyone's shrieks of excitement filled Felicity with a billowing, limitless elation. When Felicity did likewise, her eldest sister, Mercy, caught hers. Both of them had stared at each other in shock.

Mercy had worked as a nurse side by side with Clara Barton throughout the war and Felicity was very proud of her. Beside Mercy stood Indigo, the little orphaned slave whom Mercy had adopted and who was now near in age to Midge. And showing signs of becoming a lovely woman. Mercy and Indigo were on their way to begin Mercy's life's work far away in the West. Mercy had just graduated from the Female College of Medicine in Pennsylvania and was now a qualified physician.

As everyone hurried back inside, Felicity watched as Mercy handed Indigo the bouquet and slipped out of the limelight. Felicity didn't believe in omens, but then she hadn't believed that she would be a married woman on January 1, 1868, either.

When Ty came and put his arm around her, Felicity squeezed his hand. Camie stood beside her. Ty kissed the tender skin below Felicity's ear and whispered, "I love you, my bride." Her cup of joy overflowed. Ty's words came again—love changes everything for the good. Maybe love was in Mercy's future too. *Lord, let it be so.*

* * * * *

Dear Reader,

Felicity means happiness. And I think that my heroine lived up to her name. She certainly brought happiness wherever she went—even though she stirred up the status quo. It's hard for us to believe now the conditions prisoners—especially children—were subjected to in the 19th century and before. Many years passed before these were changed by people who followed Felicity's advice from Psalm 37: "Trust God and do good." And it's hard to believe that in many places around the globe, these same conditions still exist. Just in case you're wondering, Charles Dickens's book *Oliver Twist* was first published in 1838 and the term *cop* was in use from around 1850.

On a personal note, in this book, I did something fun with the names. Almost every name in the book is a name popular in my family. I used the names of my grandparents, aunts, uncles and cousins. I'll let you try to guess which ones are family names and which ones aren't.

Merry Christmas!

Lyn Cote

WE HOPE YOU
ENJOYED THIS
LOVE
INSPIRED®
BOOK.

If you were **inspired** by this

uplifting, **heartwarming** romance,

be sure to look for all six Love

Inspired® books every month.

Love Inspired®

LIIHALO2017R

"What's your name?"

The woman's eyes widened and her hand shook so that
she could barely hold the mug of tea without spilling it. She
set it carefully on the coffee table. "I don't—I don't know
my name."

"How can you not know your own name?" Caleb asked.
"Do you know where you live?"

"Nein."

"What were you doing out there?"

"Out where?"

"Where was your coat and your *kapp*?"

"Caleb, now's not the time to interrogate the poor girl."
His *mamm* stood and moved beside her on the couch. She
picked up the small book of poetry. "You were carrying this,
when Caleb found you. Do you remember it?"

"I don't. This was mine?"

"Found it in the snow," Caleb said. "Right beside where
you collapsed."

"So it must be mine."

Caleb noticed that the woman's hands trembled as she
opened the cover and stared down at the first page. With one
finger, she traced the handwriting there.

"Rachel. I think my name is Rachel."

Rachel let her fingers brush over the word again and again. Rachel. Yes, that was her name. She was sure of it. She remembered writing it in the front of the book—she'd used a pen that her *mamm* had given her. She could almost picture herself, somewhere else. She could almost see her mother.

"My *mamm* gave me the pen and the book...for my birthday, I think. I wrote my name—wrote it right here."

"Your *mamm*. So you remember her?"

"Praise be to *Gotte*," Caleb's *dat* said, a smile spreading across his face.

"Is there someone we can call? If you remember the name of your bishop..." Caleb had sat down in the rocker his mother had vacated and was staring at her intensely.

They all were.

She closed her eyes, hoping to feel the memory again. She tried to see the room or the house or the people, but the memory had receded as quickly as it had come, leaving her with a pulsing headache.

She struggled to keep the feelings of panic at bay. Her heart was hammering, and her hands were shaking, and she could barely make sense of the questions they were pelting at her.

Who were these people?

Where was she?

Who was she?

She needed to remember what had happened.

She needed to go home.

Don't miss
Amish Christmas Memories *by Vannetta Chapman,*
available December 2018 wherever
Love Inspired® books and ebooks are sold.

www.LoveInspired.com

Love Inspired®

Save $1.00

on the purchase of any
Love Inspired® or Love Inspired®
Suspense book.

Available wherever books are sold,
including most bookstores, supermarkets,
drugstores and discount stores.

Save $1.00

on the purchase of any Love Inspired® or
Love Inspired® Suspense book.

Coupon valid until April 30, 2019. Redeemable at participating retail outlets in the
U.S. and Canada only. Limit one coupon per customer.

52616033

Canadian Retailers: Harlequin Enterprises Limited will pay the face value of this coupon plus 10.25¢ if submitted by customer for this product only. Any other use constitutes fraud. Coupon is nonassignable. Void if taxed, prohibited or restricted by law. Consumer must pay any government taxes. Void if copied. Inmar Promotional Services ("IPS") customers submit coupons and proof of sales to Harlequin Enterprises Limited, P.O. Box 31000, Scarborough, ON M1R 0E7, Canada. Non-IPS retailer—for reimbursement submit coupons and proof of sales directly to Harlequin Enterprises Limited, Retail Marketing Department, Bay Adelaide Centre, East Tower, 22 Adelaide Street West, 40th Floor, Toronto, Ontario M5H 4E3, Canada.

U.S. Retailers: Harlequin Enterprises Limited will pay the face value of this coupon plus 8¢ if submitted by customer for this product only. Any other use constitutes fraud. Coupon is nonassignable. Void if taxed, prohibited or restricted by law. Consumer must pay any government taxes. Void if copied. For reimbursement submit coupons and proof of sales directly to Harlequin Enterprises, Ltd 482, NCH Marketing Services, P.O. Box 880001, El Paso, TX 88588-0001, U.S.A. Cash value 1/100 cents.

5 65373 00076 2 (8100)0 12391

® and ™ are trademarks owned and used by the trademark owner and/or its licensee.

© 2018 Harlequin Enterprises Limited

LICOUP44816

*Robin Hardy may be the only one who can help former
spy Toby Potter—but she can't remember her past with
him or who is trying to kill her.*

Read on for a sneak preview of
Holiday Amnesia *by Lynette Eason,*
the next book in the Wrangler's Corner series,
available in December 2018 from
Love Inspired Suspense.

Toby Potter watched the flames shoot toward the sky as
he raced toward the building. "Robin!"

Sirens screamed closer. Toby had been on his way home
when he'd spotted Robin's car in the parking lot of the lab.
Ever since Robin had discovered his deception—orders
to get close to her and figure out what was going on in
the lab—she'd kept him at arm's length, her narrow-eyed
stare hot enough to singe his eyebrows if he dare try to
get too close.

Tonight, he'd planned to apologize profusely—again—
and ask if there was anything he could do to earn her trust
back. Only to pull into the parking lot, be greeted by the
loud boom and watch flames shoot out of the window near
the front door.

Heart pounding, Toby scanned the front door and rushed
forward only to be forced back by the intense heat. Smoke

billowed toward the dark night sky while the fire grew hotter and bigger. Mini explosions followed. Chemicals.

"Robin!"

Toby jumped into his truck and drove around to the back only to find it not much better, although it did seem to be more smoke than flames. Robin was in that building, and he was afraid he'd failed to protect her. Big-time.

Toby parked near the tree line in case more explosions were coming.

At the back door, he grasped the handle and pulled. Locked. Of course. Using both fists, he pounded on the glass-and-metal door. "Robin!"

Another explosion from inside rocked Toby back, but he was able to keep his feet under him. He figured the blast was on the other end of the building—where he knew Robin's station was. If she was anywhere near that station, there was no way she was still alive. "No, please no," he whispered. No one was around to hear him, but maybe God was listening.

Don't miss
Holiday Amnesia *by Lynette Eason,*
available December 2018 wherever
Love Inspired® Suspense books and ebooks are sold.

www.LoveInspired.com

Looking for inspiration in tales
of hope, faith and heartfelt romance?

Check out **Love Inspired**® and
Love Inspired® **Suspense** books!

New books available every month!

LIGENRE2018R2